# ENEMY IN BLUE

## ROGUE BOOKS

This book is a work of fiction. The characters, incidents, and dialogue are drawn from the author's imagination and are not to be construed as real. Any resemblance to actual events or persons, living or dead, is entirely coincidental.

Cover design by Brianne Pickert of Izonu, Inc. You can contact Brianne at izonu@mac.com.

Special thanks to Judith Schwartz of FinalEyes Copyediting for helping with edits for this second edition.

Follow Derek on Facebook, Twitter (@DerekBlass), and his blog on Wordpress

Visit the fun, flash website for Rogue Books at www.rogue-books.com

ISBN: 978-0-615-48103-6

Printed in the United States of America

# ENEMY IN BLUE

**DEREK BLASS**

**ROGUE BOOKS**

**DENVER**

Foremost, to my beautiful wife, Meranda, who put up with various drafts and several years of writing.  To my readers, Richard Blass, Mitch Geller, and Dr. Ramon del Castillo.

To all individuals and families subjected to discrimination and brutality by police.  To the police that cross the blue line to do what's right.

# PART ONE

---

## THE REASON

# ONE

Max fingered at the pain in his stomach. It was the ulcer, same damn one since he was fourteen. His raven-black, coarse hair bounced listlessly as the armored rescue vehicle pounded through the city streets. A knot grew in his chest. All signs of weakness, nerves, stress. He looked around him at the true examples of men—at least it seemed that way.

Six years ago he had graduated from New York University, around the middle of his class in film school. He quickly learned that the middle meant "unemployable." It was a brutal industry as the big picture companies barely scraped the cream off the top of each class. One of his buddies got a job shooting a reality show and turned him onto a lead with the ubiquitous show *Police*. Working for a show like that, and not even directing, made his ulcer bleed. But, sleeping on his buddy's apartment floor and eating microwaveable noodles for nine months catalyzed him to get an interview and take the job.

Max was nestled between two men like a boy between his uncle and father—Martinez on his left and Williams on his right. It wasn't that they were older or wiser. It was that they were much bigger than Max. Martinez was probably five-foot-ten to Max's five-foot-five. He had a chiseled face, with terrain markers like defined cheekbones, a nose that had seen its share of right hooks, and thick, black eyebrows. In contrast, Max had a dumpy chin—egged on in size by his affinity for jelly stuffed donuts—pale skin rarely let out into the sun, and a physique that looked like a mason slopped wet mortar onto the ground. Williams was even bigger, stronger and better looking than Martinez. His black skin looked like battle armor, akin to breastplates worn by ancient Grecian commanders.

Williams matched his size with an enormous personality—brash, quick-witted and full of humor. He was the loose one in the group, cracking jokes that doubled Max over sometimes. The weird thing he noticed in these first few months with the group though, was that despite how good Williams' jokes were, not all of the other guys laughed. Specifically, Lindsey and Tomko would only laugh when Shaver did, and he rarely did.

Those three sat on the other side of the rumbling vehicle, conversing amongst themselves as usual. It wasn't hard to notice the dividing line.

Max's gear rested between his feet on the floor of the vehicle. He stared blankly across from himself with the sound of guns being armed, gear refitted and equipment rattling, lulling him into his trance-like state. This job had some semblance of directing, Max thought to himself. It was a half-hearted effort at self reassurance.

1

## Derek Blass

There was no need to check any of the gear as he'd already done that several times before meeting up with the team. He was meticulous by nature —a characteristic derived from anxiety...which sprung from years of getting bullied in school...which, he concluded, was his parents' fault. That over-protective mother and the typical, worrisome Jewish father. The faint squeal of brakes shook Max from his ruminations. He instinctively turned his head to Sergeant Shaver for a final briefing.

Shaver was frightening on multiple levels. For one thing, he bristled with muscles. He always sported a skin-tight shave on his head, and looked at people with unblinking, unwavering eyes. There was a violence to Shaver— certainly built and compounded by the rumors surrounding him—that left Max entirely fearful of him at all times. When you had your back to Shaver, it felt as if there was a long, cold knife pressed to the nape of your neck, waiting to slide into your body. He was like a dark pool of water under which was storied to exist something horrible.

"All right," Shaver started, "we've supposedly got a guy in this house holding his wife and his father-in-law hostage. Could have a gun, so consider him armed and dangerous. I want Martinez, Lindsey and Williams around the back. Tomko and I will take the front. When you hear our flashbangs go off, take out the back door. Max, you go with Martinez's group."

That pleased Max. It was better to film the group going in from the unexpected entrance. They would usually catch people sprinting in their direction, vision blurred and ears ringing from the flashbangs. The people's faces were priceless when they ran into a group of Special Weapons and Tactics officers. An intensely human moment as criminals, who considered themselves hard, rebellious and above the law, surrendered on the ground shaking. Society's bullies cut at their Achilles. This is what Max liked to catch on film.

He followed alongside Martinez. They both moved fluidly, silently. How to move was actually a part of Max's training. He had almost tripped, once, but Martinez caught him by the shirt collar before his second knee hit the ground. There could be no surprise if a clumsy cameraman made noise.

When they reached the back porch Martinez raised his right hand and they all came to a stop. Martinez and Lindsey straddled the door while Williams crouched at the top of the porch steps. Max steadied the camera on his shoulder. They all tensed, waiting to hear the flashbangs explode. Glass shattered and then two deafening bangs sounded.

Williams rushed forward and planted his foot on the back door. It burst open and Lindsey rushed into the house screaming, "Police!" Williams curled around the door and then Martinez slipped into the house. Max fell into line behind Martinez who was scanning rooms with his gun.

The house appeared to be well-kept, was warm and smelled like recently cooked food. There was colorful, Spanish pottery in the two rooms Max saw. Lindsey yelled out his identification again. This time a frightened cry echoed him.

"*Estamos aquí!*"

Martinez and Max approached a hallway that ran adjacent to the main living area. Shaver got there first. The six of them lined the hall and waited for Shaver's order.

"Martinez, translate," Shaver barked.

"What, just 'cause my name is Martinez? I don't speak Spanish."

"*No podemos ver! Ayudamos!*"

"So you don't speak illegal." Martinez and the Sergeant stood on either side of the door, not yet in the room. "Martinez, tell these wetbacks to put their hands up."

"Man, screw you." Max cringed at the exchange.

"All right then." The Sergeant directed his voice into the room. "Put your hands up right now! This is the police!"

"*No hablamos Inglés! No podemos ver nada!*"

"Forget this, let's go," Martinez said.

Shaver turned into the room and fixed his weapon on a woman lying on her side. Martinez followed while Max filmed through the door. Max saw a young woman crying on the floor and guessed she was probably in her twenties. A trail of tears marred her face. An older man was rigid on a couch next to her. His eyes were open, but his gaze was not fixed on anything definite. A blanket covered his body up to his neck.

All of the officers lowered their weapons and Lindsey muttered, "What the hell are we here for?"

The young woman's body convulsed as she sobbed on the ground. There was no sign of any son-in-law.

"Hey, old man, get your hands out from under the blanket," Shaver said.

"*No hablamos Inglés,*" came a moan from the woman on the floor.

"Shut up," Shaver said. He took a step toward the man, who still appeared disoriented.

"Old man, get your hands out from under that blanket!"

Max panned back to the old man and zoomed in on his face. His eyes were expressionless. Max wondered if the man was dead. At a minimum, he obviously had no idea what was going on.

Shaver turned around and gave Tomko a look of disgust. "Today's learning lesson Tomko. They come to your country, and don't speak your language." Sergeant jabbed the old man on his shoulder with the muzzle of his gun. Still no response.

"*El no te entiende!*" the woman shrieked from the floor. She started to prop herself up to say something to Shaver but he mocked her language with a barrage of "chinks" and "chongs" as he loomed over her.

"Get back on the floor."

"Sergeant, let's just cuff 'em and get out of here. They don't understand a thing," Martinez said.

"Best idea I've heard yet," Williams added.

"Forget that, these wetbacks are gonna learn a lesson."

"What the hell are you talking about?" Martinez responded.

"Just watch me." Tomko and Lindsey turned their heads and pretended to adjust their weapons.

"You're kidding, right?" Martinez said.

Shaver stepped forward and pressed the muzzle of his rifle against the old man's temple. "Move your hands old man." No response. Max pulled his shot back to capture the Sergeant. Somehow, the camera's shift in focus caught his attention.

"Scrub, shut that camera off."

"Why?"

"Just do what I fucking say!" Max set his camera down on the ground. "That better be off scrub."

"It is," Max lied.

"All right old man, you wanna fuck with me? Watch what I do to this beautiful broad you got over here."

"Sergeant, I'm not gonna let you do this to these people. They haven't done a damn thing wrong and you know it!"

The Sergeant looked at Martinez calmly. "You know what they've done wrong." Shaver sneered. His cheeks bunched up into a clown-like mask. "What you gonna do anyway, big bad Martinez? What you think Tomko and Lindsey will say? These are *my* boys. You think this scrub Jew with the camera has the balls to stand up to me?" Shaver knelt down and pressed up to the young girl's face. He grabbed her long black hair and pulled back slightly. Her chest heaved.

4

*"No, por favor, no lo dejas hacer esto! Por favor! Este hombre me va a hacer daño! Papa! Papa! Ayudame!"*

The old man stirred in his bed. The Sergeant was entirely focused on the young woman. "Ohh, speak that language to me, you filthy spic."

Shaver tilted her head back more and licked the underside of her chin. The young woman screamed.

"That's it," Martinez said while lunging at Shaver. As Shaver dodged him, the old man stirred and started to bring his hands out from under the blanket. Shaver pivoted and swung his submachine gun toward the old man. Tomko jabbed the butt of his gun at Martinez's face and landed a heavy blow. Williams came to his defense and locked into a grasp with Tomko.

Max watched like a figure inside of a shaken snow globe as bullets from Shaver's machine gun tore through plaster, then bed covers, and finally the old man's chest. In all of his time filming cops, Max had never seen someone shot. The bullet holes in the old man's chest immediately ran dark with blood. The old man gasped and then sprayed his life force out of his mouth. His eyes moved and locked on Max. Then he shuddered and his eyes lost focus. Two cold marbles.

Max stood frozen. In front of him was a chaotic picture, frozen as well. The young woman tore at Shaver's left calf with her hands. He stared down at her, emotionless. Martinez lay prone on the floor. Max felt himself gasp for air. Shaver came to life and shook the young woman off his leg. He turned towards Max and said something which was indecipherable. He stepped closer and Max could make something out. "Give me the tape." Max didn't, couldn't respond.

"Okay, how about I do this." Sergeant Shaver fired some shots into Max's camera. "All right, let's get out of here."

"What about her?" Tomko asked.

"Screw her. She ain't even legal."

"What about him?" Tomko asked pointing to Martinez.

"Forget him too. He caused this. Let's go." With that Sergeant Shaver turned and walked to the front door of the house. Tomko and Lindsey followed him out. Max slouched down to the floor and looked at the old man. Williams swore at the other officers as they left the house.

The old man's body had started to slip off the couch. Max crawled over and used his shoulder to push the old man back up. The young woman's sobs rose and fell like the lapping of waves on a beach. She intermittently let out agonizing groans, as if her soul was being wrenched from her body. Black hair matted her face. Max moved closer.

"Hey…hey there," he said while reaching out with his hand.

"*No me tocas!*" she screamed as she yanked her head back. "*Mira que hiciste a mi papa! Pinche culo Americano! Salgate de aquí!*" She stood up, staggered over to her father's broken body, and then wailed and threw herself on him. Max caught Martinez twitching on the ground. He rolled over onto his back and slowly opened his eyes.

"What the…"

"Martinez, we gotta do something." Martinez let his head fall towards Max. His right eye was cut badly and his forehead was already swelling.

"Who the hell are you?"

"Martinez…what the shit…it's Max. Shaver just shot this guy. The woman doesn't speak English. We gotta get them outta here."

Martinez groaned as he sat up. He turned around and looked at the woman laying on her father's body. "There's nothing we can do."

"What the hell are you talking about?" This caught Martinez's full attention—and made a knot grow in Max's chest. "Look, we gotta do something."

"Like what, Max? Call the cops? Get out of here." Martinez stood up with another groan.

"I filmed everything!" he blurted out.

Martinez looked down at Max's camera. "You've gotta be kiddin' me, right? Your camera looks like it turned inside out."

"Look at this." Max pulled a USB drive out of the wreck that was his camera and held it up to Martinez.

# TWO

*Q*ue paso?" Cruz said, answering his phone. He sat reclined at his desk with a white Bic pen in his hand. His desk was in the back of his office, the room a shade of brown. That 1970s type of dirty. The ceiling was low, probably not to code, and peppered with water-stained tiles. This was what he chose six years ago.

He had graduated in the top ten of his law school class, either ninth or tenth depending on who told the story. Wilmer Lopez was ninth, if you asked him. A final class, Juvenile Law, had been the equalizing factor between the two. Cruz got an "A" in the class, raising his cumulative grade point average to three-six-four. Wilmer got an A- in the class, the product of a biased teacher according to Wilmer, which lowered his average to three-six-four. Cruz argued that he had gotten the last, highest grade, and was therefore ninth in the class. Wilmer forwarded the simple argument that he was the champion, who had to be defeated and not tied. The registrar grew so sick of the beef that she finally forbade them from coming into her office.

"Hello, hello. Who's there?"

"Cruz, *es yo*. It's me man. You ain't gonna believe what just happened *hombre!*"

Cruz didn't know half of the people that called. He didn't know this caller either, despite the man claiming some mutual familiarity. It wasn't all that important anyway—the community knew him.

That was his marketing approach right out of law school. A lawyer for the community. Four of the biggest firms in the city initially courted him, but enough of his friends keyed him into the true life behind those big salaries. No recognition. No responsibility. A cog in a billing machine that was expected to spend the first six years of its career silent, researching. Cruz knew that wasn't for him.

He started his own law firm instead. It was terrifying at the beginning— the beginning being the first five years of practice. There were no clients, no money, and correspondingly no food, clothes, car (bus was a straight shot) or life. Then, the clients started to come. He would call his father every time he got a new client. The flow was slow at first, and it was enjoyable to get new clients. As word of his good work spread, that flow became an overwhelming torrent. He lived on the verge of malpractice as he struggled to learn the law, pretended he knew the law, and brought in more and more clients.

At this point he was comfortable enough to say, "Spill it bro."

"Man, *los cochinos* just murdered an old Chicano—Livan Rodriguez man. Freakin' Livan and I rallied together in the 60's! We did some militant shit together. A good brother..."

"What do you mean they murdered him?"

"Murdered him, bro! Stormed into his house on some bullshit domestic violence call and shot his ass!"

"No way."

"Hell yes, man. We gotta do something *carnal*."

"Hold on. Was anyone else there?"

"I don't know man. Livan was pretty old and beat up. I know he lived with his daughter and her husband. That *culo* was a punk-ass-wannabe-banger, but whatever. They might have been there."

Now the identity of the caller mattered. This man had information he may need. "You've got my attention, but who are you and what do you want me to do?"

"Damn man. You kidding me? Start *la Guerra* over this!" the voice exclaimed, sidestepping a part of the question. "Too much of this happens and *los cochinos no se cambian*. They never change—it's time to change them."

"Well..."

"You're the lawyer *hombre!* Bring the law down on law enforcement. Don't hesitate bro. Get your *chones* together and let's bring it."

With that, the voice stopped and the line went dead. The caller's urgency, passion and then abrupt hang-up left Cruz in limbo—his mind swirling like the wind before a heavy storm.

# THREE

A ll right then, give it here," Martinez said. He flicked a look at Williams, who shrugged his shoulders.

Max responded, "You kidding me? This tape is the story of the year. It's worth millions."

Martinez's coal black eyes narrowed, focused. "This man just died, and that's what you care about? How 'bout this." Martinez pulled his gun out of its holster and held its cold barrel to Max's temple. "How about I blow your brains out onto this wall and I just take it from you?"

Max laughed nervously. "But, you...no you wouldn't, couldn't do..."

"The hell I can't. You think I give a shit right now? Give me the drive."

"Look, the drive is password protected anyway. I need to get to a computer to unlock it, so let's go to my station and work it out there, okay?"

Martinez stood still in Max's face. He relieved the gun's pressure from Max's temple.

"Ain't gonna open it without the password," Williams said softly to Martinez.

"We can do that. I'm just a little messed up right now," Martinez said as he shook his head.

"I understand," Max said warily.

"Get your stuff together and we'll go back to your station. Call one of your news trucks to pick us up."

\* \* \* \*

Cruz stepped out of his office and felt a chill wisp around his face. He stood just outside the door to his office for a moment, enjoying the exchange of stale, musty inside air to the outside breeze. Cruz was tall for a Mexican— around five-foot eleven. A pressed, white shirt fit his slender frame, and he wore his characteristic light brown pants. It was the look of every lower to middle-class man in Mexico City, a city where every man, regardless of class or wealth, had a collared shirt and pants to wear every day.

He had a slender nose and delicate lips, which were significant traits in a culture where those of Spanish descent normally tried to separate themselves from *los indigenos*. Brown eyes and dark, coarse hair stood out from his relatively pale skin. The mix of his light-skinned father and rich, cocoa bean mother were apparent in all his physical aspects.

The moment passed, and he hopped into his car while dialing a phone number.

## Derek Blass

"Sandra, you know what's going on with this police shooting? Someone just called me, and ..."

"Of course I know Cruz. It's going to be all over the news. I'm about to go down there and tape a segment."

"What the hell happened?"

"Cruz, I gotta go. In a nutshell, some cops shot an old Latino in front of his daughter."

"How many cops were there?"

"Just come down to 11253 East Charligsen Street and we'll do some investigating together, okay?"

"Yeah, see you there."

# FOUR

After a while, a news van from Max's station showed up. The driver tried to get Max to stay and call a reporter for a piece, but Martinez quickly dispelled that possibility. He leaned back in his seat in the van and groaned. "I'm watching you. Don't do any crazy shit with that drive."

Max could faintly feel it in his shirt pocket. He had to find a way to sell its contents. After a while of silent riding, the van pulled up to the news station.

"All right, get out." Max stumbled out of the van. Williams motioned that he was going to stay put.

"My office is right this way. It's really a cubicle, not an office. I don't think they'd give me an office," Max laughed nervously.

"I don't need a tour, I just need that drive."

"Like I said, I need to unlock the drive for you to even be able to watch it."

Martinez trailed Max through the cells of news groups. He rubbed his eyes with the back of his hand. The adrenaline had faded and now he was exhausted.

"My cubicle is up here." Martinez followed Max through a seemingly unending maze of human-sized cages. "Here we go." Max plopped down into a worn, gray office chair. His cubicle walls were plastered with pictures of what looked like destination resorts. The desktop was covered with a rainbow of Post-Its, newspaper clippings and discarded plastic wrappers. "Gonna fire this beast up," Max said as he turned his computer on. Martinez looked around the office and stared down several people that were being a bit too nosy.

"How long is this gonna take?"

"No more than five minutes." Martinez looked over Max's shoulder and tried to figure out what he was doing. It was all a flurry of clicks and typing, though, nothing he could follow.

"Okay, so I've unlocked the password protection. Now, you—or someone that knows what they're doing—can just plug this into a USB drive and access its contents."

"All right."

Max turned around and handed the drive to Martinez. He lowered his voice and said, "You sure you don't want to share in the

11

proceeds of selling this with me?" Max asked. "We could get mountains of cash."

"It's evidence. I've already broken so many rules letting you come here. Now just give it to me."

Max reluctantly handed over the drive. How did he stumble across the rare instance in humanity where ethics trumped capitalistic tendencies? "If you change your mind …"

"I won't." With that Max watched as Martinez walked away from him, unaware that a slew of trouble was headed their direction.

* * * *

Shaver sat with his back pressed against a closed locker. He flexed his chest muscle which responded with a ripple. Tomko was changing into his civilian's clothes and Lindsey was sitting quietly, watching the other two interplay. It was characteristic of that damn mute, Shaver thought to himself.

"Hey Sarge, you know that crap's gonna be all over the news?"

Shaver remained focused on the bandage he was wrapping around his calf. It was an old achy injury by now. The kind that didn't bother you enough to go to the doctor because usually a good wrap and some Aspirin did the trick. He had plenty of these aches.

"Sarge, don't forget that little Jew photographer was there filming," Tomko insisted. Lindsey looked away from them, pissed. Shaver couldn't respect the guy. There he was, a freaking Jew himself, and he wouldn't even say a word to either of them. If he'd just stand up for himself once, maybe they'd change, or at least not fling around the crap in front of him.

"I told him to turn that camera off."

"And you'd trust him at his word?"

This gave Shaver reason to pause. "Fuck me. You're right."

"I think he works at Channel Four News. I can go chat with him if you want."

"Go ahead and do that. I need to have my own conversation with Martinez. That bastard. I knew I could never trust a spic on my team."

# FIVE

Cruz pulled up to an older row home and put the car into park. The place buzzed like a beehive. Cops roamed the perimeter of the house with menacing, come-close-and-I'll-kick-your-ass looks on their faces. A horde of reporters and their cameramen stood on the sidewalk out front. Cruz stepped out of his car and scanned the tumult for Sandra.

"Cruz, Cruz! Over here!"

Cruz spun to his left and saw Sandra waving. He walked towards her, ricocheting off of two fast moving cameramen in the process.

"This place is a madhouse," Cruz said.

"This is really crazy Cruz. Apparently the police were called to this house on a domestic violence complaint. They arrive, the husband is gone, but the wife is home with her father. Cops enter, and the next thing you know they've shot the old man."

"You know his name?"

"Yeah, Livan Rodriguez. Fifty-five-year-old, Mexican male. From what I've been able to gather, Mr. Rodriguez was a Mexican citizen who lived here from time to time."

"Someone I know told me he was active in the U.S. during the Chicano Movement. Seems strange that a Mexican citizen would be up here doing that."

"That is weird," Sandra mulled before moving on. "His daughter is a twenty-three-year-old. Also a Mexican citizen. Nowhere to be found now."

"The cops are going to interrogate the hell out of her when they find her."

"Yep. Hey Cruz, rumor is that a cameraman from Channel Four News was filming when this happened."

"During the shooting?"

"That's the word. Name is Max Silverman. He's a cameraman for that show, *Police*. Channel Four produces it then licenses it out."

"Talked to him?"

"Haven't gotten there yet. Feel like taking a drive?"

"Sure."

Cruz met Sandra when he was seven. Their families lived right across the street from one another. It defied odds that two kids from a poor Latino neighborhood, with the parents they had, could make it to where they were. Cruz, a relatively successful lawyer and Sandra, an anchor on late-night news.

# Derek Blass

He remembered that Sandra had always been a wickedly smart kid. Smart to the point of trouble. Add to that her stunning beauty, the kind that still made his tongue play stranger, and the reasons underlying her success started to emerge.

Cruz remembered that they became friends through other friends. He didn't hang out with her much until they were teens. Once he got that chance though, it was readily apparent that she was vibrant, funny to the point of tears, and had a depth to her soul that made her seem like an eighty-year-old woman trapped in a thirty-year-old's body. She had a glowing smile and a laugh that played in his ears. Black hair slipped down to the middle of her back until later in her life when she cut it short to the collective gasps of the women in her family. Her face was soft but well-shaped and she had a freckle under her left eye that somehow made Cruz want to protect everything pure about her.

They both came from families of fanatical activists. This created obstacles in life. Not only were they minorities, but they couldn't keep their heads down and fly under the radar. It wasn't allowed. Their fathers frequently pointed a rough, brown finger in their faces and growled, "I made this opportunity for you, go fight for it!" This common background helped them develop a strong bond. Besides, she appreciated his quirks and intelligence, and he admired her passion for life and all its folds.

When Cruz shipped off to college, things started to change in him. Like most boys, he began to fill out. His voice grew deeper. His confidence grew as he interacted with more and more women. One fall break he came home and Sandra fell in love with him. Their parallel backgrounds had brought them together, and it was also what eventually tore them apart.

They drove to the news station while catching up on each other's lives. It had been about a year since Cruz law saw her.

"So, you've been busy, huh?"

"News never stops. Neither does this type of junk."

"What junk?"

"Discrimination. Police brutality. We could run a strong discrimination story on a weekly basis." Cruz was glad to see this one thing hadn't changed. Sandra was imbued with a strong sense of justice, of a requirement to fight in defense of her community and her principles. She refused to accept any stifling of life.

"Maybe keeping it in the news would help."

"No, you know what's really going to help?"

"What's that?"

"A fundamental change. Not turning our collective cheek when we get slapped." He smiled at her unabated passion.

"You mean fighting back against the cops? That's a difficult position to take."

"What reason is there for change when you can kill a defenseless person and all you get is suspended? For an action like that, there should be an equally violent reaction."

He sighed, as they fell back into a routine as familiar as the pillow he slept on every night. "You know I don't believe in that philosophy."

"I know, I know. You are from the Ghandi-esque school of peaceful civil disobedience and kumbaya. I'm not. But, I think the wisdom is in knowing when one approach may work over another. And what has the civil disobedience approach changed? All it has done is forced discrimination to become more cunning, and generally moved it behind doors." Sandra pulled up into a visitor's spot at the news station. Her perspective flowed naturally from her upbringing, much like his flowed from his own.

"How about we continue the conversation over lunch after we talk to this cameraman?"

"Sure. But you know I'm right."

Cruz smiled. "I didn't say that."

# S I X

Tomko pulled up to the Channel Four news station and went to the front desk. He was slighter than the other guys in the team, and probably a reason he hitched onto Shaver so tightly. Scruffy, brown hair topped his rectangular face. His steps were hurried, jumpy. "You know where I can find a cameraman named Max?" He flashed his badge to move the process along.

A young, blond receptionist looked up at him and studied his badge. "Man, he's sure been popular today," she murmured.

The answer piqued Tomko's interest. "Oh yeah? Who else's been here to see him?" When she hesitated he added, "Off the record."

"Well, no one really," she said in a low whisper. "Just that he's been getting calls from a bunch of tabloids and other news agencies."

"That it?"

The young girl paused again but then said, "He came back to work earlier with another cop."

"What'd he look like?"

"I dunno...Mexican?"

"Fucking Martinez," Tomko muttered.

"Huh?"

"Nothing, show me where Max is."

"I can't show you, but I can tell you. Go down the long hall there and make your first right after the water fountain. Max's cubicle is the third on the left."

Tomko started walking towards Max's cubicle while wondering why in the hell Martinez would have come back here. As Tomko turned the corner to Max's cubicle, he noticed Max standing there talking on a cell phone. All he could catch was the tail end of a sentence, "…get you one."

"Hey, Max!" Tomko called out. Max spun around.

"Tomko?" he squeezed out. "What are you doing here?"

"I came to talk to you about today." He looked around, noticed an empty office to the right and yanked Max into it. He shut the door and crouched down in front of it.

"Calm down! What's your problem."

"Like I said, I want to talk to you about today."

"You and every other freak in the world," Max said as he readjusted his collared shirt. "You realize what you dumbasses have gotten me into? A million phone calls from reporters and journalists wanting to know what I saw."

"And what did you tell them?"

"What did I tell them?! Nothing! You think I'm an idiot? I saw what you guys did to that old Mexican!"

"Hey—lower your damn voice. Keep doing the right thing and keep your mouth shut, Max. This will be a department thing. We'll take care of it."

Max laughed. "Yeah, I'm sure you guys have an interest in helping me out."

Tomko glared at Max, but let the comment go. "Listen, I want to see the camera you had today."

"Why, it was off while all this crap went down."

"Cause I said!"

"Right there, on my desk," Max said with a flick of his wrist.

Tomko grabbed the camera and turned it around in his hands. He furrowed his eyebrows and analyzed the mangled piece of electronics.

"How does this thing store what you record?"

"A removable drive, but Martinez took it with him."

Tomko looked at him in disbelief. "Were you gonna tell me that?" Shit, Tomko thought, that's why Martinez was here.

\* \* \* \*

"Martinez, whatchu gonna do with that drive?" Williams said, his usual baritone voice tinged with a bit of nerves. They were driving in the general vicinity of the police station, but Williams noted that Martinez was taking a meandering route.

The two of them met in high school. Martinez was a scrawny sophomore when Williams exploded onto the scene. He was six inches taller than Martinez and already six-foot-five when he got to the school. They were on the high school football team, Williams playing both quarterback and linebacker while Martinez used his speed as a safety.

They both came from the 'hood, different ones though. Martinez grew up in a house of mothers, the youngest of four children. His father passed away when he was five and that left him, his mom, one aunt, and three older sisters. The overdose of estrogen made him an overly sensitive kid, slightly whiny, and definitely a mama's boy. Despite the lack of a male figure, and despite the fact none of his family played or even enjoyed sports, he always had physical ability.

Williams rode on the other side of the tracks. He ran with his brothers and male cousins all the time. He was lifting by twelve years old, already on a god-given path to play sports at the collegiate level. That was the 'hood dream —a ticket out for him and whoever else he could fit on the bus. Two games into his junior season, some jack-off rolled into his planted leg and ended the dream. His family had seen it before. Dreams shattered easily in a glass world.

There wasn't enough room for both of their egos on the team. They constantly butted heads until one day Martinez called Williams out to fight. The fight took place behind an abandoned building adjacent to the high school in a ring of cheering kids. Punches were traded until Williams landed a devastating blow that knocked one of Martinez's teeth out of his mouth. Martinez sat on his rear, stunned and slightly more humble. Williams felt so bad that he leaned down to see Martinez's mouth and that's when Martinez clocked him right back. After a few days of cooling off, the fight left them with a mutual respect. That slowly grew into a strong friendship as the wounds healed. Over time, they rubbed off on each other—Martinez developing more tenacity and Williams more temperance.

"What do you mean? It's going into evidence man. You ain't thinkin' about money like that camera guy, are you?" Martinez hoped he wasn't, because he need some affirmation that the right thing to do was turning the drive in. Ten, twenty thousand dollars could do him just fine.

"Nah man. I'm thinking beyond that shit. What you've got there is powerful."

"What you talking about?"

"Man, don't you remember what they did to Rodney King in L.A.? You think that would have had the same impact if it wasn't taped? That's a little ball of power you got there, and if you check it into evidence, it'll never be seen again."

Martinez stared ahead as he drove the SUV they had commandeered from the news station. What Williams said made sense, but he wasn't one to break protocol. The color of his skin dictated that he play by all the rules, all the time.

"I'm not used to playin' with fire, Williams."

"I know brother. But you know how this game will go."

"They'll suppress it."

"You're damn right they will. One lonely spot on the local news. One follow-up story. Then that old man will be gone forever."

Martinez thought about Williams' pitch. The cautious side of him rebelled against the idea. The other side of him, and he didn't even have a name for it because it was so foreign, liked the proposition.

# SEVEN

C ruz and Sandra arrived at the news station and on their way in a single, white cop pushed through them going the other direction.

"Watch yourselves," he snarled.

Cruz turned to Sandra, "Must be something going on." They went to the front desk receptionist and asked for the cameraman. Perhaps put off because they weren't cops, or they didn't know the cameraman's name, or just the sheer number of callers she had addressed that day for Max, the receptionist was unwilling to help.

"I'm sorry but it's too busy for me to help you," she said while typing on her computer. Sandra flashed her own news station badge to no avail. Cruz tried a charismatic smile which was greeted with the same outcome.

"Well, will you at least tell me where your bathroom is?" Sandra asked. The receptionist pointed Sandra down a hall. Sandra took a leisurely walk toward the bathroom while taking in what she could. She saw a row of cubicles and noticed that the first two were empty, but someone was in the third. As Sandra moved closer, the person wheeled around and let out a nervous, "Hello?"

"Just looking for the bathroom." Sandra kept walking toward the cubicle, hoping to engage him. He appeared to be a man in his mid-thirties, with curly black hair and a face of stubble that looked generations old. Sandra stopped behind him and struck her most enticing pose.

"Hey, who the hell are you? The bathroom is back that way," the man said pointing behind her.

Undaunted and certainly hardened by the thousands of similar rebukes she had received as a reporter, Sandra asked, "Hey, do you now the cameraman at this station that shoots for *Police*?"

"No, I don't," he said quickly. Sandra looked at the man's cubicle and saw pictures of him with all sorts of cops at different locations. She looked back at the man with a knowing smile.

"Okay," Sandra started. She pulled a business card out of her pocket. "If you do see that guy, give him this and let him know that a couple of people want to help." The man looked relieved that it was going to end there.

"All right, will do."

Sandra turned around and went back to the front desk. "I found him," she whispered to Cruz.

\* \* \* \*

Tomko got back to the police station and went straight to Shaver's office. Shaver was sitting behind his desk talking to Lindsey, but stopped and asked, "Get something good?"

"Max gave the camera's drive to Martinez. I think everything was recorded."

"So, it *was* fucking recorded!"

"He didn't say what was on the drive, just that Martinez took it."

"We know what's on the drive."

"Yeah, Sarge. Did you get a hold of Martinez?"

"No, for all I know he could be across the border by now—and with that damn drive."

"Nah, he wouldn't do that," Tomko said.

"What do you mean?"

"Martinez isn't like that. Too by the book. If anything, I bet he's struggling with coming back here or giving it to someone else."

"Well, since you've apparently mind-fucked him so much, why don't you give him a call? And speaking of our colored friends, where the hell is Williams?"

"I assume with Martinez. Those two are inseparable."

"Do this for me," Shaver started. "I'm pretty sure those two roaches have families. Let them know as delicately as you can that we don't want to have to get the families involved in the search for this drive."

Tomko smiled. "Perfect."

\* \* \* \*

Martinez and Williams circled the precinct headquarters for thirty minutes when Williams butted in, "How many times we gonna do this Martinez?"

"What's that?"

"Circle the damn station! It's getting boring, not to mention that this ain't the best place for us to be chillin' right now. You know what's inside."

Martinez pulled the car over and said, "Made my decision."

"Oh yeah? Made the right one?" Williams asked.

"Yeah man, I'm gonna keep this tape. I think you're right."

"Damn straight. Hold on." Williams pulled his cell phone out of his pocket.

"Hello...aww shit—Sarge."

"You gotta be freaking kidding me," Martinez grumbled.

21

"Nope, Martinez and I are just cruising around…nope, not planning on coming to the station for a while…we ain't gonna meet you *anywhere*, Sarge."

"What the fuck is he saying man?" Williams didn't answer.

"Nah, we'll tell you where we are when we're damn well ready. Til then, you and your Nazi posse can chill at the station." Williams hung up his phone.

"Shit Williams—now he's completely keyed into us."

"Man, you know Sarge was already onto us. He's no fool. I bet one of his punks visited Max by now."

"You coulda seen if he was willing to talk."

"You trippin'? That freak is gonna put a bullet through both of our heads if we don't give him the goods. Shit. Even giving him the drive ain't gonna solve it. We saw what happened, Martinez. It's on now—drive or not."

# EIGHT

Cruz was back at his office watching the day come to a close through the picture window in front of him. He zoned out and while he did, a formative moment of his early life leaped into his consciousness. The murder sucked it out from the recesses of repressed memories.

Harassment was normal for Cruz and his friends. The cops didn't owe him or his friends anything, but one night the usual harassment crossed well-defined lines. He and two of his friends were sitting on the porch in front of Cruz's house. It was a typical teen moment. Cruz's father, the discipline in his life, was gone to God knows where. His mother was at their church attending a community meeting about workplace discrimination. It was only natural for the three teenage boys to seek out a little trouble.

Eduardo, who had connections that Cruz didn't even ask about, brought over three bottles of Old English. Cruz remembered thinking the beer tasted like piss, but it was no time to puss out. He was already the lily-white member of their circle. Drinking was a rare event, he didn't smoke—cigarettes or pot— and he refused to bang. Eduardo called him a bookworm, but at school they called him "pendeja" or "maricon."

All of a sudden, the boys could hear whistles from about two blocks away. The whistles grew closer and closer.

"*Es la pinche policía, güey,*" Eduardo said.

Sure enough, a slow-moving black police interceptor was taking its time down the middle of the street.

"Put the beers away," Cruz warned.

"*Que se chingan,*" Eduardo said defiantly.

"No way man, don't screw with them," Cruz said. The cop car moved forward onto their block. The windows were tinted, but Cruz could tell the cops' eyes were on them.

"Look man, we gotta ditch this shit," Tony, the other member of their trio, said with a slight tremor in his voice.

"Too late bro," Eduardo responded. Just as he did, the interceptor slowed to a stop in front of them. The driver's side window rolled down. Cruz saw the cop's face. Young and angry. Burnt red face. Shaved head. A scowl that looked entrenched around his eyes and mouth.

"What's that you got? *Que tienes allí?*" The Spanish from a white cop wasn't a surprise where Cruz lived. The department trained them to "know their enemies."

"We ain't doing nothin'," Eduardo answered.

"Did I ask you what you were doing, boy?" The cop started to open his door and Eduardo took off without second thought. Cruz hesitated but when he saw the cop start to run, instincts kicked in. He remembered thinking it made no sense to run—he wasn't really in that big of trouble.

Nevertheless, he found himself directly behind Eduardo. They ran tightly bunched together, each life sparing stride falling in rhythm. Cruz had no idea where Tony went. He probably kept his cool and walked home.

Cruz remembered hearing the lumbering footsteps of the cops behind him. Between slow, steady breaths, Eduardo said, "Cruz, we got these pigs." Just as he did, the two turned a corner into the waiting muzzle of another cop's gun.

"Get down you motherfuckers!" he screamed. Cruz and Eduardo went down so fast they nearly slid into the cop's feet. The other cop came up behind them. Cruz looked around and noticed that they were in the alley behind the local grocery store.

"What's up you dumb bangers? Why'd you run, *putas?*"

Cruz curled into a fetal position on the ground. Eduardo was face down, sprawled out next to him. Dust blew up from Eduardo's breath.

"Look man, we give up, we give up," Eduardo belted out.

Cruz turned his head slightly to the right and saw the two cops standing over them. One of them was the cop from the interceptor—a burly man of medium height. He sported a thick, orange-blond mustache and looked down at the boys with cobalt blue eyes. He knelt down next to Eduardo and took off a black glove. "The time for giving up is over, *holmes*. Now, it's time for daddy to teach you a lesson." The cop stood up and stepped onto the side of Eduardo's head. He laughed as Eduardo started to squirm.

"Yo, what the hell you doing?" Eduardo screamed. His sentence trailed off as the cop put more of his weight onto Eduardo's face. The cop was lifting himself onto that one foot.

Eduardo's voice changed from its cool self to the high pitched scream of a teenage boy, "Get off me! You gonna break my face!"

Cruz watched in terror as he lay there, face to face with Eduardo. Eduardo's face was turning purple-red as tears welled up in his bulging eyes. Then he started to sob uncontrollably.

"No, no, no...Cruz...help me man..." The cop was standing with all of his weight on Eduardo's face. Cruz heard something snap and Eduardo scream. Cruz closed his eyes and began to yell.

"Look at these two pussy cholos," the cop said as he turned his head to look at Cruz. "So fucking tough, you filth of the streets." He lifted his foot from Eduardo's face. Cruz looked at Eduardo and it seemed like his jaw wasn't attached anymore. Eduardo's cries were guttural, muddled.

The cop moved to Eduardo's back and started kicking him in the kidneys. Cruz couldn't take anymore of it and he yelled out, "Stop it please! He isn't doing anything!"

The cop didn't even pause. Between kicks he said, "You spics are here, that's enough."

Cruz looked back at Eduardo whose eyes were rolling back into his head. He had vomited all over the ground in front of him. Cruz could smell that Eduardo had shit and pissed his pants.

"You're killing him!" The tears streamed down Cruz's face. He desperately wanted to get up and rip the cop apart. He sobbed on the ground and started to claw his way over to Eduardo.

"Get the hell away unless you want to be next, shithead." Cruz ignored him and threw his body over Eduardo as best as possible. He felt kicks start to rain down on his side. A rib cracked. But he wasn't going to move.

Cruz heard the voice of the other cop, "Fuck, that's enough."

The cop who had been beating the boys stopped. "You think these *putas* learned their lesson?"

"Yeah man, enough's enough."

Cruz's head dropped on Eduardo's shoulder. Short, strained breaths came from Eduardo's broken mouth. He had stopped crying, and seemed to be unconscious. Cruz closed his eyes again and passed out.

# NINE

I t was two days since the incident and Max was living like *he* was the criminal. Every loud noise made him jump. Every cross stare had him questioning what that person may know. He avoided contact with everyone.

Max went to his living room window and contemplated who he could contact for help, for support. Anyone who could listen really. He was still very close with his father, seemingly more so as he got older and his father's wisdom became apparent. However, this wasn't the situation to drag friends and family into. Max knew they may be in danger even without him voluntarily getting them involved.

As he absentmindedly perused the mail and other junk on his kitchen table, he flipped over a business card that read:

Sandra Gutierrez

Broadcast Journalist, Channel 9 News

He remembered this woman. She was the striking woman who was supposedly hunting for a bathroom. Max flipped the business card around in his hand while he thought about how he could use her. She could be exactly the help he needed.

\* \* \* \*

Martinez and Williams pulled up to Martinez's house. He saw his wife standing at the front door.

"Oh shit, what's this about?" Martinez groaned.

"Looks like you done something wrong *ese*," Williams sneered. It always irritated Martinez when Williams used Spanish slang against him.

Martinez got out of the car and screamed out to his wife, "*Que paso mujer?*" His wife kept staring him down, hands on hips and eyebrows on fire.

"What happened? How about that *loco* racist sergeant of yours calling to ask how I was doing? And his equally racist *cabron* Tomko called your wife, Williams. What the hell did you two bastards do now?"

Martinez felt a ball of fury rise from his gut. He turned to look at Williams who seemed unaffected, like he was expecting this.

"What'd you think man?" Williams asked. "You had to know those punks would pull out all the stops to get that drive back."

"Man, they're threatening our families! Screw them! We don't even know what's on the drive."

"Doesn't matter what's on there. Perception trumps reality," Williams said.

26

"They ain't gonna stop until you give them the drive or you do something with it."

"Look, let's go check out your house, just to make sure," Martinez said.

"All right, man."

"Hey *mujer*, you remember where the gun is and how to use it?" Martinez asked his wife.

"You know it."

\* \* \* \*

Tomko and Lindsey walked up the driveway to Williams' home. The sun was just falling behind the horizon, making them cast long shadows that ran up the side of the house. Lindsey stood on Tomko's right side, pressed up against the house while Tomko rang the doorbell. Tomko heard footsteps coming from the back of the house.

"Hello?"

"Alicia? It's Tomko. I got some bad news."

"Well, tell me through the door."

"Alicia, something's happened to your husband. Let me in, I don't want to tell you this through a door."

"Bullshit you pig. I just talked to him. He's on his way over."

Tomko laughed at her posturing. He looked at Lindsey and gave him a signal to go behind the home.

"I didn't say he was dead, Alicia. Look, he's got something we need and we don't want anything to happen to him. So, let me in and I'll tell you what's going on."

"Forget that!" Williams' wife screamed. "You can go to ..." A scream cut off her sentence. Tomko could hear her cry out, "What the hell are *you* doing in here?" Tomko heard more screaming and the sound of glass breaking. He took a step back and lunged through the front door. Lindsey was behind Williams' wife with one hand over her mouth and another wrapped around her chest.

"Now," Tomko started, "can we please talk?"

\* \* \* \*

Williams was driving this time as he and Martinez headed to his house.

"So, you talked to your wife?" Martinez asked.

"Yeah, yeah, man. She's doing all right."

Almost before Williams could finish the sentence, they came around a street corner and saw Tomko's car parked in the driveway.

"No way...that's Tomko's cruiser." As they drew closer, Martinez could see that the front door was open. Williams slowed the car to a stop and pulled his handgun from its holster. Martinez did the same.

Williams leaned over before they got out of the car, "Listen Martinez, I want you to go in through the front. I'm gonna go in the back of the house and see if I can't catch them by surprise."

"Why surprise? What do you think they're doing?"

"What the fuck does it matter? They're in my house with my wife!" Williams shouted.

"All right bro, just don't get crazy. Don't forget they're cops."

"Martinez, I'm blood red, just got kicked in the nuts crazy now. Just do what the fuck I tell you."

Martinez moved toward the front door while Williams crouched for cover and followed the perimeter of the house around to the back. Martinez heard faint, muffled sobs as he neared the door.

"What's that I smell?" came a voice from inside. It was Tomko. "Martinez, how's a spic like you ever gonna creep up on anyone? I can smell your ass from a hundred feet away."

Martinez stepped through the front door and said, "Fuck you Tomko. What the hell you think you're doing?"

"It's easy," Tomko started. "Give me the drive and we're done."

"You ain't gonna do shit, Tomko. You're crazy to get Williams' wife involved."

"No, Martinez! You're crazy for keeping that fucking drive! Hand it over or this bitch gets a cold one in her dome." He pulled her hair back and held the barrel of his gun to her temple. Martinez stood there for seconds that felt like an eternity. He saw Williams' head slip past a window in the back of the house. It was almost like Lindsey sensed Williams because he wheeled around and aimed his gun at the back door.

"Tomko," he started, "where do you suppose Williams is? These two don't travel solo."

"Damn good question Lindsey." Tomko turned to Martinez. "Where's your ass-buddy, Martinez? I doubt you're on a solo, charity mission here."

"Listen you shit, here's the drive. Just let his wife go." Martinez held the drive out toward Tomko. Lindsey turned around to look at the drive. Right as he did, Martinez saw Williams come out from behind the back door. He held his pistol with two hands, locked directly on Lindsey.

"Williams, don't do it!" Martinez screamed. The roar of Williams' gun drowned Martinez out. Martinez heard at least four shots bellow from the gun, and every one connected with Lindsey. The first two pierced Lindsey's torso, the third his neck and the fourth tore the top of his head off. Lindsey crumpled to the ground without even getting a shot off.

Tomko twisted his body around to aim at Williams. Martinez went to fire at Tomko but it was too late. The sound of Tomko unloading his gun shook the room. Martinez could see bullets rip through Williams' body. He stumbled forward and collapsed. Tomko coldly took aim and shot Williams in the head.

"You motherfucker!" Martinez screamed. "Put your fucking gun down!" Martinez yelled. Martinez felt his hand shake as adrenaline, rage and fear coursed through him. Tomko turned back to Martinez and aimed his gun at Williams' wife.

"Listen Martinez. Calm yourself." Tomko took a step toward the back door and pulled Williams' wife with him. "I'm gonna walk out this back door or she gets smoked." He took another couple of steps back.

"Fuck you Tomko—don't fucking move!"

Tomko kept moving in the direction of the back door. Martinez took aim at Tomko's right arm and fired. The bullet screamed through Tomko's bicep and his gun dropped to the ground.

"Fuccck!" Tomko screamed. He ducked behind Williams' wife then ran the last couple of steps to the back door and out of the house. Martinez ran over to Williams' wife who was passed out cold. He grabbed her in his arms and looked over at Williams. His eyes were open and flooded with blood.

\* \* \* \*

Max sat in his cubicle and watched his phone ring. He had dealt with so many calls in the last day that he couldn't stomach any more.

"Max!" came a voice from an adjacent cubicle. "Pick up your damn phone!"

He grabbed the phone and slowly lifted the receiver to his ear. "Yeah?"

"Maxie, how you been?"

"Who the hell is this?"

"Your old pal Max, Sergeant Shaver."

The hairs on the back of Max's neck bristled. "Oh yeah? What do you want?"

"You know what I want Max."

"Martinez has the drive—go bother him."

"You haven't heard?" Shaver asked.

"Heard what?"

"Oh man. Martinez is on the run, Max. He and Williams killed a cop. They killed Lindsey."

**Derek Blass**

"No way. I don't believe you Shaver. You can go to hell for all I care."

"Listen, you Jew prick. I'm gonna personally gut you if you don't cooperate. Let's try this again—*has Martinez contacted you*?"

Max felt his chest tighten as he tried to deal with Shaver. "No way. Why would he?" Max answered.

"Have you spoken to any newspapers about what you saw? 'Cause you understand my problem, right Max? You're a witness and I don't need anyone talking but me."

"I haven't spoken to a damn soul. Believe me, my life is more important than some payout for this story."

"See, my problem's bigger than that. What if you just tell one friend..."

"I don't have any."

"...or one family member? What if you get drunk one night and try to tell some girl you want to impress? I don't trust you to be quiet, Max. There's only one way that I know for sure."

"Goddammit, Sergeant. I'm not going to say a thing to anyone." The person in the cubicle next to him popped her head over the wall. She gave him an are-you-okay expression and he waved her away.

"We'll see, Max."

"We done, Sergeant?"

"One more thing. I want the copy of the drive that you made."

"What copy?"

"This is one of those trust-building moments, Max. Don't fail me now."

"But I didn't make a copy. Martinez took the drive right when we got back to the station."

"Why did you have to go back to the station then?" Shaver asked. "Why didn't you just give Martinez the drive at the old man's house?"

"The drive is password protected! That's the truth!"

"That's weak Maxie. Pretty weak story. I don't feel the trust so I'm gonna have to think of how to deal with you."

"Listen! Fuck you Sergeant," Max screamed but the line had gone dead before Max finished his sentence. The woman looked over the cubicle wall again.

"You fine?"

Max just stared back at her, the color in his face drained away.

# TEN

Cruz and Sandra stood outside of a fifties-style bungalow, pressed to the yellow crime scene tape that cordoned off the front of the house. A mob of journalists and neighbors jockeyed for a similar position. Cruz met Sandra after she called him to tell him there was another shooting. Maybe there wouldn't have been so much commotion except that this shooting involved two cops. The word was that these were some of the same cops involved in the Livan Rodriguez incident.

Cruz followed Sandra around as she interviewed people that looked like neighbors. She was talking to an older woman, who was speaking in an earnest, but hushed voice.

"That's Officer Williams' house. He and his wife bought it about a year ago. A nice young couple."

"Did you see anything unusual around his house today?" Sandra asked.

"Well, yes I did. A car pulled up outside of the house just a bit ago. Two men got out of the car. They stood at the front door for a minute or so, may have been longer. I don't remember exactly. Then one went around the back of the house."

"What did the person at the front door look like?"

"I knew you'd ask that, honey," the old woman answered. "But I can't tell you much. I'm certain he was a white man, with dark blond hair, close cut. I didn't see his face at all, but he was a stocky fellow, dressed all in black."

"Did you see the driver of the car?"

"No, dear. The windows were so dark you couldn't see in."

"Do you remember what kind of car it was? Was it big or small?"

"It was a navy blue car. "'Bout all I could tell, hon. Ain't much good with cars."

"And did..." Sandra's cell phone cut her off. "Just one moment please." Cruz saw Sandra's eyes widen as she listened intently.

"Now?" she asked. "I'll be there in twenty minutes." Sandra turned to the woman and said, "Thank you so much for your help. If you think of anything else, please call the number on this card."

Sandra turned to Cruz. "Guess who?"

"Who."

"The cameraman."

"No way...must be feeling the pressure. Gotta say, this is melting down quickly. I'll stay here and get the scoop," Cruz said.

"Okay, I'll see what the cameraman has to say. I get the feeling that this is about to get even more serious, Cruz."

"You just be careful," he said.

As Cruz stood amongst the throng waiting for some word of what happened, he looked around at the over-eager journalists drooling for a news bit. Their drive to turn misery into money reminded him of a conversation with his father when he was a child:

"*Mira hijo*. They say that the United Sates is the crown jewel of capitalism and it is. They say that capitalism is the most efficient path to prosperity—and so far as we know it is. But at what cost, *hijo*? Americans are defined by the constant drive to consume. And where does this leave them? It makes them the soulless handmaids of money. They work one, two and three jobs so they can go and splurge on trinkets. Every thought and every action is driven by how they will consume—whether it be food, or goods or services. They endlessly want more and run their souls dry in that pursuit. For when you aspire to something which is transitory and empty, how can you ever develop your soul?"

"Surely all Americans aren't this way *Papa*?"

"No, *mi hijo*. Not all. But, this is the symptom of capitalism—and capitalism is this country."

His dad was a professor at a local community college, and a person who had pulled himself up by his bootstraps to that position. For years, a job at a local factory served as his study, his mouth as his pen, and the streets as his paper. Finally, when the streets rebelled against his knowledge, when they became hard and insensitive to the fight that had gotten them there, he became a more formal educator.

"What's the answer then, *Papa*?"

"A better balance first. Americans can't pay for greater intellect, self-knowledge or *cultura*. Consider this example for starters. You know when we go to *el D.F.* and it's bustling, dangerous and full of rich flavors, smells and people?"

"Yeah."

"What would you call it?"

"Alive *Papa*."

"Right, *mi hijo*! It's alive because the soul of the people has not been prostituted to some economic ideal. *Los Mexicanos* don't trade one more hour in the office for a boisterous dinner *con sus familias*. They don't spend their golden years trapped in some cubicle making another person rich. They realize that their golden years are their *early* years, not their late years as these Americans would have you believe."

As this entrenched memory played before his eyes, a figure in the house caught his attention. Someone was coming to the front door. Cruz looked around at everyone else standing there. Pavlov's bell had rung. Their pens and pencils hung over small pads of paper, itching to shorthand something juicy.

He watched as a tremendously wide man strode down the path in front of Officer Williams' house. Wide in the built—not fat—sense. The man reached the crowd and stood there waiting for silence. Everyone obliged.

"As I'm sure you've all heard, we had a very unfortunate shooting here today. One officer of this city was killed in what may have been an unprovoked attack by an African-American police officer against a Caucasian officer."

Cruz heard a collective gasp from the contingency of neighbors. The speaker went on, "We can disclose no further information at this time." Cruz heard the words coming out of the speaker's mouth but was focusing more on his face. He seemed faintly familiar.

A tug on Cruz's shirt pulled him out of his thoughts. It was the old lady that Sandra had been talking to. He looked down at her and she said, "Officer Williams never would have done that."

# E L E V E N

Tomko winced as the doctor finished stitching the bullet hole in his arm. This wasn't a kosher, health care doctor. "Doc K," as Tomko and the rest of his patients knew him, was a fallback doctor. When circumstances such as legality didn't allow you to see a legitimate doctor, you went to him. He treated them like an old-school barber. You came in, exchanged a few words, sat down, and Doc K did his job. No questions asked, no explanations given.

As Doc K gathered his medical equipment he asked Tomko, "So how does it feel?"

"Decent now. But it's gonna hurt like hell soon enough," Tomko answered.

"Oh yes, it's going to be a rough one. How'd it happen?"

Tomko froze in the face of this breach of etiquette.

"Sorry Doctor?"

"Oh, nothing. Hopefully I don't see you again for some time."

Tomko relaxed, "Yeah."

His cell phone rang and he instinctively went to reach for it with his right arm but the pain reminded him that wasn't going to happen.

"Doc, I'll see you around," Tomko said as he walked out of the office which Doc K ran out of his home. Tomko flipped open his phone, "Hello?"

"What the fuck happened, Tomko? This is a royal mess." It was Shaver.

"Yeah, everything went to hell."

"Lindsey is fucking dead, Tomko—that's beyond hell."

"I was there Sarge," Tomko growled. "Williams is dead too."

"I know, Tomko. I saw the aftermath."

"Oh yeah? Was Martinez there?"

"Hell no he wasn't. I have no idea where he or Williams' wife are. I had to weave a fine tale for the media."

"What was that?" Tomko asked.

"That Williams attacked unprovoked. I'm going to leak some of Williams' Black Panther bullshit to the media and turn it into a race-related thing."

"Sarge, this is getting out of control. We've still got a drive floating around that has you shooting that old Mexican."

"Tomko, if I didn't know any better I'd say that's fear in your voice. Is that what I hear?"

"Not fear, Sarge, caution."

"They come from the same place Tomko." Shaver paused. "Listen, you get a day's rest and then we'll find out what hole that back-stabbing wetback Martinez is hiding in. With you down, I'm going to take some of this into my own hands and go scope out Martinez's house."

"All right, we'll talk in a day."

\* \* \* \*

Sandra stood outside of the cameraman's apartment. She peeked into a small window next to the front door. Two black eyes were peering back at her.

"Shit!" Sandra exclaimed as she stepped back. "Max, is that you?" A man came forward out of the darkness. "It's Sandra from News 9."

"Show me some identification."

"Sure." Sandra pulled her driver's license out and held it to the window. The man came closer to the window and scanned the driver's license. After he looked back and forth at Sandra and her license a couple of times, he popped the front door open.

"Get in here, quick," he uttered.

"Max?"

"Yeah, of course. Get the hell in here would you?"

Sandra stepped over the worn threshold into Max's apartment. There wasn't a single light on. The only illumination came from the power button on Max's computer monitor which blinked every few seconds. As Sandra's eyes adjusted to the darkness she could start to make out some furniture. The computer was on her right next to a sliding glass door leading to a second floor patio. On her left, a wall halfway covered with cardboard boxes. Max had disappeared into the recesses of the apartment, beyond Sandra's adjusting view.

"Max?" Sandra called out.

"Just one second. I'll be right back," he answered. Sandra started to feel nervous and she backed toward the front door. She put her hand behind her back and grabbed the doorknob. A figure came back out of the impenetrable darkness at Sandra.

"Hey, sit down," Max said while gesturing to a futon on Sandra's right side. Sandra exhaled. "Listen, you don't have to be scared of me. Be afraid of the people that are chasing me. Well, person really." Sandra fumbled over to the futon and sat down.

"Who's that? And why is this person chasing you?"

"His name is Colin Shaver. He's a sergeant with the police department."

"Okay, and he was at Mr. Rodriguez's house when he was killed?"

"He wasn't just there, Sandra. He did it." Max paused and sat down on a chair across from Sandra. Sandra finally got a decent look at him. He was of average height, extremely pale with contrasting, jet black curly hair. Sandra noticed dark, black bags under Max's eyes. A string of smoke danced up from his hand.

"And this wasn't the sergeant's first incident."

"You mean...he's killed other people like this before?"

"No, no. I've never seen him do anything like this before. *But*, it was all of the other, small things. The looks, the harassment, the threats and the use of excessive but not deadly force. I've been around the sergeant for three years now and it was coming."

"Then why don't you report anything?" Sandra asked.

"Shit—who are you to judge?" Sandra could feel Max pull back. "Believe me that in retrospect I wish I had done something. It's been eating me alive. I feel like a goddamn accomplice. But, it's hard when even his fellow officers weren't doing anything. That made it feel... well... kind of normal."

Sandra sat listening to Max. Judging him wasn't going to help create trust. Plus, she could kind of understand where he was coming from. Society had developed this sentiment that someone else would take care of its problems.

"A part of me...a part of me was just a damn coward too. Sergeant Shaver is scary as hell. I was able to hide behind my camera. Voyeurs have no obligation to act. At least that's what I thought. This time is different though."

"How so?" Sandra asked.

"He *killed* someone. This wasn't an extra twist when putting cuffs on. He killed that old man for *no reason*."

"How do you want me to help?"

"I want you to take the damn drive and do a report on it," Max said.

"Reporter to semi-reporter for a minute, okay?" Sandra asked. Max ashed his cigarette onto the floor and nodded. "You're giving me this story for free?"

Max chuckled. "Crazy, huh?" He shook his head and groaned. "Don't think I'm long for this world anymore, Sandra.

"You think Sergeant Shaver is already after you?"

"Hell yes! I can't believe he hasn't shown up yet. I keep waiting for a knock and him to be behind that door."

"But, he couldn't do anything to you at this point. It would be so obvious," Sandra said, trying her best to reassure Max.

"Sandra, you still don't get it. He doesn't give a shit. He thinks he's invincible."

"I just can't believe he would come here and hurt you after all this."

"Believe it, because he would. This is enough talk though."

"But wait," Sandra interrupted, "I need to know your account of what happened."

Max had turned to his computer. Without turning around he said, "We don't have time for that. You're just going to have to watch the recording." Max reached down and pulled a drive out of what appeared to be one of the USB ports on his computer. All of a sudden he froze and sat stiff in his chair. He turned to Sandra.

"Did you hear that?"

"What? I think you're being paranoid..." But before she could finish her sentence a shadow passed in front of the window next to the front door. Her heart fell into her stomach.

"No fucking way," Max seethed through his teeth. "He can't be here now." Max spun around once, apparently trying to figure out what to do. He grabbed Sandra's elbow and pulled her to a back room. "Get in here," he said as he pushed her into a closet. "Stay *quiet* and take this," he said as he handed her the drive. Sandra knelt down in the back corner of the closet. She was partially hidden by hanging clothes. Someone knocked on the front door.

"Who...who is it?" Max asked.

Sandra heard a lowered voice pierce the front door. "Max, you know who it is."

# T W E L V E

M artinez stood next to Williams' wife. The hum of the florescent lights in the station were the only thing breaking the utter silence. Martinez looked over at her. She was focused on the worn linoleum floor, her hair disheveled, eyes red and moist.

"Alicia," Martinez started, "I got to tell you something."

Without looking up, she said, "What's that, Jo-Jo?" Martinez smiled when she said that. She had called him that since he could remember.

"I made your husband a promise—a promise that's gonna be dangerous to keep."

"What did you promise?" she asked while taking a second to look at him.

"Can't tell you, Alicia. You're already in danger and more information would just make it worse."

"So why the hell bring it up then?"

"Well, I need you to know that this isn't going to get better. You should consider leaving for a bit."

"Leaving?" Alicia asked incredulously. "We have…I…I have a house and a job here. Don't make me say 'I' anymore Jo-Jo! I'm not going anywhere. You do what you need to do, but I'm not going anywhere."

Martinez started to respond but was distracted by a bald-headed man poking his head out of a doorway. It was the Chief.

"I'm ready for you two," he said.

Martinez waited as Alicia gathered her purse and jacket. He had known Alicia for over twenty years. They went to the same elementary school and then they both met Williams in high school. Despite being the same age, Alicia was always more like a big sister to Martinez than just a peer. She was an accomplished psychologist —a perfect complement to Williams' fiery and brash personality. This situation was unique to Martinez because Alicia was always their rock, but now it was his turn.

He grabbed Alicia's arm as she started to walk to the Chief's office. "Alicia, I want you to realize this fool ain't our friend. He's a snake—so watch what you say."

Martinez didn't actually know much about the Chief apart from the stories. Extortion, hits, political corruption to stay in power. Possibly—but it was never as concrete as the other rumors. Some said he was high up in some white supremacy organization. It was a rumor as fleeting as a distant dog bark, but some people said he was a Lone Wolf.

"All right Jo-Jo. But you know I'm going to give him a piece of my mind."

"Just be careful." They reached the Chief's door and stepped inside.

"Welcome, welcome Ms. Williams. Sit down, please," the Chief said gesturing to a faded, brown chair. "Martinez, take a seat," he said a bit more sternly.

The Chief sat back in his chair and lit a pipe. He drew a few times and let the thick smoke roll out of his mouth.

Directing his gaze at Alicia he said, "Now, Ms. Williams, I'm sure you've questions for me. I do of you as well. Why don't you go first and we'll see where we get."

"Okay, I want to know what you are going to do about that racist Tomko. You see, he came to our house to do me harm."

The Chief raised his hand to stop Alicia and smiled politely. "Why would you say all that, Ms. Williams? Why call Officer Tomko a racist? That's a bad foot to start out on." He smiled but his eyes didn't crinkle, and he puffed on his pipe again.

"Because the bigot messed with Alvin so many times before. And Jo... Officer Martinez too."

"So this happened before and no one reported it?" the Chief asked, mock incredulity rolling off his tongue like the pipe smoke.

"No sir. My husband has not been shot and killed before while trying to protect me," she answered sarcastically.

The Chief took his pipe out of his mouth and leaned across the desk. He was imposing, not necessarily physically, but certainly imposing.

"Ms. Williams, I understand your grief. However, you will respect me and this department or you will get the fuck out. Understood?" Both Alicia and Martinez recoiled at the Chief's sudden change in tone. Martinez grabbed Alicia's wrist in an attempt to calm and reassure her.

She bit her quivering lip. "Fine," Alicia started, "this was not the first altercation between the two."

"Thank you. Was their supervisor aware of the altercations between your husband and Officer Tomko?"

Alicia laughed. "Sergeant Shaver? Aren't you in charge here? He's notoriously inept and a bigot." The Chief's face turned red.

"And from what I understand your husband was notoriously hot-headed and antagonistic. In fact, we have reason to believe that your husband was responsible for the bloodshed at your house."

This time Alicia leaned forward. She thrust a finger in the Chief's face.

Martinez tried to shoot her a look but it was too late. "You look here *Chief*. Those two pigs were in my house pointing their guns at my head and asking for some goddamn drive."

The Chief's eyes glittered. "A drive?"

Martinez took a deep breath and lowered his head.

\* \* \* \*

Sandra heard Max arguing with Shaver. "You can't come in here...show me a warrant...no goddammit get out!" Sandra heard a grunt and a thump. "You asshole!" Max screamed.

"Maxie, your apartment looks like shit," the Sergeant paused, "but something sure does smell sweet." Shaver's comment made Sandra tense and pull back even further into the corner of the closet. She noticed her thighs were shaking uncontrollably. Beads of sweat formed on her forehead. The front door slammed shut.

"You know why I'm here. Cough it up."

"Wow, are you idiots for real? Tomko already asked for the same thing."

Shaver lowered his voice, "Look here you little Jew. Sit the fuck down."

"I don't want to." Sandra heard a thud and then Max yelled, "Fuck you Shaver! That hurt!"

"It's only gonna get worse. Now sit down." Sandra's entire body was shaking now. She ran her hand down her suit jacket and pulled her cell phone out. The phone lit up and Sandra scrolled down to Cruz's contact. She sent a text message:

"Need help @ cameraman's apt

1248 Lilly St #204"

She shoved the cell phone back into her pocket.

"Max, let's cut to the chase. I'm giving you two minutes to get me the video from your camera. If you don't, I'll kill you. Period."

"You're crazy Shaver. You can't get away with all of this. Plus, I told you Martinez followed me back to work that day and took the drive! What do you want me to do Shaver?"

"That whiny plea took ten seconds of your two minutes. It's a strange way to waste the last seconds of your life, but to each his own."

"Shaver! Martinez fucking has it!"

"Then I'd suggest you call him, eh?"

"Oh my God! I don't have his number!"

Sandra's phone vibrated in her pocket. She pulled it out and looked down.

"BRT"

Then she heard a strange, muffled whistle followed by a horrendous screech from Max.

"What the …!? You shot me! You shot my …"

"Stay awake you little prick," Shaver said. "It's just your knee, you'll live. That was slightly rude of me though Max, so I'll add two more minutes to your little lifetimer."

Sandra heard Max groan. Sweat was dripping down her chest. The closet suddenly felt like a coffin.

"Max, wakie wakie. Tell me where I can find that video…purty please," Shaver mocked in a slurred southern accent.

"Okay…okay. I saved a copy of the video onto this computer here."

"And how did you get it to this computer?" Shaver asked.

"Email."

"Really, something that size?"

"Yes." Sandra could hear Max's voice trailing off. "Shaver, you gotta help me out. I'm bleeding all over the place."

"Don't worry, Maxie. I've got an old friend coming to help you out."

"I need a doctor! Not a friend."

"Shhh, shhh, Maxie, don't waste your precious energy." Sandra faintly heard the tapping of keyboard buttons being pushed. "Tomko? It's Shaver. I've got our video. Come over to Max's apartment to get his computer and send a tech over to Max's work to get that computer too."

"Tomko?! That's no goddamn friend! Oh shit, shit. I'm gonna die." Sandra heard Max start to sob. "I'm going to die. This is bullshit. I'm so young Shaver."

"Shush Maxie, you aren't gonna die! Who would we have to film all of our exploits?"

"Then why are you pointing your gun at me?"

"Christ Max, am I? I'm conflicted. I've got this nagging feeling that I should get rid of all the witnesses to that unfortunate event a couple days ago."

"No, Shaver…"

"But part of me also knows it wasn't your fault you were there. You were just doing your job, right?"

"Exactly," Max groaned. "Just my job…I won't say anything."

"See, I'd love to believe that Max, but I bet you made a similar promise to yourself that you wouldn't tell me where that video was. And, you caved on that promise."

"You *shot* me!"

"True, Max. But, I just don't know if you would really protect our little secret. I think we should let Mr. Colt decide, okay? He's typically a good judge..."

Sandra heard another of those muffled whistles and then a gurgle.

"Oh shit, Max! That was...man. Mr. Colt, you're a bastard, ain't ya?" Sandra heard a gurgle. She stifled a cry that tried to emanate from her soul.

"What a mess you've made, Mr. Colt. Such a travesty. Now, let's see what you've got around this place, Maxie." Sandra heard footsteps come down the hall to the room where she was hiding. A switch clicked and Sandra could faintly see light stream under the closet door. Terror gripped her as the footsteps continued toward her room. She pressed into the corner of the closet as she heard Shaver take a deep breath through his nose.

"I just don't get it Max. You're such a smelly shit but I'm catching the faintest trace of sweet woman. It's really confusing me. Whatchu hiding in this place? You get laid at lunch?" Another switch clicked and Sandra's room lit up.

"Sweet, sweet woman. Let me see you princess." Sandra's skin crawled as tears streamed silently down her face.

"Mr. Colt, you check the closet." Sandra saw the end of a gun slide in at the far end of the closet. She dug her nails into her shins and took a deep breath. All of a sudden the far closet door slammed in front of her. Shaver's shadow crept along the closet wall.

"Eh, hello?" Sandra caught a glimpse of the monster through hanging clothes. He had a freckled, red face and sported a tight buzz cut. His jaws were more like jowls, two protruding muscles. He had deep-set, liquid blue eyes. She closed her eyes and remained dead still.

"Hmm, trail went cold Mr. Colt." The closet door closed. Sandra quietly exhaled. She guessed that the clothes in the closet masked her smell. Footsteps trailed away toward the front of the apartment. She heard rustling at Max's computer.

"What's this, Max? Sandra Gutierrez...Station 9 News Reporter?" Sandra squirmed and held back a gasp. It must have been the business card she gave Max. "You don't work there though. Interesting."

After a few seconds, Sandra heard the front door open. "All right, Maxie. Remember to keep our little secret." The front door slammed shut. Sandra waited in the closet for what seemed like an eternity. She grew stiff but her body would not release its clench. As more time passed, she swore she heard footsteps on the stairs outside of the apartment. The front door seemed to creak open slowly.

"Hello?" came a voice. "Hellooo?" A footstep hit the linoleum in the entry way. "Oh my God," Sandra heard the person gag and step back out of the apartment.

"Sandra? Sandy, are you there?" Sandra wanted to scream, "Yes! I'm in here," but the terror of what just happened seized her vocal cords. Footsteps ran into the apartment. "Sandra? Where the hell are you?"

This time Sandra managed a weak, "Here."

"Sandra!" The footsteps neared the room she was in. She could tell it was Cruz's voice. She kicked out her right foot and struck the closet door in front of her. The footsteps stopped and the closet door flew open. Cruz stood there, mouth agape.

\* \* \* \*

Tomko sat in the middle of his living room listening to Shaver.

"You fucking *shot* him?"

"Had to."

"What do you mean you had to?"

"He was a witness, Tomko."

"So what the hell then—am I next? This is out of hand, Shaver. All of this has been to protect your ass! I got shot for you!"

"Tomko, Tomko—calm yourself. I appreciate what you've done and no, I'm not going to hurt you. I need you."

"And what about when you don't need me?"

"Let's cross that bridge when we come to it," Shaver said with a disturbed laugh.

"That's not funny!"

"Oh chill out. Look, you were there too and didn't do anything. You've aided and abetted me in this and are now helping me get away with it. So, you're in the same damn boat."

"Forget that Shaver. You shot him."

"Sure Tomko, but that's not the whole picture, is it? If I go down, you go down. I promise."

Tomko grunted.

"Our tech should be in the process of scrubbing the hard drive on Max's work computer. After that, we just need to find that crook Martinez and get that copy of the video back. Simple."

"Look, Shaver, we need to stop the violence. We're gonna catch a ton of shit soon if we aren't more careful."

"I agree, Tomko. Let's not forget that it was your little hostage situation with Mrs. Williams that really turned ugly. That's where the real heat is going to come from." Not hearing anything from Tomko, Shaver added, "Follow up with the tech and we'll meet at my place tomorrow to figure out how to get to Martinez."

\* \* \* \*

Martinez and Alicia climbed into his car, a solemn net cast about them.

"Was it that big of a screw up?" Alicia asked.

"It's...I know you were doin' your best. It just adds another layer of shit. Shaver would be plenty on his own, but now he's in the Chief's crosshairs. That drive would destroy the police department. The Chief won't let it happen."

"I'm sorry Martinez. The trauma of it all was too much. We haven't even buried Alvin and I've got to..." Martinez leaned over and took Alicia into his arms as she broke down.

"I know Alicia. Don't worry 'bout it. We're gonna bring it to these punks. I still need your help though."

Alicia collected herself between sobs. She managed to take some deep breaths and look up at Martinez.

"You're one of Carmen's best friends and I'm gonna need your help in convincing her to leave town. You know she won't accept leaving her own home. But, it's not just her in danger." Martinez stopped, softened his face and lowered his voice, "I know you said you wouldn't leave, but do you understand the danger here? Do you understand why I need the two people I love the most out of here?

Alicia thought about it and then nodded her head.

"Alvin was your husband and basically my brother. We share that grief but we also share the weight of the fight that's coming—and I need your help getting Carmen and yourself to safety."

"I can do it."

"Good," Martinez said as he started the car. "When we get to our house I'll fill you in on the plan." He was putting on a courageous front but the truth was that Martinez had no idea what the next step was.

\* \* \* \*

Cruz stood slack jawed in front of Sandra.

"Are you okay? What happened...did someone hurt you?" He knelt down and took Sandra by her hands, gently pulling her out of the closet. She was pale and limp. As Cruz started to lead Sandra to the front door she pulled away and ran into the bathroom. Cruz heard the toilet seat slam and Sandra vomiting. He pulled out his cell phone and started to dial "911" but then stopped and looked at the body in the living room. Blood pooled behind the cameraman's body. Every few seconds Cruz heard a drip.

Cruz closed his phone and moved back to the closet where Sandra had hidden. He opened the closet door and knelt down on the carpet.

"What are you doing?" Sandra asked.

Cruz jumped up, "Shit Sandra. You scared the hell out of me!" He looked at Sandra who had hair pasted to both of her cheeks. She was always so put together that this vulnerable look was startling. "I'm making sure no one knows we were here."

"You aren't going to call the cops?"

"I thought about it, but no way. If that cop is crazy enough to shoot an innocent person, he'll have no problem pinning this on us. Hell, he's probably waiting for the call to come back here and kill us too." Sandra lowered her head. "I need your help taking care of anything that could identify us. Scrub down all door handles and the bathroom you were just in, then ..."

"I've got something," Sandra interrupted.

"Okay," Cruz responded a bit impatiently. "What is it?" Sandra handed him a USB drive for a computer. "It's the video of the shooting." Cruz stared at the drive in disbelief.

"How'd you get this?"

"The cameraman, Max, gave it to me before the Sergeant got here. Literally, as the Sergeant got to the door."

Cruz still could not believe they had the drive. After a moment he gathered himself and said, "That's amazing work Sandra...truly. We've got to get this cleaned up and get out of here. You clean anywhere that may have prints. I'll check for anything we may have dropped. I don't want to meet this Sergeant or leave him a calling card to come find us."

"I think he already has one..."

"What do you mean?"

"I gave Max my business card, and the Sergeant picked it up before he left."

Cruz's heart dropped when he heard the news, but he tried to maintain a calm demeanor. "Don't worry, Sandra, I'll protect you," he said, hoping his voice didn't betray his doubt. "Let's get this place cleaned up and then worry about that problem next."

The two scoured the apartment for the next ten minutes. Cruz collected two pieces of Sandra's hair from the closet and crept along the floor looking for more identifying evidence as Sandra wiped down surfaces where they may have left fingerprints.

When Cruz reached the front door, he said, "Let's get out of here. Close the door with a paper towel." He watched Sandra come out of the apartment and close the door. Cruz put his arm around her as they walked to his car. When they got into his car, Cruz turned on his phone.

"Who are you calling?" Sandra asked.

"A doctor who can take a look at you."

"No, no. I'm fine Cruz, just a little shaken up." When he didn't respond she said, "Really, I'm fine."

He hesitated to let it go that easily. "You sure?" She nodded her head. "Okay, but I've got to make one other call then." Sandra let out a breath of air that she had been storing since the Sergeant was in the apartment.

"Who's that?"

"Diego," Cruz answered as he backed the car out of its stall. "Hey Diego...it's Cruz. I've got something you are definitely going to want to see... yeah, yeah, I'll meet you there in an hour." He hung up the phone.

"Diego Archuleta?" Sandra asked.

"Yeah...you remember him?"

Sandra laid her head back on the seat. "How could I forget?"

# THIRTEEN

Tomko paused at the door to Shaver's house and listened. He could hear Shaver yelling inside but could not quite make the words out. He gently turned the doorknob until he heard a click and edged the door open. As he started to peek his head through the crack something cold touched his forehead.

Shaver's voice seethed through the darkness, "Are you fucking nuts, man?" All Tomko could see was one of Shaver's ice-blue eyes.

"Sorry, I heard you yelling and didn't know what was going on."

Shaver lowered his gun from Tomko's head. "Have I satisfied your silly curiosity?"

"Kind of. Who were you talking to?" Tomko asked. Shaver turned around and walked into the darkness, beckoning Tomko as he moved away.

"Shut that door."

Tomko did and asked again, "So who wher..."

"I heard you the first time," Shaver snapped. He sat down on a couch and put his gun on a table in front of him. The room was barely lit by an overhead light in the kitchen. "It was the Chief."

"No fucking way. The cluster bomb has officially gone off," Tomko muttered.

"Yeah, you can put it that way."

"What did he want?"

"What the hell do you think he wanted Tomko? The goddamn drive."

Tomko laughed. "How did that old dog catch wind of this?"

"Who knows. He's got ears in all corners of this city. Shit, I may have told him in my sleep. Persuasive little shit."

"Did he give you a deadline?"

"No, but he didn't have to. When he asks for something, God turns over his hourglass."

Tomko sighed and sat down on the couch next to Shaver. "Well, he wants what we want, right?" Tomko looked over at Shaver whom he had never seen so visibly distressed. Shaver usually didn't get shaken by things like this because he didn't care about much. Apparently the Chief's call had some serious bite behind it. Tomko went on, "So, if we get him what he wants, we're saving our own hides. Whatever he decides to do with the drive after that sure as hell ain't our problem."

## Derek Blass

Shaver shifted uneasily in his spot. Tomko saw him lean forward and grab the handgun on the table. "Tomko," Shaver started, "I don't think you understand how much of a snake he is."

* * * *

Cruz and Sandra sat on Diego Archuleta's back patio. Diego was a short, stocky Chicano. He sported a full beard that was always borderline unkempt, silver jewelry on his wrists and neck, and thick glasses that perched halfway down his nose. Diego had fought for Latino rights in the streets, the schools, the town halls, the capitol...and it all showed in his burdened gait. But his eyes and voice told a different, more alive story.

"You two *conejos* have gotten into a bit of trouble, huh?" He looked mostly at Sandra as he said this. "You, *princesa*, look like you've just seen the *chupacabra*!"

"It's been a rough day," she responded quietly, without looking at Diego.

He shook his head, less than surprised that events of the past did not evaporate so quickly. He stepped towards her and put one of his hands on her shoulder, "Muchacha, you can let it go. It was just a difference of opinion."

Actually, Cruz recalled it had been a bit more than a difference of opinion. Diego was about the same age as Cruz and Sandra's parents. Their parents were activists in their own rights. However, about six years ago a schism developed between Diego and Sandra's father.

Diego was a hardcore activist. He lived in the streets and fought for rights in the fields. He was a devout, outspoken Marxist. On the other hand, Sandra's dad took a moderate approach and attempted to integrate capitalism into his life while still serving the general good of the community. To Diego, capitalismo would slowly turn the whole world over into "sheeple," as he called them. Sandra's father was skeptical of capitalism, but figured that a better path than fighting it was to use it to advance the goals of the community. While Diego would have everyone live on a farm and support one another, Sandra's dad would have people be productive members of the great, capitalist machine.

In any event, the two men used to co-exist amicably. They were two great champions who respected each other's intelligence and their joint dedication to their shared community.

That amicable relationship ended abruptly when Diego published a column in a local newspaper slamming the fact that Sandra's father endorsed the development of a research facility for an oil and gas company on land owned by community members. In turn, Sandra's father used his connections

48

as a professor at a national university to lambast Diego in the local media. What followed was an Ali-Foreman throw down between the two men which ended on a hot July night when Diego cracked Sandra's father across the forehead with a half-full bottle of Dos Equis.

When Sandra didn't respond, Diego turned around and moved back to study his rose garden.

"So," he started slowly, "what do you two need from me? Or, let me rephrase. What do you two need from me that your own families could not provide?" Cruz could see the left side of Diego's long mustache flicker, most likely in light amusement.

"What we've got is a little less ivory tower and a bit more..."

"Zapatista?" Diego asked, finishing Cruz's sentence.

"Yeah, you could say that. We're going to need some protection."

Diego stopped scanning his flowers and without turning said, "It's that serious?"

"Yes," Sandra answered. "I was two steps from dying today!"

"Ayy," Diego groaned, "who would harm a hair on your pretty head?"

"The Sergeant in the police department who wants what we have." That piqued Diego's interest enough to get him to turn around.

"*La policía?*"

"Yeah," Cruz answered. "This is connected to the slaying of Livan Rodriguez."

"*El Caballo?*"

"Who?"

"Livan Rodriguez—*El Caballo*. He got that name because back in the day, and I'm talking way back, he used to come to protests on a horse. Freakin' crazy dude," Diego said with a reminiscent smile on his face.

"Well, I'm sure you've heard about it."

"*Por supuesto...*of course I've heard. Don't forget who's green around here!"

"Listen, Diego," Sandra said raising her voice, "we are here despite my better judgment and we aren't goddamn kids anymore. So treat us with some respect, especially in a situation like this."

He shrugged off her attitude. "You know that coming to me for something related to *la policía* is dangerous, right? *Esos cochinos* and I don't get along. Look, look here!" Diego said excitedly drawing them to a particular rose bush.

"See that?" Diego asked pointing to a stem on the rose bush.

"No, what are you looking at?" Cruz asked impatiently.

"It's an aphid."

"Okay, why the hell does that matter?" Sandra asked.

"Because the cops are like these damn aphids. We build beautiful things in our community. We start beautiful families. We raise beautiful families. But, it's all as delicate as this rose." Diego reached towards the stem and held it up as the aphid moved slowly in the opposite direction of his hand.

"Then these little *putos* come along and start to destroy what we've built. It isn't fast or visible. If it was, our reaction would be violent and they can't have that. It's slow, degrading. Small bite by small bite. Once you recognize that they are there though, they *must* be dealt with." Diego pinched the aphid between his fingernails. "Understanding my philosophy, are you still interested in my help?"

Cruz and Sandra looked at one another. They knew Diego was the only alternative. He was the only one that would fight fire with fire. Nothing else would do. They turned back to Diego at the same time and said, "Yes."

\* \* \* \*

Carmen ran to the car and took Alicia into her arms. They stood there for some time before Carmen led Alicia inside the house.

"Sit down *preciosa*," Carmen said as she directed Alicia into a lazy chair. "I want you to know we're here for anything you need, okay?"

"Yes Carmen, I know," Alicia said as she wiped tears from her face.

Carmen turned to Martinez, her face changed instantaneously, "*Que paso aqui?* How did you let this happen?"

"It's not really that simple Carmen. This…this situation…"

"It was Shaver and his racist punks, huh?" she asked.

Martinez took a second to gather himself before responding, "Yeah, and it's Shaver and Tomko after us."

"Not to mention the Chief now," Alicia added.

"She's right," Martinez said. "We just met with the Chief and he knows what we got."

"*Pues*, are you going to finally tell me what you have?"

"It's a video of Shaver killing that old man a couple days ago."

"*No puede ser!*" Carmen said as she sat down. "No wonder he's going nuts trying to get it."

"Right, and that's why we need to figure out a game plan," Martinez said as he went to the kitchen. He grabbed a glass of water and rejoined the women. "I only see one option for you two, which is for both of you to leave."

"No way *hombre*—this is our home and I'm not running!" Carmen exclaimed.

Martinez cherished how strong Carmen could be. However, a companion of strength is usually stubbornness—and she was no exception. He knew this mini-battle would erupt and that he would have to win. He looked Carmen directly in the eyes and said, "I'm not giving you a choice. What's up is bigger than both of us. It was bigger than us when Shaver murdered that innocent man, and became even bigger after they killed Alvin."

"I know this is bigger than us! That's why I want to stay and help!"

"Any help you give by staying is outweighed by the risk of having you here. If Shaver is able to leverage me through you, the whole situation is fucked."

Martinez could see the disappointment in Carmen's eyes as she considered what he was saying. "The greatest sacrifice is for you to leave what you know, what is yours, and where you feel safe. But it's necessary." Martinez looked at both women without an ounce of doubt. They sat near to each other on the couch as this all set in.

"Let's say we do leave," Alicia began, "what are you going to do here all alone?"

Martinez looked at Alicia. "Fight. Fight for your husband and against that bastard Shaver. It's time to strike back."

# FOURTEEN

The Chief watched as his phone blinked with each ring-tone. He was a small, wiry man with a busy mustache and salt and pepper hair. He impatiently tapped his fingers on his desk.

The Chief was an unlikely person for his position. He wasn't a jock, or excessively predisposed to violence or "action." He didn't come from a police or military family. But, what he lacked in physical prowess he made up for in mental ruthlessness. His mind and his willingness to use his mind as a weapon helped him rise through the ranks and beyond other candidates.

This was his ninth year as the department's chief, so plenty of instances of police brutality crossed his desk. None of them were ever filmed though. This was novel, but the challenge would drive him. The chance to wield his nearly limitless power was also attractive.

The other line picked up, "Who is this?"

"It's your old friend from the department."

"No shit...haven't I repaid my debt to you?"

"Not quite. Hell, maybe not ever!" The Chief had an extensive list of debtors. Looking the other way, filing "half-truth" reports, and letting guys slide all came with a price—and the Chief never forgot who owed or how much. The how much part was always open to his interpretation.

"What is it?" The Chief laughed at this game Tyler played. The "no-you-are-twisting-my-arm-to-do-this" game. The truth, which both of them knew, was that Tyler was a lifelong criminal with a lust for violence. When he could get his rocks off *and* have the Chief's backing, well, there was nothing better.

"I've got two sets of problems, both emanating from my department. All of them are connected to the shooting of that old Mexican guy a few days ago. Five of my men were there, and two of 'em just killed each other yesterday. That leaves three: Roman Martinez, Ben Tomko and Sergeant Colin Shaver. The whopper here is that Sergeant Shaver shot and killed that old man while a cameramen was filming an episode of *Police*."

"So you want me to take 'em all out?"

"No, no...not yet, tiger. If you kill them all, then I never get my video. No, I'm hoping Shaver can do his job and recover that video. But, you know what my grandpa used to say to me?" Tyler was silent. "Hope in one hand and shit in the other and see which fills up first. I'm not counting on anyone coming through for me—except you."

"Then, you've got nothing for me to do?"

"Not yet, but I want you to be eager, willing and ready the next time I call you."

"Eager is for the weak," Tyler responded, "I'll be willing and ready."

* * * *

Tomko laughed nervously at what Shaver said but then stopped.

"No way, Shaver—he asked you to do what?"

"To kill you, Tomko. And he didn't ask, he told me." Tomko watched Shaver play with the gun in his hand. His own gun was on the coffee table, too far for him to reach before Shaver could make his move.

"You've done so much for me Tomko..."

"I know! I just killed another cop to protect you!" Tomko blurted out.

Shaver grimaced. "I've already explained you are helping yourself just as much as me Tomko. Nothing more I can do anyway man, this is out of my hands."

"Out of your hands?" Tomko asked incredulously. "No... it's actually right in your fucking hands!"

"Well, what I mean is that the decision of whether to kill you or not is not up to me."

"Who the hell is it up to then?"

"Some would say the Chief. But, in this case he just planted the seed." Holding his gun up Shaver added, "It's up to Mr. Colt to decide whether to water."

"What the fuck—you're crazy."

"Bad tone Tomko. Harsh words. That's *probably* the wrong route to take given your current situation. But, I've got to tell you that Mr. Colt has always had a particular affinity for you and your loyalty."

"Well, thank God for Mr. Fucking Colt's *feelings*," Tomko retorted sarcastically.

"Tomko," Shaver snapped, "I told you to watch it. You'll hurt his feelings."

"Jesus, you *are* crazy."

"Guilty as charged!" Shaver said with an enormous smile. "I talk to a gun, and it makes life and death decisions for me. That's why you are so shit-your-pants afraid of me, Tomko."

Shaver stood up and circled Tomko. "You see, my old friend, this meek shall inherit the Earth bullshit is just that. Power rules. Inspiring fear in others creates power. People whine that if you rule with an iron fist no one will like

**53**

you...waaa fucking waaa..." Shaver's face had become red and contorted. The veins in his head bulged. "Since when did a man's value come from how fucking popular or well-liked he was? That's a tool of the weak, Tomko. They create fictions, values—for self-preservation. I've gone beyond what society tells me is good or bad. I just ask Mr. Colt." Tomko could say nothing and just stared at Shaver. "And...he says...well lucky you..." Shaver looked at the gun. "Really?" Shaver put the it back into the holster on his hip and turned to Tomko. He whispered, "Mr. Colt must be feeling especially fucking generous today." Shaver sat down on the couch to his left.

"You're a goddamn lunatic!" Tomko yelled.

"Again...no argument here Tomko. Maybe, just maybe though, you'll realize that *you* are actually the lunatic for believing in all this *shit*," he spat as he waived a big paw in the general vicinity of the world. Shaver stopped and studied Tomko's face. "Back to business, it's time we get that drive. If we can deliver the drive, the Chief may let you live. If we don't get it, he'll kill us both."

# FIFTEEN

O kay then," Diego said, "We'll fight together. But, it isn't going to be pretty or easy."

"We know," Sandra said.

"Let's see this drive you two have."

Sandra pulled a small USB drive out of her purse.

"Do you have a computer?" Cruz asked.

"I may be old, Cruz, but I'm no dummy." Diego walked slowly into his house, beckoning the other two to follow. What Cruz saw when he got into the house was more like a shrine. There were pictures and posters of Dr. Martin Luther King, Jr. and John F. Kennedy. There was a large oil painting of Emiliano Zapata hanging on the wall to their left.

"Diego," Cruz started, "how do you reconcile these different positions? You've got MLK next to Zapata and I see a small picture of Che right over there."

"Reconcile to whom, Cruz?" Diego turned like an aged merry-go-round as a smile lit on his face.

"Well, you are presenting two very different philosophies by mashing these historical figures together."

"That's a narrow view. Their goals were all *el mismo*. They all fought in the same, timeless battle against *la injusticia*. The only difference is how they got there. It's just like our present situation. You came to me instead of, say, Sandra's papa. Why? Sometimes you need the olive branch and sometimes you need the hammer." They continued moving on, back into a den. This area was filled with pictures of Diego—tons of pictures of Diego with other people.

Sandra picked up a picture and asked, "You knew Cesar Chavez?"

"*Si*. We worked on a lettuce boycott together many, many years ago now. It was the first bit of organizing I had ever done." Diego switched his computer on. As it fired up he stood with his back to the two, but both could see a tremendous sense of pride welled up in Diego.

"This *pelea*…this fight has taken so many resources for so many years. People have sacrificed their time, their money, their families, and even their own lives." Diego stopped and looked at the pictures around him. "I understand why there has to be such a fight for true equal rights. But it's a shame that so much has been wasted on gaining equality when so much more could be done if people just treated each other with dignity and respect."

"There has always been discrimination, and there always will be," Cruz said.

"Most likely," Diego started, "but perhaps someday soon, the tables will be turned."

Cruz looked over at Sandra who flashed him a sweet smile. Pinpricks of nerves jabbed him in the chest. Cruz smiled back but quickly turned away in embarrassment. What a strange reaction, he thought to himself. He had never felt like that around Sandra in all the time he had known her. Her smile and look were filled with a depth she had never directed at him before. He regrouped and asked, "Is your computer ready?"

"Yes. Let me see that drive." Cruz turned back to Sandra who handed the drive over with a clenched fist.

"You are going to have to let it go *muchacha*."

Sandra unclenched her hand. In a fit of selfishness she said, "You know this drive could make my career! Any other reporter would be at the press with it already."

"I know Sandra...but you aren't just any other reporter," Diego said.

"Even in the short time I have had it, it has been such a fight to keep it safe," Sandra added.

"*Yo entiendo*," Diego said as he plugged the USB drive into the computer. Just as he did, they all heard a click come from the front of the house. Diego spun around in his chair. "*Quién es?*" he called out. He waited a few seconds and then called out again, "Who is it?" Diego started to open a drawer behind him just as a shadow moved on the wall outside of their room.

"Diego?" a voice asked.

"Man...who the fuck is it?" Diego growled. A head peeked around the wall.

"Soy yo, Alfonso," the man said as he finished entering the room.

"*Caramba Alfonso!* You're crazy to come in here like a goddamn ghost. Here I am reaching for the damn *pistola!*" Diego slammed the drawer shut.

"Sorry, papa. I heard you talking and didn't want to interrupt."

"You are going to get shot acting like that," Diego said staring at Alfonso. "Well, don't just stand there! Introduce yourself *hombre*."

Alfonso turned to Cruz with a wary look. "Alfonso Archuleta...who are you two?" Alfonso's face was still but his eyes were fiery. Cruz guessed that Alfonso was in his early twenties. He was medium height, a bit shorter than Cruz himself. His hair was jet black and pushed back, and the look matched the black, army-style jacket and pants he was wearing. What

**56**

stood out the most was a scar that ran diagonally almost the length of Alfonso's forehead.

Cruz extended his hand toward Alfonso who grabbed it cautiously but firmly. "Cruz Marquez, and this is my friend Sandra Gutierrez."

"Nice to meet you," Alfonso said. "Now, I hope you don't mind me asking, but what are you doing here?"

"Well..." Cruz started before stopping to ask Diego a question. "Are you sure you want him privy to what's going on? It could make this dangerous for him too."

"I appreciate your concern," Diego said, "but he is my partner in my work. In fact, the work I do is now driven by my son and what was done to him." Diego turned back toward the computer. "Do you see the scar on Alfonso's forehead?" Not knowing how to respond to the question, Cruz and Sandra remained quiet. "Go ahead, Alfonso, tell them what happened."

Alfonso again looked at Cruz and Sandra with distrust, but said quietly, "A cop bashed me across my forehead with a billy club."

"And why did she do that Alfonso?"

"She said she saw a weapon in my hand."

"And what was actually in your hand Alfonso?"

"A pencil and a pager. I was just coming out of class and was hanging out with some friends..."

"Friends?!" Diego exclaimed, cutting his son off. "Tel them who these *friends* were."

"They were certainly the wrong crowd. Bangers, dealers, users. It was a bad time for me."

"For us!"

Alfonso waited to make sure the commentary was over. Diego angrily organized pens into a neat pile, apparently a coping mechanism. "The cop stopped to ask us questions. She focused on me for some reason, and told me to put down what she thought were weapons. When I opened my hand to show the cop what I had, one of the guys in the group started to make a run for it. The cop swung her billy club at him, missed, and hit me on the forehead."

"How old were you?"

"I was fourteen. I've had two surgeries to correct the damage and doctors said I may have cognitive problems at some point. None to report now though," Alfonso said with a half smile.

"So you see, Alfonso is one significant reason why I do what I do," Diego said. "The department took no responsibility for what happened and refused to contribute to his medical bills. We filed suit against the city but some judge decided the case wasn't worth the time and dismissed it. We've appealed but the stress of the medical bills and litigation drove my wife and I apart. This happened eight years ago and we still haven't seen an ounce of justice—so we fight for it."

They all contemplated the story. "Enough of that," Diego said. "You know us better now and you know why my son stays."

"Sure," Cruz said. A media player popped up on the computer screen.

"All right, push play," Sandra said.

# SIXTEEN

Martinez stood at the top of his driveway watching Carmen and Alicia pull away. His heart filled with anxiety. He just lost Williams, his partner and best friend away from home. Now his wife was leaving, and with her the last layer of external security that he had in his life.

He wiped his eyes dry and went back into the house. As he walked into the house he remembered Williams' words and his challenge to fight back. The reality of the matter kept popping into his mind. Him—one man versus an enraged police department. His so-called brothers in blue all taking aim.

He went to his bedroom and pulled a board out from the closet floor. Underneath the board was a space, about the size of a cereal box with a miniature safe in it. He entered the code and checked to make sure the drive was still there.

"My God, this couldn't be more perfect!" came a voice from behind Martinez. He froze as the familiarity of that voice struck him and he felt a cold object press against the back of his head.

"Put the safe down and get on your stomach," the voice said.

"Shaver?" Martinez asked incredulously.

"Who else sunshine? Why so surprised? Did you really think your house was a good hideout? Figures, for a dumb wetback."

"Amazing what a dumb honky you are to think I would just keep the drive at my house."

"What the fuck are you talking about?"

"It ain't here, Shaver." Martinez felt what must have been the muzzle of Shaver's gun relax ever so slightly from his neck. "All that's in here is this...!" Martinez spun around with his left arm and knocked the gun from his neck. With his right hand he hurled the safe at Shaver's face. The safe connected with a dull but devastatingly solid thud. Shaver immediately hit the floor. He picked up Shaver's gun and the safe and ran for the front door. He heard someone call in, "Shaver? What the hell is going on in there?" It was Tomko's voice.

Martinez turned the corner for the front door and was about fifteen feet from Tomko, who hardly had time to adjust with Martinez charging at him. Martinez pulled his arms into his body and lowered his shoulders as he bowled through Tomko. Tomko fired off two errant shots. Martinez scrambled to his motorcycle on the side of his house.

"Please, please, please! Fucking start!" He turned the keys in the ignition and pressed the starter. The motorcycle began to turn over and then shuddered. Just as Martinez was going to give up hope, the engine turned over and the exhaust roared to life. Martinez pulled the clutch in, stomped on the shift lever and pegged the throttle. As the motorcycle's tire caught traction he could hear Tomko screaming his name.

"Maartinezzzz! You're fucking dead!" Martinez was already passing Tomko and he could see him raise his gun to take aim as the motorcycle flew down the driveway. Martinez pressed tightly against the gas tank to slim down his profile. He heard a shot ring out and then another. As soon as the second shot sounded, Martinez felt a searing pain in his right calf. He let out a muffled groan, realizing he was shot. His right leg became loose and almost fell off the foot peg. He shoved the gun and safe into his jacket and grabbed the pants on the shin area of his right leg. The bike quickly decelerated as he let go of the throttle. Martinez dropped his foot onto the peg and grabbed the throttle. Just as he did he heard one more shot ring out. This time Martinez felt no pain and he wrenched the throttle back again. The thousand cubic centimeter engine screamed and lifted the front wheel off the ground. Martinez raced down residential streets at eighty miles per hour. Parked cars on both sides of Martinez became blurred, solid sheets of metal.

Martinez let off the throttle about five blocks from his house to check his side mirror. Seeing nothing he slowed down a bit more to re-adjust his leg on the motorcycle. Just as he did, he heard glass pop behind him. Martinez turned around and saw a black SUV barreling down the street in his direction. Martinez shot down the road again and headed towards the highway. He cut through alleys, ran over front lawns and dodged cars on the way. Shaver's black SUV traced his path the whole time.

As Martinez approached the highway he knew something drastic was necessary to escape Shaver. There was a railroad track two miles east of the highway, but riding his sport bike next to the track would be extremely dangerous at best, and fatal at worst. As he pulled onto the highway he looked down and saw his speed top one hundred, then one-twenty and then a hundred and forty miles per hour. Though he pulled away from Shaver, he could still see the outline of his SUV in the distance behind him. Martinez made a split-second decision and took the next exit off of the highway. At the bottom of the ramp he squeezed through three parked cars and narrowly avoided being plastered by an oncoming truck as he merged onto the street.

He raced down the beat-up street, running red lights where he could and blowing through stop signs. Two enormous headlights continued to track his moves. He could see the glimmer of the railroad crossing sign coming up fast in front of him. He cut back on his speed, and after he crossed the second track he yanked the bike to the left. Now his fate was ninety percent luck. If he could catch up to a train in the next five minutes, he may have a chance. If not, the advantage of Shaver's SUV would surely overwhelm him.

* * * *

Diego pushed play in the media player and a black screen popped up. The length of the video showed eight minutes and forty seconds. After a few seconds of nothing, the screen lit up with a shot of Shaver's squad leaving the back of their transport. The camera bumped along as Max scampered to keep up with three of the cops as they maneuvered to the back of the home.

"The Latino must be Martinez," Cruz said.

"How many cops were there?" Diego asked.

Cruz turned to Sandra, not remembering exactly how many cops there were. "Uhm, I think there were five total. Martinez was the only Latino. Then there was a black cop named Williams..."

"Oh, the one who was just killed in his own home?" Diego interrupted.

"Yeah. Then Shaver, Tomko and another one." All of their attention reverted to the computer screen which showed Martinez breaching the back door and stepping aside as the other two cops entered the home.

The camera was partially obstructed by Martinez's shoulder. As the other cops pushed in, Martinez stood still with his gun drawn. When Martinez moved in, Max followed closely behind him. The camera picked up glimpses of the home between shifts in Martinez's body. The group traveled down a long hall with doors off to each side. Suddenly the whole train stopped and Max stuck the camera around Martinez's right shoulder.

Martinez seemed to relax a bit and lowered his gun while still holding it with two hands. He motioned Max to move forward, and when he did, the room came into plain view. Max pushed back into a corner to capture the whole scene.

"Pause it there. That's obviously Williams," Cruz said, pointing to a figure on the right side of the room. "On the left you can see Lindsey and Tomko. I recognize Lindsey from the photos in the news after he died at Williams' house."

"So, that leaves Shaver then," Sandra said as she pointed to the figure looming in the center of the screen. His gun was drawn and pointed directly at Livan Rodriguez. Shaver seemed huge. Shaved blond hair gleamed from the

61

overhead light. His pit bull neck bulged out of his Kevlar vest. She knew that profile all too well.

"Start it again," Cruz said. Diego restarted the video and they all watched, simultaneously entranced and braced for what was coming. The young woman at Shaver's left leg clawed at his ankle. Her face was awash with anguish and glistening from tears. Shaver pulled his leg back from her grip and pushed her away by placing his foot on her shoulder.

Max panned in on the young woman. Without turning around, Shaver gave a sign which seemed to be directed at Max. Max put the camera on the ground but still managed to catch a good portion of the scene.

"Wow," Cruz started, "I wonder if there was something under the camera to prop it up."

But Sandra noticed that the camera was still moving and it dawned on her what Max had done. "It's on his foot," she said.

Diego paused the video and turned around, "What is?"

"The camera. Look at how it keeps jostling around."

Diego restarted the video and almost as soon as he did, the computer player went black and displayed an error message.

"What the hell!" he swore. Diego clicked on various things to try to fix the problem. He pulled another disc out and inserted it into the computer. It played fine. "I have no idea what just happened."

"It's almost like the file is corrupted," Alfonso said.

"That's what I was thinking too," Diego responded. "Who got this drive?" Diego asked.

"I did," Sandra answered.

"From who?"

"From the cameraman himself."

"Well, let's go talk to him."

Sandra looked at Cruz. "We can't...he's dead."

"How do you know that? I haven't seen anything about it on the news."

"I was at the cameraman's apartment when it happened."

"My God, did you see it happen?" Diego asked.

"No, I was hiding in the closet when it happened. The cameraman, Max, contacted me to give me the drive. He wanted to make sure someone else had the drive in case something happened to him. When I was over there, Shaver came to his apartment and...well, he shot him in the head."

"How did you know it was Shaver if you were hiding?"

Sandra was starting to get exasperated with all of the questions. The trauma of the murder still tormented her. "Because Max said his name, all right?" Cruz noticed Sandra's distress and put his arm around her.

"Let's just move on."

"Well, we can't because we have no video," Diego said. "Without that, what's next?"

"I think we need to talk to Martinez. I have a feeling there may be more than just this copy," Cruz said.

"What makes you think this was a copy?" Alfonso asked.

"For starters, I don't think any cameraman would simply give up a video of this magnitude. I think Max made a copy and that when he did something became corrupted. And what if Max didn't have the original? If I was Shaver, I sure wouldn't let that drive get way from me—we may need to get the original from him."

Diego rolled his eyes and laughed, "Get the drive from the police officer and murderer? Good luck with that!"

"Fucking listen here!" Cruz bristled. "You said you were going to help. A negative attitude is about the last thing we need. You're either in or not!"

Diego's face turned red and Alfonso squared his shoulders to Cruz. "You need to watch how you talk to me, *hijo*. I understand your frustration and fear. But, you're in my house and you need my help. That's the last time you disrespect me in my fucking house in front of my fucking son! Got it?"

Cruz felt his pride well up in his throat. He took a deep breath and told himself to swallow it. Diego was right. They needed his help. Any more fighting and Diego wouldn't help them at all. He backed down and both Diego and Alfonso pulled back a bit.

"I still think we need to find Martinez and see what he knows," Cruz said.

"Okay, I agree. I've got some friends who are investigators. They can tell me where Martinez lives. You and Sandra will start there once I get the info," Diego said.

\* \* \* \*

Martinez squinted his eyes as dirt and dust kicked up around the motorcycle. He didn't look down at the speedometer—it probably would have scared the hell out of him. Objects were flying by so fast that any change in focus could certainly spell death. As he struggled to see ahead he caught the vague outline of a train about a mile in the distance.

He lowered his body to become more aerodynamic. Shaver was still somewhere behind him, and Martinez knew that jumping on a train was an imperfect plan. But, he needed a chance to rest, even for the slightest time. His leg throbbed with every strained heartbeat. If he didn't stop the blood flow soon it would mean big trouble.

As Martinez closed in on the lumbering train, specks of debris flew back at him and pelted his face. He clenched his teeth and pulled up alongside the last car of the train. The roar of the wind almost completely drowned out the sharp, metallic sound of the train churning along its tracks. The first car Martinez came alongside didn't have its doors open but the next one did. He pulled forward and steeled himself for the jump. One slip, the slightest hesitation, and he would die.

Martinez drew the bike as close to the swaying car as he could, planted his left leg on the motorcycle's peg and pushed off. To Martinez it seemed like he floated slowly in the air. His hand reached out for the handle on the car's door. His left foot caught the step going up to the car. Just as it did he grabbed onto the handle. Martinez's body swung open from the force of the wind and slammed against the car. Nearly every ounce of his energy had been drained in the pursuit. As he mustered what was left, he saw a plume of dirt shoot up behind the train. The headlights of Shaver's SUV first spun horizontally and then they started to tumble end over end. It was a spectacle. Light shown through shattered glass. Martinez's motorcycle was spit out to the right of Shaver's SUV. He swung himself into the train's car and collapsed onto his stomach.

The taste of dirt caked onto his teeth and permeated his mouth. His eyes were blurry and stinging from the debris swimming in them. Martinez rolled over and put the safe on the floor. He took off his hoodie and shirt, tore the shirt and tied it tightly on the upper part of his calf. Searing pain shot down his foot and made his toes curl. He screamed out, "Goddammit!!" Martinez threw himself back and tried to focus on the ceiling of the train car.

The car steadily swayed from side to side, like a giant metal crib. He turned his head and looked at the passing landscape. The sun had almost set, leaving only the faintest glow to illuminate passing buildings. Streetlights shed a faint yellow on industrial structures and lit up vehicles as the train plodded eastward. The swaying of the car and double thud every ten seconds gently led Martinez to sleep.

The car's floor was uneven and a raised beam in the floor pressed into the middle of his back. That discomfort, even with the cold graininess of the dirty car floor, was not enough to keep him awake.

# SEVENTEEN

Shaver gasped for air and cracked his eyes open. Light flooded his right eye, which immediately closed. His left eye felt dead. A voice came from somewhere far away.

"Sergeant? Sergeant Shaver, can you hear me?" Shaver groaned and turned his head from side to side. Then, as if a light was switched on, the pain kicked in. It ripped up and through Shaver's chest. He opened his right eye again and realized that he was actually upside down. The passenger seat was empty.

"Wha…where's Tomko? What the fuck what happened…" Shaver asked in a strained voice.

"Sergeant, my name is Clive Toussel and I'm an EMT. We're going to get you out of there in just a moment. You were involved in a significant vehicular accident. Your partner, Tomko, is out of the vehicle and doing okay. We found a motorcycle about one hundred feet behind your vehicle but have not found the…"

"What the hell is wrong with my eye? I can't feel my left eye and I can't see out of it."

"Sergeant, you have sustained serious injuries…"

"I fucking know that!" Shaver screamed out. Pain started to stand out in localities around his body. The pain in his left knee was excruciating. Every time he took a breath it felt like someone was stabbing him between the ribs. But his left eye was the most alarming to him. He still couldn't see out of it. "What the hell is wrong with my left eye!" Shaver could feel liquid running down his face and over his lips.

"Let's just get you out of here first, Sergeant."

"I want to know now!" All of a sudden Shaver heard Tomko's voice come from his other side.

"Sergeant, no mincing words. You're a mess," Tomko said.

"I can fucking feel that, Tomko. Bones will heal. I'm worried about my eye."

"I don't know what to say…" Tomko took a deep breath. "It looks like some debris embedded in your eye. Honestly, there isn't much left there."

"Sergeant, we have an ambulance here ready to transfer you to an emergency room just a mile away. We have to unbuckle you first…"

"You mean my eye, it's gone?"

"Excuse me, Sergeant."

"It doesn't look good, Sarge," Tomko said.

The EMT chimed in, "Doctors really can perform miracles these days, you never know. Maybe they can fix it."

Shaver screamed out and started thrashing his arms. The EMT called for something and Shaver barely felt a pinch on his shoulder, then everything went black again.

\* \* \* \*

The Chief ground his teeth as he watched the news. A helicopter provided an aerial shot. Its high-powered light focused on an overturned, black SUV. A reporter was relaying some facts the Chief halfway paid attention to.

"Appears to be a city vehicle…two survivors motorcycle involved…no apparent survivor from the motorcycle…"

The Chief sighed and turned off the television. His hand steadily increased its pressure on the remote control until he hurled it against the wall. The shattered remote drew his wife's attention.

"Honey, you all right in there?" Hearing no answer but a grunt, and having learned to leave that temperamental man alone after twenty-two years of marriage, she returned to what she was doing.

The Chief picked up his cell phone and walked outside.

"It's me and it's time. I want you to go to 76th and Delmuth. Confirm for me what I already know—that Shaver and Tomko were in the accident. I'm going to go back to the office to deal with this fucking disaster. I'm sure those two were already taken to the hospital, so make that your second visit."

The Chief hung up the phone and set it on the window sill behind him. His slight storm was now a hurricane.

\* \* \* \*

It was about seven at night as Cruz and Sandra set out for Martinez's home. Earlier that day Diego used his resources to trace the address.

"You remember that time you and I got arrested while marching downtown?" Sandra asked with a knowing smile. Again, Cruz took in more than just Sandra's words as he listened. There was a new intensity to how he thought of her.

"Uh, yeah. That almost got me disbarred." Cruz answered.

"Really?" Sandra asked.

"Yeah! I had to go before the Office of Attorney Regulation. Those bastards grilled me for three hours before they let me go."

"I'm surprised you took it that long."

"Well," Cruz paused, "my Dad always told me people have to earn your respect. But, he also taught me that pride can be a great motivator or a great destroyer. Sometimes you've got to swallow it, just like you and I did by seeing Diego. My license is worth too much for me to piss it away on some notion of pride."

"It's a strange balance," Sandra mused. "Having to check your pride when you need something. And yes, I had to check my pride—hard—when we went back to Diego."

"Your control surprised me. When he and your father got into it like that, I figured it was the last time we would ever see Diego."

"It probably would have been except there was no one else to turn to," Sandra said, her sentence trailing off at the end.

The conversation stopped as they pulled up to Martinez's address. It was dark now and the home was eerily quiet. Cruz and Sandra got out of the car and walked up to the house. Nothing stirred in or around the area. The deadness made the hairs stand on the back of Cruz's neck.

"Feels weird," he said.

"Feels like someone left in a hurry," Sandra said as she stepped through the open front door. "Hello?" she called out.

Cruz put his hand on Sandra's shoulder and stepped in front of her. He stepped forward and felt glass crack under his foot. "We need to find a light switch." Both Cruz and Sandra slid their hands along the narrow hall walls as they moved forward. Cruz's hand touched something slick and cool.

"Huh, wonder what that was."

"What?" Sandra asked.

"Just felt something strange on the wall."

"Now we really need to find a switch."

They struggled through the home until Sandra cried out, "Ah-ha! Found one." The light switch clicked and illuminated the kitchen. The condition of the house was startling. Cruz looked down at his hand in dismay as he saw that the slippery substance he felt was half dried blood. He quickly washed his hand in the kitchen sink while Sandra continued to poke around.

"Wow, there was quite a struggle here," Sandra said as she moved a chair out of the way to get to a living room. Cruz dried his hands as he took in the blood-splattered broken glass, the plants lying on their sides, the hole in the wall. Cruz followed the path of destruction into a back bedroom that appeared to be the master bedroom. He flicked on the light, which dimly lit the room. One of the light bulbs was broken in the melee.

Cruz stumbled upon a cubbyhole in the closet while moving around the room. A tile was removed, but there was nothing in the space below.

"Hey Sandra, come check this out." Cruz heard Sandra crunching in his direction.

"Check out this little hiding space," he said, pointing to the empty hole.

"Yeah?"

"Looks like whoever raided this house got what they wanted."

"You think someone made this mess searching for something?" Sandra asked.

"Possibly. I mean, what if I was wrong, and it wasn't Shaver with the original?"

"But look at all of the dressers and storage in the house. Nothing else is touched. If this really was a raid to find something, we'd see drawers pulled out and closets ransacked—not the neat removal of an inconspicuous tile."

"Well, maybe they knew where it was."

"Hmm, I don't know Cruz. I think Martinez was here when this happened."

"What makes you say that?"

"You may be right about Shaver not having the original." Cruz looked at Sandra. Going on, she said, "This doesn't look like a ransack—it looks like Martinez had to fight to get out of here. The blood on the wall and glass in the hall. The hole in the drywall. Overturned plants. Furniture on its side. This all points to a struggle and not a search."

"And Martinez had to get something out of his hiding place?" Cruz asked, jumping onto Sandra's theory.

"Yes, look at that hiding space. A camera certainly wouldn't fit in there."

"The video...Martinez has the original copy..."

"That's what I'd say," Sandra answered. "And Shaver has the most to lose from that video."

"But..." Cruz started before they heard a noise by the front door.

"Did you hear that?" Sandra whispered. Cruz nodded and started to move in that direction. Cruz picked up a chair leg and crept as quietly as he could through the debris. They heard a sound again and froze.

"Who's there?" Sandra called out. They remained frozen and strained for some sort of response. Cruz resumed moving forward until he reached the end of the hall. The front door was on his right, about fifteen feet away. He held the chair leg behind him and peeked around the corner.

"Oh, shit," Cruz said with a bit of a laugh. "It's a damn raccoon!" Cruz straightened up and moved around the corner. Sandra stepped out to his side. They watched the raccoon scurry out of the front door. What they both missed was the man watching them from the darkness.

# EIGHTEEN

Tyler arrived at the scene of the accident. He was a tall, lanky man, whose ghostlike silence and pale complexion made him deathly. He had dark black hair and black pools for eyes. A worn, black leather duster swamped his wiry frame. He slithered past an officer who jumped when he caught Tyler's shadow on the ground.

"Damn! You can't come in here!" Tyler flashed a badge the Chief provided him for just these occasions. "Oh geez, sorry Detective."

"What happened here?" Tyler asked. Even his voice was icy enough to make the young officer shudder.

"Well, this black SUV must have rolled six to seven times before it came to a stop on its roof. Pretty amazing the two officers inside survived." Tyler surveyed the torn body of the SUV. A tow truck was in the process of loading the SUV onto its bed.

"Do you know the names of the officers in the vehicle?"

"Yeah, Shaver and Tomko," the young cop answered. "Say," he went on, "you work in our department? Never seen you around before."

"Pretty big city, wouldn't you say?" Tyler said as he turned and gave the cop a stare that was enough to cut off further prodding.

"So, yeah. Shaver and Tomko. Tomko walked but Shaver was in pretty bad shape. They said he was gonna make it but, man, losing an eye probably. That's horrible, don't you think?"

Tyler didn't answer. Instead he crossed the train tracks and looked back. Remnants of the SUV were strewn along the tracks in the dirt stretching away from him. The young cop followed Tyler.

"The tire marks go back about a quarter-mile or so over there," he said pointing to a group of bushes on an embankment, "That's where we found the motorcycle. Well, what was left."

"How'd the rider of that bike turn out?" Tyler asked.

"Shoot, we haven't found him yet. You figure no one would've been able to survive an accident like this on a motorcycle. They'd have to be Jesus to walk away."

"Yes, Jesus indeed," Tyler echoed. "Where is that motorcycle?"

"Over by the tow truck." Tyler walked back to the tow truck with the young officer still at his heels. The accident had reduced the motorcycle to essentially two wheels and a metal frame. He took out a pad of paper and wrote down the motorcycle's vehicle identification number, then went back to his car and got in.

The young officer called to him, "Hey, that's it?" Tyler nodded. "All right, well I guess I'll see you around then."

"You hope not," Tyler said under his breath. The young officer went back to his work. Tyler picked up his cell phone and dialed a number, "It's me. I need you to run a vehicle identification number. It's 1M8GDM9AXKP042788...yeah, I'll wait." Tyler sat stoically and stared straight ahead while he waited. His eyes were calm, rarely looking at anything around him.

"Still here...who owns it?" Tyler got his answer and hung up. He put the car in gear and pulled away from the accident. He called the Chief next.

"It was Shaver and Tomko."

"And the person on the motorcycle?" the Chief asked.

"Martinez."

"So you know what Martinez has then. Go check his home first. You aren't that far away anyway. I'll text you the address."

"Got it." Tyler flipped the phone shut. He thought about Shaver's ineptness as he drove. He never would have let Martinez get his hands on that drive. But, Tyler thought, people always get emotional right after killing someone. Plenty of experience taught him that those who could control their emotions would own the world and everything in it. That was one lesson his prick of an adoptive uncle taught him. He wailed on Tyler without a semblance of emotion. It wasn't until Tyler stopped caring about the beatings, accepting them as robotically as his uncle doled them out, that his uncle stopped. They never talked again after that day.

Tyler's personality kept him isolated from other people as a young man. Studying them from isolation, he began to develop the feeling that they were all weak and powerless creatures. He made efforts to sit among them and observe any redeeming qualities. He never saw one. Instead, he saw weakness. He saw compensation. He would choke as he breathed in their fake cheer. A teeming, parasitic bunch of lemmings who walked, nose to neck and crotch to ass, on their way to his slaughterhouse. With time and tens of murders, he began to view himself as their savior—their cultivator. Like children, they didn't know just how bad it all was. But, unlike children, they had some sense that something was wrong. They dared not ask though— instead they stayed plugged into the system, content to rot away.

These thoughts ran through Tyler's mind as he drove to Martinez's house.

# Derek Blass

He slowed down to try to read addresses illuminated by solitary lights. He stopped a few houses away and turned his car and lights off. There was a car in Martinez's driveway. Martinez could not have come back, he thought. On the other hand, if that video was still in the house, he may have. He opened the car door and softly closed it. From a distance he could see that the front door was open. Some light spilled out from it.

He moved closer and saw the shadow of a person on the wall just inside the front door. Tyler moved behind a tree as two people came out. They shut the front door and started toward their car. It was a man and a woman. The man was tall but probably a few inches shorter than Tyler. The woman was about six inches shorter than the man. Both were well dressed and looked relatively young—maybe late twenties or early thirties. They started their car and backed out of the driveway. Tyler pulled out his pen and paper and took down their license plate number.

\* \* \* \*

Martinez stirred out of his sleep and then sat upright. Dawn was just beginning to break outside on the third day since the incident took place. His leg throbbed intensely. Taking care not to disturb the wound, he pulled his pant leg up and saw that the skin was glossy smooth from being stretched. His leg was discolored a plumish purple from his knee down, and the color deepened to caked, black blood around the bullet wound. Martinez knew that he didn't have much time before infection set in. He slid over to the train car's door and peered out.

All that he saw were plains intermittently broken by oil wells. Despair filled him a bit as he looked at the barren landscape. He took a breath and tried to calculate how many miles he had traveled. At an average of twenty miles per hour, he figured about a hundred and twenty miles. That distance placed him about fifty more miles from the next city. It was doable.

Martinez pulled the safe out of his jacket, which he guarded neurotically even alone in the train car. He typed in a code and opened it. The drive was still inside—peering back at him as if it had a life of its own.

"I'm going to give you life just as soon as we get out of his mess." He closed the safe back up and set it aside. His body swayed gently from side to side in rhythm with the train. Suddenly one of his pockets began to vibrate.

"What the hell?" He reached into his pocket and felt his cell phone. "Forgot I even had it." He answered, "Yes?"

"Roman Martinez! How the *hell* do you go this long without answering. We thought you were dead you bastard!"

It was his wife. Martinez looked at the screen and saw sixteen missed calls.

"Shit—I'm sorry baby, but..."

"Sorry? Sorry? I almost called the damn police station to find what the hell happened."

Martinez's tone immediately changed, "Carmen, don't call the station or any police officer for that matter."

"But I had no idea..."

"Just listen to me—that's the worst thing you could do. If they find you, you're dead and they'll get this drive. Where are you two?"

"We've almost reached the border," Carmen answered. "Probably another three hours." His "master plan" had been for Carmen and Alicia to head for the border.

"Okay, listen to me honey. I want you to drive straight through until you cross. Then call me."

"You doing all right baby?" Carmen asked, her tone softening some. "You don't sound so good."

"I'm doing all right, just a little beat up," he said, masking the nauseating pain he was feeling.

"Have you talked to Shaver?"

Martinez hesitated, "Kinda."

"Are you at home?"

"No," he answered, "just stepped out for a couple."

"Well, I want you to get home and barricade yourself in there until this passes over. I assume you got the video to the local news?"

"Not yet. That's two stops from now."

"I hate when you're vague like this," Carmen said. She was used to it though. There was plenty of vagueness being married to a cop for twelve years. "Well, get home."

"Okay, love you," Martinez said as he hung up the phone. All of the sounds which he tuned out during the call came rushing back. His leg throbbed for good measure, not to be forgotten. Martinez rolled onto his side and stared out at the golden plains, waiting for his exit.

# NINETEEN

Shaver lay on his back looking at the ceiling in his hospital room. Fractured bone in his left leg. Three cracked ribs. Punctured lung. Concussion. One lost eye.

A piece of debris apparently flew in through the shattered window of his SUV during the crash. It cut a line from above his eyebrow, diagonally across his eye and stopped on the middle of his nose. The damage was too severe to save his eye. The doctor said he was lucky to be alive. Shaver didn't care about luck. All that he felt was rage dripping from his mouth. He longed to see Martinez again so that he could dissect him alive. That bitch had gotten away, Shaver thought, but not for long.

Tomko stirred next to his bed, momentarily drawing Shaver's attention away from his thoughts. Then his phone rang. He picked it up off the end of the table next to his bed.

"Hello," he croaked out with an unused voice.

"How bad is it?"

"Chief...well, I should be all right in a couple weeks."

"Don't fuck with me Shaver. A fractured leg and a missing eye is going to have you out a lot longer than that," the Chief said.

"How the hell do you know my injuries?"

"Come on—did your concussion make you an idiot too?"

"Fuck you."

"No, Shaver...fuck you. Did you get that goddamn drive?"

"No." A long pause ensued before the Chief broke it.

"I'm not quite sure what to tell you, Shaver. Old dogs get put to sleep. I can't wait for you to recover and get that drive back. And, if you have no stake in getting that drive back because I'm going to do it for you, then I don't see what good you are to me. You're nothing but a liability."

"Bullshit, Chief. You try to kill me and I'll just go to the news with this."

"Sink the whole ship, just like that, huh?" the Chief asked.

"Fuck yeah. I've got reporters that'll die for this story. You know what, Chief? How 'bout I just start by telling this nurse in my doorway?"

"No, no...wait! Is it a man?"

"Yeah, but you had a fifty-fifty..."

"Promise to tell him one thing for me, okay Shaver?"

"What's that, you prick?"

"Hello," the Chief said flatly.

* * * *

Tyler walked down the hospital's main entrance. Incandescent lights hummed and flickered overhead, making shadows play on the walls. He had donned a nurse's uniform and moved amongst the hospital's staff with serpentine fluidity. He stopped behind a nurse's station and picked up a clipboard with a patient list on it. Tyler stood behind the station as he slowly scanned the list until he got to Shaver—Room 439.

"Excuse me, sir?"

Tyler looked up calmly at a nurse. "Yes?"

"Do I know you?" she asked.

"Oh no, no. I've just been transferred here and I'm trying to get my bearings."

"Where from?"

"What's that?"

"Where'd you get transferred from?"

"Oh! Mercy—up north."

"Okay...I figured they would have told me if I was getting new staff," the nurse said while coming out from behind the nurse's desk. "But then again, why would they tell *me* anything," she added snidely.

"So," Tyler started, "can you point me in the direction of the 400 rooms?"

"Why don't I just take you? You'll need a tour of the place anyways."

"That'd be fantastic!" Tyler cooed.

The nurse grabbed some documents and then moved off. Tyler fell in behind her as she began to point out landmarks such as the cafeteria and the employee locker room.

"I'm sure you know where Human Resources is by now..."

"Yes, of course."

"Just around this corner are the 300 and 400 rooms." Tyler followed her, scanning the door numbers as they went. 408...409...410...

"This is generally where we house the trauma patients, so it can be a pretty stressful place. Do you know where you're going to be assigned?" the nurse asked. 422 ...423...424.

"All my experience is in trauma so probably here." 427... 428...429...

"Well, you're gonna need to buckle down because trauma here is much busier than at Mercy. I used to work up at Mercy and it was a pretty light flow." 433...434...435... "That reminds me. When did you work up there? You must be my same age and I don't remember ever seeing you." 438. Tyler itched inside. He wanted to grab the nurse's face and slam her into a wall. Annoying bitch.

"I was up there for the last three years, after I graduated," he answered.

"Ah, that explains it. I've been here for five years," she said as she moved down the corridor again.

"Say, where's the closest bathroom?" Tyler asked.

"Right around the corner up here on the left."

"Okay. Something I ate just reared its head. How about I meet you back at the nurse's station?" The nurse gave Tyler a bit of a grossed-out look and then nodded her head and walked away from him. He went into the bathroom and stooped over a sink where he ran some cold water and lightly patted it on his face. He waved his hands under a towel dispenser, grabbed one and dried himself off.

Tyler pushed through the bathroom door and headed back to Shaver's room. He looked behind him to confirm no one was there and then pulled a silenced handgun from a side holster and let his arm hang loosely at his side. He entered Shaver's room and saw Shaver in the hospital bed just hanging up his cell phone. There was a younger man asleep in a chair next to the bed.

Shaver looked up. "I'm supposed to tell you hello." The comment startled the man in the chair enough to wake him up. Tomko went to draw his gun but Tyler lifted his own and trained it on Tomko.

"Please—don't try," Tyler said.

Shaver put his hand out to Tomko in a motion meant to stand him down. "What do you want, you demented asshole?" Shaver said.

"Save it Shaver. Just because I kill doesn't mean I'm demented. In fact, I feel wholly rational and collected right now. Tell me, is this how you felt when you murdered that old man in his bed?"

"What the fuck does it matter?"

"Well, you start with attacks, but I don't think you've turned that magnifying lens on your own actions yet. I'm solely a consequence. I am a product of a course of action you set in motion. Being a product, I have no desire, anger, or remorse associated with what I am about to do. Can you say the same of your slaying of an innocent man?"

"What—what are you about to do? Do you know this guy, Shaver?" Tomko asked with a crack in his voice.

"Know *of* him."

"That's all you're supposed to know."

"Get over yourself," Shaver said, "you're no fucking angel of death.

You're just a prick like your boss. You're a killer and just because you don't have emotion attached to your killing doesn't make you any different than me."

"In any event, that's about as philosophical as we need to get," Tyler said, shutting the door to the room. He went over to Tomko with his gun still fixed on Tomko's face. "Give me your gun." Tomko handed his gun over to Tyler who then moved back around the bed.

"Before I kill both of you I need information."

"Kill us? What the fuck, man?" Tomko cried as he looked back and forth at Tyler and Shaver. "But I didn't do a damn thing!"

"Guilt by association. It's a hard lesson to learn—especially when it's your last one. Now, what I need to know is where that drive is."

"And that's why you can't kill either of us—we're the only ones who know where it is," Shaver said. Tyler raised his gun again and shot Tomko in the left shoulder.

"Ohhh fuck!!!" Tomko screamed as he folded forward. "What the fuck!!"

"Don't fuck with me, Shaver," Tyler warned.

"Fuck you," Shaver said, staring into Tyler's eyes.

"No, no—I'll fucking tell you!" Tomko yelled. "Kill him but fucking leave me. I'll tell you what you want to know."

"Let's hear it then," Tyler said.

"Don't do it Tomko, it's the only leverage we've got."

"Fuck leverage, Shaver—I just got shot! This lunatic is gonna kill us if we don't cooperate."

"He's going to kill us anyway—so tell him to go fuck himself instead."

"No...no way. Listen here, man," Tomko said, turning his misty gaze to Tyler. "If I tell you what you want to know, will you let me go? I was just there; I didn't do anything!"

"Sure," Tyler answered, "tell me what I want to know and I won't kill you."

"It's a lie, Tomko," Shaver said.

"Fuck it," Tomko said in a half cry, half exclamation. "Another cop named Martinez has the drive. We tried to get it from him at his house but he got away. That's when we started chasing him and he went to the railroad tracks. We think he managed to hop onto a train while it was moving but we weren't sure because the next thing we know our SUV was somersaulting through the fucking air. So there—you've got all the info we have. Now will you let me..."

## Derek Blass

Tyler pointed his gun at Tomko's head and shot. Tomko's mouth dropped open and his eyes widened. Blood, hair and skull fragments sprayed on the window behind him. His body slumped and his lifeless arms fell on both sides of the chair.

"You cocksucker...he didn't have anything to do with this," Shaver said.

Tyler waited for a moment and listened to blood gurgle in Tomko's mouth. "You know that didn't matter," Tyler responded, turning his gun on Shaver.

"One question before you do this."

"Yes?"

"Do you know someone named Mr. Colt?"

"What are you talking about?" Tyler asked, his voice straining a bit. Tyler saw a movement below the covers of Shaver's bed and immediately lunged to his left. A shot bellowed out from Shaver's gun and grazed Tyler's right shoulder. Tyler's ears rang as he regained his bearings.

"Hahaha! You pussy, look at you go!" Shaver screamed. Tyler scurried toward the door and another shot rang out. This shot missed Tyler entirely as he yanked the door open and ran out into the hall. He saw the head nurse running down the hall toward him.

"What's going on down here?" Tyler ignored her, and as they met he pushed her aside to the ground. "Hey! What are you doing?" she cried. Tyler kept running until he got to his car a few blocks away. He started the car, still panicking a bit but then stopped himself.

"Deep breath," he said to himself. He put the gun back in his side holster and pulled a handkerchief out of his back pocket. He dabbed his forehead and took several deep breaths. It had been sometime since he had a struggle like that. Adrenaline was flowing through his body. As he checked his face in the rearview mirror, Tyler noticed that he was aroused. He smiled and pulled away.

# TWENTY

Cruz and Sandra were headed back to Diego's house when Cruz's phone rang. "Hi Diego. We found some interesting information at Martinez's place." As Cruz listened, the car slowed and came to a stop.

"What's going on?" Sandra asked.

"Here," Cruz said as he turned on the speakerphone. "Diego, I put you on speakerphone. Start from the beginning again if you would."

"I was telling Cruz I may know where your Martinez is."

"Oh yeah? How?" Sandra asked.

"I can't get into my sources too much, but the more important question is where." Sandra flashed Cruz an exasperated look. He smiled back at her and rolled his eyes. "I was watching the news and saw a pretty significant accident between a SUV and a motorcycle out by the old Ranch Store near the railroad tracks. Turns out that the people in the SUV were none other than your white cops."

"Shaver and Tomko," Sandra said, finishing Diego's thought.

"That's right. What's most interesting about this accident is that they never found the motorcyclist. No body in the vicinity. No motorcyclist injuries reported at any hospitals in the vicinity. No results from a five-mile radius search."

"Okay," Cruz started, "so what are you thinking?"

"The only person I think those two miscreants would be chasing fast and recklessly enough to nearly kill themselves would be Martinez. Now, and this may seem far-fetched, but bear with me. No body."

"Right."

"Quite honestly, no one would survive getting run over on a motorcycle."

"Agreed."

"Only other thing possibly moving in that area? A train."

"Ehh, yeah, but what does that..."

"What if Martinez jumped on a train to get away?"

"From his motorcycle?"

"Why not," Diego answered indignantly.

"I mean, I guess trains don't travel that fast and it wouldn't be that hard to catch up with one. Seems pretty incredible," Cruz said.

"Wait, wait, wait!" Sandra cried. "Think about what we just saw at Martinez's house!"

**Derek Blass**

"What?" Diego asked.

"Well, when we got there the door was open and the house was pretty trashed. But, and I said this to Cruz, it looked like a struggle took place in the house—not a ransack. If Shaver and Tomko went to that house looking for the drive, they would have turned it upside down," Sandra explained.

"You think Martinez was there when Shaver and Tomko went to look for the drive?" Diego asked.

"Yep, and I bet Martinez got out with the drive and those two chased him down."

"Couldn't catch him though," Cruz said.

"No, they didn't," Diego said. "You know, I think you two should head east down those railroad tracks to the next town. I would check the local hospital first. He's got to be banged up if there was a struggle. If that's a no-go, then check local pharmacies or drug stores."

"I think that's a good plan. We're already on our way," Cruz said.

"Okay, Alfonso and I are trying to figure out if we can fix the video we have here. I wouldn't count on it though."

"We'll call you when we get there," Cruz said. He hung up the phone.

"Feels like we're a couple steps behind," Sandra said.

"We are, but that's to be expected. We aren't a part of the action, and the way things are going I'd say we keep it that way for as long as possible."

\* \* \* \*

Martinez leaned out of the train car and saw a city looming in the horizon. That was his stop. He pulled his cell phone out and texted Carmen: Almost there. Call when you cross border.

He leaned back and figured it to be about an hour until the train got near the city. It was his first bit of downtime since all the shit hit the fan. As he thought about what happened, and how Williams had died, he began to cry. Martinez pulled his legs in close and put his head on his knees. It was a raw moment like none he had ever experienced before, but he was unimaginably alone.

He realized he never even had the opportunity to mourn the loss. Except in the strictest sense, Martinez and Williams were brothers. They had spent five years together as partners. The stress, loss of life and tragedy involved in their jobs were enough to bond the two eternally. Outside of work, they planned on being godfathers for each other's kids and organizing family events on scorching summer days.

Martinez wasn't sure if he could even remember what it was like before he and Williams became partners. While he would never admit it, with Williams dead and Carmen gone, he felt naked. Ultimately, he didn't know what to do with the video, just that he had to protect it. More than ever, he intended to fulfill Williams' mandate and disseminate the contents of the video, but stumbled on how to do that or who to trust in the process. He was sure that media types would just want to make a quick buck on the video, while he wanted to assure its maximum impact. This was all foreign to Martinez. The whole situation clawed at his confidence.

Martinez tried to shake off the feelings—blaming them on the stress of the situation. He pulled his pant leg up and realized that his calf was more swollen. The point of entry of the bullet was shriveled and raised. The wound smelled. Initial signs of infection, Martinez thought to himself as he gently touched the area. Nothing to become crazy about though. He would be at the hospital soon.

He rolled his pant leg down and looked out of the car again. Those thoughts must have immersed him longer than he knew because the city was now visible. The conductor blew the train's whistle as they made their way over intersections. The beast lumbered on into the outskirts of the city and slowed down by about fifty percent. Martinez watched a sign approach slowly and then pass with a glint from the sun: "Westchester—Pop. 42,156—Elev. 4341."

Martinez readjusted the homemade tourniquet on his leg. He gritted his teeth as the tightening made his bloated calf feel like it was going to burst. Some sort of liquid ran down to over his ankle.

The train ventured in from the city's outskirts, but still not into its heart. Martinez was fairly certain that this was as close as he could get to the hospital on the train. He pushed the bulky car door open some more and stood on the edge. Wind swept Martinez's hair back enough to cause him to worry about hitting the ground at high speed. He planned on jumping onto his left side to avoid his injured leg, but knew that even the best laid plan was bound to fail in circumstances like these.

People waiting at railroad crossings shot him astonished stares. He looked ahead for a softer patch of ground than either cement or glass-ridden dirt. There was a spot, about four hundred feet ahead, that appeared to have some bushes and growth around it. Martinez braced himself and watched with growing apprehension as his spot approached. The "growth" was just tall, reed-like weeds. It seemed he wasn't going to avoid glass or other trash as the whole path along the railroad was littered with debris. Figuring that this was the best place to jump, Martinez bent down on his left knee and sprung as far as he could from the perilous wheels of the train. He landed on his left side but his momentum immediately spun him and his right leg crashed down onto the ground. He screamed in pain as he lay on his back in a cloud of dust.

Another scream came from somewhere behind him. "Holy shit! Wha—what the shit!!" Martinez opened his eyes and all he saw were two blood red eyes. He immediately tried to pull back and sit up but there was a hand on his shoulder.

"Calm, calm down man. Shit. You crazy bastard, whatchudoin' jumping from trains?" As the passing train blew the dust away, the outline of this stranger's face began to appear.

"Whoooeee!" he screamed and then emitted a hellacious belly laugh. "I swear I couldn't tell if you was the whiskey playing tricks or for real—but you sure as shit for real!"

"What?" Martinez managed to mumble.

"You just jumped from a moving train, that's what! Musta been goin' 'bout twenty or so. Here, lemme help you git up." The stranger grabbed Martinez's hand and next thing Martinez knew he was half standing and half crouched over. Rib pain could now be added to the list.

"Here, here—come sit over here. I got a nice little setup over next to this abandoned warehouse." Martinez looked up at the voice and saw an older, ragged bum. "Come on man!" The bum put his arm around Martinez's shoulder in an apparent attempt to help him walk. Suddenly, Martinez couldn't tell if he was dreaming but he felt a hand brush his back pant pockets.

"What the fuck you think you're doing?" Martinez screamed as he tried to spin away. The move wasn't so successful with a bum leg.

"Damn! Whatcha talkin' 'bout?" Martinez got a better look at the bum who threw his encrusted mitts back into the air. A mouth half full of rotted teeth flashed an I-didn't-do-it smile. "Just tryin' to help! Say." His attention turned to something on the ground, "What's this?" Martinez instinctively felt his jacket pockets and noted that his mini-safe was not there.

"What? What is it?" Martinez asked as he began to gain his bearings.

"Shiny little box. Looks like someone left me a gift."

Martinez looked and saw the bum holding his safe. "Hand that over please," Martinez said as he tried to straighten up. Pain darted up his leg throughout his body.

"Shit—hell no man. You landed in my fuckin' territory. This here shit mine."

"Listen to me," Martinez implored, "I'm having a pretty shitty day, okay? I'll repeat this once, nicely...give it to me or you are fucked for real."

"Hell *no*. This shit's mine." Martinez heard a click and saw a reflection off of a knife blade. He started laughing. The laughter built until Martinez was laughing so uncontrollably that the pain in his ribs made him stop.

"What the fuck you laughin' 'bout?"

"Man, fuck that bitch-ass knife," Martinez said as he spit at the bum and pulled out his gun. "You wanna fuck with me?"

The tip of the knife blade dropped. "Shit—put the whip away."

"I told you not to fuck with me. Now hand the fucking safe over!" The bum hesitated, weighing the perceived riches in the safe against guaranteed bodily injury.

"You want this shit? You're gonna have to go get it, you lame-ass bitch." With that the bum hurled the safe over the train tracks into what looked like an enormous mound of trash. "That's where I shit," the bum said, staring Martinez down defiantly. Martinez stared back at the bum but started to hobble over the train tracks. He saw the safe sitting in between some cans of soda.

"Didn't I tell you not to fuck with me?" Martinez shouted over the tracks.

"Aww man, you're just a punk," the bum said dismissively.

"You think so?" Martinez said to himself as he turned to go back across the tracks. "How 'bout I show you what I got?" Martinez felt rage building and reasoning failing. Pain had whittled his patience away. He still teemed over Williams' death. "You wanna see what I got?" Martinez repeated as he crossed the tracks.

"Huh? Man, I'm done with you. You ain't shit."

The chiding was too much. Martinez's better judgment was overwhelmed and he raised his gun at the bum. He pulled the trigger and shot the bum in his hip. The man collapsed to the ground, clenching the area. As he rolled around Martinez hovered over him, taunting him and asking if he still thought Martinez was a punk.

"No man—no!! Leave me the fuck alone!" Martinez was jabbing the gun into the bum's cheek.

"Still a punk motherfucker? Am I still a fucking punk?"

"No!"

Martinez's eyes refocused and he saw the man cowering below him. Fresh blood stained the bum's pants. The return to reality made Martinez ashamed of his actions.

"Goddammit man," he muttered. Martinez swiveled away from the bum and started to walk toward the hospital.

"Hey! You can't just shoot me and leave me here!" When Martinez didn't respond, he added, "This shit'll come back to get you! Just wait." By this point, the bum was fully tuned out. Martinez was spent and needed to take care of his leg.

* * * *

Tyler sat in a chair in the Chief's office, motionless and meditating. He could still taste the violence and rolled it around in his mouth. He replayed Tomko's horrified gaze over and over in his mind. The thrill of killing Tomko sent fantastic sensations to all regions of his body.

"Tyler—how are you?"

"Doing just fine."

The Chief came up next to him. "What's that in your pants, you sick fuck?" Tyler's face turned crimson but he didn't respond. The Chief shook his head in disgust.

"I know how things went at the hospital, but why don't you tell me your side of the story. I'm delirious to find out how you managed to kill Tomko, but the invalid with one eye is still *fucking alive!*" The Chief pounded his fists on the desk as he finished his sentence.

"Shaver had a gun hidden under the sheets of his bed. If you want to be so critical, go kill these bastards on your own."

"Really?" the Chief said, moving around his desk toward Tyler. "You really think you can come into my office, my lair, and fucking talk to me like that?"

"You're a step too close to me," Tyler said. Just as he did, the Chief let a telescoping baton fall from his side and he swung it at Tyler's left shin. The baton connected with a hollow thud and sent Tyler reeling onto the ground. He pulled his gun out from its holster and fixed it on the Chief.

"You asshole! What the hell do you think you're doing?"

"Put that gun away, son."

"Fuck that—I'm about to splatter your teeth."

The Chief emitted a hearty laugh. "You can't kill me! I'm your dealer Tyler. I'm your pimp. The second you betray me is the last time you get to shoot up. Think about that and then put your gun down." Tyler grimaced. "See, you can feel the truth. Imagine your life without me. You'll be tossing salads in jail so soon that you won't be able to tell anything else ever existed." The Chief smiled as Tyler slowly lowered his gun.

"You're going to track Shaver down and kill him this time. But, time is of the essence, my dearest Tyler," the Chief said as he sat down on the edge of his desk. "The true prize we're chasing here is that fuck Martinez. We can silence voices, but that video is infinitely reproducible."

"Shaver should be easy, I'll just go back to the hospital."

"I think your anger has clouded your judgment, Tyler. First, there's no chance in hell that you would be able to get back into that hospital anytime soon. Second, it's a moot point because Shaver isn't at the hospital anymore."

Even in his anger Tyler had to acknowledge the scope of what the Chief knew. "Where is he then?"

"Like I said, you need to track him down."

Tyler gathered himself and rose up, using the chair as support. He gingerly tested weight on his left leg. "There's one thing I haven't had the chance to tell you. When I went to Martinez's house, I saw two people leaving."

"Did you recognize them?" the Chief asked.

"No, but I got their car's license plate number."

"Okay, give it to me and I'll follow up on them. You focus on finishing off Shaver. If you can't track him down and kill him in the next twenty-four hours, I want you to back off and find Martinez instead. I don't know what he intends to do with that video but..." A phone rang in the Chief's breast pocket.

Tyler watched as the Chief listened intently to the caller. When the murmur from the phone stopped, the Chief slowly closed the phone and looked at Tyler.

"Change of plans."

# TWENTY-ONE

"All right Diego, we just got to the hospital. Will call you if we find anything," Cruz said, ending the phone conversation. Cruz and Sandra were still in their car. Dusk had drawn down on the city. Cruz watched exhaust fumes rising behind the car and looked down at his watch—four days since the incident. Fall was in full bloom all around them. The trees varied in colors from maple brown to pumpkin orange to bright gold. He felt a bit of disappointment because he had missed the start of his favorite season.

"How do you suggest we go about finding Martinez?" Sandra asked.

"Well, you're the hotshot so I think you'll have a better chance at getting information than me."

Sandra blushed and tucked her hair behind her ear. "I've got a few journalist tricks up my sleeve."

"Sounds good—let's go then."

They stepped out of the car and walked toward the hospital's main entrance. It was a medium-sized hospital teeming with people. Doctors and nurses passed each other. The ones leaving were grim from a hard day's battle, while those entering carried a renewed sense of hope. Patients in gowns stood outside smoking cigarettes. Others were pushed around in wheelchairs, taking in the last remnants of another nearly forgotten summer. Sandra and Cruz passed through the front entrance and walked to a reception desk. The line must have stretched forty people long and Cruz looked at Sandra in dismay.

"Don't worry," Sandra told him. "I've got some tricks—remember?" Cruz took a place in the line while Sandra moved up to the front. Each person she passed flashed her a contemptuous look.

"Hey!" someone screamed. "What the hell you think you're doing? We've been waiting here for over an hour. Get to the back!" The people in the line murmured their assent. As if on stage, Sandra wheeled around with a flashy reporter smile already affixed to her face. Her eyes twinkled with a freshness as if they had never been opened before.

"Everyone, I understand your frustration. My name is Sandy Gutierrez and I'm with 9 News." Cruz heard a woman shriek behind him and whisper, "Oh my God! I watch her every night." Sandra continued, "I know you've all heard about the murder of those two policemen and we're here to investigate it. We need to get some information before the cops get here though, so I'd appreciate it if you let me talk to the station attendant here first."

"You mean the double killing connected to the murder of that old Hispanic man?" asked the same man who had just yelled at Sandra.

"We aren't sure they're connected yet, but that's why I'm here," she responded.

"You must have some sense of it," a woman behind Cruz said. Cruz smiled. Sandra played to these people's nature, and curiosity overrode any sense of injustice.

"Off the record?" Sandra said with a smile. "Off the record, I think something is going on." Everyone in the line started chattering amongst themselves. "I knew it!" someone said from behind Cruz. In the distracted moment, the line's occupants forgot they were even waiting around. Cruz saw Sandra talking to the attendant, who pointed to a corridor to his right. Sandra waived Cruz up.

"Off the record?" Cruz asked with a questioning but playful look on his face.

"Told you I had some tricks."

Cruz laughed, "More like abuse of power!" They walked down the hospital's corridor in tandem. "Where we going?" Cruz asked.

"Down to the end, turn right and then third room on the right."

"The attendant just told you where he was?"

"Yep," she said lightheartedly, naïve to the effect she had on people.

"I'm pretty interested to see what Martinez is like," Cruz thought out loud. They turned the corner and stopped in front of Martinez's room.

"Geez..." Sandra said. Martinez was sprawled out on his back. His leg was elevated and an IV bag hung next to his bed. They crept into Martinez's room and when Martinez stirred, Sandra clutched Cruz's arm and started to turn around.

"Who the fuck are you two?" Martinez growled without opening his eyes. His hands stirred beneath the sheets. Both of them stopped in their tracks, caught and without an answer.

"I'm really sorry—we thought this was..." Sandra started.

Cruz picked up the slack, "My name is Cruz Marquez and I'm here with my friend Sandra." Martinez slowly opened his eyes, which were encrusted with dirt and stuck together as he tried to peel them open.

"Fuck off."

"Hold on, we've been investigating the Rodriguez killing," Cruz said. "We saw a part of a video taken by a cameraman..."

"Max."

"Yeah, Max."

"How's he?" Martinez asked.

"Uhm, he's dead," Sandra answered. "Shaver killed him."

Martinez's head sunk. "It'll come back 'round to him sometime."

"Almost did, we think ..." Cruz said while glancing at Sandra.

"What do you mean?" Martinez inquired, his interest rising.

"Well, our guess was that you and Shaver got into a pretty intense chase, is that right?" Cruz asked.

Martinez had become more alert and looked at Cruz and Sandra warily. "Timeout—I just told you all to fuck off. Why the hell should I trust you?"

"There's really no reason, I guess. I'm a lawyer activist in the Latino community. Sandra is a reporter with 9 News."

Martinez laughed. "Okay...that doesn't help."

Cruz frowned and said, "I can't get you to trust us this fast I guess. But, what happened that day is...it's of extreme importance to the community." Cruz said.

"So what do you need me for, activist lawyer? I'm just a little cop."

"We need to see if you know where the original video is." Martinez visibly tensed.

"What do you mean original?"

"Well, we got our hands on a copy but something was wrong with the file."

Martinez managed to pull himself up and leaned on his pillows with a sigh. "What are you planning to do with the video?" he asked. Sandra and Cruz looked at each other. In the midst of chasing the video, they hadn't really thought about what they would do with it if they got it. Martinez sensed their hesitation and added, "I mean, a lawyer and a reporter. You two are here to make a quick fucking buck."

"No, no, no!" Cruz said quickly. "I guess we hesitated because we just haven't talked about it yet, but..."

"But what we want to do is use the video to show the kind of injustice that exists," Sandra finished. Martinez smiled inside as he heard her words and thought about what Williams asked of him before dying. Just as Martinez stopped to think about what they were saying, a male nurse came into the room. He went over to the IV bag hanging next to Martinez's bed and switched it out for a new one.

"Is everything okay in here, sir?" the nurse asked. Martinez looked at the male nurse suspiciously.

"What happened to the nurse that was just in here an hour ago?" Martinez asked.

"Shift change," the male nurse answered as he walked out of the room. That's when Martinez noticed the nurse was wearing heavy work boots. Mud had fallen off of the boots and was on the floor.

Martinez looked at Sandra and Cruz and yelled, "Get down!" They looked at him in surprise and stood stupefied instead of dropping. He repeated his command and they hit the ground and covered their heads with their hands. Martinez flung the bed sheet off and aimed his gun at the door. Cruz saw the male nurse come back into the room at the same time, his uniform gone and brandishing two guns of his own. When the nurse saw Martinez's gun, he dove down toward Sandra while firing shots in Martinez's direction. Martinez returned fire and Cruz struggled to move to Sandra. He looked up and saw a gun aimed between his eyes.

"Let her go!" Cruz screamed. Plaster and dust rained down on them. The pungent smell of spent casings burnt his nose. The four of them sat in a triangle of pistols. One gun pointed at Cruz and the other at Martinez by the nurse. Martinez locked onto the nurse. The nurse was gauntly built, deathly looking. His eyes were the ominous dark gray of storm clouds.

"Now, you're going to lower your gun," the nurse said while looking at Martinez.

"Let her fucking go!!" Cruz screamed again. Spit flew out of his mouth and landed on the nurse's forehead who gave him a look of disgust.

"Why would I do that?" Martinez asked the nurse coolly.

"I'm going to blow both of these bitches away if you don't."

"What makes you think I give a shit? I just met them." Cruz's body was shaking as fear and rage engulfed him. Sandra was sobbing with her head in her hands. The nurse had her in a choke hold.

"If you want the blood of these two maggots on your hands, then go ahead and try to shoot me. Otherwise I'd suggest that you lower that *fucking* gun!"

"Let the girl go first," Martinez said.

"No chance in hell," the nurse said. "She's coming with me for security. Or, you can hand over the drive and I'll leave everyone here as they were."

Martinez hesitated before responding, "What drive?"

"Don't fuck with me Martinez," the nurse said.

"You have the drive here?" Cruz asked, surprised.

"Just who the hell are you to know my name and where I was?" Martinez asked the nurse.

"All in good time Martinez. Now decide. I get this bitch or the drive."

"Fuck you asshole!" Cruz screamed.

"I don't have the drive," Martinez said slowly, "so it looks like you're gonna have to take her."

"No, please no..." Sandra cried.

"Martinez, you can't let him do this!"

"Do what? I've got nothing here! You want me to pull this drive out of my ass? Ain't gonna happen."

"Okay then," the nurse said as he stood up while pulling Sandra with him. "No struggle now, sweetheart. I've got a really twitchy finger," he said with a sinister laugh. "I'll keep her until you come to your senses and give me that drive. Get your cell phone charged up because I'll be calling you with your deadline to decide." With that the nurse started backing out of the room, using Sandra as a shield. Cruz watched as he pulled her into the hallway and then pushed her in front of him. The nurse jabbed his gun into Sandra's back. Cruz instinctively lunged forward but stopped when the nurse whispered, "One more motion toward me and your little girlfriend is dead." They moved away as Cruz fell to the ground, exhausted and distraught.

"Hey...hey!" Martinez yelled at him.

"What?" Cruz said despondently.

"Do you know that creep?"

"Never seen him before."

"Was anyone following you here? And, for that matter, how the hell did you know I was here?" Martinez asked.

"No, didn't see anyone following us and ours was just a lucky guess."

"Did anyone know where you were going?"

"No...well, yes actually. One person but he is...he's...he would never rat us out. I mean, who the hell would he even tell we were coming here?"

"That guy that just took your girlfriend."

"First," Cruz began and turned around to Martinez, "she isn't my girlfriend. Second, it's a helluva lot more likely that guy just guessed lucky like us."

"That many people don't get lucky."

"Look, enough talking. I've got to go after Sandra now!"

"You can go ahead, but I'm not moving," Martinez said. "I've got what they want."

"You've got the drive?!"

"Of course." Cruz stood up and approached Martinez as menacingly as he could considering Martinez had a gun out. "Chill out. It had to go like that."

"Fuck that! This isn't Sandra's fault!"

"But you two came here and so now you're in it, aren't you?" Martinez said, staring at Cruz directly into his eyes. "I didn't fucking invite you two here!"

"I've got to get her back."

"You need to realize that they don't want her, she's just leverage. If you give me a damn second to recover here, I may be able to help you out."

Cruz brushed himself off. "Look, I'm quickly getting out of my league here. I'll accept your help wholeheartedly, but I have one question first."

"What's that?"

"Why would you help us out at all? And...why'd you keep the video? You could've stayed out of all of this—hidden behind the blue line."

Martinez looked at Cruz for an uncomfortable length of time. Why *was* it? It was Williams but it was more than that too. Then, he remembered a saying. It captured his sentiment.

"Because it's better to spend one day as a lion than to be a lamb for a thousand years."

# TWENTY-TWO

Carmen and Alicia pulled up to the border crossing. The sun beat down and scorched the surrounding area. The air conditioner blew at full tilt but it still felt like a hand-held fan in the desert. A patrolman monopolized the sliver of shade provided by the border checkpoint structure.

"*Vamonos mujer*! *Pasale*! *Y, bienvenidos a Mexico!*" he said sarcastically. Carmen looked at Alicia who shrugged her shoulders, not understanding a word.

"How about we take a break?" Carmen asked. They had been driving for fourteen hours without rest.

"Sounds good. By the way, what's the plan now that we're here?"

"Not sure what we are going to do. I've got a brother who is active in politics down here and who is an anchor for the local news channel. I'll warn you though, he can be a little...well...passionate is probably the right way to put it. Some may say radical."

"A radical reporter on television?" Alicia asked, surprised.

Carmen laughed, "Yeah, it's different down here. The reporters aren't as...they aren't as whitewashed is probably the way to put it."

"What do you mean?" Carmen smiled at Alicia. Alicia was a nice person and the two had known each other for quite some time now. But, Carmen had never felt that she could fully connect with Alicia because she just didn't quite get it. She either hadn't experienced the world's injustice or she ignored it.

Alicia was into arts and crafts and cooking and taking kids to soccer and baking and hosting social functions and all sorts of other, noble activities. She wasn't a fighter though, and Carmen wondered if all those activities weren't just a coping mechanism to avoid confronting the world's harsh realities. Most people use hobbies to get away. To get away from what, she wondered. Why not stay and deal with reality? Tackle the world with both arms and then hug the hell out of it on the ground. Get filthy in the trenches and fix the world.

"I'm sorry Alicia, what did you say?" Carmen asked.

"What did you mean about people being whitewashed?"

What she meant was people's great rush to be inoffensive, placating robots living in the ever-growing morass of the middle world. Elected officials serving as voice boxes, tap-dancing from one constituent issue to the next without ever taking a position. In the country's desire to become absolutely, unequivocally politically correct, it has lost its soul. Instead, she tried to focus on the positive, "That's something you'll see down here Alicia—the souls of these people are strong. Their cars aren't as nice and their clothes don't always fit right. But, they don't lack these material things because they're poor. It's because they haven't sold their souls for them—yet."

Alicia stared out of the window. "Well, I like our boring, middle of the road country already," Alicia said while pointing at a rundown, rusted tin-top store on the side of the road.

Carmen grinned.

* * * *

Anytime Sandra slowed down she felt the nurse's gun jab her in the back.

"I'm going, you ass!" she seethed through clenched teeth.

"Cooperate and you *might* live, if the Chief doesn't let me have you."

"The Chief? The Chief of what, you freak?" And then it hit her, "Oh my God! The Chief of Police?"

Pissed off at his own slip, Tyler said, "Just keep walking and shut up."

"I don't even know where I'm going, you idiot."

"All of these words will come back to haunt you. Maybe I'll pull a fingernail off with pliers for every name—or maybe I'll just use the pliers to twist all of your teeth out. How does that sound, you dumb bitch?!"

And so they walked in silence, their way dimly lit by overhead lights flickering in the dusk. A cold wind gusted every few steps and Sandra would correspondingly get a jab in her back.

"The white sedan, over there," he said pointing at an inconspicuous vehicle in front of them. Sandra started to move toward the front passenger seat. Tyler reached out and grabbed her by the hair.

"What the hell?!" she screamed.

"Think again...you're going in the trunk," he said as he popped the trunk and tried to shove her in.

"No way!" she cried as she struggled with him.

"I thought we just talked about this!" he yelled as he forced her into the trunk. Before he could close the trunk, Sandra saw a man walk up to the car.

"What's going on here?" the man asked.

"What's it fucking look like?" Tyler answered. "I'm shoving a woman into a trunk before I go kill her."

The man started to take a step toward Tyler, but before he could get close all Sandra heard was a shot, and then a thump as the stranger collapsed to the ground.

Sandra sobbed silently in the trunk. Tyler leaned in and said, "The only reason you aren't sharing that bastard's fate is that you have something we need. So, it's best for you to shut the fuck up and cooperate!" With that he slammed the trunk down and closed Sandra in darkness.

Sandra heard the car start and then she rocked forward as the car backed out. She could hear Tyler entering numbers into a phone.

"Hello? It's me...I didn't get Martinez but...no, *wait*...I got us some bait, juicy bait...."

\* \* \* \*

Shaver sat in a reclining chair tucked away in Doc K's waiting room. The doctor brought him a glass of water and said, "Tomko is dead?"

"Yeah Doc—lost all but one in a team of four guys in just under a week. I don't know what's going on," Shaver said.

"Who's left?"

"Fucking Martinez. That slippery little wetback is the only survivor except for me. All of this is because of him and that goddamn drive."

"Sure, but it's what's on that drive that really started this, isn't it?"

Shaver shot the doctor a menacing stare. "Listen, I don't need a fucking philosopher right now. Just take care of me and let's leave it at that." Shaver was pissed about the trip to the emergency room to begin with. Wished he had come straight to Dr. K, but he wasn't left with much of a choice at the scene of the accident. Once that freak Tyler showed up though, he knew it was time to get off the public grid.

"All right, Sergeant." The doctor walked out and went to his main office. He closed the door which doubled as a soundproof barrier, grabbed his phone and pressed a speed dial button. Someone picked up and asked, "Did he come to you?"

"Just like water down a hill," the doctor answered. After a pause, Doc K asked, "What do you want me to do with him?"

"Nothing right now. He's one tough son of a bitch and maybe we'll need him. Plus, he's still teeming with desire to exact revenge on Martinez. Guaranteed I'll need that kind of emotion to get this mess resolved."

\* \* \* \*

Diego sat back in his chair and looked at Alfonso. "It's no good."

"I told you we couldn't fix it. I don't even know why you spent so much time trying."

"Are you kidding me?" Diego asked scornfully. "Do you know what this video is worth?"

"Well, if I didn't at first I do now with how much you've brought it up," Alfonso retorted.

They both heard the front door swing open. "Who is it?" Diego called out.

"Me, Cruz." Cruz walked into the room followed by a man sporting a limp.

"Who's he?" Alfonso asked.

"Diego, Alfonso—this is Officer Martinez." Diego looked Martinez over. His right leg was heavily bandaged and he had fresh cuts on his face and hands.

"Been a rough few days, huh?" Diego said.

"You can say that again," Martinez answered.

"Don't just sit there Alfonso, help the man to some food and drink. Oh, show him the guest room too." Diego ordered. "Are you tired?" Diego asked Martinez.

"Deprived, hallucinating. Yeah."

"Well, make yourself at home. You know the saying."

"Thank you very much," Martinez said as he followed Alfonso out of the room.

"Where's Sandra?" Diego said. The pain Diego had failed to notice on Cruz's face became apparent. "What happened Cruz?" Cruz sat on a chair next to Diego, crossed his arms over his chest and bent at the waist.

"Someone kidnapped her when we were at the hospital," Cruz stammered.

"What?!" Diego shrieked. "Then what the hell are you doing here?"

"There's no point—he said that he was going to contact Martinez."

"What the hell does Sandra have to do with calling Martinez? Again let me ask you why we aren't doing something. No, no, no! I'm going to call the police and get them..." Cruz put his hand on Diego's shoulder as Diego went to pick up the phone.

"Diego, the police want to kill Martinez. Police involvement is the *last* thing we need."

"Why didn't you do anything?!!" Diego yelled.

"There was *nothing to do!*" Cruz yelled back. "The guy had Sandra at gunpoint and us by the balls. It's a fucking ransom situation and we've got to wait until they contact *us*." As he said that, Cruz heard a phone ring in the guest bedroom. He bolted to the bedroom with Diego close behind him.

When he got to the bedroom he asked Martinez, "Who is it?" Martinez rolled over and shook his head. "Who is it then?"

"Doesn't matter to you," Martinez snapped back.

Both Cruz and Diego retreated from the room a bit miffed by Martinez's reaction. They went back and sat down in Diego's office. Cruz stared through a picture on Diego's desk as they both sat in silence.

"You know what I don't quite get?" Cruz began.

"What's that?"

"How that guy knew we'd be there. I thought it was lucky enough that we were able to find Martinez—let alone for it to happen to another person."

"I don't think it's such a surprise. You think you want this video? Imagine what the people who will lose everything because of this video are willing to do to get it back."

"I think I know now," Cruz said sullenly.

"So...does Martinez have the video?" Diego asked. Cruz missed the slight flutter of excitement in Diego's voice.

"He does." Diego sat quietly rotating his thumbs around each other.

Alfonso came in during this last exchange and jumped in, "Why don't we watch it then?" Diego was relieved that he hadn't had to display his overriding desire to see the video. It was so close to him—it was all he wanted.

"I guess we can go ask Martinez," Cruz said hesitantly. They all got up and went to Martinez's room again. Cruz knocked on the wall outside of the room.

"What now?" Martinez grunted.

"Wondering if we could see that video?" Cruz asked.

"You know what's on it. Don't bother."

"We don't know what's on it—that's the point of all this," Cruz said earnestly.

"It's an execution, okay? Now you know," Martinez responded. But the men didn't leave the room. He could feel them all staring into the back of his head. "Okay, you know what? Here, I'm going to give it to you," Martinez said as he tossed a mini safe with the drive at them. Cruz stayed where he was but Diego and Alfonso jumped forward. They hit shoulders and Alfonso caught the mini safe. Cruz went up to him and took it away, looking at both of them quizzically.

"Your eagerness is getting a bit disconcerting," Cruz said looking at both of them. "Martinez, this is password protected."

"I know. Figure it out and it's all yours," he answered.

"That's ridiculous," Diego said, "give us the password!"

"Old man—you're probably the last person I'd give that to right now. Well, there are some exceptions to that but you get my drift. Much blood's been shed over that drive and I'm not about to cough it up to just anyone."

Cruz turned the mini safe around in his hands. "Who are you going to give it to then?" he asked.

"Haven't figured that out yet. Listen guys, my leg is killing me and what I need is rest. Give me that mini safe back and I'll get my sleep," Martinez said with his hand extended. Cruz walked over and handed it to Martinez.

"Thank you, Cruz. While I rest let's all think of what the shit we're going to do when we get the call." He seemed to be asleep when he said, "It shouldn't be long."

# TWENTY-THREE

Sandra felt the car stop and the engine turn off. She was light headed, sweating through her clothes and prepared for that trunk to be her tomb. Footsteps headed her direction, scuttling through loose gravel. The trunk opened and cool, fresh air rushed into Sandra's lungs. She opened her eyes but was immediately blinded by a flashlight.

"Come here darling," Tyler said. Sandra was beyond resisting and hung limp while Tyler tied something around her eyes. He picked her up around her waist and pulled her out of the trunk. She felt Tyler throw her on his shoulder and slam the trunk lid shut. As he moved, she bounced on his shoulder. "My, my little one. You are quite the catch." He walked with Sandra on his back for a good distance before stopping and ringing a door bell. She heard the door open.

"Is it okay to come in?" Tyler asked.

"Yes," answered a relatively squeamish voice. Sandra felt Tyler take a few more steps and then she was set down, immobilized with her hands tied behind her back and feet bound. She felt a mix of terror and tears well up in her again as feet shuffled around her. She was powerless against the will of these men. The darkness was no friend and only magnified her terror. Instinctively, she curled into a ball in a hopeless attempt to stave off harm.

"Who is this little gem?"

"She was with Martinez and another man. Remember when I told you I saw two people leaving his home the other night?"

"Yes."

"This was one of them."

"Hmmmm...let's see what you've got here," the high-pitched voice man said as his hands thrust along the top and inside of her legs, rummaging with disregard in her pockets. She clammed up as much more as she could. His hand stopped in her jacket pocket and pulled its contents out. "Sandra Gutierrez...is that your name? 9 News credentials. A reporter, huh Sandy?" All of a sudden she felt tugging at the cloth covering her eyes and light flooded her vision. She could barely make out the man standing over her. He had a thick mustache on a small, round face. His glasses hung low on his nose.

"You're snooping around in the wrong neighborhood today Sandy!! We're gonna kill youuuuuu!" Sandy was shut off in darkness again. "Load her back up, let's take her to the doctor."

\* \* \* \*

It came upon him rather quickly—Shaver didn't trust the feel of the doctor's office. He took a good look around and noted that the room must be underground. The walls were smooth and appeared freshly painted. Some dark spots still managed to bleed through the new paint. Call it a cop's instincts, but it suddenly felt wrong. Where was the doc anyway?

"What the fuck is this?" Shaver whispered to himself. He was still getting used to seeing the world with one eye. Not much changed, except that depth perception was off and he had to turn his head more. The eeriness of the room was something he really didn't need sight to pick up on. He tried to roll over but a surge of pain halted him.

There was nothing in the room except for the hospital-style bed and the support stand for his IV bag. An overhead light hummed relentlessly, flickered, and then went back to humming. Shaver pulled the stand over to him and tested its weight. Not too heavy to pick up. Shaver heard the *whoosh* of a door pulled open down the hall. Then the slow rattle of wheels on a cart being pushed. Whistling, step step, rattle, whistle. Shaver set his head down on his pillow and pretended to be asleep.

"Sergeant?" the doctor asked as he came around the corner. Shaver didn't answer. "Hmmm, fast asleep, you brute. Sleep like the cow you are." Shaver heard the doctor rattle his cart over toward the bed and stop. "So many *fun* toys!" Objects clinked and clanked on the cart. Something wisped and then Shaver heard two taps of fingernail on glass. He stirred and opened his eyes.

"Well, well, Shaver! Thought you were fast asleep. Let's see if we can't take care of that." The doctor raised a needle and went for Shaver's arm. Shaver grabbed onto the stand he had pulled next to the bed and flung it at the doctor. The doctor dropped the needle and looked up stunned at Shaver. The drip line on the IV bag reached it maximum length and pulled out of Shaver's arm.

"Ahhhhhhhhhhhh!" Shaver screamed, but he reached out and just caught the end of the line. He pulled the stand back and grabbed it with both hands. The doctor, sensing what was about to happen, tried to move away but Shaver was already swinging the heavy metal stand. The circular base of the stand connected with the doctor's temple and he dropped to the ground like a stone. He moaned on the ground, barely conscious.

# Derek Blass

"Stop...sto..."

"Fuck you, sicko. What the hell were you going to do to me?" Shaver leaned his weight onto the side of the bed and used the stand to leverage himself up. Nearly intolerable pain coursed through his body. He couldn't put an ounce of weight on his left leg, which was still in bad shape from the car crash. The doctor started to convulse on the floor. "Oh man, gotcha good, huh Doc?" He hovered over the doctor, both hands on the stand holding himself up. Blood dripped out of the doctor's nose, running across his upper lip and onto the floor. Shaver put all of his weight onto his right leg and lifted the stand over his head. He slammed the stand down on the doctor's head, over and over.

"You were gonna fuck me up good, weren't you Doc?!" he spit out as he pounded the doctor's head. The doctor coughed blood out onto the floor and his feet started to quiver. "I've had a bad couple of fucking days and I thought I could trust you!!" Shaver set the stand down next to the doctor's head and rested on it again. He was panting. "Shiiiiiiiiit!!!" he screamed in frustration.

Even though the door was only a few feet away, it seemed like a chasm to Shaver. He rested on the bed and used the stand for support as he caught his breath and tried to figure out what to do. A glint from the key on a carabiner hanging from the doctor's waist caught his attention. Shaver scooted over and grabbed the keys. There were probably twenty-five different keys on the key ring.

"You're just gonna have to manage this pain," he said out loud to himself. He gripped the stand until his knuckles turned white, trying to keep his left leg as immobile as possible. Even with the cast, the slightest movements or bumps were excruciating. He roared with pain as he got to a full standing position. Moving was the next problem. He tried hopping a few steps but it was too much. He set the stand out in front of him and pulled himself forward, shuffling on his right foot. Pain, but not unbearable.

In that manner he made a slow path to the door and out into the hall. Left was a dead end. There were three doors to his right. He crept toward them. The first one was sealed shut with an electronic keypad. He moved onto the next door which had a keyhole. Shaver fumbled for the keys while trying to keep his balance. Key after key failed until one slid in all the way. Shaver felt each tumbler give way and he turned the key. The door glided open and the room breathed out a metallic vapor. Shaver covered his mouth and nose. His eyes watered. "Christ," he muttered.

The room was pitch black except for the sparse light from the hall. That was enough to reveal a light switch. Shaver flipped the switch and a low, yellow glow lit the room. A stainless steel operating table dominated the room. It sat facing the door, pulsating with evil. The left side of the room was taken up by cabinets above a long, sanitized work table. Shaver could see vials, boxes and medical equipment through the glass doors of the cabinets. He slowly moved over toward two closet doors on his right side, opened one of the doors and recoiled at the sight. Heads, fingers, noses and a mélange of other body parts were neatly organized in formaldehyde-filled jars.

"I knew it! Damn freak!"

Shaver opened the other door and to his delight he saw two sets of crutches and a wheelchair folded up against the back wall. He pulled the wheelchair out, and balancing on his right leg alone, opened it. He set the leg rest and sat down, emitting a long, "ahhhhhhhhhhhhh." Immensely more mobile now, he went over to the other side of the room and started rummaging through the drawers under the worktable. He pulled out some bandages, gauze and medical tape. He stretched to reach a cabinet full of vials—ultram, vicodin, oxycontin—those would do. Shaver popped two vicodin.

The wheelchair squeaked as Shaver rolled back out into the hall, his lap full of medical supplies. There was one more room in the hall he hadn't investigated. The door was slightly ajar and Shaver gingerly pushed in. He flipped the light switch and a somber office came to life. A metal desk was pushed toward the back wall and covered with neatly organized piles of documents. Shaver wheeled over to the desk and searched through its drawers. They were surprisingly messy, given the state of the rest of the rooms. As Shaver fingered through Post-its and pens and binder clips, a small, wallet-size organizer caught his eye. He grabbed it and flipped through its pages until he came across a page with the words "her head" written on it in ink. "Just weird," Shaver whispered. He studied the rest of the organizer for any clues as to what the words could mean, although he already had one idea. Seeing no clues, he wheeled into the hall and moved back toward the room with the electronic keypad.

He punched in numbers corresponding to the words "her," "head" and the combination of the two. The digital screen on the keypad flashed "DENIED" each time. Shaver shook his head and sat in front of the door contemplating what those words could stand for. He sorted through the rooms he had been in and tried to think of any bits of evidence that fit. And then it came to him. He went back to the first room and opened the closet full of preserved human remains. Jars glistened, unfamiliar to light. One jar stood out. It contained the preserved head of a female whose hair had been removed. Her eyes were locked in a deathly stare and her mouth had pulled back to reveal a permanent grimace.

Shaver reached for the jar and pulled it down. He set it on the cold operating table and opened it. The fumes from the formaldehyde burned Shaver's nose and eyes and made him gag. Still, he dipped his hand into the jar and slowly lifted the head out. It dripped on the operating table, making it extremely slippery. Shaver wheeled over to an auxiliary table and set the head down. He turned it around and looked at her neck. He pulled each eyelid down. He grabbed the woman's lower lip and pulled it down. "Bingo!" A five digit number was tattooed on her lip.

Shaver spun around and headed back to the door with the electronic keypad. He entered the number and the door clicked open, "ACCESS GRANTED." The door was vacuum sealed and so took some effort to push open. Shaver wheeled in and lights automatically turned on. He looked around in astonishment at the setup in the room. There were eight monitors arranged in a rectangle on a wall to Shaver's left. Three of the monitors showed shots in the operating room. The other five seemed to be located in other parts of the home.

An L-shaped desk framed the other side of the room and Shaver wheeled behind it. He started to pull drawers out until he found a stack of journals tied together with a rubber band. The top journal had "patients" listed on it. Shaver pulled the journal out from the stack and opened it.

"Oh shit...gotcha," he said.

# TWENTY-FOUR

C armen and Alicia sat in the car as a gas station attendant filled their tank. Carmen heard two taps on the trunk and looked back at the attendant who was smiling at her as if he knew something she didn't. She started the car and made it a few blocks away when she noticed his nasty trick. The gas gauge hardly budged. Oh well, she thought, just a few more miles to her brother's house.

They passed through what had been a continuous, rocky and arid landscape. Every twenty miles or so, rundown buildings dotted the bareness— *tiendas, farmacias* and the like. They cruised along an empty highway until Carmen slammed on the brakes. "Missed it," she said. She turned the car around and made a right onto a dusty, dirt road. Alicia tensed as Carmen plowed down the road, throwing plumes of dust high into the air around them. They finally arrived at a medium-sized adobe home, nestled into the surrounding environment.

Someone immediately came out of the home to greet them. "*Hermana!! Que paso?!*" The person was a man, forty years old. He had a head of thick, brown hair, combed back. He was about average height but possessed lumberjack arms and butcher's hands. A bushy mustache curled over his lips and rounded out the package.

Raul embraced Carmen almost before she could get out of the car. "*Que bueno verte!*" he exclaimed. "*Y quién es esto?*"

"This is my friend Alicia," Carmen said as she hugged Raul. Alicia stuck her hand out and Raul promptly engulfed it with his own.

"So nice to meet you," he said with a thick accent.

"Likewise," Alicia answered with a smile.

"Welcome to my little home," Raul said as he swung his arm around. They followed him toward his house along a meandering path lined with stones. Blood-red Spanish tile floors greeted the visitors, and the inside was replete with bright oranges and yellows. Pots, plates and art gave the home a sense of life. Alicia noticed that the art ranged from depictions of Native American scenes to Santa Clara pottery. She stopped in front of a specific painting. It was of a man with a beard and a cigar in his hand.

"Who's this?" Alicia asked.

"*En serio?*" Raul asked. He looked at Alicia in amazement and then playfully rolled his eyes and stuck an imaginary dagger into his heart. "That is Che. Maybe someday I will tell you about him."

"So, *hermana*, what brings you to this border barrio?" He directed them to sit in his sunlit living room.

"Well," Carmen said, not knowing quite where to start, "there was recently an incident of police brutality, and Roman happened to be there."

"How long ago did this happen?" he asked.

"A week."

"Why didn't you come to me sooner? Is he okay?"

"He was okay last I saw him, but I haven't heard from him in two days," Carmen said as her lip quivered. She looked over at Alicia, who was holding back tears. "It might not have been so significant except that the incident was videotaped."

This drew Raul's attention. "Have you seen the video?"

"No, I don't even know where it is. Roman won't tell me."

"That's smart," Raul said. "Do you know what he plans on doing with it...if he has it?"

"I don't, but let me tell you the rest of the story so you really understand how serious this is," Carmen said.

"It gets more serious than this?" Raul quipped with a slight smile until he saw the expression on both women's faces. *"Perdon."*

"Shortly after the incident, Roman and his partner, Alvin Williams, were coming back to Williams' home when they noticed that other police officers were already there. When they rushed into the home, they found two of the other officers who were at the murder attacking Alicia."

"They were questioning me to try to figure out where the video was," Alicia added. Raul nodded.

"It was more than just questioning," Carmen chastised. "In the ensuing exchange, Alicia's husband killed one of the police officers but also died." At this point tears had built up so much in Alicia's eyes that they began to pour out. Her shoulders heaved and Carmen reached over to hold her tight. Alicia cried into her shoulder. Raul got up and came back with several tissues.

"At that point, Roman basically told us to pack up and get out of the country to be safe. I didn't tell him we were going to come here. He probably assumed it though."

"You said there were two policía at Ms. Alicia's house...what happened to the other?" Raul asked.

"I don't know what happened to the other officer," Carmen answered. "Do you?" she asked turning to Alicia.

"I barely saw him run out—I was more concerned about Alvin."

"This other officer that got away, he may still be after Roman?"

"Yes," Carmen answered. "But, it's not just that officer. In fact, he isn't the greatest danger. There's another one that's a menace. I never trusted him, Raul. His name is Shaver. He's pretty much loathed in the community because despite leading a vicious attack on a young man about fifteen years ago, he was allowed to stay on the force. Shaver is the one Roman needs to watch out for."

Raul stood up, *"Quieres algo de tomar?"* he asked Carmen. She shook her head no. "You, Alicia, do you want something to drink?"

"Yes, thank you. I'll take a water." Alicia turned to Carmen. "We aren't just here to hide out, are we?"

"No," Carmen answered.

"So, why are we here? We could have stayed at a hotel."

"First off, this place is the safest place for us. Second, we are going to need Raul."

"For what?"

Carmen paused and tried to analyze Alicia's commitment to exposing this incident. She just wasn't ready, Carmen thought. Carmen, on the other hand, almost as if telepathically connected to Martinez, was ready to do what she could to expose the contents of the drive. Alicia was too entrenched in the regime to flip around one hundred and eighty degrees. Carmen decided to dodge the question instead.

"Raul," she called, "Why don't you come over here and tell Alicia the story of Che Guevara?"

\* \* \* \*

The phone rang like a siren and all of the men ran to the room where Martinez was waking up.

"Hello?" he strained. After a pause he said, "Yes, there are others here." Martinez set the phone down on the bed and turned the speaker phone on. A man on the other end of the line said, "Go ahead...introduce yourselves."

Enraged, Cruz blurted out, "We don't need to fucking know each other— just give Sandra back!"

"Slow down, stallion," the man said. "If you cooperate, this little beauty will be returned to you with, perhaps, a scratch or two. But I extend my invitation again, introduce yourselves."

The men hesitated and looked at Martinez, who nodded at them.

"Cruz Marquez."

"Diego and Alfonso Archuleta."

"And Martinez, I certainly don't need you to introduce yourself." The other men looked at Martinez.

"You know this guy?" Diego pressed.

"I do."

"Who is he?"

"Allow me," the man said. "I am the Chief of Police for your beloved little city. What I have for you is a very, very simple proposition. The video for the girl. If that transaction does not take place within six hours, your friend here will lose a digit for every fifteen minutes of delay. I have an...acquaintance...who will be more than happy to take Sandy apart, piece by precious piece."

"You fucking hurt her at all and I'll kill you!!" Cruz screamed.

"Watch your tone, my brown friend," the Chief admonished. "People have been hurt for less than disrespectful language. In any event, the last thing I want is Sandy in fifty pieces. The acquaintance, on the other hand..." the Chief mused. "The bottom line is for you all to use logic. I want the video, not your doll. She is meaningless to me otherwise. Comply, cooperate and she will be fine. Don't, and she will be the first in a long line of victims to your collective stubbornness, or stupidity, whichever would drive you to ignore my direction. Oh, and Martinez? Don't think we'll leave your precious wife out of this."

"I don't have a clue what you're talking about Chief."

"Sure you don't. I'll call you all back in exactly one hour, and as for Sandra...does she like to go by Sandra or Sandy, Mr. Marquez? It's a difficult enough situation without being called by the wrong name!"

"Fuck you," Cruz said.

"Haven't really learned your lesson yet, huh? I'll see you soon enough. One hour gentlemen. *Ciao!*" The Chief hung up and Martinez's phone emitted an empty dial tone for a few seconds as they sat around in silence.

"What the hell are we gonna do?" Cruz asked.

"Give the video to the Chief in exchange for Sandra," Diego said.

"Ain't gonna happen," Martinez said coolly. The other men looked at him in astonishment.

"What do you mean ain't gonna happen?" Diego asked incredulously. "Listen, we *have* to get Sandra back."

"Doesn't mean that anyone is getting this video. I'm about to be very blunt with you guys—one more life lost to ensure this video gets publicized isn't a problem for me. I don't even know why you all got involved. But, you have and now it looks like you all may pay for that shit." Martinez shifted his weight where he sat and grimaced.

"Timeout, there's an easy solution," Cruz began, "we make a copy."

"That's not gonna happen either Cruz. I'm not opening this safe for anything other than it's final recipient," Martinez responded.

"And who the fuck may that be?!" Cruz yelled.

"You're pretty wound up...probably 'bout time to settle down," Martinez said.

"Sandra's being held captive and is about to get tortured! I don't know how anyone expects me to be calm right now!"

"I understand what you're feeling Cruz, and you have to believe me, I'm angry too. My best friend was killed over this video. I narrowly escaped death over this video. Believe me, I understand." Cruz looked at Martinez, judging his sincerity.

"We can't let this happen to her Martinez," Cruz pled.

"Who said we're gonna let anything happen? I'm still a cop and it's not in me to let innocent people die. I know the Chief. His weakness is his ego. We've got to try to exploit that to get Sandra back. He wants the video for Sandra. I'm gonna give him a bullet instead of the video," Martinez said. This made Cruz feel a little bit better.

"I'm interested to know one thing," Diego said. "What do you plan on doing with that video?"

"Publicize it...make sure as many people are impacted by it as possible. How'm I gonna do that? Not sure yet. It's a good reason to get Sandra back though —she may be able to help."

* * * *

Shaver wheeled over to an elevator at the end of the hall. Ending up in the doctor's office had been a coup because he had a full lap of medical supplies and the journal. He hit the button for the first floor. The old elevator groaned as it started moving up. It reached the first floor with a thump and the rickety, metal doors slid open.

The upstairs portion of the doctor's home was welcoming—a perfect front. Shaver rolled over to a phone and called for a cab.

His mind raced with what his next step would be. The list in his hands could guarantee the Chief's demise. He knew he couldn't trust that bastard for shit. In fact, he was surprised one of the Chief's henchmen hadn't been around to kill him since he had failed to recover the video. That thing was more important now more than ever—to preserve his hide and to avoid spending the rest of his life in an eight-by-four-foot cell.

Shaver wheeled around the doctor's home. He found a set of locked drawers in a cabinet in the master bedroom. Shaver pulled the set of keys out of his shirt pocket and tested the drawers. Finally, the right key slipped in and Shaver pulled a drawer open.

"Nice, the doctor that keeps on giving," Shaver said as he looked at a variety of handguns. He noted that one of them was his beloved Colt. The next drawer contained boxes of ammunition. "Too good to be true." He heard a horn beep outside and quickly gathered his ever-growing bundle of supplies. As Shaver wheeled his way outside, he decided that his next step was to get that video back. Maybe the Chief would cut him some slack if he did that, especially with what Shaver had on him now.

* * * *

The Chief and Tyler knocked on the doctor's front door. They backed their car up to the garage door and were getting antsy the longer the doctor didn't answer. The Chief knew that sometimes the doctor holed-up downstairs, engrossed in his sick experiments, so he tested the door knob. It surprised him a bit that the door opened freely. Tyler pulled his gun out.

"You stay here with the girl, I'm going inside to see what the hell's going on. I'll open the garage door too so we can get her inside," the Chief said, drawing his own gun. The Chief raised his gun and moved into the doctor's home. He scanned left and right as he stepped through the threshold. Everything appeared to be in order, except for one thing. The elevator was open and on the first floor at the far side of the home. Doctor couldn't be downstairs then.

The Chief moved from room to room until he got to the doctor's bedroom. This was the only sign of disorder. Two drawers were open. The top drawer was lined with red, crushed velvet and had indentations resembling handguns. The drawer underneath it had some boxes of ammunition. It didn't appear that anyone was around on this level.

"What made you run out of here so fast, Doc?" the Chief wondered. He moved back through the kitchen, into the garage and hit a button to open it. Tyler backed the car in and got out.

"Where's the doctor?" Tyler asked.

"Hell if I know. I haven't gone down to the basement level yet."

"What? Well I'm sure he's down there."

"Don't be so sure. The elevator is up here on the main floor. Shaver is a crafty bastard. I don't like the feel of this."

"No way. Shaver just about died in that accident."

"Don't underestimate him or his will to stay alive and serve up some revenge. Get the girl inside, I'm going to the basement." The Chief moved back into the house and stepped onto the elevator. He held his gun up at eye level. His body temperature started to rise. This was not his strong suit. Wreaking havoc from behind a desk was a much different way of getting his hands dirty. The elevator bounced to a stop and its doors opened, revealing a poorly lit corridor with doors on each side. All of the doors were open, including one that had an electronic keypad.

"Doctor?" the Chief called. Beads of sweat were now gathered enough to roll down the Chief's face. He wiped them off with his forearm and pressed his back against the wall opposite the first room. As he slid in front of the room it became apparent no one was in there. Medical supplies were scattered on the floor though, and the preserved head of a woman sat on a desk in the middle of the room.

The Chief performed the same maneuver as he checked the other rooms. When he slid in front of the last room he couldn't believe what he saw. The doctor was sprawled on the ground in a pool of his own blood. The side of his face swollen and deformed. A hanging stand for an IV bag was lying next to the doctor. He went to the room with the electronic keypad. This room had the most signs of rummaging. Papers and journals were strewn about on the floor. As the Chief sorted through journals, sweat began to collect even faster on his face.

"Goddammit!!" he screamed and raced back towards the elevator. He got to the first floor and went straight to the kitchen.

"What the hell's wrong?" Tyler called out.

The Chief grabbed a glass and filled it with water. "The doctor's dead."

"Shaver?"

"Gone."

"Holy shit. He should be fucking dead!"

The Chief looked at Sandra who was half-in and half-out of consciousness. "I told you not to underestimate him. He's a tough son of a bitch."

"What now?"

"Nothing changed, Tyler. We still need to get that video back." The Chief's phone rang and Tyler watched him as he turned his back and spoke in a low voice.

"Who was that?" Tyler asked after the Chief hung up.

"Never mind who it was," the Chief answered. "What matters is the message."

"Well, what was the message?"

"Get ready for an attack."

\* \* \* \*

Martinez held a black gun out to Cruz, "You ever handled one of these before?"

"Can't say I have," Cruz answered.

"It's a Glock 22.  You can't use a heavy finger on this puppy, so be mindful of that."

Cruz held the short, black gun in his hand.

"Pretty lightweight," he said.

"It's a great gun.  Easy to aim, most of us use them."

"What's that you got?" Cruz asked Martinez.

"That's a SIG 226," Diego chimed in.

"You know guns?" Martinez asked.

"Sure.  You don't fight your whole life without knowing guns," Diego answered.  "I've got a few myself," he said as he pulled open a safe, which happened to be a war chest.  There were at least ten guns in the six foot high safe, ranging from rifles to shotguns to handguns.

"Christ.  Prepared for battle, huh Diego?"

"Whatever it takes."  He handed two guns to Alfonso and took one for himself.

"So—what's the plan with all this firepower?" Cruz asked Martinez.

"Pretty basic.  We ambush the Chief and his sidekick when we go to hand off the video."

"You don't think he'll be expecting that?"

"Maybe, but one thing about the Chief is that he's a total pussy in direct combat.  He's a master at all those psychological games.  In person, I'm not worried about him."

"What about the other guy that's helping him out?  The sidekick," Cruz asked.

"I don't know much about him.  We've heard rumors before of the people the Chief uses, but it's such a wide network that it's hard to pin anyone down.  He literally has people *everywhere*."

"Entrenched," Alfonso grunted.

"Yeah, you can say that," Martinez answered.  Cruz stood in the middle of the room as the other men packed gear and ammunition into a black duffel bag.  "I'll be right back," Martinez said while he walked out of the room.

"Gonna hit the head," Diego said, following Martinez.  The room that

Martinez went to was right next to the bathroom.  He dialed his wife's phone number and connected after a few rings.

"Carmen?" he asked in a hushed voice.

"Roman!  Why has it taken you so long to call me?!"

"Some crazy stuff has been going on baby.  This is the earliest I could call you."

"Are you okay?" she asked with some panic in her voice.

"Yeah, baby—just a little banged up."

"What happened??  When are you coming down here?"

"Did you go to your brother's in Mexico?" he asked.

"You sure you want to know exactly where I am?"

"I guess that's a yes.  Tell Raul I said hello...and thanks.  How's Alicia?"

"Oh, she's hanging in there.  She has periodic bouts of crying, to be expected.  How are you dealing?"

"Haven't had much of a chance to think about anything.  It's been tough not seeing you in awhile."

"I know, honey," she answered.

"Carmen, I need to tell you something then I gotta get going."

"Okay..." she said hesitantly.

"It's...it's about to get ugly.  I want you to know that I love you with all my heart."

"What?!" Carmen cried out.  "Why the hell are you talking like this?  I'm coming back up there right now.  You aren't gonna pull any crazy shit on me and get killed, Roman!"

"You aren't going anywhere," Martinez answered calmly.  "I need you to stay down there until this is over."  Carmen stayed silent on the other end of the phone.  "I promise I'll be just fine, Carmen.  I love you."

After a moment she responded, "I love you too, Roman.  Please, please be safe."  He could hear the frustration in her voice.

"Will do...bye," Martinez said.  He went back toward the living room and bumped into Diego coming out of the bathroom.  Diego flashed him an odd look which Martinez wrote off quickly, too quickly.

# TWENTY-FIVE

Tyler and the Chief went around the doctor's house securing doors and windows. Their plan was to create a single, defensible point of entry into the home. Sandra had recovered a good amount of her energy and was spitting venomous comments at the men when they walked anywhere near her.

"What the hell are you two cowards getting ready for?" she asked.

"Put the gag back in her mouth Tyler, this is getting ridiculous. I'm about to kill her and that would be a mistake right now," the Chief said. Tyler walked over to Sandra and pulled the cloth up that was hanging around her neck. He put the cloth in between her teeth and tightened the knot. She focused a piercing stare at him.

Feeling generous, the Chief added, "To respond to your question, we are getting ready for your friend, or boyfriend or whatever he is, and Martinez to come storming in here and try to rescue you." The Chief turned to Tyler, "You can call them now, by the way. Let them know where this place is and tell them to be here in exactly one hour." Tyler went to another room in the house to get his phone. "You see," the Chief started after concentrating on Sandra again, "a little bird has told me that your friend and Martinez don't intend to give the video up. It's such a shame because this really could be an expeditious transaction." With that, the Chief spun around and took the elevator down to the basement.

Sandra wondered how the Chief could know all of this. What "bird" had this kind of inside knowledge? It seemed doubtful that Martinez would feed the Chief information. Cruz didn't even know the Chief. And then it dawned on Sandra. She tried to figure out how this creep Tyler got to the hospital where Martinez was nearly as fast as she and Cruz. The only person that knew where they were going? Diego. Same thing here. The common denominator is Diego. But why? Why would he stab both her and Cruz in the back? Sandra had no answer to that question.

As Sandra thought about this she wiggled her wrists and ankles in an attempt to loosen her bindings. It was no use, though, as there was hardly any play between the bindings and her body. She heard the elevator start up. When it reached the top the Chief stepped off and called for Tyler. He whispered something in Tyler's ear, who then came her way.

Tyler hooked his arms in Sandra's armpits and dragged her to the elevator. At first she struggled, but then stopped as there was no purpose. "Given up, have you?" Tyler said with a smirk. Sandra glared at him. "It'll all be over soon, princess." The elevator reached the basement and Tyler pulled her out. She hung loosely as the hall they were in took shape backwards. It was cold, disturbingly sanitary and humming with overhead lights. Sandra watched as one, then two, then three doors passed. Tyler pulled her into a room and went to turn a light on. Sandra turned her upper body to see what was behind her, and when Tyler flicked the light on she shrieked. It was a stainless steel operating table.

"Let's get you up there," Tyler groaned as he tried to pick Sandra up. Now she struggled. With every ounce of energy in her body she kicked, head butted and tried to shoulder Tyler away. "This...isn't going...to stop the inevitable," Tyler gasped as he worked to contain her struggle. Eventually the fight in Sandra died down, although not from desire. Her body was exhausted.

Tyler lifted her onto the operating table and put her on her back. He first strapped her down to the table with duct tape around her chest. Then he wrapped the tape around her waist and ankles. Finally, he wrapped tape around her forehead, completely immobilizing her.

This was horror. At least before she was only bound by her hands and her feet. She could move, shift and struggle, albeit in vain. Now, Sandra was essentially in a straight jacket. Tyler leaned over her and smiled. The fear in her eyes made him excited. He ran his hand over her neck and watched as goosebumps rose. He got closer, breathed her fear in and then licked her forehead.

"My God," he said, "I love that taste." Tyler grabbed the piece of cloth tied in Sandra's mouth and pulled it down a bit. She whimpered and he pulled it down some more. "If you don't scream I'll take this out," he said as he looked at her. "Are you going to scream?" Sandra shook her head no. Tyler reached behind her head and untied the cloth. Sandra drew a long breath in.

"There...see, I'm not all bad." Tyler stayed close to Sandra and put his ear close to her mouth. Her short, shallow breaths aroused him even more. "Oh yeah, that's nice," he whispered. He put his hand in his pants and started to rub himself. Just as he did Sandra thrust her chin up and bit through the bottom half of his earlobe.

"Fuck!!!!!!!" he screamed as he pulled back. Blood streamed down his neck and into his shirt. She cackled as he spun in a circle. "You bitch!! I fucking did you a favor! Now I'm gonna make this reallllly fucking uncomfortable." Tyler pulled the light over the operating table down to just inches above Sandra's face. He turned it on and Sandra was instantly blinded.

"Turn it off!" she shrieked.

"Screw you. Fucking die under that light." Tyler left the room muttering about killing Sandra as he ascended to the first floor in the elevator. The Chief was there to greet him when he got to the top.

"What the hell happened to you?" the Chief asked.

"That bitch bit me."

"What were you doing that close to her and why was her gag out?" the Chief asked even though he already knew the answer. "Your sickness is a liability, Tyler. Start barring up the doors and let's get this wrapped up. I'd expect them here any..."

A loud crash from the front door interrupted the Chief's sentence. He saw Martinez rush into the house with his gun raised. Tyler started firing his gun as Martinez dove behind a couch. The bullets from Tyler's gun ripped through walls and furniture in search of Martinez. The Chief kept his gun fixed on the front door. He heard Martinez scream, "Stay back!!"

In the dusky light the Chief was able to see a head pass by a window on his left.

"Tyler, it's time to get out of here."

"What about the girl?"

"Forget her, there are more people outside. We're about to get cornered. Plus, this isn't the only card up my sleeve." He turned and ran out of a back door with Tyler following close behind him. As Tyler came out of the house he caught a figure in his peripheral vision. He instinctively hit the ground and was about to fire when the Chief yelled, "No!" The figure was about twenty feet from Tyler, with his gun raised as well. No one fired. Tyler jumped up and followed the Chief to their car which was parked around the block. They both fell in and the Chief hurriedly started it.

"Where are we going?"

The Chief took a second to catch his breath and then responded, "Mexico."

\* \* \* \*

Martinez crouched down and leaned on the front door of the house the Chief designated as the meeting place. Cruz was on the left side of the door. Martinez noticed that he looked pale and shaky.

"You okay?" Martinez whispered.

"Yeah, yeah," Cruz answered. "Shit, are *you* okay? You're the one that's hurt."

He looked down at his bandaged leg. It hurt like hell, but adrenaline currently outweighed sense. "Nah, this is nothing. Don't forget the game plan. I go in first, then you wait for me to give the signal before you come in. If you break that rule I can almost guarantee you'll get killed." Cruz nodded his head. "You two," Martinez started while looking at Diego and Alfonso, "you two head around the back. I expect the Chief to make a break for it."

"How do you know that?" Diego asked.

"'Cause he's a coward." Martinez shifted his weight onto his other leg. "Head around to the back of the house." While those two moved slowly around to their position, Martinez looked at Cruz and said, "Go time." With that he sprung up and kicked the front door near the handle with such force that the jamb splintered and sent wood shards flying. Cruz watched as Martinez calmly moved into the home. It seemed like gunshots simultaneously rang out and Cruz slid down to the ground. He peeked around into the house and saw Martinez taking cover behind a couch.

"Stay back!!" Martinez screamed at him. Martinez held his gun up to the couch and fired three blind shots through it. Two shots rang back at him and then an unsettling silence took over.

"Martinez? What's going on?" Cruz looked into the house again and saw Martinez crawl to one end of the couch. Cruz decided it was time to jump in and bolted through the doorway. He slid behind the couch. The silence remained unchanged.

"What the hell, Martinez?"

"I don't know. I think they left."

"Nothing back here!" Cruz heard Diego yell from the back of the house.

Martinez rose cautiously and scanned the room in front of them. "I think it's all right to get up," he said.

Cruz stood up slowly and looked at the room. There didn't appear to be any signs of people. "Martinez, where is she?"

"No idea, check the rooms over there," he answered, pointing to two rooms in the corner of the house. Cruz checked the first room which was empty. As he came out of the room he ran into Diego and Alfonso.

"You see Sandra?" Cruz asked.

"Nothing," Diego answered.

"There was an elevator when we came in the back of the house though," Alfonso said.

"Okay...what the hell are you doing up here then?" Cruz said as he moved to the back of the house. Martinez was already on the elevator. Cruz could hear a faint, high-pitched noise coming from below him.

"Get in!" Martinez yelled.

"Coming...coming," Cruz panted as he ran to get in.

"You and Alfonso stay up here and make sure no one comes back," Martinez said to Diego as the elevator descended. The high-pitched noise grew louder. The elevator reached a basement floor and Martinez stepped off in front of Cruz. Cruz pushed past Martinez towards the noise, which was now distinguishable as Sandra screaming. He ran into the room where the screaming was coming from and froze in horror. Sandra was duct-taped to an operating table. An overhead light was pulled down just over her face. The exposed areas of her face were red and blistered.

"Sandra!" Cruz shouted as he ran to her. He shoved the light away when he saw Sandra and screamed to Martinez. "Martinez, get in here!!" Martinez came running in and pulled a knife out. He cut the tape securing Sandra to the operating table and Cruz pulled her off. Sandra still had her eyes shut and was screaming unintelligibly every few seconds.

"It's me Sandra...Cruz! You're all right, you're all right Sandra. Take a breath," Cruz said as he held Sandra close to him.

"Let's get her out of here," Martinez said. "The shock won't wear off until we get her out."

"Tell Diego to call an ambulance." Sandra's eyes suddenly opened wide.

"No...no, Cruz. No Diego," Sandra cried.

"What?"

"Keep him away. He's...he betrayed us..." Sandra's head fell onto Cruz's shoulder as she got this out.

"She fainted," Martinez said. "Let me tell Diego to get that ambulance here."

"No! Didn't you hear her?"

"Cruz, she's in shock, she's just been tortured. Who knows what she was talking about."

"Listen, I've been having some weird feelings about Diego anyways. I think she may know something we don't."

"Well, Diego isn't gonna do shit to us right now, so let's move upstairs, okay?"

"Sure, we'll go upstairs, but don't let Diego call the ambulance."

Cruz carried Sandra to the elevator and they went upstairs. Diego and

Alfonso were waiting on the top floor.

"How is she?" Diego asked.

"Not good...not good at all." They all looked down at Sandra's face which had blister bubbles all over it. Her eyes were just starting to flutter. "She fainted almost as soon as we got down there."

"What the hell did those *perros* do to her?" Diego asked angrily as he gently touched Sandra's wrist. Cruz and Martinez were silent. "Let's go set her down in the room with the bed." Cruz followed with Sandra in his arms and set her down on the bed. Alfonso came in with a damp towel and gently placed it on Sandra's forehead.

"I'm gonna call an ambulance," Cruz said.

"Are you sure?" Diego asked. "I can do that so you can stay here with Sandra."

Cruz looked at Diego apprehensively, "No, I'll do it." He stepped right outside of the room and dialed 9-1-1. Sandra screamed in the room just as Cruz finished telling the dispatcher the address they were at.

"What the hell is going on?" Cruz shouted as he bolted back into the room. Sandra was wide-eyed.

"Cruz, Cruz, get him...get me to home...he's dangerous, Cruz...he knows!" Sandra whimpered.

"She screamed as soon as she saw me. I don't know what's going on," Diego said. Martinez came into the room and stood silently behind Cruz.

"What's going on is that you betrayed us!" Cruz blurted out.

Diego laughed but Cruz noted that his face reddened a bit, "You've got to be kidding me. Why would I betray you two? I've known you two since you were little kids!"

"You tell me, Diego," Cruz said as he took a menacing step toward Diego. Alfonso pulled his shoulders back and took a step forward as well. "You don't need to get involved in this, you fucking ape," Cruz seethed at Alfonso. "You tell me how the hell that goon knew we were going to be at the hospital to find Martinez."

"Really? All they had to do was make the same deductions we made. There's no magic to that," Diego responded.

"And then how did they know we were going to be here when we got here? They were ready for us! They were ready for us to attack!"

"How the hell would I know? They probably heard us pull up."

"Bullshit!"

"He called him a bird..." Sandra whispered.

"What?" Diego asked.

Cruz moved over to Sandra and pushed Diego aside. Sandra looked at him and motioned for him to get closer, "The Chief, he called Diego his little bird. They knew you were coming and that you weren't going to make the exchange." Diego strained to hear what Sandra was saying.

"What's she saying?" Diego inquired. Cruz spun around with his gun drawn on Diego. Alfonso raised his gun and pointed it at Cruz.

"Put it down Cruz!" he screamed.

"Please," Diego said with a laugh, "you don't even know how to use that Cruz."

"She said that the Chief called you his little bird and that you told him we weren't coming here to exchange the video."

"Again, show me a motive," Diego said.

"I don't need a motive. Coincidence is quite enough."

"You're going to shoot me? Go to jail for the rest of your life for *coincidence*?" Cruz considered what Diego said.

"Wait a second," Martinez jumped in. "What else did you tell them?"

"Listen up kids. I didn't tell those two anything!" It was Martinez's turn as he raised his gun and placed it on Alfonso's temple. Cruz's hand started to shake. Diego shook his head and looked sideways at Cruz.

"Come clean old man, or your son gets lit up. I'm fucking crazy right now, so you don't need to ask me about jail. I'm ready!" Martinez exclaimed.

Diego looked at all of the guns. The one pointed in between his eyes. The one pointed at his son's head. Most importantly, he considered Sandra, who was now unconscious on the floor. His actions led to the harm she had faced—that beautiful, little girl. That and the weight of living with lies and guilt for so many years finally broke his resolve. "Alfonso," he said, "put your gun down."

"Hell no Dad."

"*Do what I said!*" Alfonso hesitated but then slowly lowered his gun.

"Lower your guns too and I'll tell you what's going on," Diego said.

"Tell Alfonso to drop his first," Martinez demanded.

"Go ahead Alfonso, do what he said." Alfonso threw his gun on the ground. Martinez put a hand out to Cruz and they both lowered their guns as well.

"I can't believe it came to this..." Diego lamented.

"Well it has, so let's hear it," Martinez retorted.

Diego paused and then took a deep breath, "It was a long time ago now.

If Alfonso is twenty-three...it must have been about twenty years ago." Diego dropped into a chair next to the bed. "I was a pretty radical activist back in the day. We took a war-is-first approach. Police brutality was no rare occurrence back then. The cops beat up one of the members of the radical organization I was a part of so badly he ended up dying. In retaliation, I was part of a group that bombed the police station and killed several cops."

"What's that have to do with the Chief?" Cruz asked.

"The Chief was newly appointed back then and something he's always been smart about is getting people to owe him. When the ensuing investigation was about to reveal that I led the bombing, the Chief contacted me to see if I wanted to make a deal."

"What kind of a deal?"

"He would impede the investigation enough that my involvement would never come out. In return, I was to be his informant."

"You work for the cops?" Alfonso asked incredulously.

"I don't *work* for them. I was indebted to the Chief...he owned me. *If you had just given him the drive this wouldn't have happened!* But, you had to go all fucking warrior on them, Martinez."

"Look, this story is fucking scintillating but I still want to know what the hell else you told the Chief," Martinez said.

Diego looked down at the ground.

"Well?? What the hell did you tell them?!"

Without looking up Diego said, "I told them where your wife is."

# TWENTY-SIX

Tyler and the Chief split up shortly after leaving the doctor's house. Tyler was to go finish Shaver off, while the Chief jetted down to Mexico to find Martinez's wife.

It was the middle of an especially dark night as Tyler drove to Shaver's home. He was starting to feel the effects of going nearly two days without sleep. Objects in his periphery startled him. His vision was blurred. Sounds were distorted, distant and haunting. He was having cognitive problems. The steering wheel felt like a writhing snake in his hands.

A computerized, female voice spoke through the speakers of his car, "Turn left in two hundred feet." Tyler took the left and then followed a long, dark country road for another mile. The headlights of his vehicle were the only source of illumination. They lit a swath in front of him that seemed to promise something menacing around every corner. The female voice spoke to him again, "Your destination is five hundred feet away."

Tyler brought the vehicle to a stop and shut off the headlights. He grabbed a flashlight out of the center console and checked the clip in his gun to make sure it was loaded. A bitter, fall wind blasted Tyler when he opened the door and stepped out onto the dirt road. He closed the door quietly and stood next to the car as his eyes adjusted to the dark. A solitary dog bark in the distance stole through the still night.

Tyler's breath rose in front of him as he moved toward Shaver's house. When he was about a hundred feet away he could make out the outline of a long, ranch-style house set back from the dirt road. He stopped at the top of the driveway behind a hedge that ran the front length of the home. There were no lights on, either inside or outside of the house. Cloud-obscured beams of light spilled down from the moon and bathed certain areas around Tyler in a milky ash.

He slipped down the driveway until he came to the front door. The screen door slipped open just enough to wriggle his hand in to see if the front door was locked. The doorknob turned and Tyler felt little resistance as the door cracked open. He pulled the screen door back more and winced when it creaked. One foot ventured into the house and then he slid the rest of his body in while slowly closing the screen door.

Pitch black blanketed Tyler. He stood motionless for several minutes, straining to hear any signs of life. There was nothing to give away Shaver's location. To his left, Tyler saw the green glow of a microwave clock. He was in a hallway that seemed to open into a large living room. The faint whir of electronics murmured about ten paces in front of him. Tyler knelt down and felt the floor. Rug, good.

He crept forward while staying crouched. Stop and listen. Creep forward some more. Stop, strain ears to listen. Tyler started to move forward again when he heard a rustle from down a hall to his left. There was nothing more than the rustle and then complete silence. No buzz from a refrigerator. No clock ticking. Nothing but silence and the uncanny feeling that he was moving deeper into a spider's web.

There was just one door at the end of the hall. A faint, yellow light filtered out from it. Tyler hesitantly put one foot in front of the other as he made his way to the room. The hair on the back of his neck stood up and he felt his heart pound. The rough grip on his gun became slippery with sweat. He stopped at the threshold to the room and tried to figure out its layout. A crack in the door provided a limited view.

A bed was pressed into the back corner of the room. There was a window on each wall the bed touched. Moonlight barely made it through to the room, as the pines surrounding the house provided a natural barrier to any light. Tyler could see the figure of a person lying in the bed.

"Shaver," he barely whispered. He nudged the door and took two delicate steps into the room. It was clear. Tyler took two more steps to the center of the room. He had infiltrated into Shaver's house undetected. Shaver was laying in front of him, motionless and unknowing. Perfect.

Tyler took his next step but before his foot hit the floor closet doors erupted behind him. He rolled forward and as he spun around he felt something strike his head. He was immediately dazed, struggling to push up off of the ground. A hand clasped around his neck and pinned him to the floor. Tyler felt the muzzle of a gun on his cheekbone.

"Are you fucking crazy?" a steely voice came from the dark above him. Tyler groaned as he tried to focus his fuzzy vision. "This is *my* house you dumbshit. Just what were you trying to do? *Kill me? Me?* One eye and I still fuck you up." Tyler's vision started to normalize. He heard the sound of duct tape being pulled from a roll. Tyler struggled but it was too late. Shaver bound his hands and was on his legs next, stopping any attempt at movement. Shaver worked with the meticulous fury of a spider wrapping a newly caught insect. He let out an *argh* as he got up off of Tyler, breathing heavily while hobbling over to a light switch.

"The Chief sent you on a suicide mission, buddy," Shaver said as he sat down on the bed. "You see that over there?" he asked, pointing at a group of monitors. "I saw you before you even got to the driveway. Shit, with the microphones I've got planted out there I *heard* you before I could even see you." Shaver took a second to catch his breath. "The Chief's main assassin. Not much to you, is there?

Shaver rolled over onto his elbow and looked at Tyler. "You know I'm gonna fuck you up badly, yeah? You see me? Missing one fucking eye. A messed-up leg. Countless other injuries that you could call miscellaneous. I'm pissed man! You shits have tried to kill me three times now, once with the doctor and twice with you. And look at me! All fucked up—trying to take advantage of a beat-up old shit! It's about goddamn time the tables are turned!"

Shaver rummaged through Tyler's pockets and grabbed his cell phone. Tyler bounced on his shoulders in an attempt to scoot away. Shaver just laughed as he flipped through the contact list until he reached the entry for the Chief. He pushed the send button and waited as the phone rang. The Chief picked up.

"You done yet?"

"No, not quite," Shaver answered.

"Well, tickle me silly Shaver. One eye and all and you're still alive, huh?"

"Just couldn't let it end now," Shaver answered.

"You got some hard-on to call and let me know what you've done?"

"I've got your lackey here, and I figured you'd want to come collect your garbage."

"Nahhhh, you can have him."

"You hear that buddy? The Chief couldn't give a shit less about you," he directed at Tyler. "There's one other thing you may care about."

"What's that?"

"It was an interesting find at the doctor's office. By the way, hire some good help Chief. You've got some real incompetence around you."

"Would seem that started with you, big man."

Shaver grimaced. "Anyway, I found this detailed journal at the doctor's office. It was a list of all the people he had killed. When he did it, what method he used and if he was paid to do it. Guess whose name showed up a lot?"

"Doesn't mean a thing Shaver."

Shaver let out a hearty laugh. "Sure Chief, doesn't mean a thing. You're chasing for some video that may damage your career, when I've got information here that's going to end your *life*." The Chief didn't respond. "Listen, I've got to get some rest. I was in the middle of catching up on all that missed sleep when your bitch stumbled into here. You call this phone when you've decided what your priority is." Shaver hung the phone up and threw it on the bed. He looked at Tyler again.

"Get some rest my friend. You got hell in front of ya."

* * * *

Cruz stared down at Diego, who was prostrate in front of him, Martinez and Alfonso. He analyzed Diego's face. Years of struggle, deception and anxiety had battered his face. His speckled gray mustache twitched nervously. His deep-set brown eyes flicked up and down. What a poor man, Cruz thought. Decades of a phantom struggle. The reaper hanging over him all this time waiting to call his favor in. Powerless to resist. Shackled by the past and required to do whatever was asked—even if it meant betraying his own people. Diego's chest heaved as he spewed a plea none of the men listened to.

Cruz glanced at Alfonso. His face was gaunt, slightly yellow looking. Black hair fell over one of his eyes, failing to obscure the hatred lying therein.

"You fucking sellout!" Alfonso screamed, breaking the ice-thin silence. "How could you do this to us?"

"*Vendido*..." Cruz muttered.

"Damn right he is a *vendido*. My own father. My hero. Again, how could you do this to us!?

"I had no choice Alfonso! I was captive."

"Fucking excuses," Martinez growled. "I need to get the hell out of here."

"To Mexico?" Cruz asked.

"Of course," Martinez answered. "They've got a head start."

"Listen, I can still..."

"Give it up old man," Alfonso said. Diego's shoulders crumbled under the weight of his son's words.

"Alfonso, please, *por favor*, my son. I love you so much, please don't leave me like this. We can't leave each other like this! You're all I've ever had!!" Diego threw himself at Alfonso's feet and clawed at the floor.

"It was *no love*, father! It was *fake* love. You preached a philosophy to me my whole life, a philosophy you *never* practiced! I have no respect left for you, and so no love."

123

The exchange made Cruz feel sick. "What did you expect, Diego?" Cruz asked him.

"Forgiveness! Understanding!"

"You put my wife in jeopardy!" Martinez exclaimed.

"I had no choice..." Diego said. He started pounding his hands on the floor. "Give me a chance!!"

"Of course you had a choice! You had a choice to sacrifice my wife or protect yourself. You chose the path of cowardice, you sellout."

Alfonso pulled his foot away from his dad's hands. "Can I come with you guys?"

"Just like that? Like an old towel you can discard me?"

"All right...we could use another hand," Martinez answered.

Cruz picked Sandra up in his arms and they all started to walk out of the house. He turned around to look at Diego who was still kneeling on the floor. The two men locked eyes and Cruz felt a wave of remorse. It was almost too much to bear. Traitor or not, he knew Diego for a long time. And the lack of forgiveness from his only son, who clearly meant the universe to Diego, brought tears to his eyes. He turned around and as Martinez closed the front door, a scream and then a bang filled his ears. He turned to go back into the house but Alfonso grabbed his shoulder. Cruz looked at Alfonso's face, which was eerily calm.

"*Dejalo*. Leave him. At least that choice was honorable."

The harshness of Alfonso's decision left Cruz feeling disconnected. This was not humanity. This was a young man raised in a mercenary environment, where truth was paramount to love and forgiveness. Diego's own methodologies led to the instantaneous abandonment by his son. Martinez called him away from his trance by screaming, "Let's go!" They all hopped into Martinez's vehicle and sped away for Mexico. For battle. To escape.

# TWENTY-SEVEN

The Chief hauled down the highway with his lights flashing. The sparse number of cars on the road moved to his right and left, opening a black path of tar in front of him. By his calculations, he was already too far on his way when Shaver called him to turn back. Tyler would be dead—that didn't bother him. Shaver wouldn't do anything with the journal by the time the Chief was able to make it back with Martinez's wife. Then he'd negotiate with Martinez for the video and Shaver for the journal. Easy, he thought, to comfort himself while knowing the situation was a lot harder than a couple days ago.

Dawn broke. The Chief had been driving for several hours without stopping. He unzipped his pants and relieved himself into an empty can which he then threw out of the window. Diego told the Chief approximately where Martinez's wife was hiding, and with what person. Raul Santiago Dominguez. He was her brother and a well-known anchor on television, according to the Chief's people. He lived just across the Mexican border.

The Chief saw the border crossing in the orange haze in front of him. "At fucking last." There was already a line of cars stretching back several hundred feet. He pulled in between two lines of cars and moved forward as drivers of other cars yelled at him and flipped him off. The Chief looked at them and marveled at how stereotypes formed the basis of truth. He passed a lowered, white pickup truck with small wheels and a print of the Lady of Guadalupe plastered on its back window. Another car had an entire circus act packed into it—five people stuffed in the back seat of a sedan. A nicer car had several young, white girls in it, undoubtedly off to some border town to lose all notions of personal and public respect.

A border patrolman with an assault rifle walked out and stepped in front of the Chief's car. He held his hand up and the Chief came to a stop. "What the hell are you doing?" the patrolman asked in broken English. The Chief flashed his police badge to which the patrolman responded, "*Tu no mandas aquí jefe*. This isn't your jurisdiction."

"I know," the Chief responded. "I've got to get across due to an emergency."

"Next time you wait in line like the other *gringos*, okay?"

"Sure." The patrolman stepped aside and the Chief headed into Mexico. After a few minutes he stopped in front of a pharmacy fronted by two old dogs. They were both females, the same brown as the street, whose teats hung low off their mangy undersides. He rolled his window down and asked a passerby where Calle Roblado was. The man looked at the Chief warily and said, *"Dos quadras para allí y te das la izquierda—eso es Roblado."*

"Any chance of getting that in English?" The man just shook his head and went on walking. The Chief headed to where the man had pointed and eventually found the street. He drove a while before seeing the house. It was set back a good hundred yards from the road, fronted by a waist-high stucco wall. The Chief kept driving down the street which eventually doubled back and started to go up the side of a large hill. After about ten minutes of going up switchbacks, he stopped on the side of the road where he had a good view of the house and pulled out binoculars.

Cars whizzed past him and sent up clouds of dust. An hour passed when he saw some movement at the front and back of the house. A man came out of the back of the house with a shotgun in his hand. He walked the perimeter of the backyard which was hemmed in by the natural flora. Two women came out of the front of the house and cautiously approached the top of the driveway. They looked both directions as they moved. The Chief zoomed in on the women and recognized one of them. It was the wife of the cop that had died. He didn't recognize the other woman, but judged it to be Martinez's wife.

The Chief watched the people move around the house before the women finally went back inside. The man in the backyard made his way to the front and sat down on the front porch, his shotgun draped across his lap. The Chief tapped his fingers slowly on the steering wheel as time passed. He faced a dilemma. Move in on the house now, when the occupants were clearly alert and it was full daylight, or wait until night fell but when Martinez was sure to have arrived. The Chief picked up his phone, figuring it would be best to make a move before Martinez and whoever he decided to bring arrived.

"Hey, I need a favor."

"Now what," answered the gruff voice of a man.

"I need you and another gun to help me secure a hostage. They're located in a house not that far from where you're usually at."

"You're down here, *cabron*?"

"Sure am. I've been watching the house where the hostage is located for a while and it looks like the occupants are on guard."

"Listen, before you start with your shit, my debt to you is gone. This, *te va a costar*. You're going to pay." The Chief winced at the answer but knew he was in no position to drive a hard bargain. The man on the other end of the line was Jorge "El Tiburon" Lopez, a notorious drug dealer and human trafficker. Jorge escaped charges in the United States thanks to the Chief. He was another in the long list of criminals the Chief brought onto the books.

That was how the Chief built his list of connections over the last twenty-five years—a debt collector of criminals. These exchanges undoubtedly corrupted his soul, but it wasn't like he fought it off. The Chief was always bent the wrong way. As a child he recalled torturing his family's dog for pleasure, for the feeling of control. Growing up he would manipulate the dumber children in his classes to do things like steal money for him from other kids. It was a natural transition to manipulating the generally dumb confederacy of criminals.

None of that mattered to Jorge. A person unafraid to kill or be killed was not easily manipulated, and the Chief did not have time to work him over right now.

"How much is it gonna cost?" the Chief asked.

"Five grand a person."

"Come on! It's only an hour. Two grand a piece is more than fair."

Jorge laughed, "You are funny *jefe*. You are on *my* home court and you must be desperate to come to the barrio desert. Five thousand each or you can die in this *pinche hell hole* of Mexico. Plus, I'm good company and you know it."

"Bastard," the Chief said, only because he knew both statements were true. "I've got the money."

"Where do you want me to meet you?"

"I've gone a little beyond the end of Calle Roblado, up a hill overlooking the house."

"Exciting! You sound like James Bond, *jefe*. There is a small bar up the hill. I will meet you there in twenty minutes."

The Chief threw his cell phone onto the passenger seat and picked up his binoculars again. The man sitting in front of the house was still there, but close to sleeping. The Chief studied his tiny face through the binoculars, grunted and set the binoculars down. A short time later a black pickup truck tore up the road behind him and passed, sending rocks clanging into the side of his car. The Chief pulled out onto the road and followed up to the meeting place.

It was a very old, small bar. The kind a movie director would kill to find. A triangular sign hung from two cords over the door, "Lookout Saloon." Boards were missing from the steps leading up to the front door. The Chief avoided the rotted handrail for fear of toppling over.

"You like it?!" Jorge bellowed.

"Fancy."

"It's been here for ninety-seven years."

"Looks like two hundred."

The Chief stepped past Jorge's broad frame into the bar. "A whiskey," he called out. The barman looked at him and then at Jorge who nodded his head.

"*El dinero* first."

"Here," the Chief said while handing Jorge a thick, white envelope. Jorge stared at the Chief as he put the envelope in his jacket pocket.

"So what the hell is this about?"

"Is it just you? There's ten thousand in there. You said that would buy you and someone else."

Jorge flung his head back in the direction of the barman. "Chico will come too." The barman lifted his head up when he heard his name, but went back to his work when they didn't call for him. "What's it about?"

"A kidnapping."

"Oh shit, I thought this was serious, *hombre!*"

"It's a cop's wife. Some unfortunate things took place over the last week and it's time to burn the loose ends."

"A fellow officer? Another member of the blue crew? Cold *hombre*. Must be some serious shit for you to fuck over one of your own like this."

"Serious enough. I expect there to be several men defending the place..."

"What place?"

"The home of some Raul Dominguez..."

"*Ay chingao*! Raul? You crazy shit!"

"You said five thousand a person," the Chief said, cutting off the impending renegotiation.

"But you didn't say Raul's place."

The Chief moved his glass of whiskey around in his hand. "What's the big deal?"

"Shit—you can expect more than several men defending Raul's place. He usually has a bunch of people just chillin', 'specially if he knows he's gotta defend."

"I've only seen one guy working the perimeter."

"You don't know how many are inside."

"I haven't seen a ton of movement inside, even after watching for a while," the Chief responded.

Jorge leaned across the narrow table, "Look *hombre*, you can wish or you can believe. I am telling you what the fuck exists in that place." Jorge paused and then sat back in his chair. "What about the husband, he gonna be there?"

"By the time we get moving, I expect so."

"Good cop?"

"Morally?"

"What the hell do I care about morals? No. Is he a good fighter."

"One of our best. Morally and the other way."

"Damn *jefe*, even if you get out of this you know you're fucked."

The Chief gave Jorge a long look. "Been fucked for a while, you know, Jorge?" Jorge looked away and called for Chico.

"How about one of these *jefe*. Take that edge off," he said handing the Chief a pack of Marlboro Reds.

"I can't inhale that crap." Jorge kept his hand extended and nodded his head at the pack. Two years since the Chief had quit, cold turkey, after seventeen years of smoking. Finely rolled cigarette, brown tobacco leaves puckering their sweet, brown lips at him. He grabbed the pack, pulled one out, lit it using a worn candle on the table and vomited up a lung coughing. Jorge roared. "Fucking Reds."

\* \* \* \*

Cruz sat in the back of Martinez's vehicle, speeding through time. Staring at Sandra who quivered when they hit large bumps. He brushed her forehead with the back of his hand.

"How's she doing?" Martinez asked.

"Same."

"We're about to cross the border. If they ask, she's sleeping."

"She is."

"You know what I mean." Cruz did know what he meant and wondered why he chose to be semantic. Stress like this turned him into a demon. He looked up from Sandra and saw the border checkpoint ahead. There was no line and they flowed on through. The only mark of their passage into Mexico were two thumps.

Sandra stirred and opened her brown eyes, currently blood red and searching.

"Where are we?"

"Mexico," Cruz answered. Alfonso peered around from the front seat to see what was going on.

"Who's that?" Sandra asked while clamping onto Cruz's arm.

The question unnerved Cruz a bit. He reassured himself that the

129

shock affected her memory. "That's Diego's son, Alfonso. Remember?"

"The traitor's son?"

"Yes." Alfonso shifted uneasily in his seat.

"My head is killing me. Does my face look that bad?" Sandra asked, finding a moment to be a woman.

Cruz paused, experienced enough to carefully word his response. "Those blisters will heal."

"My eyes still aren't adjusted from that light," she said as she repositioned herself on Cruz. With that, she was back asleep. Cruz looked out the window at the just-inside-the-border mess around them. Men in straw hats and tired sandals pushing little carts around with bells on the handle. Calling out *"helado"* every few steps. Women in pressed white shirts and red skirts riding up their thick thighs stood on street corners. Every other store was a pharmacy. The delicious irony of a Mexican border town providing life support to the first world. They arrived a few minutes later.

The house was set back in the lot. A man sat solemnly on the front porch. His face was a series of hems, time strewn across his face. Brown skin hardened and sheened from the sun. A pristine, white hat, pulled down just above his eyes.

The front door sprung open and a woman came running out. She went straight to Martinez and jumped on his hips, straddling his waist and deluging him with kisses. A tall, stout man came out next. He stood in the doorway and smiled at Martinez.

*"Cómo estas hermano?"*

"Man, it's been a long time Raul," Martinez said while returning the smile. So this was Raul, Cruz thought to himself. Martinez told Cruz a bit about his brother-in-law during the car ride. He grew up in the Chicano Movement during the late 60s. Father—a revolutionary and leader in the movement. Mother—educator and medic to the warriors. Martinez said—and it was all conjecture—that he worked with revolutionary groups in Mexico like the Zapatistas. Wooden stairs creaked as he made his way off of the porch and came down to shake Martinez's hand.

Martinez set his wife down and turned to Cruz and Sandra, who had just edged past the open car door.

"Carmen and Raul, this is Cruz, Sandra and Alfonso there in the front seat." Martinez gestured for Alfonso to come out of the car.

"Who are they?" Raul asked. He looked at them guardedly. A black cowboy hat with a red insignia on the front was in his hand. He wore a black, western-style shirt neatly tucked into his blue jeans. Cruz saw the same insignia on Raul's belt buckle, which was reflecting the setting sun.

"Cruz is a lawyer where we live. Sandra is a reporter for one of the local news stations up there too."

"Ahhh, a fellow media person," Raul noted. Cruz watched as they smiled at each other. "And him?" Raul asked looking at Alfonso.

"That's a longer story. Let's just say he's an interested bystander with a debt to repay."

Raul looked around them at the surrounding hills. "Let's get your car in the garage and go inside. These hills have eyes." Cruz supported Sandra by her arm and followed Raul into the home. The man on the porch sat motionless. Not a twitch as they passed with Cruz wondering if he wasn't one of those sculpted Indian figures you see outside of smoke shops. To his surprise, there was a whole group of men inside the house when they entered. They sat around a big, circular pine table littered with bottles and chips and cards and packs of cigarettes. It was the moment in the dream when a whole roomfull of people looks up at you.

"*Todos, estos son amigos de Carmen y Martinez,*" Raul announced. The people in the room collectively grunted and went back to their activities.

One woman stood out. She was seated on a couch with her back to them, watching a news station. Raul pointed toward the same couch and invited them to sit down. They did but the woman still didn't acknowledge them. Instead, she sat focused on the television and without looking at them said, "It's riveting. We're sitting in a war zone. Evil fighting a little less evil in a struggle over a multibillion-dollar drug trade. Bodies found limbless in the middle of the street. Tongues delivered in boxes. Decapitated heads lined on fences. Skeletons resting in metal cans full of acid. Kidnapping, rape, murder, extortion, bribery. Riveting."

"She hasn't taken her eyes off that set since getting here," Raul whispered to Cruz.

"I hear you, and no, I haven't," Alicia answered. "This is the eye of the storm delivered on a seventeen-inch rabbit ear television." Raul just shook his head and pulled up an old wood chair next to Cruz.

"It's true, you know?"

"What's that?"

"These border towns are at the center of a colossal struggle. The government, supposedly cracking down on the drug trade they facilitated for fifty years. The drug lords fighting back with armies of their own. No one is safe. These monsters dump mutilated bodies at schools' doorsteps to intimidate children. Mind control, *hombre*. Inculcating the youth. The streets are *vacio* by seven every night. Any surviving businesses either pay off the government or the drug lords or both. *Burros* line up to make border runs and shit out *la cocaina* and *la marijuana* on the other side for rich *gringos* to consume. And that's what it is brother, the destruction of human life just to get highhhhhhhhhhh."

"You working to stop it?"

"Man...there's no stopping this. No revolutionary group has the might of capitalism behind it. When money is at issue, ideals and politics take a back seat. No, we will let them fight and kill each other until all of those *cabrones* are dead." Cruz looked at the television which showed a report on the kidnapping of a teenage girl from right in front of her school. She was some politician's daughter.

"You seen that video Martinez has?" Raul asked, changing the subject.

"Not all the way through," Cruz answered hesitantly. He was relieved when the door to the garage opened and Martinez came into the house with Alfonso and Carmen.

"So what's the plan, brother?" Raul asked Martinez.

"First, sit down. I'm beat up to hell."

"No shit."

"Then, figure out what to do with this," he said as he flung the safe with the video to Raul.

"This it?"

"That's it. Fucking blood-stained video. The life lost over that video..." Alicia broke her focus on the television and looked at Martinez. "Just don't know what to say, man, other than I've got an obligation to make the contents of that video matter."

"You watched it yet?"

"Why? I was there."

"More to make sure it's even got what you expect it to have."

"No. Pandora's box opened in the last two weeks. I've been surviving."

"You mind if we watch it?"

"Nope." Raul handed the mini-safe back to Martinez so he could open it. Martinez punched a few digits into the electronic keypad and opened the safe.

Cruz noticed him handle the drive delicately, seemingly in reverence to its contents, the lives lost protecting it. Then he turned his attention to Alicia. "Excuse me, but who are you?" Cruz asked her.

Martinez answered for her, slightly protective, "That's Alicia Williams. She is—was—my partner's wife."

"I'm still his wife. It's just that God separated us." Cruz sat quietly and looked at her until she changed her position, relieving him of his unspoken duty to be mournful.

Sensing the tension Raul said, "Let's go downstairs to watch it. I've got another television and a laptop set up." Cruz, Martinez, and Alfonso followed him. Carmen sat with Sandra and Alicia on the couch.

Downstairs was a fortress. Steel lined the four walls. A generator sat silently in a corner. One wall was full of canned fruits, vegetables and meats. Another wall had a workbench laden with boxes of ammunition. Guns of all types were mounted on the wall.

"We don't fuck around," Raul said to Cruz. Cruz smiled sheepishly at him. The firepower was humbling. Raul pulled some folding chairs into the middle of the room and gestured to everyone to sit down. They did and Raul went about setting up the video.

"Okay, here we go," Raul said. He turned the lights in the room off and pulled up his own chair. Cruz half expected him to start a popcorn machine. The screen went from black to slightly colorful. The house in the jostling picture was run down, a whiteish-gray with peeling paint. Weeds grew around the perimeter of the house, about a month tall. The camera followed three officers around the side of the house while a separate group took place at the front of the house.

"Is your sound broken?" Martinez asked.

"No, no. Must just be the video." They watched in silence as one of the officers with Martinez used a devastating kick to break in the back door. The cameraman stormed into the home directly behind the last officer. Martinez led the group, checking rooms off the hall while moving to the front of the house. The group stopped at the end of the hall, which opened into a larger living area. The camera peeked around the officers who were pressed against the wall.

Martinez lowered his gun. The rest of his group did the same. They walked into the room and the camera focused on a young woman crying on the ground, her eyes squinted and her hands over her forehead. An old man lay motionless on a couch next to her. The camera panned up to one of the officers who was making agitated gestures at the camera with his finger.

"That's Shaver," Martinez said, identifying him although his back was to the camera.

133

The camera dropped to floor level but something kept it tilted up.

"Smart," Raul murmured.

"What's that?"

"He's got the camera propped up on his foot."

They watched as the young woman grabbed onto Shaver's leg. He kicked her off and she went reeling like a stuffed doll toward the wall behind her. After some seconds Shaver pointed his gun at the old man, who was still motionless. He jabbed his gun into the old man, which is when Martinez made his move toward Shaver. When he did, Shaver's gun unleashed several rounds into the old man. The camera shook from the shots and as if to coincide with real life, a man's voice from upstairs cried out to all of them, "*Oye!*"

A cannon-like boom sounded from upstairs, followed by the splintering of a door. Cruz jumped out of his seat and instinctively went toward the stairs. He saw Sandra on her stomach at the top of the stairs.

"Sandra, get down here!" he screamed out as he rushed up the stairs. She sat still, immobilized by the blast. Cruz got to the top step and grabbed Sandra under her arms. He got a glimpse of the men at the pine table. It was now turned on its side, functioning as a shield from the bullets. A *rattlle, rattlle tat tat tat* came from the front door and pieces of the table flew around the room. Cruz hauled Sandra down the stairs just as Raul and Martinez came rushing in his direction, guns in hand.

"Where's Carmen?!" Martinez screamed.

"Still up there!"

Sandra crawled to the middle of the room where she rested on her knees bawling. Alfonso was crouched, frog-like, behind a chair. Alicia remained in the upstairs room, sitting still in her chair and staring at the screen in front of her. Cruz pointed at Alfonso and said, "You grab one of these guns and protect these women!" He nodded and pushed his chair up to the stairway as Martinez brought Carmen downstairs.

Sounds of material being broken surrounded them. Wood splintered. Glass shattered. Ceramic ware exploded as both sides exchanged fire. Martinez crouched at the top of the stairs and urgently called to Alicia.

"Alicia...Alicia! Get over here!" She turned around and stared blankly at him.

"What the fuck is her problem?" Cruz asked from right behind Martinez.

"She's fucking traumatized."

Cruz looked behind him at Alfonso and the women. Alfonso was still behind the chair with his gun pointed up the stairway. As Cruz turned back around, he heard a thump and then a scream. Alicia's eyes were peeled back wide. Blood shot out from her throat and nose.

"Oh my god," Martinez said. He crawled to the couch and pulled Alicia down in front of it. "Goddammit!" Martinez cried out as he put his hands on her neck. It was no use. Blood streamed through his hands and Alicia went limp.

The rest of the room was in similar disarray. Several of the men Cruz had seen at the poker table were either shot or taking cover behind objects. Then something startling happened. Cruz watched as Martinez started to wipe Alicia's blood on his face and chest.

"Martinez...what the hell?"

"Just stay down there Cruz!"

Raul was pinned down behind the couch where he had been trying to return fire. Cruz covered his mouth and gagged when he saw Alicia exhale her last breath. The gunfire subsided some. Cruz heard moaning and the occasional piece of glass fall to the floor in the main part of the house.

Martinez was pointing furiously at the security room. "Get in that room. Fucking trust me Raul!" Raul scurried from the couch to the stairs and squeezed past Cruz. He went and checked on Carmen and Sandra, who were huddled in the back corner of the room. Cruz saw Martinez lay down on the ground next to Alicia and put one of her legs over his head.

"Check that side room!" Cruz heard someone scream from the front of the house. A set of footsteps crunched toward him. After several tense seconds, a shadow appeared around the corner and Cruz slowly backed down the steps. The only sound was the muffled cry of Carmen and Sandra. The three men knelt in the center of the room, hearts slamming against their sternums as they waited for the final showdown.

Cruz could hear someone rubbing against the wall while advancing. The noise stopped at the top of the steps.

"We know you're down there! Might as well give it up, *hijitos*." There was a pause followed by, "I hear your bitches crying. If you don't surrender it's gonna be a hell of a lot worse for them!" The men pointed their guns at the stairs. Cruz's hands were shaking.

"I'll give you three seconds. Make a smart decision, would you? One...two...thr..."

"Three motherfucker," Cruz heard Martinez say. Now Martinez's plan came to fruition. The men had taken the bait and thought Martinez was dead.

## Derek Blass

"Get your fucking hands above your head!  Tell that fucker over there to get his hands up too!  Guys, get the hell up here now!"  The three of them bolted up the stairs and came upon the blood-smeared Martinez with his gun held to a weaselly looking middle-aged man's head.  There was another man in the center of the room, dark, criminal-looking, with a sneer on his face.

"Take care of that one," Martinez said to Cruz.  Alfonso and Cruz went and grabbed the man's hands and held them behind his back.  Martinez put his arm around his prisoner's neck and spun him towards the other men.

"Pot of gold here, gentlemen."

"Who is it?" Raul asked, slightly out of breath.

"Our police chief."

# TWENTY-EIGHT

Tyler's hands and ankles were bound. He tested the bindings, but they were rock solid. Shaver circled around him in the small room. Tyler could see him getting more and more agitated. His face started to turn red and his breathing shortened. He was a bull of a man, with biceps the size of Tyler's thighs. He wore an army camouflage jacket and black tactical pants. This only added to the intimidation level. Tyler spent the last hour praying that he would get out of this...somehow.

"The longer your sponsor doesn't call the closer you get to hell buddy," Shaver barked. There would be no physical overtaking of the brute. Instead, Tyler knew he had to overcome Shaver mentally—something that was possible given his frazzled state.

"You know they're coming for you, right?" Tyler hissed. Shaver stopped his pacing.

"Who the fuck is gonna come for *me*?"

"The Chief is barreling into their trap. He's out of his territory and pretty much alone. I'd say the odds are heavily against him and that he gets nabbed."

"Nabbed by cops?"

"No, nabbed by the cop with the video."

"Martinez?"

"Yes, man!" Tyler said in exasperation. He twisted his body to take some of the pressure off of his shoulder. "Listen, could you at least sit me up? I'm no threat. I'm bound, weaponless and quite honestly, outclassed by your size." Tyler watched as Shaver considered the request. It may have been the semi-veiled compliment that compelled Shaver to sit Tyler up on a chair.

"The Chief can't give me up. This journal will ruin him more than any video ever would," Shaver said while holding up the journal from the doctor's house.

"I agree that the journal is critical, but the remorseless end of a muzzle in your mouth tends to produce illogical actions. Plus, what if he's made a deal to give you up and to get the journal in return? That way, he stays out of jail and at most loses his job." This possibility visibly affected Shaver. Sensing a quarried prey, Tyler added, "Having killed, you don't have that option. Shaver shot him a vicious glance and then went back to pacing around the small room, interrupting the silence every so often by pounding his fist on a wall.

"What's your suggestion then, fucking smart guy?"

"Start getting ready. Start getting ready as of ten damn minutes ago." Tyler hesitated before he supplemented the next part, not sure if he had coaxed Shaver enough yet. "Problem is you can't set this up alone."

Shaver let out a chortle. "Who then...you? I ain't gonna let you out of those bindings. Have you jack me from behind while I'm not expecting it? I don't think so."

"Listen, you know you can't do this alone. You've got open land on all four sides of the house. Little tree cover. No natural obstacles. It's the middle of a god damn field."

"Why would you give a shit to help?"

Tyler laughed this time. "Look at me. Either you kill me or I help you fight these bastards. If we win, I get to walk." Tyler cocked his head to the side and watched Shaver mull over the proposal. "Clock's ticking."

"I know," Shaver answered shortly. He pulled out a combat knife from a sheath on his belt and moved behind Tyler. A shiver went up Tyler's back as the hulk stood behind him, one stroke from spilling Tyler's blood out onto his lap. He felt Shaver's warm breath wrap around his ear and the cold knife blade under his chin.

"If you try to fuck me—even if I just think you are—I'm gonna rape you with this eight-inch serrated hunting knife. You fucking got me?" Tyler moved his head affirmatively. Shaver cut the bindings off of Tyler's hands and feet.

"I've got about twelve grenades and three proximity mines. A complete arsenal of handguns, semis, fully auto rifles. Shit, I've even got a Barrett."

"Sounds like enough for a Waterloo to me," Tyler said as he cracked his wrists.

\* \* \* \*

Martinez stood over the cowering Chief, watching him quiver. The sounds in the home died down to intermittent sobs, people shifting in their places. The adrenaline rush and then come-down bashed his mental capability. A recurring dream that he'd had since all the proverbial shit hit the fan asserted itself in his consciousness.

He is in a room with hundreds of faceless people, all in suits, all with drinks in their hands. The room is completely and utterly silent. As he stands there, the faintest murmur begins to emerge from these people. Their bodies start to move, almost imperceptibly. At that point a knot builds in his chest and nervous spikes shoot out from his stomach. He's standing in the middle of that mass, that crowd of potentiality.

They start to move a little bit faster. Some move from faceless person to faceless person, each identifiable only by the shape of their body. Some raise their glass to drink. Some don't move at all but only stare at him. The talking gets a little bit louder, like someone is turning the volume knob up at an excruciatingly slow, but consistent, rate. Movements are increasing in speed at the same rate. His heart pounds as this beehive of faceless people thaws out and comes to thundering life around him. Eventually, the sound of people talking and clanking glasses and moving around the room is deafening. Even with his hands over his ears the sound cripples him. People move in blurs, contorting the image of their blank faces. In the end, he's balled up, fetal, and crying as the sound and movement keep increasing.

He looked down at the Chief, blinking and returning to reality—wondering how long he had been staring silently at the man. "I've had these weird dreams about a beehive of people since Shaver killed that man. Can't tell who the hell they are. It made me wonder what the hell's going on. I never used to have dreams. Every night was a blank slate. Now, this vivid-fucking-dream wakes me up in a warm bath of sweat every night. You know what I think it is?" The Chief didn't respond. Martinez didn't know it because he was locked onto the Chief, but everyone was holding their breath and looking at him, wondering if he was about to kill the Chief.

"All these pieces came together. The different treatment growing up because my last name is Mexican. The difficulty moving up in the force because of that same thing. The fact that time after fucking time people of color can be mistreated, beaten up and even killed by cops. And now this dream makes sense.

The people in the dream *are* those people of color—faceless, nameless, voiceless people. But those people are getting active, fighting the system, *moving*. Developing a voice. And that person in the middle of the room, it's not me. It's *you,* and every other ignorant fuck who sees what's coming up on you. The motion and the voice will overwhelm you. You are the one curled up in the middle of the room as the tide rises around you, drowned by people like me."

Martinez knelt closer to the Chief and adjusted the bandage on his right leg. "What you gotta realize is that you can't just end us. This is slow-motion revolution. Every year the news will bring you one step closer to the new reality, a reality dominated by another face. My fucking face."

"So what's the fucking point of this? You spics take over. You bring your black and your yellow and your women friends and you run the country into the ground because you are all a bunch of fucking idiots. Great. But, what's it got to do with me here, now?"

"Glad you asked. See this trigger?" Martinez asked while holding his gun sideways for the Chief. "Starts a reaction, doesn't it? Shaver killing the old man, a trigger. The *video* of Shaver killing that old man, a trigger. I'm going to show this video to the country. It will be shown and read on every local and national website, print media and television station. And then people will know their enemy."

"Brilliant, just fucking brilliant," the Chief said throwing his head back and laughing. "You see, this is what I'm talking about. You're going to take physical evidence and release it to the world before Shaver is prosecuted? Genius, Martinez. You'll completely blow the case against Shaver out of the water."

Martinez looked over at Cruz who half shrugged, half pulled his eyebrows back, implicitly agreeing with the Chief. "The trial *will be* the release," Martinez said in an effort to regain his correctness.

"Whatever. My question stands—what the hell do you want from me?"

"Shaver."

"That's it? That's all you want?"

"Yep."

"Hell, *I want him too.* Let's go get him!" The Chief grinned at Martinez who was slightly confused by the ease of this.

"All right...let's go then."

"Hold on there, brown boy. There's some negotiation involved in this. You know me."

Martinez raised an eyebrow and crossed his arms on his chest. "Don't think you're in a position to negotiate. "

"And neither are you if you want Shaver."

"I could find him."

"Sure you could, but that would take time. I'm kinda gathering you don't have much of that, seeing as you are wanting to start a revolution and all." This jab pissed Martinez off enough that he thrust his right hand in between the Chief's legs and squeezed his balls. The Chief grimaced and his face turned bright red.

"Fuck you Martinez," he spit out.

"Fuck me?" Rage blurred Martinez's vision and he held his gun up to the Chief's face.

"Wait, wait, wait!" Cruz screamed as he jumped up from the couch and put his hands up in Martinez' face. "This is *not* what we want."

Raul stepped closer to Martinez and put a hand on his shoulder. "I know you're *loco* from the stress right now, but this won't help. Spending the rest of your life in a Mexican prison is no way to live."

Martinez's vision cleared up. He lowered his gun and stepped away from the Chief. "Look," Cruz started, "tell me what you want."

The Chief used his shoulder to wipe perspiration from his forehead. "Just one thing Shaver has."

"What is it?"

"That doesn't matter. One thing, very important to me and completely irrelevant to any of you. You promise I get it and you get Shaver." Cruz looked at Raul and Martinez. Raul seemed indifferent. Martinez had turned his back to all of them.

"Fine. I promise you get what you want from Shaver. Now tell us where to find him."

* * * *

Cruz and the rest of the convoy spent most of the trip to Shaver's place in silence. They encountered a brief issue at the border. Bringing in a cache of weapons was frowned upon. The Chief came in handy though, because he "knew" a border supervisor. Another pawn in the pocket.

One of Raul's men drove Sandra and Carmen back to Sandra's place. Martinez drove himself, Cruz, Raul and the Chief. The group had held a small memorial for Alicia before arranging to have her shipped back to the States. Another car followed them with Alfonso and three more of Raul's men. Everyone was bandaged, bruised, beat up and exhausted.

Cruz tried to sleep but couldn't. He felt raw and energized, but thin as paper. He laid his head back on the headrest and thought about what had been going on. The violence replayed in his mind with photographic vividness. Sandra's blistered face. The confrontation at the hospital. Alicia's chest exploding. The old man and his daughter begging for their lives. He shook his head, wondering if this really represented humanity—if he could call it that.

Martinez saw Cruz shake his head in the low glow of the car's instrument clusters. "What's wrong?" The question caught Cruz off guard. He had assumed he was alone in those thoughts. He looked over at Martinez and wondered if this was a conversation he could share.

"Just contemplating whether this is it. If this is what people are about."

"Good versus evil?"

"That...but more. The violence is startling."

Martinez shifted in his seat and grabbed a bottle of water in the center console. "I've gotten used to it."

"I'm sure you have, but is that healthy? Isn't it insane to say you are acclimated to two innocent people being slaughtered right in front of you?"

"I didn't say I was used to the injustice or the evil of it. The violence though, the blood, guts and that look a person gets right before they are about to die. You get used to that or you can't go on. It's a fact of life for someone in my line of work."

"That's my problem. It's a fact of life for all of us. Maybe there are varying degrees. Some people have never seen a dead person other than in a movie. But violence and death are a fact of life for everyone. Media pumps it into our veins every day. Local news is about assaults and rapes and murders. National news is about serial killers and mass shootings. International news is about civilian death counts in war and the latest number of people blown up by some self-proclaimed martyr. They used to strap bombs to men and blow up in markets. Now they strap bombs to women and detonate in mosques. Next, children in daycare. Then, chemical weapons. I'm waiting for the first dirty bomb to be set off in the States."

"The area around the Mexican border is the same," Raul piped in. "Except, we are in the dark ages of violence. Hand-to-hand brutality. You have reached the renaissance age in your country. You can direct a drone to attack from a ship at sea—brilliant. We will make ourselves obsolete at some point."

"Is this my punishment?" the Chief asked. "To listen to three wetbacks ruminating about the fate of my world?"

"Your punishment hasn't begun," Martinez answered. "And if you drop any more slurs, I'm gonna pinch one of your balls and slice it off."

They spent the rest of the trip in silence, letting the weight of their conversation lay over them. The topography changed as they neared Shaver's house. Rangy mountains flattened to rolling hills and then to expansive plains. Evergreens became junipers and pine which gave way to sparse vegetation cover. The car's headlights illuminated a calm, desolate and beautiful nothingness in front of them.

The navigation system broke their silence.

"How far should we approach on foot?" Raul asked.

"We have no cover at all. Our lights are visible from hundreds of feet away, so I'd say we walk the last mile or so." Martinez slowed down and let the car with Alfonso in it pull alongside. He rolled down the window and waited for Alfonso to do the same before saying, "Follow me up the road, then we'll stop and hoof it the last mile." Alfonso nodded his head. Cruz noted a steeled look on the young man's face. It was remarkable that just a short time ago his father was sabotaging them. Now he was ready to die for their cause. Powerful emotion, that guilt thing.

The two cars kept moving up the road. Martinez left the window down and Cruz could hear the crunch of gravel under the cars' tires. Soon the crunch turned into the raspy sound of dirt passing under the cars and they stopped. The pitch-black night sky was all encompassing. A few crickets made lazy calls in the knee-high grass. Cruz gently opened the door and stepped out. Alfonso and his full car of mercenaries gathered around where Martinez was standing. Raul pulled the Chief out of the car by his collar and set him on the ground next to the back tire. Cruz stood alone for a moment, admiring the heft of darkness that created its own silence.

"We're going to split into three teams," Cruz heard Martinez start. "Team A will be the reconnaissance team; Team B will be the diversionary team; and Team C will be the strike team. Alfonso, I want you to lead the reconnaissance team, which will be one of Raul's men, the Chief and you. Team B is going to be Raul and Cruz. Team C is me and the rest of Raul's men. Team A is going to advance up the road to Shaver's house while Teams B and C take positions on opposite sides of the house. Teams B and C will swing in wide arcs to the house so that not all of the teams can be detected at once. When recon gets fifty yards from the front of the house, I want you to get down on the ground and lay low. Team B, your primary tactic will be using flashbangs in order to disorient Shaver and whoever else he's got in there."

"Probably Tyler," the Chief said.

"When we hear your flashbangs, Team C will gain entry and attack from the other side of the house. Plain and simple," Martinez said with a smile as he looked around at everyone. "Raul, these guys of yours speak English, right?"

"Not so much."

"Well, the...then why the hell didn't you tell me before I went through all of that?"

"You seemed so excited."

"Shit...I was." While Raul translated Martinez's plan into Spanish, Cruz approached Martinez to hopefully take care of some frayed nerves.

"You know I've never done anything like this?" Cruz said scratching the back of his head. "I mean, I'm a lawyer. I yell at people and write some nasty letters, but that's about the scope of my violence."

"You'll be fine." Martinez grabbed one of the flashbangs and showed him how it worked. "Once you release the flashbang, it will do three things. First, cause a flash of light equal to 300,000 candlepower. Second, emit 150 decibels of sound. Third, because these ain't the bargain-basement variety, the flashbang will emit CN tear gas. The effect is a complete loss of balance and orientation."

"Can Shaver fight these off?"

"Sure, with the right equipment—and he's been trained to counteract the various effects. But I don't necessarily care if the flashbangs actually work on him. The diversion is what I want. The few seconds those flashbangs buy will be important." Cruz stood staring blankly at the dense piece of metal in his hand.

"What do I do after that?"

"Wait. The house would be too crowded with you and Raul in it too."

"You'll need all the help you can get," the Chief smugly added.

Martinez knelt down next to the Chief, his nose inches from the Chief's crimson cheek. "That's a fine suggestion. I think I'll use you as a human shield. Any more of 'em?"

"Of what?"

"Suggestions." The Chief sat silently and turned his head away from Martinez.

"Get your gear and nuts together. Three minutes and we'll head in." Cruz looked on as the other men moved around, clipping clips, adjusting straps, snapping weapons. He pulled his windbreaker on and leaned against Martinez's car, analyzing the cylindrical flashbang in his right hand and squeezing it a few times. Raul saw him and grinned.

"Not exactly combat-ready?"

"You could say that. I'll just follow your lead."

"It won't be a big deal. Squeeze, pull pin, throw through window." Raul paused his gearing up to add, "Just make sure to get it through the window. If that lands in your lap, well, you know..."

Cruz watched the others and noticed his hands were shaking again. Martinez saw it and held his hand up to Cruz, "See...mine does it too." Cruz's countenance changed for the better. He squatted down and ran his hands through his hair, emitting a loan groan as he did. He grabbed a chunk of dirt and grass, held it to his nose and breathed in deeply. The richness of the soil mixed with the pungent odor of the grass woke his senses and grounded him. The clicking around him stopped.

"On our way then," Martinez ordered. Raul led the group out while Martinez brought up the rear. They walked in single file, every now and again the rhythm of their footsteps was broken by someone dragging a foot. As they made their way, the pitch-black sky around them began to transform in color. Cruz noted the minute change from black to deep purple and watched as the deep purple yielded to a shade of lighter purple. "*Cuidado!*" came a hushed warning when Cruz bumped into the man in front of him.

The line had stopped. Cruz made out the shape of Shaver's home. It was like a bunker, low and square. The windows were dark and there were no streetlights on the dirt road. The quarter moon provided the only illumination and tended to make the home look more daunting than it probably was. They moved closer as Martinez sped up to the front of the line. They stopped again when Martinez held up one finger and pointed to the left of the house, held up two fingers and pointed at the driveway, held up three fingers flicked them toward the right side of the house.

Cruz and Raul crouch-ran in an arc while staying several hundred feet from the house. Cruz felt more rugged than he ever had in his life, crouch-running. Where was Sandra to see him now? He breathed heavily as they both came to a stop, the flashbang pressing its cold, steel body against his leg. Very rugged. They both watched as Alfonso and the Chief slowly made their way down the driveway, slightly hunched over. Martinez and his group were barely visible on their side. They sat silently, chests heaving in unison, gazing intently until an eruption forced them backwards onto the ground. Cruz's ears rung and he fought to take a breath but it felt like someone was sitting on his chest. Raul was laying next to him, sprawled out on the ground. He was making futile attempts to get up, drunk attempts. The taste of blood filled Cruz's mouth. Seconds later he sucked in a lungful of air and rolled onto his side. Raul managed to get onto all fours and was coughing violently.

Cruz pushed up off of the ground and rested on one knee. He ran a finger in his mouth, and when he pulled it out could see a dark stain. There were no figures standing in the driveway anymore. As the ringing cleared from Cruz's ears, a ghastly screaming replaced it. It sounded like Alfonso. The screams penetrated the still of the night and then faded as he drew another breath. Cruz started to head toward the noise but Raul grabbed the back of his foot.

"Don't move that way."

"What do you mean? We've got to go help Alfonso."

"We have no idea what's out there—it could be a trap. That was either a set explosive or a mine and we have no idea where the rest of them are."

The thought of stepping on a mine confounded Cruz. "A mine?"

"May have been."

"What the fuck is this?"

"I don't know Cruz, but we can't go that direction." The screams were spaced out further now and had transformed into wails. Cruz didn't realize it but he kept running a hand over his body to make sure everything was intact.

"What now?" Cruz asked with a heavy feeling of regret and guilt. Leaving Alfonso out there to suffer alone seemed inhuman.

"We move to our position, carefully. There may be more mines to look out for. Stay directly behind me as I move and only step where I step." Raul stood up slowly and stretched his legs. He stood up and bent down, stood up and bent down. "Damn...damn!"

"What is it?" Cruz whispered.

"I'm having trouble putting any weight on my right leg. I've got an old knee injury. I think that blast aggravated it."

"That means you want me to go first?"

"Not want—you have to."

Cruz shook his head and a small helping of dust fluttered off. "Can you tell me what the hell I'm looking for?" The ridiculousness of the situation frustrated Cruz. Two men possibly dead a hundred feet away. Raul standing in front of him with a knee injury. God-knows-what other fucking booby traps laid out in front, around or behind them. Through all of this, the flashbang grenade hung relentlessly out in his pocket—a reminder of further conflict and possible fuckups to come.

"Wires, laser lines, small circular objects. Look for piles of leaves, mounds of dirt or anything else that doesn't look flat."

Cruz took his first step, muttering "Hail Mary, full of grace..." while extending one leg in front of the other as if the bottom half of his body was immersed in quicksand. Some remote quadrant of his brain—not paralyzed by fear—was tickled to hear the prayer come out of his mouth. A firm nonbeliever temporarily transformed on these solitary, moonlit plains. Cruz took step after step while watching for anything that looked out of the ordinary. He stopped several times and unsuccessfully tried to slow his breathing. The beat of his heart filled his ears like a rubber mallet pounding on an empty metal tank. Everything looked like a threat. Simple piles of dirt became land mines. Leaves were hiding trip wires. He felt light-headed and nauseous as the threat of death loomed over him. Raul's hand was on his shoulder providing a mixture of support and condolence.

"Steady as she goes, steady, steady, steady as she goes..." Cruz hummed.

"We are almost there," Raul said.

Cruz stopped and wiped sweat off of his forehead. He looked back to see Raul's status. Just as he did, a red dot fluttered on Raul's chest and then disappeared.

"Down, get down!" Cruz yelled as he ducked to the ground and pulled Raul down with him. They heard a puff of air and then dirt kicked up right next to them. Both of them started a mad rush to the house. They re-prioritized dangers and brushed aside the possibility of stepping onto something explosive. Cruz heard one more puff of air and felt something burning his right shoulder. The front of the house was feet away. Cruz vaulted a row of shrubs wrapped around the perimeter of the home and dove to the corner of the house. He turned his head and watched Raul tumble over the shrub, an accelerated trip to the ground, and then crawl the last few feet to Cruz's side.

The two men sat against the side of the house, chests heaving, their chins in their chests. Raul looked over at Cruz, "You're shot," he said matter-of-factly.

"Where?" Then the pain returned. "Oh shit. That happened when we were running," Cruz said as he put a finger onto the wound.

"Doesn't look too bad—let me feel it." Raul touched the wound. "Grazed."

"That's a first."

"Shaver popped your cherry," Raul laughed. Cruz snickered before they both sobered up and realized where they were sitting. Raul climbed over Cruz and looked around the edge of the house. "I don't see Martinez."

"How do we know when to move?"

Raul didn't respond immediately. He continued to look around the side of the house for Martinez. Cruz tuned his ears into the sounds around him. The house was silent. Insects made noises barely audible above the buzz of the world. Plains stretched out in front of him into a pitch black. Stars filled almost every inch of the globe over him. He felt Raul climb back over him and rest against the house with a sigh.

"We'll have to wait for some sign of..." Both men snapped their heads to the right.

"Did you hear that?" Cruz asked.

"Yes."

They sat dead still, straining their eyes to pick up some movement down the length of the house. Seconds seemingly stretched into minutes before they saw it. A face popped out around the corner and then slid back into the darkness.

"Fuck—fucking-a, who is that?!" Cruz exclaimed. Raul shook his head and pulled his gun out. He shifted down onto his stomach and took aim down to where they had seen the face. As he did Cruz heard something from around the corner of the house next to them.

"I heard something else, Raul."

"I'm not taking my eyes of this corner. You deal with the other shit."

"Cruz?? Raul??"

"Who is it?"

"I'm not taking my eyes off it."

"It's Martinez."

"Martinez! Hey, what the hell happened to Alfonso and the Chief?"

"Not sure, but we don't have time for that now. Give me thirty seconds to get back on the other side of the house and we'll charge in."

"There's no fucking deception anymore, Martinez. Something freakish just saw us from over there," Cruz said, pointing to where Raul was transfixed.

"Stick to the fucking plan, Cruz. It's what we got and we aren't changing."

"You two shut the fuck up and let's do this shit," Raul stammered. His Spanish accent sounded whiny when emphasizing English swear words.

"Thirty seconds."

"Okay, then I'll toss this into the house..."

"Yes, thirty seconds." Martinez bolted back to the other side of the house.

"Twenty...ten...five..." Cruz pulled the pin, stood up and turned to the window behind him. He lifted his hand up just as someone's face moved back from the window. It was the same face he had seen peek out from behind the house. Pale skin, long black hair, egg-white eyes. There was no body, just a white face in the darkness.

"Throw the fucking grenade!" Raul yelled.

Cruz threw the grenade. It crashed through the window and bounced inside the house. He knelt down just as the grenade exploded and burst light out onto the plains behind them. Raul ran to the front of the house with Cruz in tow. They both stopped next to the front door. Martinez and his group busted through a side door and were greeted by a chorus of bullets. Despite Martinez's orders, Raul shouldered his way through the front door and into the house. Cruz stayed perched on the front porch, his own gun rattling in his hands. He saw Raul backing out to him, dragging something big.

"It's him, it's the freak we saw," Raul gasped as he pulled the body through the threshold and next to Cruz.

"Is he dead?"

"Stunned. I'll be right back."

"Wait!! Give me something to keep him here!" But Raul was already back in the house. Cruz looked at the man. He was slender but muscular. Jet black hair fell over his face in a mess. A streak of blood from a wound on his head streamed down his cheek, a crimson ribbon down the otherwise pale canvas. The man's lips quivered and startled Cruz. He looked around and picked up a stone.

Several more gunshots rang out, followed by silence, then more gunshots and a deafening explosion. Cruz jumped up and peered down into the house. He saw a person stumbling down the hall toward him, banging into walls while moving. As the person neared, Cruz tried to pick out who it was. It didn't appear to be any of their people.

"Who is that?"

The person kept stumbling down the hall. The moment Cruz realized who it was, Shaver opened his bloody eyes and raised his gun at Cruz. Frozen in place, Cruz could only draw what he thought would be his last breath. Shaver pulled the trigger and his gun clicked. Click, click-click. Then Shaver tripped over the doorway and fell onto the ground in front of Cruz.

And there he was, the man Cruz didn't know he knew.

# PART TWO

## THE TRIAL

# TWENTY-NINE

$S$andra stood behind Cruz rubbing his shoulders. Her face was nearly healed. Only upon the closest scrutiny were light pink spots visible.

The two had grown closer in the weeks following the raid on Shaver's home. After the run in with Shaver and Cruz's recognition of who he was, Cruz took some time off from work to unwind. Sandra stopped by his house, often bringing him little gifts of pastries or meals until he recovered his energy. The care they demonstrated for each other in those stressful times sparked the beginnings of strong emotion.

"So who is Shaver?"

"The same pig that beat me and Eduardo—you remember Eduardo—when I was a teenager."

"You're sure of it?"

"Positive. Same face. Same eyes...same hate."

"Wow. He's always been like this then."

"A powerful one."

Cruz also went to visit Martinez when he had the chance, and visa versa. Martinez recounted what happened once he kicked open Shaver's side door.

"It was a hail of bullets. Something fully automatic and the bullets just tore through everything in the doorway. I was hit two times—once in the leg and the chest. The Kevlar vest is why I'm here. Two out of three of Raul's men were killed almost instantaneously. I ducked into the house and was basically immobilized. It was so dark I couldn't see a damn thing, to tell you the truth."

"So if Shaver had the upper hand, why'd he come out like he did?"

"Raul—Raul flanked him. Shit, Raul saved the day. He grabbed that freak Tyler out of a side room..."

"That part I saw."

"..and then went back in and flanked Shaver. I think Shaver was slightly disoriented from the combination of the flashbang you threw and our attack on the side of the house. Raul managed to land a shot on him before he charged. That's when he shot Raul...and...well, you know how that turned out."

"How's Carmen?"

"Oh, she's hanging in there as much as possible. She's been by Raul's bedside night and day, hoping for some sign of life."

"Anything?"

"Nothing so far."

Their conversations vacillated between sharing bits and pieces of the joint trauma and the more mundane topics. They could only revisit those details so often and for so long before they were overwhelmed. Like any trauma, those moments were as vivid as life itself.

"What happens next for Shaver?" Sandra asked, bringing Cruz back into the present.

"Huh?"

"Shaver...what next?"

"He's sitting in the city jail right now awaiting processing." Sandra stopped rubbing his shoulders and played with the tag on his shirt. He discounted this as hapless drifting off, fiddling, but he still felt blood rush to his face. As if she caught herself being too personal, she tousled his normally brushed back black hair, which was unkempt and disheveled. Cruz heard her walking around his office. Instead of turning around, he imagined how she moved. Her legs close together in her tight, black skirt. Heels clicking on the tile floor as she strolled around the office. She paused and he imagined her rubbing her soft neckline.

"Did you go to Alfonso's service?"

"No." Cruz let his answer bounce around the room to get a feel of whether he felt guilty. "It was so soon after we caught Shaver—I wanted to get as far away from all of it as possible." He felt her turn back around to him. He thought of them stepping close together. Warm breaths barely reaching each other. Slow, rhythmic breathing, tantric, in time. Absolution through touch.

"Cruz?...Cruz?" A hand on his shoulder. He turned his head around to her. "Are you okay?"

Cruz let out a long, slow breath, pursing his lips and pushing air out. "I've hardly slept since we caught him. My head feels foreign, pressure from within pushing out. Weirdest dreams too. I see Shaver everywhere. Awake and asleep. I'm sorry." She rubbed his shoulders again.

"Don't be sorry. I understand what you're talking about."

"You do?"

"Please." The corner of her red lips quivered, shining in the overhead light, a small, celestial movement. "I see Shaver too, even though I've never seen him in person. I've been able to construct him from his voice, his actions. He's a newborn in my mind. I build him and then he hovers over me. They all do, light pressed close to my face. Just glare and hum as I feel my skin start to boil, literally ripple as it pulls away." A glistening tear escaped from her long eyelashes and wound a black course across her cheekbone and to her chin where she wiped it away. "They wake me every night. Or, I wake and they scurry back into where they woke me up from...I don't think they'll ever leave."

* * * *

Shaver slumped in the back of the squad car. His shoulders ached from being pinned behind his back. The trip from the hospital to the city jail was fifteen minutes, or about twenty-five with traffic. He'd run back and forth to that goddamn jail so many times when he was a rookie. Now, irony and shame drizzled over him as he made his own way there.

"Could you roll your windows down some? It's hot as hell back here."

"Sure, Sarge," the young cop answered. The over-filled city only added to the summer swell. Exhaust fumes plus engine heat plus thousands of swarming bodies. As Shaver jostled on the black vinyl seat he felt the range of his wounds. Each brought back the tumult of the last several weeks. The gunshot wounds he suffered at his house stood out as the most painful, but his whole body felt brittle and worn down.

He didn't know if it was Martinez or the other spic that had inflicted the wounds. He remembered hearing the explosion out in his driveway, figuring that had taken care of most of the ensemble. That's when he sent Tyler out the back of the house via a passageway in his basement. Shaver set up his M14 assault rifle in the only hallway leading to the back of his house. Down an offshoot to his right was the front door. Directly in front of him, probably six or seven man-length paces, the side door. He would cover both.

Tyler came running back in and shouted to him that there were guys on both sides of the house. Shaver noticed Tyler was frantic so he clamped a bear-like hand around Tyler's neck and slammed him against a wall.

"You're gonna calm down because if you don't, we're fucked," Shaver growled, an inch away from Tyler's face. "Now, go to the front room of the house and ambush anyone that comes in the front door." And this was his mistake, Shaver recognized. Putting that prick in charge of something as significant as protecting a point of entry.

Although it wasn't all Tyler's fault, Shaver thought. Soon after Tyler took his position in the room, Shaver heard a bang and an artificial sun lit the front of the house. Shaver's ears rang and he soon inhaled the fumes of a flashbang. The side door burst open. Shaver remembered seeing black silhouettes pouring into his house. He pulled the trigger on his assault rifle and felt it recoil into his shoulder as it pumped out rounds. Bullets tore through men, splashing blood on walls as limbs exploded. The still night just outside the door swallowed bullets that missed their mark.

155

# Derek Blass

The first gunshot that hit him came from some sort of handgun. It shattered his left forearm, exited, bounced on the floor and ricocheted into his left shin. He continued to fire the assault rifle, trying to rotate to his right. That's when he felt the next bullet enter his body. This one was clean, quiet, into his right midsection. Shaver couldn't decide whether the bullet or the surprise of where it came from was more alarming. That bullet slid through ribs and punctured his right lung before coming to a rest in the inner sanctum of his body. Doctors said he was lucky that one didn't do the job. He told them it was a fucking shame it didn't. Next thing he remembered, he was toppled over on his front porch.

He spent a month in the ICU, although it was hard to tell time. There was nothing to distinguish the passing days. Today was a visit back to his doctor for a checkup of his wounds. Doctor called him bionic.

The squad car wound its way through the city. They passed vivid memories, places Shaver tried to lock in his mind. He figured he'd never see them again. His favorite Chinese restaurant polluting almost a whole block with its pungent food. The cigar lounge, where he'd spent hours upon hours with other cops. Every speck of matter in that place touched by cigar smoke. Rolling a Maduro in his fingers before sliding the tightly rolled cigar into his wet mouth. It was more painful than the wounds to his body—knowing this was it. His last view of the world. Forty-two years in this world soon to be gone, never touched or seen again. A shitty friend, but one he'd miss nonetheless.

"If you turn to the right here, you'll cut off five minutes."

"All right, Sarge," the officer responded mechanically. It was a lie though, and they both knew it. A right would add ten minutes to the trip. A small consolation for a dead man.

\* \* \* \*

Martinez sat alone in his living room. The television was on, but muted. He watched the news, making up his own headlines and reports in his head. That inner voice set up reports, bantered between newscasters, threw in the ubiquitous, "That's a great story." Mournful voice for the stories involving violence against women and children. Resentful voice for the local robber. Happy voice for the one story in twenty dealing with something positive. Mournful, resentful, happy...lather, rinse, repeat.

Carmen was out shopping for food. Her resolve and toughness came through since the mess with Shaver ended. She was already leading the charge with Cruz to investigate further into Shaver and the Chief. He, on the other hand, was crippled since then. Hated to admit it, but *emotionally* crippled. The loss of Williams finally surged from the recesses of his consciousness to terrorize him on a daily basis. His retinas burned with the image of Alicia's chest exploding.

Someone pulled up into the driveway. He struggled to push himself up off of the chair. No part of his body was unscathed from injury. His cradled his left arm in a sling. Little pockets of pain manifested every few hours and then went away, mortal reminders. Cruz and Sandra were getting out of their car. Martinez popped the door open and went back to his chair, gently took a seat, and shifted around until his body parts were comfortably placed in the chair's crevices.

"Hello?" he heard Cruz ask from the doorway.

"Yeah, in here." The door creaked open as Cruz entered.

"Damn, Martinez, you want a light on or something? Martinez just shook his head. Sandra came over to him and gave him a peck on his left cheek. Cruz approached and they did the shake-to-thumb-grasp-to-fist-punch handshake.

"Where's Carmen?" Sandra asked.

"She just went to the grocery." They sat in the wake of Martinez's brief answers.

"Martinez, you're gonna have to snap out of this," Cruz said.

"Why?"

"We need you."

Martinez flashed a look of disdain at them and asked, "What for now?"

"You know what's going on. We need to put Shaver away for good."

"Look, I've done my job, protecting that video. The district attorney's got it now. It's their job to build a case."

"But we've..."

"And I'm not goin' on some crazy winter adventure with you to find out about his past. He'll stand trial for what he did recently, that's good enough for me."

"Come on Martinez. Reports are surfacing from all over the city that the depth of Shaver and the Chief's collective crimes run very, very deep. I get people calling me all the time to give me their Shaver abuse reports."

"You know what? The truth is that everyday things like this happen. Have you ever stopped to imagine the number of cops around this country? Fact of the matter is that people get beat and taken advantage of by cops all the damn time. At least in this case they were caught. So, I don't know what the hell else you want from me. I'm not a lawyer, the case is over for me."

"There's proof that Shaver has been involved in several beatings of minorities, Martinez. For years this guy preyed on our community. We need someone like you who knows the city, who has contacts and informants throughout the city to help us." Martinez gave Cruz a cross look. "Plus, wasn't your whole purpose in protecting the video to make sure it would get disclosed to avenge your partner's death?"

The recent struggles and Martinez's constant pain made him close off. He recognized it and changed his tone. "You can't play the race card on a minority."

"I just did."

"Dammit," Martinez muttered. "I'm all screwed up right now so I can't help right away."

Sandra smiled at him and said, "I knew you'd help."

# THIRTY

Shaver sat in his cell, the "rubber room" as it was called. The rubber room was normally reserved for loons or inmates on death watch. Putting Shaver in it was a favor from his fellow cops. If they put him in with the rest of the population, with men he'd put away himself, they all knew what would happen.

The rubber room was eight-feet wide by eight-feet high by twelve-feet long. The walls weren't actually bouncy and they didn't have much give. Instead, they were coated with a rubber-like substance that took away sharp edges or rough surfaces. Shaver lay on his bunk. The mattress was hardly better than the cold floor. To his right were a small toilet and a mirror set back in protective plastic.

The weight of the future was slowly settling on his shoulders. Of all the emotions he ever felt—few in his life—this grief was certainly the strongest. It was completely unrelated to the old man he killed. Instead, it was the claustrophobia of confinement and the darkness that filled him when he thought about the rest of his life like this. No, it wasn't about the old man, Shaver thought to himself.

Killing was of no import. The first time he did it was twenty-two years earlier. He grew up in a small, rural town several hours from anything that could be called a city or even civilization. He remembered that as he grew up, more and more of the Mexicans showed up each year. They came for certain seasons, taking farming jobs from his family and friends. They were like brown locusts.

There came a point when none of the town's residents were hired for the seasonal farming jobs. When they accosted the local farmers for hiring Mexicans, the farmers responded that the Mexicans were willing to work for ten cents on the dollar and they would do the jobs townsfolk wouldn't. It didn't take much time after that for the town's hatred to flare up.

Shaver remembered that it was a peaceful, late-summer day when the attack began. The Mexican workers were out in the fields, as they were every day during this season. A faint murmur grew from the country store in the middle of the town. It spread from store to store and then house to house. Soon most of the residents were gathered in front of the country store. A tall, lean man named Alan stood on the top step of the store. Alan owned the adjacent farm tool store. He kept pushing his glasses up the wet bridge of his nose, shouting to the crowd.

## Derek Blass

"For years we've let this inferior race invade our town and take our jobs! Now, all of the land around us is infested with these wetbacks!" The loosely assembled crowd of white faces booed. Some held shovels, others rakes. Most were weaponless. Shaver remembered feeling in his pocket and palming the four-inch switchblade that he always carried.

"It's time we take this town back!" Alan continued to yell. People in the crowd cheered and pumped their fists in the air. It was just talk at this point, a group of small-town people angry about the operation of free market capitalism. That all changed when Todd White, Shaver's neighbor, screamed, "Les go git 'em then!" The crowd collectively weighed this proposition—the change from talk to action. Mere words to physical confrontation. In this split second, the crowd tipped toward action and started to move to the fields with another cheer.

Shaver enjoyed imagining how those Mexicans must have felt as they heard the crowd's rumble and shouting grow closer. Slowly, they must have stopped their work, looking at each other while trying to figure out what they were hearing. Hoping it wasn't what it sounded like, but fearfully straining their ears. Then they must have seen the crowd churn over the hill that fronted the fields. Shaver recalled seeing one or two of the Mexicans start to run away into the growth behind the fields. Others were slower to react.

The crowd went from a fast walk to an all-out run. The workers nearest the crowd turned and attempted to run but were quickly engulfed. This was the first time Shaver heard the dull thump of a shovel caving in someone's head. Small pockets of violence developed and wrapped around Mexican men and women of varying ages like the devastating embrace of an octopus. As Shaver looked around he remembered seeing a figure crouched just beyond the field, about two hundred feet away. He charged and let out a yell.

She popped up out of the growth and stumbled on heavy feet. Shaver laughed and sprinted the last few feet until he was on top of her, smothering her and putting his face next to hers. He breathed heavily into her ear as he caught his breath. She squirmed and whimpered under him. She clawed at the ground in a futile attempt to escape.

"You ain't getting away from me." He pulled his knife from his pocket and flipped it open. "See this?" he asked as he put it on her lips. "I'm gonna make you hurt." He slid the blade to her cheek and pressed down enough to barely cut her skin. Then he grabbed a handful of her dress with his other hand and lifted it to her waist.

"Fucking dirty, aren't you?" The girl kicked him with her heel and squirmed some more but she wasn't going anywhere. Shaver looked down and put his hand in between her legs. When she screamed he pressed the knife to her neck until she shut up. "I'm gonna kill you so *shut the fuck up!*" Shaver grabbed the top of the girl's panties and pulled them down to reveal the left side of her butt. Her skin goose-bumped, sending Shaver's raging hormones into a frenzy. He used his free hand to unbuckle his pants. That's when he heard a rustle in the growth to his side and felt a kick into his right ribs. The force of the kick rolled him off of the girl and onto his back where he struggled for air. He saw the girl run farther into the growth with her dress still hiked up on one side of her waist.

A man's shadow covered Shaver and blocked out the sun. He clearly remembered the man's fatherly face, infused with rage, more than ready to kill Shaver. The man put his hand on Shaver's chest and punched him on the side of his face. The blow stunned Shaver and filled his mouth with the taste of blood. As the man reached up to punch him again, Shaver lifted his knife. The man could not stop his arm's momentum and his fist surged down on the knife. He screamed out as the knife embedded between two of his knuckles.

Shaver caught his breath and pounced on the wounded man. The knife slid neatly out of the man's bloody fingers.

"*Déjenos en paz, cobarde!*"

Shaver smiled a yellow-toothed grin and danced the knife across the man's neck. Blood flowed from the wound. The man coughed on the flood in his mouth and vomited blood vertically in a spray all over Shaver's face. Shaver didn't flinch. His face bore the same smile.

Hooting and hollering came up behind the two. Shaver watched as the man's arm fell to the ground. Probably wasn't the loss of blood, Shaver thought to himself. Must've been drowning.

The noise drew closer. Shaver wiped off his face and put his blade back into his pocket. He stepped back from the body, working to imprint the image in his mind. Someone tapped him on the shoulder.

"Shaver?"

He turned around to a group of three townies. Their smiles disappeared when they saw his face and clothes.

"Well, fuck, Shaver...what'dja do back here?" Shaver said nothing as he pushed through the middle of the group and walked back into town.

Shaver rolled onto his other side as he lay daydreaming about that day. The piece of loosely sewn cloth called his mattress did nothing to soften the bed frame's steel coils. Despite what it seemed, the killing wasn't about race. He didn't mind wiping some filth out of of the world every now and again, but the thrill was the control. Ending something that took so long to nourish and grow. And then the reactions. That was key too. Shocked, pissed, literally scared shitless.

So no, it wasn't about killing the old man. It was the claustrophobia.

# THIRTY-ONE

Mason West. He kind of looked like his name. Copperish brown hair. Thick and without a hint of thinning. Always perfectly combed, dry, to the side. A warm, bushy mustache. The husky, Selleck thickness men envy. His face was solid, wide, with few but well-placed angles. Mason West was the county's district attorney. That was a relatively prominent job in a county of over half a million people.

Mason knew he wanted to be a lawyer when other options ran out. He toyed with writing but never seriously enough. A short stint in construction was enough to make him study harder in school. Working for a nonprofit—or for free—never appealed to his ambitions. So he went to law school after taking a year to travel around the States. People asked him why he didn't go somewhere more exotic, and he never had a good answer.

He coasted through law school, pushing the right buttons at approximately the right time to get through. It wasn't until a trial advocacy class that he awoke from the stupor. CN: 4076 "Trial Advocacy: Becoming a DA or a PD." He remembers some snotty classmates chuckling, "You don't *become* a DA or a PD. You have to be *born* one." Mason always appreciated the fact that he wasn't born a lawyer.

He spent most of his time drafting and performing mock direct and cross examinations, openings and closings. Something noticeable started to develop in him. Interest, passion. More and more often he planted himself in front of a fantasy jury, comprised of two well-worn couch pillows, his favorite dish, a potted plant named Horatio (often the most difficult juror to sway), a baseball card of Aaron Boone and his dog, Simon. That, believe it or not, is where Mason started flourishing.

He began reading books on constructing arguments. He scoured through McElhaney on everything. Tuesday and Thursday mornings he went to the state district court and watched the docket churn through Courtroom 11. Classmates in the trial advocacy class began to show him their arguments, asking for his thoughts. His professor awoke from his open-eyed nap when Mason began his opening statements. Five months after starting the class, Mason won the state mock trial competition and received the American Jurisprudence award in his trial advocacy class.

Upon graduation, Mason faced a difficult prospect—lawyers hardly ever go to court anymore. The days of trying a case were washed away by enormous judgments. Astronomical billing rates for attorneys didn't help either. He knew he'd rather be a janitor than languish in some back room of a stuffy law firm. Facing that reality, he had one of two options. Become a district attorney or a public defender.

There should be no confusion. Those in either camp agree on one thing, and one thing only—one can't be the other. There's nothing so reviling to a public defender as to suggest he or she could be a district attorney. Visa versa. It's a distinction based upon principle, way of life, manner of dressing, patterns of thought, and just about any other human characteristic or tendency imaginable. Yet, Mason found himself wavering between the two until he had a conversation with his professor.

"Where do you stand on capital punishment?"

"Appropriate in some circumstances," Mason answered.

"That's that then."

So it was settled. For no self-respecting public defender would ever think, let alone admit, that he or she was amenable to the death penalty.

Mason applied for a job as a first-year district attorney. He met with the county's district attorney in a relatively dingy office. Mason sat attentively across the desk as the district attorney pelted him with probing questions. Questions that went beyond the "what-are-your-qualifications" interview questions. More into the realm of what constitutes you and does that parallel our mission. After two hours of scrutiny, the district attorney bid Mason goodbye.

Mason muddled for the next sixteen days. He saw the district attorney once at a function in that timespan. The district attorney shook his hand as if the two hadn't met before and walked away to get a drink. Some other interviews popped up. One with a law firm that practiced family law. The thought of dealing with infantile adults was unappealing.

Another interview was with a prestigious, national law firm. He remembered looking around at the interviewers, four of them in total, in dark suits with recently pressed, highly starched shirts and power ties. The attorneys told him he would get a much better salary at their firm than as a district attorney, and would even get some court time. They asked him questions about his past, what he expected from himself in the future, and to describe his greatest weakness in painstaking detail. This was his second such interview with a firm of this caliber, and both times it felt like he was interviewing with morticians.

That's when his phone rang—literally, in the middle of the interview.

Mason scrambled through his pockets to find out where the startling noise came from. He found the phone, pulled it out and was about to silence it when something in him said, "Answer it." With a finger held up to the astonished lawyers, Mason turned around and whispered, "Hello?"

"Mason, this is Jerome Visgil."

"Oh, hi, Mr. Visgil." Mason shot a pleading look over his shoulder to the attorneys waiting on him.

"You want a job?"

"Well, yes, of course."

"I'm going to give you a chance. I'm not sure if you're really a district attorney, tried and true, through and through, et cetera. But, I'm going to give you a chance."

"All right! Thanks Mr. Visgil." The line went dead. Mason turned around to the interviewers, "I've...well, you see I just got a job, so I've got to go." They all continued to stare at him and mutter as he gathered his notepad, resume and pen. He walked out of the law firm a district attorney.

In his first three years as a district attorney, only one other lawyer who began at about the same time as Mason was still around. Young district attorneys dropped like leaves off a dead tree. Bad pay, an overwhelming caseload, poor supervision, and the stressful types of cases they were dealing with drove even attorneys with the noblest intentions away.

Mason excelled. He began trying misdemeanors almost as soon as his foot crossed into the state office. Because the cases dealt with small offenses—minors in possession, DUIs—his caseload was voluminous. Probably around two hundred and fifty case files at any time.

His practice developed a cadence of its own. The judges became familiar and mildly receptive to him. The courthouse began to feel more like a comfortable sweater than an ill-fitting suit. He even got along with the public defenders on his cases, although this was something kept quiet.

The rate of attrition had a positive side effect—Mason moved up the ranks quickly. Within a year he was trying felonies. Not murders or rapes, but assault and robbery cases. The stakes changed. His caseload dropped but the ramifications of the cases themselves more than made up for that drop. Mason would have weeks, rather than hours, to prepare for cases now. He got the benefit of investigators and the development of evidence.

This was about the time Jerome Visgil noticed Mason rising through the ranks. He sat in on one of Mason's trials, which racked Mason's nerves. It was a pretty significant case for Mason. Man robbed a store clerk at gunpoint.

# Derek Blass

Despite the nerves, when Mason stepped into the courtroom, he was setting up in his office. Tools were there—pens, pads of paper, exhibits, redwells. The familiar players were there—judge, opposing counsel. Soon the prospective jurors would come in for voir dire. He loved the repartee as he tried to figure out who amongst these strangers would be most receptive to the state's case. This was comfortable to him.

Jerome summoned Mason into his office soon after the trial. "You did well, Mason. You have a calmness and accessibility that jurors like. It was a tough conviction, but you nailed it."

"Thanks, Jerome."

"I'm getting tired, Mason. Physically, I mean shit, I'm fifty-eight. But, also tired of the gig. It's a wearing, constant grind. I've got two people in the office that I'd like to groom as my successor, and you're one of them."

Despite knowing Jerome for several years at this point, and being familiar with his directness, the scope of what Jerome said hit like a ton of bricks.

"Me? There are plenty of other district attorneys that have practiced for a lot longer here. Why me?"

"Listen Mason, I've stroked your ego as much as I'm gonna. You've either got the nuts to go ahead with this or you don't. I pegged you as the nuts type. Your call, get back to me by tomorrow."

Mason walked out of Jerome's office in a cloud of possibilities. Of course it wouldn't be that easy. He'd still have to run for the position. But, with the incumbent district attorney supporting him, chances were that he'd get elected. The next day Mason told Jerome he was game. Seventeen months later he was sitting in Jerome's old chair.

\* \* \* \*

"Who's the district attorney again?" Sandra asked.

"Mason West."

"*Ay cabron*, I've heard some terrible things about him."

Cruz thought about his impression of Mason before responding. "He's tough, and any district attorney is going to hate a case against a cop. But, Mason is...well...he's principled."

"Principles or not I don't trust the blue or the men behind the blue, and that's the district attorneys." He knew what she meant. Cruz was uneasy about the suggested partnership too.

Mason called Cruz earlier that morning to see if he wanted to be a part of Shaver's prosecution. It was an unprecedented, seemingly magnanimous overture. Cruz couldn't figure out what Mason's motives were. Did he want to seem like he was including the Latino community? Would that make a circus of the prosecution?

"I mean, aren't you supposed to hate each other? Ex-public defender and current district attorney? Lions and hyenas, no?"

"That's the way it's supposed to be," Cruz said, "but, that's not the way it always works out." Cruz stood up and paced around his office, lightly clapping his hands together from time to time. "Our community is usually left out of the big decisions. Why would I turn my back, and the back of the community, to a request like this?"

"I don't know, Cruz—I'm telling you I don't trust them. I'd worry this is a trap."

"Yeah...I just don't think that's Mason's style."

After a pause, Sandra said, "I've got to get down to the station. We're developing a multi-segment story to air next week on this case."

"You covering all of it?"

"Every last detail."

"You know, that's fine, but be careful about how you treat the video. I'm not sure you even mention it exists."

"How could I not? It's the key to the case against Shaver."

"Exactly. Between you and me, and off the record, the prosecution is gonna have some hurdles to clear with introducing that video into evidence. I mean, the damn thing was all over the place, bouncing from hands to hands, in a motorcycle chase, on a train, in a hospital. Chain of custody will be an issue. If you report there's a video out there, someone is gonna pay enough money to have it leaked. I can promise you that won't be good for the case against Shaver."

"I hadn't thought of all that...I'll talk to the news editor and see what he wants to do."

"Okay." Cruz waited as Sandra stood up and grabbed her coat from beside the door. He held his hand just off her back, escorting her outside. As she stepped out of the door she turned around to hug him. She slipped her arms under his and clasped them behind his back.

"You've done a great job, Cruz."

The show of affection made Cruz's heart jump into his throat. All he could muster was, "You too." Sandra let go of him, hopped into her car and drove away.

Cruz looked up and realized it was a beautiful day outside. He decided to take a walk to clear his mind. The streets were full of mid-day bustle.

People entranced, perhaps entrapped, in their own worlds. They sped down the sidewalks in their impenetrable bubbles, annoyed if they had to dodge other people or if someone dared make a verbal connection. Cruz wondered—like he always did—how the world had come to this sanitized, headphones-in-ear loneliness. He also wondered how Shaver's trial would change their city, if at all. Martinez was sure it would. "That video!" Cruz could hear Martinez exclaim. But a nagging feeling had Cruz concerned that people were too far gone. Disconnected from life and excessively connected to their iPods or their reality television shows. Cruz heard a car's brakes squeal lightly beside him.

"Hey! Hey, you Cruz?" Cruz looked at the car. It was a clean, Grand Marquis-looking car. Blacked out windows with two guys inside.

"Yeah."

"Hop on in."

Cruz laughed and kept walking. "You've got to be kidding me."

The car sped ahead a bit and then stopped abruptly, chirping the tires. The bubble people paid the regular city sound no mind. Cruz slowed down, drawing the ire of a woman behind him. He watched as a bulky white man got out of the passenger side of the car. The guy was wearing a black, leather trench coat with a white shirt and blue jeans underneath. He smiled and gestured to Cruz.

"Cruz, come on. Stop being such a fucking pussy."

Cruz halted a few steps from the man. "Some brute asks you to get into his car and you're a pussy for saying no?"

"Listen, you little shit," the man said, lowering his voice, "Get into the fucking car. I ain't playing." The man flipped open the right side of his trench coat to reveal a gun. "One word, one raised voice, and I'll bury you in your own shit to die. Get in."

"Guess I don't have much of a choice. I'd rather not have to shit that much, honestly."

The man grinned. "No, you wouldn't."

# THIRTY-TWO

Martinez watched from the dark as Sandra prepared to go on air. Cameramen scurried around. A woman brushed off Sandra's suit while another put the finishing touches on her makeup. Screens glowed around the room. The parts and players moved in unison, their tempo hidden under a heavy silence.

"Thirty seconds Sandra. Don't forget what I told you," said a man seated right in front of the news desk. Must be the producer, Martinez thought. The dark enveloped him too. His shrill voice was all that identified a person. Someone else shouted out, "In five...four...three..."

Sandra took dead aim at the camera in front of her and began her report.

"It has been just over a month since Sergeant Colin Shaver allegedly shot Livan Rodriguez in his home—the victim of a horrible incident of police brutality. In the time since, I have been covering the chase, the hunt for Sergeant Shaver." The broadcast switched to a pre-prepared piece.

"That wasn't what I told you to say!"

"I'm not going to bring the video up."

"What? You're going to deliver this story like I fucking tell you. That video is what matters, all right?"

"No, the *innocent victim* is what matters, you jerk." Sandra seemed stunned by what came out of her mouth. She shuffled the papers in front of her and adjusted her suit jacket. The man stood up and strode to the news desk.

"Forty-five seconds till we're back on," someone else said.

"You do what I say, or you lose your job. Got it?"

Martinez stepped out of the shadows. "Back away from her." The producer spun on one foot, startled by the voice.

"Just who the hell are you?"

Martinez held up his badge. "Back away." Sandra looked warmly at Martinez and then went back to reading her notes. The man descended back into darkness and reappeared close to Martinez.

"We didn't hire any security. What're you doing here?"

"Watching."

"This is a closed set."

"Not for me. This is all part of an ongoing investigation."

## Derek Blass

The man screamed out to Sandra, "Is *he* why you won't say anything about the tape right now? I'll kick his ass out, Sandy!"

"Five...four...three..." The two men glared at each other.

"Sergeant Shaver is currently being held at the county jail where he will remain until his preliminary hearing. If you or anyone you know has information pertinent to this matter, call Viewer Report Line Nine." She held her gaze until given the signal that the broadcast had stopped. The producer scrambled back to the news desk.

"You ever do that again, and you'll lose this job! You get me?!"

"Fire me and you'll lose the best story of the year. Guess where that'll land you?"

Martinez walked up and stood in the middle of the two. "Let's grab some lunch, Sandra."

"I'm not done here," Sandra said menacingly.

"Probably best to cool down. Come on," Martinez said as he gently tugged on her elbow. This time she acquiesced and followed him out of the studio. They walked in silence as Sandra regained her composure.

"That McMahon is a real jerk. I told him I wasn't going to bring up the video yet."

"Why not?"

"Cruz warned me not to. He said it could affect the case against Shaver."

"You did what's right then. We'll get this video out in time—all of us have a reason to make sure that happens."

"It's not just the video though. This job leaves me feeling filthy. All that producer and the news director care about is making money. The more depraved the story the better. Ten seconds, fifteen seconds, whatever sells the most. People like Mr. Rodriguez get lost in the shuffle."

"Maybe it's not all about the producer."

"What do you mean?" Sandra asked.

Noting exasperation in her voice, Martinez went on to explain, "They'd put puppy dogs and angels on the tube if that sold advertising space. Truth is, they're just tools. You need to be mad at the public. We—and I'll throw both of us in there—we die for quicker, more violent and more shocking news."

"I guess," Sandra said after a pause. "I don't like the perspective that puts my job in."

Martinez shrugged his shoulders and opened the door to the street for her. "You heard from Cruz today?"

"I just saw him a little while ago."

"He hasn't answered any of my calls today."

"Maybe he's in court?"

"Could be."

"What were you calling him about?"

"I got a call...from an ex-cop. Said he wanted to tell me some things about Shaver that only he knew about."

"Gets better every day, doesn't it?"

"It's hard to imagine that a cop like him existed, doing damage to the world for so long. As a cop, you hear about some toeing of the line. You just don't imagine anything on this level."

"Why'd you come see me?"

"Just found myself in the neighborhood," Martinez answered. "You want to go meet this guy with me?"

"Sure, where at?"

"Joe's Diner. Just a few blocks from here. We can walk."

They came around the corner and Joe's burst into sight. The one o'clock sun reflected off the chrome exterior. The two saw commotion around the diner as they neared. Four cop cars were parked at angles in front of it. People lined up around the makeshift perimeter set up by the cars. A cop strung a roll of yellow crime scene tape along the sidewalk. Martinez pushed through the crowd with Sandra tucked in behind him.

"Hey—hey, where do you think you're going?" a cop said to Martinez. Martinez took his badge out.

"You're in plain clothes. What business you got here?"

"What happened inside?"

"Like I said," the cop said while leaning in towards Martinez, "What...business...you...got...here?"

Then it dawned on Martinez that it could be a hit. "Is there a dead cop in there?" The cop didn't respond. Martinez shook his head, "Fuck! Let me in!" He pushed past the cop who stiffened and looked the other way.

"Hold, hold, hold on there, sweetie. You ain't goin' in there with him." Sandra rested on his outstretched arm. She turned back into the swelling mass of people.

"They tell you what happened?" When she didn't respond, the person asked again, "I said, did they tell you what happened?"

Sandra looked up and saw a well-dressed business man standing in front of her. "No, they didn't tell me anything." The people crammed around her were itching, like fiends, for a body to be wheeled by them or some loud noise

**Derek Blass**

to make them jump.  Anything to help them briefly forget the linearity of their lives.

A tap on Sandra's shoulder made her jump.  It was Martinez.  "Let's go."

"Hey, did they tell *you* what happened?"  They ignored the man and walked away.  When they were away from the crowd, Sandra stopped and asked, "Was it him?"

"Yes."

"My God.  I thought we hit the bottom of the rabbit hole."

"Apparently not," Martinez said as he handed her a file.

"What's this?"

"Take a look inside."  She did, and as she turned the pages inside Martinez could see the terror grow on her face.

"Who are these people Martinez?"

"I don't know.  That's the part he was gonna fill in."

"They're all brown, or black.  Martinez, who did this?"

"My guess?  Shaver."

\* \* \* \*

Cruz bounced around in the back of the Town Car as it sped down an unpaved road.  The beast to his left, the one who had *gently* persuaded him to get into the car, kept looking over and smiling politely.  A polite but glaringly false smile.

"I'm surprised you're letting me see where we're going."

"This is not a full-fledged kidnapping.  You're just gonna meet someone."

"He, or she...it...could have just called me."

Cruz turned his head and looked out the window.  Mansions set back from the road loomed behind ancient-looking trees.  The car moved to the left to accommodate a horseback rider and then began to slow.  They pulled into a driveway that was also the end of the road.  The driver typed in a number on the gate.  Horse stalls and a barn appeared to the right as they made their way down the driveway.  The car edged around a bend and the house started to take shape from behind a lazily sloping hill.  It was a magnificently styled Tudor, bordered by manicured hedges and bushes.  The driveway ended in a circle centered with a fountain.

The man to Cruz's left got out of the car and went around to open his door.  Cruz stepped out and stretched.

"Home sweet home, huh?"  The man smiled his polite smile again and took a position behind Cruz.  He assumed this meant move, so he headed toward the two huge front doors.  They lurched open before he could knock.

"Master Cruz, I presume?"

"I'm no master. Just Cruz."

"This way then, please," the butler said as he pointed to a waiting room. Cruz entered the room and stood by a window.

"Won't you sit down...Cruz?"

"I'm fine standing." In reality, he felt altogether too out of place to sit down. The chairs in the room looked like they were out of a seventeenth-century French palace. A far cry from the yeoman-like furniture he was used to.

"As you wish. Mr. Sphinx will be down momentarily."

Mr. Sphinx? Cruz recognized the name. There was a locally famous attorney named Sphinx, but this couldn't be him. An attorney kidnapping another attorney? That was so far removed from the bounds of ethics.

"Mr. Marquez!" a voice boomed from behind him. "What a pleasure to meet you!"

Cruz turned around to meet the voice. "Holy shit! It *is* you! Are you nuts? Do you realize I'm going to have you disbarred for this crap!"

"For what? For sending a Town Car to pick you up for a meeting at my house?"

"What?! That guy..." Cruz said as he searched for the man who sat next to him in the car, "...I don't know where he went, but that guy, the big one, told me he would 'bury me in my own shit' if I didn't come. Some fucking invitation."

"My goodness, he said *that* to you?"

"Yeah!"

"Tomas!! Tomas, come here!"

"See, that's the one I was talking about!" Cruz said when Tomas came into the waiting room.

"Tomas, you're fired. Please pack your belongings and leave."

"But, what the hell? You told me..."

"*Tomas!*" Tomas shot Cruz a look of disdain and then left the room. "I apologize, Mr. Marquez, I truly do. Please, won't you sit?" Sphinx said while gesturing to one of the many chairs in the room. Cruz cautiously slid into one of them.

"What the hell are you doing with this kind of a setup anyways? Aren't you a criminal defense attorney?"

"Why would that preclude this decor?"

"Well, I just assume you'd have something a bit more down to earth.

Enough of the small talk though. Why'd you kidnap me?"

"A meeting, Cruz, simply a meeting."

"Forget that. Next time you call."

"The gravity of the situation called for a more immediate..."

"Let me guess, you're representing Sergeant Shaver? Right?"

"Why, yes."

"Hey, while we're at this, how about you kick this fake English accent you've got going. I don't know a ton about you, but I do know you aren't fucking royalty."

Sphinx half-smiled, half-scowled. "All right...you want the down-to-earth talk?"

Cruz burst out laughing. "I knew it, I knew it man. You even talk that fake way in your commercials." Cruz pushed enough buttons. Sphinx stood up. His three-piece, pinstripe suit fell neatly over his body. He must have been at least six-foot-five, Cruz guessed. He had a closely shaved hairdo and a menacing goatee. Cruz swallowed slowly. Sphinx came over to his chair and put both of his hands on the armrests.

"Let's get real then, all right Cruz? Remember Tomas, who told you he'd bury you in your own shit? That'd just be the beginning. That was merciful. Don't think you can come into my fucking house and disrespect me." Pause. "We clear?"

Cruz squeezed back into his chair. Seeing no other option, he responded, "Crystal."

"Good, now I've come to talk to you about Sergeant Shaver's case."

"But why me? I'm not the DA."

"Believe me, I'm talking to Mason too. I've reached out to you because of your personal involvement in this case and the connections you have in your community. Sergeant Shaver is interested in settling this case with as little fanfare as possible."

"Again, I have no control..."

"Bullshit you don't. I know you and Mason have spoken regarding this case. Don't play me for a fool, and realize that I know everything you think I don't." Sphinx went over to a small cocktail table in the corner of the room. "Scotch?"

"No." Sphinx finished pouring his own drink and then sat down across from Cruz. "If you know everything, then I don't need to tell you that Shaver's case is about much more than his murder of Livan Rodriguez. First, the community has been at a boiling point for a while now. Second, this isn't

Shaver's only instance of unlawful use of force. You're mistaken if you think this case will go away easily."

Sphinx shook his head and said, "The state's case against Sergeant Shaver is terrible. I am giving you and the state a chance to get out without embarrassing yourselves."

"Terrible? How's that?"

"All of your witnesses are dead, how about that for starters?"

"Dead because of Shaver and his hitmen! You think that's going to help him? Plus, Officer Martinez and Livan Rodriguez's daughter were there— they're both alive and more than willing to testify."

"You've been away for too long Cruz. His daughter conveniently relocated to Mexico."

"What?"

"Everyone has a price Cruz."

"We'll bring her back here to testify in the trial."

"I doubt it." Sphinx swirled the scotch around in his glass. "As for Martinez, you mean the same Martinez that hunted down Shaver and the chief of police? The same Martinez that kept the only video of the incident on his person instead of checking it into evidence?"

"He couldn't check it in—it would have been 'lost' for eternity."

"That would be your argument, naturally, but we'll see how much traction you get out of it. That is a serious breach in the chain of custody. We will be moving to keep that video out of evidence."

"You haven't told me anything unanticipated, Sphinx. What's the real purpose of this meeting? To intimidate me? I've dealt with much more than you before."

"I know all about you, Cruz. What's wrong with wanting to meet face-to-face?"

"Now that we have, are we done?" Cruz stood up from his chair.

"I suppose, unless you want to stay and get acquainted even more."

"Please," Cruz said sarcastically.

"Joffrey!" The butler stepped into the waiting room. "Please show Cruz out." Sphinx extended his hand to Cruz. "See you soon, Cruz." Cruz reluctantly shook his hand and walked to the front door.

"Do I get a Town Car home too?" Cruz asked. Sphinx had disappeared. "Guess not." Cruz walked outside and down the long driveway to Sphinx's home. He dialed Sandra's number on his cell phone and started walking in the direction of the city.

## Derek Blass

Sandra picked up, "Where are you?  Martinez and I have been trying to get in touch with you.  We've got something you'll want to see."

"Out near Bellevue.  What is it?"

"Tell you when we pick you up."

# THIRTY-THREE

Morning light spilled over Mason's desk as he sat in silence. Files, manila folders and case documents covered his desk. He organized the mess at the start of each day and by the end of each one it was like the same bomb exploded in his office.

He faced significant backlash from his own office since reaching out to Cruz Marquez. The local papers ran two articles on whether the state could try a fair case against Sergeant Shaver with Cruz in the loop. Attorneys in his office asked how Cruz could help on the case—shouldn't he be a witness? Then there was that prick Sphinx. That was all Mason needed on the other side of the ledger.

Sphinx and Mason knew each other well. They came up in the same law school class. Where Mason was measured, Sphinx was loose. Where Mason was ethical, Sphinx manipulated rules like a three-year-old with absent parents. The first time Mason argued a case against Sphinx was actually in law school. The two had a trial advocacy class together with a mock case called State v. Outlander. Mason initially represented Outlander, a young man who had hit and killed two pedestrians while driving drunk. Sphinx appeared on behalf of the state. The two were so lackluster in their representation that the trial advocacy teacher switched their sides. It was a battle from then on that continued to this day.

Sphinx graduated with a higher class rank than Mason, but only by a few percentage points. Both were in the top ten percent of their class. Both had offers from major downtown firms—the silk-stocking, mahogany desk, thirty-second floor types—and both turned those firms down. Mason on account of wanting to get into trial, Sphinx on account of "not wanting to be someone's bitch for the rest of his life." Then, Sphinx incomprehensibly joined the public defender's office and he was the state's bitch, and a much poorer one at that.

The state's public defender and district attorney offices had a high turnover rate in common. The low pay, long hours and hugely stressful caseloads quickly culled the weak and half-hearted. Like Mason, Sphinx rose through the ranks quickly. He was trying felony cases within a year. Within three years he tried seven murder cases. That was when Sphinx got the thought that inevitably comes to all attorneys—"I can do this, do it alone and do it better." Except there was a greater priority for Sphinx. "I can do this and make a ton of money." Certainly, that feeling was further magnified by his paltry salary.

## Derek Blass

Mason remembered that just before Sphinx left the public defender's office, the two had a murder trial against each other. Sphinx was a master in the art of persuasion bordering on guile. Mason was polished, but always felt compelled to let the facts speak for themselves. After two days of deliberation, the jury returned a guilty verdict. Sphinx came over to Mason while he was packing up his documents.

"Full circle, isn't it, Mason?"

"Kind of feels that way Sphinx," Mason said. He looked up and saw the anger in Sphinx's eyes. "I thought you did a good job, if it helps." Sphinx kept silent.

"Is there anything else, Sphinx? You've lost before, this isn't..." But before Mason could finish his sentence Sphinx clocked him across the chin. "What the hell?!" Bailiffs ran up and grabbed Sphinx but Mason told them to hold on. Mason eventually decided not to press charges. He was initially angry, but then felt more sorry for Sphinx than anything else. It was the act of a spoiled adult.

Sphinx went on to open his own practice after that trial and the rest is history. Mason toiled away at a modest salary, in a modest office, with a modest home. Sphinx defended some of the most notorious criminals in the country, from mob bosses to chief executive officers of Fortune 500 companies. Nothing was modest in Sphinx's life.

The sigh that Mason let out when he heard Sphinx would be representing Shaver was not out of fear of losing. Instead, it was an old warrior's sigh, from full knowledge of the impending battle and the toll it would inevitably take. Mason kept the effects of the years to himself, but felt it creeping up every day. The seemingly endless reserve of energy that Mason had through his twenties and thirties was starting to fail him. Like the old warrior, he had the vague feeling, emanating from a combination of his gut instinct and years of experience, that this could be the last fight as a district attorney.

It was Christmas morning. Mason looked over a three-inch thick manila folder one of his investigators created for him. The office was silent—which often accompanied his hard work. Mason used to go to church, and the Catholic guilt never left him, especially when he was doing something like missing church on Christmas morning. His wife tried to prod and poke him into going to church more. Too many years of questioning and too few signs of existence of a God had him as far from religion as ever in his life. If anything, he saw signs on a daily basis that confirmed no God existed. The scurvy crew he dealt with—the rapists, pedophiles, kid-killers, abusers of the elderly, serial killers—numbed the would-be effect of any religion, let alone Catholicism. But the guilt persisted.

The folder was full of newspaper clippings, some recorded transcripts, and notes from his investigator. He picked up the newspaper clippings first even though they were most often useless. Repetition of things he already knew. Mason scanned the articles to make sure he didn't missed anything and jotted down the names of the journalists. Nuggets of information sometimes hid with the journalists.

A couple of the articles were written by Sandra Gutierrez. Mason dug into the cobwebbed recesses of his mind to figure out how he knew her. He had a brief moment of frustration as he stared through the clipping in front of him until it broke, "Channel 9 News." She was a reporter for Channel Nine News. Looks like she also contributed to the local papers. Then he remembered seeing some of Sandra's reports on television about Livan Rodriguez's death. He liked watching her reports. They had an air of sincerity, innocence and purity. The news mattered to her, the content. He wrote her name down on his fresh pad of yellow legal paper.

He picked up the recorded transcripts next. Again, these were generally not helpful from a substantive perspective. As soon as a person is asked, "What did you see?" or "What do you think happened?" or any other permutation of the typical interview question, a floodgate holding back cranial trash opens.

"Well, you know I saw a man and he looked dark and then he ran to a car that looked like an old American car, but you know I knew the person he shot, Livan, and he was a good man, we used to have neighborhood breakfasts together at his house and eat *huevos con salsa* and drink *horchata*, it's so sad he is gone..."

"Did you see how tall the man was?"

"Ohhh no. Tall. But everyone is tall to me."

"Did you see his face well enough to describe it?"

"Yes!"

"Okay, describe it."

"It was round, no mustache or beard or anything like that."

"Any marks, could you see the color of his eyes?"

"Goodness no! I was too far away. Just round, that's what I remember."

"What about the car, what color was it?"

"Dark."

"Black dark?"

Thinking. "Maybe black with some blue and purple. Dark."

"Was it big?"

"Yes, very big, a car with four doors."

That's how they usually went. The people always wanted to get back to the person involved. Natural human reaction. Who cares about the details of the car driving away—besides Mason and his investigator—when a person was just killed? So again, Mason would scan the transcripts to make sure he didn't miss anything. He could also tell from that scan which people he needed to follow up with. Nothing from the transcripts stood out. He would have his investigator contact them in the next few days. The passage of time eventually separated those with actual information from the others.

Finally, he got to the notes from his investigator. He stood up and stretched. Eleven a.m. The morning had flown by.

Background

Deceased was a sixty-two-year-old male. Hispanic descent. Cause of death: bullet wounds to stomach and sternum areas.

Witnesses

Sergeant Colin Shaver

Officer Roman Martinez

Officer Benjamin Tomko (deceased)

Officer Alvin Williams (deceased)

Officer Ted Lindsey (deceased)

Max Silverman (deceased)

Flores Rodriguez (daughter of Livan Rodriguez, address currently unknown)

No other witnesses. Incident took place inside home of Livan Rodriguez.

Mason picked up the phone and dialed his investigator's cell phone number.

"Hello?" answered a groggy voice.

"Todd?"

"Yeah."

"It's Mason. Wake up man, it's after eleven."

"It's also Christmas morning, Mason. What do you want?"

"Few questions. Max was a cameraman for the show *Police*, right?"

"Uh, what are you talking about?"

"The Rodriguez case. Max Silverman."

"Oh, right. Yeah, he was a cameraman."

"What happened to him?"

"Shot dead in his apartment."

"When?"

"They estimate shortly after Mr. Rodriguez was killed because the landlord found the body three days later when it stunk up the apartment."

"Any leads on the killer?"

"None that I know of."

"Who's handling the investigation?"

"I'm not sure but I'll find out for you."

"Now, how about this Flores Rodriguez. Have you talked to her?"

"No, I wasn't able to track her down. Some neighbors suggested that she went back to Mexico. One day she was there, they said, and the next she was gone. No moving trucks, no family or friends to say goodbye, just gone."

"You know Esteban Herrera right?"

"Of course."

"He specializes in skip-tracing to Mexico. Talk to him and see what he can find."

"Okay."

"I'm going to set up a meeting with Officer Martinez and I want you to be there. Also, did you see that Sandra Gutierrez popped up a lot in those newspaper clippings you gave me?"

"Didn't notice it, who is she?"

"Channel 9 News reporter. Dark hair, good looking..."

"Oh yeah! Yeah, I like her."

"I'll talk to her too."

"I'm sure you will."

"Last thing. Who was the guy Officer Martinez brought in with Sergeant Shaver?"

"You have the file in front of you?"

Mason looked down. "I expected you to have this on the tip of your tongue," Mason said, buying himself some time as he rummaged to the police report. "Tyler Smith," he muttered. "What do we know about him?"

"We don't know anything other than his name. There was nothing in the file and my name search yielded nothing."

"I'll ask Martinez about this when we meet him. Who knows how deep this goes, freakin' ghosts."

Mason hung up the phone, reorganized the documents and shoved them back into the manila folder. He picked up a business card propped up in his keyboard. Cruz Marquez. He hadn't heard from Cruz since he called last week. Mason grabbed the phone again and dialed his number. No answer. It was Sunday, Christmas morning, Mason reminded himself. He picked up his jacket and shut the light off in his office. His church had a twelve-fifteen service.

* * * *

Martinez and Sandra picked Cruz up along the side of a dirt road in Bellevue. They were now seated around a small dining room table at Martinez's house. Carmen came into the room and gave Cruz a hug.

"Glad to see you're doing all right, Cruz."

"Did you hear the latest?"

"No, what now?"

"Shaver's defense attorney kidnapped me."

"Really!?"

"Yeah, some sort of weak effort at intimidation. Although I have to say I *was* pretty intimidated until I knew it was Sphinx."

"Leyton Sphinx? The lawyer who defended Antonio Viscutti?"

"Yeah, that Sphinx."

"He's good, huh?"

"If you're willing to kidnap other attorneys, then I'd say you have a hand up on the competition."

"Okay, I'll let you all get back to work," Carmen said.

"Wait," Cruz started, "How's Raul?"

Carmen paused before answering. "He's with family in Mexico. I go back there tomorrow." It didn't answer his question, but Cruz figured that was intentional. Raul had been in a coma since they captured Shaver, almost three weeks now. Cruz wasn't sure how long they kept comatose people alive these days.

Martinez spread the photographs of the victims across the table. They shared the same calm, bluish pallor. They all looked like that, Cruz thought to himself. All the dead. They photographed the same.

"Do we have any idea who these people are, or when they died?" Sandra asked. They were men and women, young and old. All looked to be ethnic minorities.

"I recognize these two," Martinez said, pointing to the pictures of two young, Latino men. "Gang bangers. I remember where they live but nothing else. And, there wasn't anything in the folder to indicate when any of these people died. We can go down to the city morgue though. A friend down there will help us cross-reference the photos with records."

It was a relatively short trip down to the city morgue from Martinez's house. Martinez probed Cruz about the district attorney's request during the ride.

"It's a difficult decision, and I'm not even sure how it will work out logistically."

"What's so difficult?" Martinez said. "You have the opportunity to put a damn monster away."

"The hard part is that I may need to be called as a witness."

"You didn't witness the murder, I did."

"Sure, but I was involved in getting the video. We may need a witness to testify that the video was not tampered with or altered."

Martinez pointed at Sandra, "She can testify. Carmen can testify." He stopped, visibly affected by something.

"What's the matter?" Cruz asked.

"I almost said Alicia and Raul could testify. It's not real yet, the death of my closest friends in the world." Silence fell like a shroud around them. Martinez's demeanor suddenly changed. "I lost my best friend and his wife over this. My wife may have lost her brother. Just figure something out, all right?"

Cruz didn't answer. He knew Mason would do a fine job. Mason's office had excellent attorneys and staff. Something nagged him though. Cruz analyzed whether it was a desire to fulfill some personal vendetta for what Shaver did to him and Eduardo so many years ago. While an inkling of that emotion existed, it certainly wasn't enough for him to put the case in jeopardy. The judicial system could work the case out itself. He decided any desire to help derived more from a sense of duty than vengeance.

"I still don't know," Cruz murmured.

"What was that?" Martinez asked.

"I don't know, Martinez. The case is fragile enough as it is."

"I don't understand how you could do it, even if you wanted to," Sandra interjected.

"Do what?"

"You aren't even a district attorney. In fact, you used to be a public defender. How could you possibly be a part of the prosecution?"

"There is a way..." Cruz began, "...there is a way to bring co-counsel on or have a special prosecutor assist. That's usually reserved for different types of cases though."

"Like what?"

"A small town that has a district attorney with limited resources.

But the district attorney in this case has all the resources he could need."

"Why would he have asked you to help then?"

"That's something I've been asking myself. I barely know him—just met in person a couple of times. Plus, it seems like he's adding a layer of uncertainty to the case by asking me to help."

"Nah man," Martinez said. "You know the case. You have a big connection with our community, so if anyone is going to help him investigate the case you're the one," Martinez said. The car stopped in front of the city morgue. "Maybe identifying some of these people will make your decision easier," Martinez said in an attempt to soften the edge of the moment. "You can do some good for them," he added.

They all stepped out of the car and approached the morgue. Its morose paint job, flecking away with every wind burst, conveyed the weight of what took place inside. A long flight of steps led up to the building, giving the entrant time to change their mind. Cruz lagged behind Martinez and Sandra, who were caught up in conversation.

They entered the building and Cruz waited with Sandra while Martinez went to the reception desk. She put her hand on the middle of his back and rubbed up and down a few times.

"You'll make the right decision." Cruz smiled back at her, his spirits somewhat lifted.

"Martinez!" a raspy voice bellowed. Cruz looked up to see a middle-aged white man, heavy set, breathing as if the matter around him was constantly pressing inward. He walked pigeon-toed, but with a certain gaiety that was willfully ignorant of his surroundings. The two men embraced.

"These two wit' you?" he asked.

"Sure are. This is Cruz, and this is Sandra."

"Pleasure to meet you," he said. "Joseph Tallinder's the name. Go by Joe." He shook Cruz's hand vigorously. "I 'preciate the visit, I really do Martinez, but if you're *here*, this ain't social s'it?" Cruz noted that Joe chopped words and sentences down to their most efficient usage of air.

"'Fraid not. We've been through a lot in the last few weeks...to say the least."

"Uh-know! Saw some of yer reports there, darlin'," he said while flashing a toothy smile at Sandra.

"I got a hold of some pictures, some shots of corpses. We need some help identifying them."

Joe laughed and Cruz watched as his gelatinous stomach rolled along. "That ain't no easy task, Martinez. Ya know how many bodies come tru' hir?"

"I know, I know. But, even if you could set us up to do the research ourselves, we'd be happy to."

Joe laughed again, "Ya think I was gonna d'it?!" He slapped Martinez on the back and pulled him past the receptionist's desk. A wall blocked off the public view behind the desk. They walked around it and came to a set of two elevators. The elevators took them down a floor to a long hall with evenly spaced doors on each side, all the way down.

"Y'all ever bin down hir?" Cruz and Sandra shook their heads. "Welp, the firs' three doors on each side are autopsy rums. After tha', two admin offices and then a storage rum and a research rum. Thas where y'all be spendin' yer time." Cruz couldn't help but stare into each autopsy room as they passed. They were all empty, no bodies out, no blood and guts. Not that there would be, Cruz chastised himself.

They got to the research room and Joe fumbled with some keys. He opened the door and held it open for them. Four computers hummed in the room, all as archaic and governmental looking as the morgue itself.

Joe must have caught the look on Cruz's face, "Welp, they ain't exactly fassst, but they'll work for y'alls purpose." Joe moved the mouse at each computer and then came back down the row to type in a password. "Hey Martinez, lemme see them photos, maybe I'll 'member one of 'em."

Cruz sat down and adjusted the computer in front of him. "What's the best way to search your database?" Cruz asked.

"Nope, nope. Dun recognize any of 'em, Martinez. Like I's said, jus' too many come tru' here, ya'know?"

"I do, Joe. What about Cruz's question? I've never been down here myself."

"Seems like these ar' all blacks or Mexicans, huh? Y'all can search the database by etnicity." Joe's speech entranced Cruz. So utilitarian and nearly indecipherable.

"Okay," Martinez said, taking back the pictures. There were ten pictures of Latino people, five of blacks. He handed the ten to Sandra and Cruz, "How about we split them this way. Let's each start with a search back ten years. Hopefully we'll get some hits in that time frame."

"Y'all can also add identifyin' marks like tattoos or scars, if those people hav'em. That shud cut the time down."

"All right, looks we're set here then Joe," Martinez said.

"If y'all need anything, jus' dial extension 102 from tha' phone. We got water and such." He slapped his hands together and rubbed them fast, signaling his work was done. Sandra and Martinez settled into their respective work stations with five pictures each.

Cruz picked up his pictures to see if any of the people had identifying marks. Unfortunately, none of them did.

"By the way, we may not be able to find all of these people in this database. Not everyone who dies in the state comes through here, obviously. I don't even know if all of these people died in this state, could have been from who-knows-where-else. Wish we had more info to go along with the photos, but..." Martinez trailed off.

Cruz grabbed his first picture and looked at it closely. He entered "Latina," "Brown hair." She had green eyes, possibly helpful. The search yielded five hundred and ninety-four results. "Damn!"

"What?"

"Almost six hundred results from this first search, and she's got green eyes," Cruz said despondently.

"It's gonna be a pain-in-the-ass, no doubt."

Sandra lifted one of her pictures and held it next to the computer screen. She leaned toward the screen. "Look guys." Both of them moved over to her computer. "Looks like a match, huh?"

Martinez read the statistics out loud, "Isabella Cordoba, born May 17, 1978, five-foot-two, one hundred eighteen pounds, last known residence..."

"Near where I grew up," Cruz finished.

"Where *we* grew up," Sandra added.

"Print that out—that's one match. Let's keep searching," Martinez said. They searched fruitlessly with picture after picture until Martinez came to his last one.

"This may be another match. Take a look. Jerome Miller. Born August 4, 1983. Last known residence was on the east side of town."

"Is that all the pictures?"

"That's my last one, you guys done too?"

"Yep."

"I think it's time to split up then," Cruz said. "Martinez and I can go follow up regarding Jerome. Sandra you go investigate what you can find out about Isabella."

"Sounds good to me," she answered.

"You'll get to go stomp around the old haunt anyways," Cruz said. She smiled at him, leaving Martinez to notice the less and less hidden undercurrents.

# THIRTY-FOUR

Several weeks passed in the jail. No visitors, none that Shaver expected. The only people he could possibly hope for would be from the force, and none of them wanted near his stink right now.

He had no family. Shortly after his incident in the fields a group of Mexican men attacked his family's farm, killing all the livestock, fatally wounding his father. His mother had no skills or work experience to fall back on and the family fell into desolate poverty. Shaver, the oldest of three children, tried his hand at odd jobs around the town, mainly provided by people who pitied his family.

The town itself chilled to Shaver after his attack. Something he had not surmised, most likely an error of youth, was the undrawn line that people were not supposed to cross. The town's attack on the Mexican farmers was supposed to intimidate, strike fear, but not kill. The county never prosecuted Shaver, but his act cast a somber mist over the town that never quite lifted.

Counterattacks from the Mexicans came more frequently. As they did, more and more townsfolk shut their doors to Shaver. The blame for bad times shifted from the Mexicans to him. At least before Shaver killed that Mexican man the two groups co-existed. Now a veritable civil war raged.

Shaver's mother died three years after his father. His brother and sister went to live with his aunt. Shaver was alone, tired, and eventually homeless. He spent days panhandling, while early afternoons involved finding somewhere to camp out. Sometimes that was under a bridge, other days he could find a cot in a shelter. It was there that Shaver found out about the Police Explorers.

A local church ran the shelter, and one of the priests was especially adamant about helping the young homeless. This priest approached Shaver, who was a physically fit, able-bodied young man of nineteen, and asked him if he knew about the Police Explorers. Shaver recoiled at the thought of becoming a police officer. They were the enemies of a homeless kid, kicking them out of camp areas, turning them into state offices and foster care. The priest wouldn't give up though and the persistence worked to whittle down Shaver's guard until one day he agreed to talk to a recruiter.

Shaver graduated about average in his Police Explorer class, and got a job at a rural county jail. His instructor explained that Shaver would have to work his way up before applying to the police academy, since he had no high school diploma. Shaver got to spend a year watching drunks at the county

187

jail before moving to a higher security facility in the southern part of the state.

The time in corrections definitively set Shaver's mind against minorities. All he saw in those facilities was some shade of nonwhite. The car thieves, the drug dealers, the pimps, the murdering gang members. They hurled feces at him and spit in his eyes while screaming they had AIDS. Hatred grew. He took liberties with certain prisoners, leaning down extra hard on a pressure point, making holds tighter. This escalated until one day he beat a mouthy black inmate nearly to death. Shaver claimed self-defense, the other correctional officers with him backed his story, and the warden eventually dropped the investigation.

It was also at this point that Shaver learned where the blue, or gray, or whatever color line existed. You never crossed or betrayed one of your fellow officers. This principle developed from the constant stress the officers were under, a necessary sense of team in the face of threat. It also developed from the power that came with the position. Without a rat, a traitor, the officers were untouchable. Shaver found that this principle applied just as readily to the police force once he made it to the academy.

Keys rattled, perking Shaver's ears.

"Shaver...visitor." He stood up and put his hands through the open hatch in the door. The officer cuffed him and then opened his cell door to let Shaver out. They walked with another officer in a line to the visitor's center. It was his lawyer, Sphinx.

Sphinx picked up the phone on the other side of the glass partition, "Shaver, good to see you." Shaver nodded. He wasn't sure about Sphinx yet. Sphinx had a celebrity reputation, having gotten Viscutti off so many years before. He was skeptical of celebrity. It implied individuality, and one of the rules behind the blue line, something imbued in Shaver, was that there is no individual. Plus, things hadn't gone well so far. At his first advisement hearing, Sphinx lost his plea to have Shaver let out on his own recognizance. The second advisement hearing wasn't better. Shaver found out that he was being charged with second degree murder of that old man. Sphinx promised Shaver that he'd be able to plea that down, that there was no way the District Attorney would maintain that charge. Nothing had come of the promise yet.

Shaver's case before the Civil Service Commission wasn't going well either. He was suspended without pay, a rare measure. The rest of the Commission's investigation was stayed pending the resolution of his criminal case. The Commission did not want to prejudice the criminal case with their own investigation. Based on all of that, Shaver greeted the visit skeptically.

"How they treating you in there?" Shaver shrugged his shoulders. "I mean, are they harassing you? The guards or the inmates?"

"The guards? Those are my people. I know half of them from my time in corrections. Besides, what do you care?"

"Your health is critical to our case. If they're mistreating you, we can make special requests of the court."

"Like I said, the guards are fine. Four fucking stars."

"The inmates?"

"They're treating me like a cop, what do you expect? I get death threats on a daily basis, especially from the pricks that I've locked up before. The officers set me up in my own cell though, because of the threats. I'm in a pussy section of the place, with the rapists and peds, so I doubt anything's gonna happen to me. You never know though, and I don't give a shit."

The jail was medium-security, meant mainly to be a holding area until inmates knew where they would be going. It was an old design—probably sometime in the late sixties—a telephone layout prison. There was a main corridor from which cells and program rooms branched out. The seats in the waiting room were teal, gum-laden and cracked. The jail reeked of use, the worst bodily functions and odors collected in a tight, enclosed space. Blood caked the floors of some cells, left there until the understaffed facility could get around to cleaning them. Some inmates refused to bathe, others ate their own feces, while others pissed themselves and didn't tell anyone. This return to primitive nature was inevitable when all of life's hope and freedom was stripped away. A chime sounded in their phones, five minutes.

"We are going to get you out of here Shaver. I need you to cooperate though."

"What the hell do you think I'm doing?"

"I consider appreciation to be a part of cooperation, so start there."

"Fuck you! Appreciation? You'll sap every dime I have defending me. You should fucking appreciate me!"

"That's where you've got it wrong Shaver. I'm the best defense attorney in this state and you're lucky to have me helping. Who gives a shit about your money. Without me you'll spend the rest of your already wasted life in a cell. You have no family, no friends to speak of, not even fucking pets. Your money is useless except if I get you out. So, from this goddamn moment, you have a choice. Start to fucking appreciate me, or get a new lawyer."

Shaver glared through the glass at Sphinx. He had really reached the point of not giving a shit. Even if he got out, there was no guarantee that he would ever be allowed to rejoin the force. Working security at a mall wasn't going to cut it. On the other hand, thirty more years or so in some dump of a prison didn't sound that enticing to him either. He decided to stroke Sphinx's ego, because that's all this was about.

"I'll appreciate you, you man-baby. If that's what you need. I'll never kiss your sandy, Persian ass though, so get that shit out of your head." Sphinx stared back at Shaver. He already hated this man, but the case was too juicy for him to abandon. Fame was Sphinx's primary motivation, with money a very close second. He could take some verbal abuse from Shaver to further those two motivations.

"Good, glad we got that straightened out. You'll recall that the judge denied your bail..."

"Yeah, that was a good start for you, huh?"

"It was completely a product of what you're accused of. I had nothing to do with the outcome."

"That's convenient."

"You mean the truth, Shaver? It sure is. Moving on, the judge also found that there was probable cause for your arrest at the preliminary hearing. The next step is your arraignment at the end of this week."

"Not guilty."

"Right, good. We'll get a trial date then too. Listen, this is going to be your word against Officer Martinez's."

"What about the video?"

"It'll never see the light of day in court." Sphinx's assertiveness was enough to give Shaver pause.

"From what I've heard, that video shows everything that happened."

"Nah, won't get in. It was never checked into evidence, who knows if it's even the actual video. Martinez or anyone else could have doctored the thing. It's not coming in. You let me worry about that part. That's the legal part. Start to prepare yourself for court. You have to be remorseful looking, but credibly. No one wanted this to happen, but you were acting in self-defense. Attentive. Alert. Don't make faces, don't react to testimony you hear. I'll give you a pad of paper and a pen, all you do is take notes. Like when you were a good student in school, remember that?"

"Fuck you."

Sphinx let out a hearty laugh. "That reminds me," he said as he stood up, "clean out your fucking mouth. I'll see you in a few days." A corrections officer put her hand on Shaver's shoulder, signaling the return to his cell.

* * * *

Mason pushed open the big, oak doors to the courtroom. The courthouse was situated near the center of the city, set above the buildings around it. Eight columns supported the front porch of the building where people gathered to smoke and meet their attorneys. The inside of the courthouse was semi-illuminated. The lighting that existed was high up in vaulted ceilings and spaced sparingly in meager wall fixtures. Marble floors butted up against old, handcrafted woodwork. There were sixteen courtrooms, eight on each floor.

Some of the most notorious judges in the state presided in this courthouse. They were old judges, screamers. Mason landed one of these cantankerous judges, Judge Melburn.

Judge Melburn had to be in his eighties, Mason thought to himself. In fact, Mason was afraid that the old guy would die any time he was in the courtroom. The judge was a public defender for twenty-two years before winning an election to preside in the city's district court. He was a merciless jurist and engaged in conduct all attorneys despised—yelling at them in front of their clients and in front of the jury. While any attorney could expect to be grilled by a judge, getting screamed at was unanimously considered unprofessional. Didn't stop it from happening.

Unfortunately for Mason, Judge Melburn was also known to be bent against prosecutors. That bias could exist may seem implausible, especially from the only person in the courtroom who should be as unbiased as possible. Again, didn't stop it from happening. To Mason's dismay, Judge Melburn was sitting at the bench when he entered the courtroom. Judge Melburn looked up and then back down without any sign of acknowledgment.

He was a small, Napoleonic man. Mason surmised he was an abused child, picked on by other children growing up, who now had the luxury and the forum to forever turn the tables. It was strange for the judge to be in his courtroom before the hearing started. Usually judges stayed in their chambers until it was time to appear. Nothing was normal with Judge Melburn, though.

Mason opened up his briefcase and pulled out a pad of legal paper and several folders. He sat down in the plush leather chair on the prosecution's side of the courtroom and flipped through his documents. The flipping was a time-passer. Mason knew what he wanted to say, what he would argue.

A cool draft flew into the room. Mason looked behind him and saw Sphinx enter, two associates in tow.

"Sphinx."

"Mason. How have you been?"

Mason set his documents down, "Getting old, Sphinx. Too old for any of your games. You gonna play this one by the book?"

Sphinx smiled as he set his briefcase on the defendant's table. "You know me too well to think I play games, Mason. Everything is legal, within legal bounds. I'm just *creative*."

Creative at figuring out how to skirt the law, Mason thought. "Your client going to plead guilty and get this over with?"

"Is the State going to drop its charges on account of a lack of evidence?" Both of them focused on their documents, acting busy and contemplative although the time for preparation was long passed.

Sphinx looked up and said, "Hello, Judge Melburn."

"Mr. Sphinx."

"Mason, you got a moment to step outside of the courtroom?"

Mason pursed his lips as if to say "sure" and walked out with Sphinx.

"What do you want?"

"We haven't talked plea bargain yet."

"No need to, I've got a rock solid case against your client."

Sphinx crossed his arms and leaned against the wall. "Listen, Mason, I'm going to try to spare you here. You've got *no* case against my client. All of the witnesses are dead except for Officer Martinez."

"We're working on that."

"What, to bring them back like Lazarus?"

"I'll find where you've hidden the daughter. Besides, Officer Martinez has been an honorable and accountable officer on the force for six years. He'll be enough."

"You mean the officer that went ape-shit, stole evidence, and performed an illegal arrest of my client? Is that really what you're pinning this on, Mason?"

"Spin it all you want, Sphinx. I'm confident that Officer Martinez will be a credible witness, especially in comparison to your client. In any event, there were exigent circumstances warranting the arrest."

Sphinx bellowed, "Exigent circumstances?! You mean my client holed up and afraid for his life because of Officer Martinez's lynch mob?"

"Spin, spin. Your client had a man with him that he was holding hostage. Your client demonstrated that he was willing to kill witnesses to save his own life. Exigent, actionable circumstances."

"Whatever, Mason." Both men had their arms crossed now, faced off. Sphinx's face contorted with frustration. Mason started to turn away. "You know you can't pin second degree on him though. We'll take criminal negligence and five years."

"You're nuts. I'd like to kill someone and only get five years."

"Take it Mason, or you're going to be embarrassed. You don't have the strength for this anymore."

"The hell I don't," Mason said, as much to himself as to Sphinx, as he walked back into the courtroom. Judge Melburn watched both men return to their respective tables.

"Did you reach an agreement?"

"No," Sphinx answered.

The judge shook his head while he chewed on a pen. "Don't turn this into a cockfight and waste my time, gentlemen. This courtroom has no place for your egos." He whispered something to his clerk, who left the courtroom. When the clerk returned, she was with the bailiff and Sergeant Shaver. Mason noted that the coldness in Shaver's eyes remained intact. It was something Mason analyzed every time he saw the man. There wasn't a shred of remorse in him. Mason figured this would help with the jury. Shaver took his place next to Sphinx silently except for the clanking of his leg chains.

"Enter your appearances and we will get started," Judge Melburn said.

"Mason West for the state Your Honor."

"Sphinx for the defendant Your Honor." Mason bristled at the familiarity and slack Sphinx was afforded.

"Simple arraignment here gentlemen. How does your client plead, Mr. Sphinx?"

"Not guilty," Shaver answered.

"So he has a voice..." the judge said. A cell phone rang at the end of his sentence. Mason froze, mortified it was his. But the "Oh my God," from behind him and to his right allayed that fear. He glanced up at the judge, whose face was blood-red.

"Just who's...just who's damn phone is that?" One of Sphinx's associates stood up slowly. Mason turned around to look at the associate, both out of curiosity and to deflect the ensuing barrage. "This is a courtroom, not a goddamn lobby! You turn your cell phone off and if I hear another cell phone ring, from any of you," the judge said as he looked at everyone, "I'll hold you in contempt of court. Do you understand me?" The associate nodded but dropped a redwell while trying to stuff the phone into her briefcase.

Judge Melburn shuffled paper around on his desk to regroup. "Now, I'm going to set this for trial in March, or about two months from now. I think three days will be sufficient. Your motions date will be in the middle of February. Have the parties reached a plea deal?"

Mason stood up and answered, "No, Your Honor."

"So noted. Is there anything else, counsel?"

This time Sphinx stood up, "Your Honor, I foresee a substantial evidentiary issue, related to a video allegedly capturing what occurred in this case. The video was never..."

Mason shot up and interrupted, "Your Honor! This is not the time or place for oral arguments related to exclusion of evidence. This is the arraignment, not a motions hearing." Adrenaline coursed through Mason and he felt his temper start to flare.

"I agree, Mr. West. Mr. Sphinx, you will save your arguments for hearings on the matter." Mason knew Sphinx got what he wanted. The issue was now on Judge Melburn's radar. The judge banged his gavel and ended the arraignment.

Mason waited for him to leave the courtroom before admonishing Sphinx, "No games?? You're a loose cannon, Sphinx, and it's gonna bite you soon."

Sphinx shrugged his shoulders. "I got what I wanted."

"I know you did," Mason answered as he hurriedly gathered his documents and walked out of the courtroom. He strode through the courthouse and through the front doors. His phone rang.

"Hello?"

"Mason?"

"Him. Who is this?"

"Mason, it's Cruz Marquez."

"Hi, Cruz. Did you make a decision?"

"Yeah ... I'll help."

"Good to hear. I just got a taste of why I'll be happy to have you on this case."

"I've got some information for you. Startling information. Let's meet."

"Name the time and place and I'll be there." Mason took down the information and shot down the courthouse stairs.

# THIRTY-FIVE

Tyler walked out to his mailbox, one in a group of over fifty. He watched two men exit their car and head up to an apartment. He was always watching people—out of fear, desire to learn, and readiness. He sorted through a hefty stack of mail while heading back to his apartment. After getting through the usual junk, he came to a piece of mail with no return address. He pushed open his apartment door and set the rest of the mail down.

"Tyler:

It's Shaver. I'm not sure what happened to you after they caught us in my house. A couple bullet wounds screwed up my ability to figure out what was up and what was down. I think one of the cops that ultimately booked me said you were booked too, but released. Would make sense, since they've got nothing to pin on you—yet. I've got something that you may want unless those asses ransacked my apartment and took it. It's a loose end someone like you should take care of. Come see me, you know where I'm at."

"Fuck you, Shaver, coming at me from the grave like this."

The Chief's death, the capture by the cops, it was all enough to put a scare into Tyler. A lonely, usually quiet part of himself wanted to end the killing. It wanted some peace. How could you change a monster though? Tyler was no Hannah-fucking-Montana. He'd killed thirty-eight people. A murderer, cold, disconnected and dissociated from society. Violence, especially death, aroused him. A sociopath, as one shrink told him. There comes a point in life where change is not only extremely difficult, but probably not worth the effort. Whether you're a fifty-year-old book salesman or a thirty-something-year-old assassin, some things can't be changed. Tyler was sick, and he knew it. His options were to keep killing, commit suicide in some grandiose but hopelessly alone fashion, or check into an insane asylum.

In the few short weeks since Martinez captured them, the lust to kill resurfaced with vigor. Every day was worse. He just wanted to straddle someone's body, knees on their arms, his hands around their neck, slowly constricting, the familiar smells, the veins bursting, blood in their eyes.

Tyler shook his head. When he was released Tyler thought this may all be over. Shaver implied the opposite. He knew what Shaver wanted. Blackmail was a familiar friend and foe in Tyler's line of business. Shaver had something Tyler needed. A message. A phone call. Something to tie him to something he'd done. So he jumped into his car and headed to the prison. He was just an eventuality, why fight the force?

# Derek Blass

The prison guard told him to wait in stall number eight. He tapped his fingers and played with the cord on the phone. After thirty minutes of waiting he looked around, wondering if this was some sort of joke. Then a door on the other side of his stall opened and Shaver shuffled through. Even after a short time in jail, Shaver looked tired, a bit emaciated.

"That didn't take you long," Shaver said.

"Not like I'm up to much. My employer is otherwise indisposed."

"Yeah, what was the final verdict on him?"

"I guess you could say verdicts. He stepped on a mine, ka-boom. Nothing to bring back really. There was a little bit left of that kid who was following him, but not much more."

"Now you're out of work."

"You can say that. We had a plant closure," Tyler said with a mechanical chuckle.

"That's not natural for you, is it?"

"Laughing? No, not really."

"Me neither."

"I smile, but usually at the wrong moments, or at things that disgust people. I'm all fucked in the head."

"Aren't we all..."

"Not that spending time with you in this shit hole isn't scintillating, but what did you want from me? What do you have that I so *desperately* need?"

"Your former employer was a busy man. His doctor, Dr. Xavier Kastenoff, especially. Perhaps busier than even you in the same profession."

Tyler raised his eyebrows. "You don't say?"

"I do, I do. This doctor was quite active, for a long time."

"Good for him...why do I care?"

"Getting there. Remember that journal I told you about? This doctor kept an accounting of his...*patients*."

"Okay, again, what's that got to do with me?"

"This list makes several references to you, as an alternative source of patient care." There it was. A list, with him in it.

"Shaver, why should I trust you? You've got nothing to lose and a real craving to get out of here. This list could have nothing related to me. Hell, it may not even exist."

Shaver had prepared for this. He wasn't book smart, but his upbringing taught him to be cunning. Persuasion and manipulation included. Shaver pulled a torn piece of graph paper from his pocket and held it up to the glass.

Tyler started to read the meticulous handwriting. "The Chief declined my services for Lucy Hahn, stating that he would use Mr. Smith instead. Disappointing, as the Chief is using Mr. Smith more and more."

"Hey! You! What the hell do you think you're doing?!" a guard screamed as he came over and wrenched the piece of paper out of Shaver's hand. The guard then grabbed Shaver by the shoulder and started to pull him away.

"All right, all right, I shouldn't have done it." The guard relaxed his grip on Shaver, seemed to contemplate his next move, and finally decided on letting Shaver get away with the transgression. Shaver put the phone back to his ear. "Was that glimpse enough?"

"Enough for what?"

"Enough to know that I'm not bullshitting you and to get you to do me some favors?"

"I'm not in a position to do favors, Shaver."

"Well, then how about no favors, but just do the only thing you know how to do. There's nothing else out there for you Tyler. No better life. No flipping burgers at a restaurant. The sickness will drive you forever. I'm just helping you release it. Plus, if you don't, that list is sure to get leaked. You'll end up spending more time in here than Charlie Manson."

Checkmate, Tyler thought. Why resist; this is all he wanted. It was what consumed him in the middle of empty nights. "What kind of work are you talking about?"

"You know exactly what I'm talking about. Three little piggies."

Tyler shrugged his shoulders, "I'll think about it."

"You go ahead and think, but if I haven't heard from you in a week, consider the list published." Shaver hung up the phone and rotated away to the door behind him. Tyler walked out of the jail, the same man, back to square one.

\* \* \* \*

Cruz sat in Mason's office, waiting for him to come back from a meeting. The past few days were eventful. Cruz and Martinez followed up on the lead they generated at the morgue. Jerome Miller was twenty when he died. Eight days from his twenty-first birthday, his mother explained to them.

Jerome's family still lived at the address that came up at the morgue. It was a dilapidated section of town, an area built up in the 1950s with small bungalows and row homes. Abandoned cars, or cars that should have been abandoned, lined the streets and driveways. Teal and white translucent porch covers hung on by single screws. The brick finishes of the homes were cracked and the lawns overrun with weeds.

Mr. and Mrs. Miller, probably both in their mid-fifties, were the core of the family. Jerome was their second child; his sister Donella was the oldest. Mr. Miller told them that Jerome had two other siblings, but said nothing else about them. Cruz saw no sign of them in the house, which was clean inside, although a funereal film hung about. The Millers showed Cruz and Martinez to Jerome's old room. Everything was intact four years later. The bed was made. The room vacuumed. Posters of athletes hung taut on the wall. The room shocked Cruz—the Millers hadn't let go at all.

"He was our only boy," Mr. Miller said from behind them. He was standing between them and the hall, apparently requiring them to respect this statement by staying in the room for longer than comfortable. Mrs. Miller put a hand on his arm and he stepped sideways, letting Cruz and Martinez squeeze by. "You told me you're a cop, and you're a lawyer. What's this all about? Jerome died a long time ago now. We've been through the rigmarole." Mrs. Miller directed all of them back to the living room where a pitcher of lemonade and some glasses were waiting.

"It's about just that, Mr. Miller. How Jerome died."

"But why would you want to know that? Especially now?" Cruz could sense some frustration and rightful indignation coming from Mr. Miller.

"Have you followed the reports on this shooting involving one of the city's cops?"

"I don't watch the news anymore. What happened?"

"A sergeant in the city's police department, Sergeant Shaver, shot and killed an unarmed, elderly man from the Latino community."

Mr. Miller tried to wave the importance of it away. "What's new? Police brutality? Look where we live, my friend. That's as old a game as dice."

Martinez went on to supplement Cruz's explanation, "We're investigating some leads that I got—leads that may connect this sergeant to more deaths. We have reason to believe that your son may have been one of his victims."

Mr. Miller's hand shook and spilled his glass of lemonade on the table. Mrs. Miller darted to the kitchen and returned with several towels. He looked at her as she cleaned up his mess. "I'm sorry, it's just...so startling." He started off into another time, aching to put pieces of the puzzle together. "The police were never able to tell us what happened. Jerome died of a gunshot wound to his chest, but there were also signs of choking. I've always told Mrs. Miller something was wrong, foul. The coroner had no answers for us. He cut our son up, a big "Y" on his chest, his head, cut him all open and couldn't give us a *damn answer*. The coroner and the police chief met with us, told us they would keep investigating the death until they found a killer. After several months they labeled the case cold and told us they wouldn't be able to do anything else unless they got more leads."

"That's kind of quick to shut a case down," Martinez said.

"We thought so too!" Mr. Miller exclaimed, his whole body trembling now. Mrs. Miller poured him another glass of lemonade and stood there, making him take a sip. "What the hell were we going to do? Look around," he said while gesturing to their house. "We aren't rich. We live in a rundown neighborhood. They could have just blamed it on the drug dealers that infest these areas, like they always do."

"We just kept our memories of him," Mrs. Miller said, her first uttered words. Mr. Miller took the interruption as an opportunity to gather himself.

"It's all we got," Mr. Miller said.

"Was anyone with Jerome when this happened?"

"As far as I know, Jerome and a friend, Lamont, were coming home from watching their high school play a football game. We heard frantic rapping on our front door that night. When we opened it, Lamont was standing there, out of breath. He grabbed my wrist and hauled me five blocks while I asked him what was going on. He wouldn't talk, he just ran. We got to an alley, behind the old Smoky's Grocery and there he was, my beautiful son. Still warm, laying in a slowly growing puddle of his own blood." Mr. Miller cut himself off. He grabbed his knees to stop his hands from shaking. Sobs welled up from his chest. "My boy...*my only boy!*" Tears welled up in Mr. Miller's eyes and ran down his face. "You'll have to excuse me," he barely got out as he left the room.

Mrs. Miller stood by Cruz and Martinez, her eyes damp. "Maybe it's time for a break," she said softly. They both nodded at her and stood up.

"We're very grateful for you taking the time to talk with us Mrs. Miller. Here's my card," Cruz said, "Please, please call me and maybe you can come into my office to talk some more. I think we may be on a track to figure out what happened to Jerome." She smiled, took the card and then opened the front door. They walked out and Martinez let out a long, held breath.

"What do you think?" Cruz asked.

Martinez shook his head. "I don't know. Certainly sounds suspicious to me. Why would the chief and the coroner meet with them at the same time?

Why was he choked *and* shot? There's definitely something to this."

The world started to take shape around him again as the memory drew to a close. Mason stormed into his office and completely broke Cruz from his thoughts. After telling Mason about Jerome Miller, he said, "Sandra came across equally alarming information." Mason was busy taking down notes as Cruz spoke. When he caught up, he looked at Cruz.

"What did she find?"

"She went to investigate the death of a young woman named Isabella Cordoba. Isabella was a college junior here in the city. Her mother is still alive, widowed last year. She explained that Isabella died of an apparent drug overdose, but she adamantly denied that Isabella ever did drugs. Said she was nearly a straight-A student, never hung out with the wrong crowd."

"Pretty common for kids to successfully hide things from their parents."

"Didn't seem like that here, Mason. At least from what Sandra told me. This was an old-school Spanish household. Parents are very, very involved with their kids, especially the girls. They protect them."

"Let's assume what you're saying is right, what's the connection?"

"We got these leads, in the form of photographs, from a cop. Martinez did. Apparently, this cop knew that Martinez was digging deeper into Sergeant Shaver's past. That's why he gave Martinez the photos. When Martinez went to get the photos, at the place and time the two had agreed to, the cop was dead. Shot while waiting in a diner for Martinez. We took the photos..."

"Wait, what happened with the cop?"

"Once he died? I don't know. Haven't had the time to look into it either." Cruz took a breath. "We took the photos to the city morgue, then got access to the morgue's databases and searched for the deceased people in the photos. Two of them were matches—Jerome and Isabella."

"The others?"

"No matches or leads."

"Can you get those other photos to me? I'll have my investigator try his luck too."

"Sure. To get back to your question, how this connects, well, that cop gave Martinez the photos and we assume the people in them are somehow connected to Shaver. Our investigation lends support to that assumption. Just consider how Jerome and Isabella died. Unexplained...inexplicable."

"I don't know, Cruz. I certainly wouldn't go so far as to say inexplicable. Jerome could have died any number of ways, and if Isabella died of a drug overdose, then that's it. Hold on one sec." Mason picked up his phone, "Todd, do me a favor. Pull the coroner's reports for a Jerome Miller and Isabella Cordoba. They both died within the last five years. If you need more information, call me and I'll have Cruz talk to you." Mason returned his attention to Cruz. "Let's talk about something else until Todd pulls those reports."

"All right."

"How the hell do you suppose we're gonna get that video into evidence? Without that, this case is just a 'he said-he said', pitting Martinez against Shaver."

"What obstacles do you see?"

"Hearsay, for one. Chain of custody, two."

"Hearsay?"

"Could the video be considered an out-of-court statement used to prove the truth of what is asserted?"

Cruz thought about the question. "I don't think you even get to the statement part. The video isn't a statement, it's a recording of an incident. Even if you want to address the statements contained in the video, the dialogue that occurred, they aren't being offered to prove the truth of anything. There doesn't seem to be a hearsay problem. The chain of custody issue is a problem."

"The requirements that the physical evidence be documented, who handled it be documented, and the number of transfers be kept to a minimum —all of those are blown."

"We know Sphinx is gonna challenge the admissibility of the video on those grounds. That means we have to prove the video offered into testimony is the same as the one Max recorded. Martinez can testify that he never doctored or otherwise edited the video. Have you subpoenaed Max's records, specifically the files on his work and home computers?"

Todd came into the office while Cruz was speaking and handed Mason some documents. "Todd can tell you what happened there."

"We did subpoena those files, and we got access to the computers. Unfortunately, Max had put a self-executing virus on both computers. If he didn't log on for a certain amount of time, the virus eradicated everything on the computers' hard drives."

"Guess you didn't get to them before that happened?"

"Nope. There was nothing left for us to recover. Our best computer techs tried to, but unsuccessfully."

"You see? It's going to be tenuous," Mason said.

"It certainly would have been more of a slam dunk if we could have pulled the video off of his computer. There's no choice though, we've simply got to present Martinez's testimony about the video and let the judge decide. Who's the judge in this case, by the way?"

"Melburn."

Cruz shook his head. "That's no help."

"I'm going to get back to work," Todd said as he left the office.

"I know," Mason said, answering Cruz.

"Melburn's a pain in the ass," Cruz said. "We've got no alternatives though. Plan A is Martinez's testimony against Shaver plus the video. Plan B is the testimony by itself. That's one more reason why we've got to keep investigating these other deaths. The problem is I just don't see how we connect Shaver to them. We'll have to pull the cold case files and see if we can match any physical evidence."

"Or we can start here," Mason said while handing one of the coroner's reports to Cruz.

"What is it?"

"Look at the last page of that report, the coroner's signature."

"Okay."

"Now look at the same page on this other report."

"Same signatures. That would make sense, to have the same coroner drafting and signing these reports."

"It certainly would make sense—if that was the city's coroner." Cruz did a double take and looked at the signature lines again. "Dr. Xavier Kastenoff is not the city's coroner. I've never heard of that doctor."

"Bingo."

Mason picked up his phone again and asked Todd to pull the medical bar's records on Dr. Kastenoff. Todd returned with the results quickly.

"Dr. Xavier Kastenoff, originally licensed to practice medicine in 1972. Had his license revoked in 1996 for multiple investigations into unnecessary surgeries. He ran his last office out of a small clinic established in his home."

"Oh my God," Cruz said.

"What is it?"

"I've been there."

# THIRTY-SIX

Shaver walked around the perimeter of the "yard." After nineteen days in relative isolation, ostensibly for his own protection, he couldn't take it anymore. The walls started to creep in on him. His muscles cramped and ached from lack of activity. He felt his mind evolve toward feelings of depression, even suicide. Those thoughts were flashes, almost like a single image cut into the reel of a film, hardly noticeable but disturbingly present. He persisted in getting out to the yard despite the guards' admonitions.

Circling felt great, a chance to stretch his legs. Fresh air removed the asbestos-like contagion from his lungs. Small, random shoots of grass were starting to spring up in the otherwise golden grass. The yard had three basketball courts, the requisite workout section with bench press, pull-up bars, stations for curling, a seated row machine, and bleachers in every corner. It was further divided by skin color. The blacks worked out at a certain time then went to the basketball courts where races actually mixed—more out of a sense of competition than amnesty. When they were done working out, the Latinos would transition in, then the whites. There were a few Asians, but their numbers were too small to assert rights over any of the facilities.

Shaver just circled. He recognized several faces. They didn't seem to recognize him, yet. He knew eyes were on him though. He represented new blood, a potential new threat or ally, a potential new source of weed or coke or sex. A new "bitch" to steal coffee or other goods from. Shaver mainly kept his head down, walking at a slow but confident pace. This introduction was critical, and he knew it. Appear weak and he'd be someone's slave—appear too cocky and he'd most certainly be attacked or even killed. So he circled, around the blacks' benches, the whites' benches, and the Latinos' benches.

Everyone was tatted up, but the whites took the most effort to show them. Mainly swastikas, or "white power" scrawled on a bristling chest. The Latinos sported 13's, or last names in Old English on their backs..."Gonzalez", "MS," broken bottles, sneering clowns with blood dripping off of bared teeth.

"You better not step there *ese.*" The low hiss broke Shaver out of his trance. He looked up to see an older Mexican, maybe late forties, tats running from his forehead down both sides of his face. Shaver recognized the tats as a form of Mexica design, something the Mexican gangs often paid reverence to. The man was in his prison blues with a white T-shirt. He leaned on his knee with a hand, hugging the edge of the bleachers. "That's *La Eme* ground."

The organizational structure of these gangs didn't differ much from the streets to the prison. Shaver was familiar with most of them, although new ones frequently attempted to spring up. The Mexican Mafia was what this man referred to. A rival gang to *Nuestra Familia*. Shaver looked back down at the ground and detoured to the right to continue walking.

"*Ese*, that's *Eme* ground *too!*" the same man yelled to him. "Shit," the man said as he got off of the bleachers and came toward Shaver, "You're already standing on *Eme* ground."

Shaver squared up to the man, who was about the same height, definitely broader in every other aspect. Shaver guessed he must be at least a lieutenant. Several younger men looked at the two from the bleachers, probably soldiers or *carnales*. Shaver remained silent.

"See, you can go over there, where you got some white *putas* to hang with. This part of the yard is taken." Confrontation, to be expected. It was a test and would be determinative.

"I'm walking."

"I know what the fuck you're doing, *ese*," the man said while tilting his head. "You think I'm dumb?" Shaver didn't respond, it was an attempt to escalate. "You mute, *puta*?"

Shaver shook his head and started to walk away, in the direction that was *La Eme* ground. It was a questionable move. He had no allies, no back. The collective eye of the yard watched. All of them would take the cue from this interaction. He knew his only chance was for the whites to intervene if he ignored this lieutenant. The lieutenant would have to take action if Shaver didn't listen to him. He couldn't be perceived as letting Shaver ignore an order.

"*Oye, oye! Mira esta puta!* He's gonna get his shit waxed first day out!" the lieutenant said back to his *carnales*. Shaver didn't turn around to look but could feel that the lieutenant and several other men followed him now. His heart pounded in his chest. He could see guards start to perk up in the towers around the yard. That's the last thing he wanted—to be perceived as a guard bitch. He kept walking at the same speed, trailed by the *La Eme* members.

After turning a corner he heard another shout out, "Yo muthafucka, you 'bout to step into Guerilla territory. Best go back where you came from." Now Shaver was stuck, in between a black prison gang and the *La Eme*. He stopped, feeling the presence of the men behind him. "And what the fuck you muthafuckas doin' here?" the black gang member yelled out to *La Eme*.

Muscles tensed, fists clenched and walls of chest began to form. Just as the mood started to boil, three white men walked up into the mix.

"He got lost," one of them said.

"Fuckin' right he did," retorted the Guerilla member. "Better take that white boy to the Brotherhood before I fuck him and make him mine."

Shaver looked behind him. Four members of the *La Eme* stood with their arms crossed, ready to pounce. The lieutenant said, "Same thing goes for us, *cabrones*. Make sure that white *puta* knows where he's going."

The white man who had spoken up gestured his head towards the other side of the yard and Shaver followed. When they were out of earshot, he asked Shaver, "You fuggin crazy?" He shook his head, "You gonna stawt a fuggin war."

The man talking to him was short, only coming up to Shaver's shoulder. He had swastikas tattooed up his right arm and another one on his forehead. His jaw was in constant motion whether talking or not. Grinding, clenching. The hallmarks of some sort of drug addiction. His right shoulder hung slightly lower than his left as he walked in a sped-up gimp, his right foot scratching the ground every few steps. Two other men walked with them, absolute hulks. Both taller than Shaver, both wider, meaner. They all had sandy hair and blue eyes. The ideal Aryans.

"Listen, you owe us now."

"Who's us?"

The short man paused. "Yous kiddin' me, right? Fuggin Aryan Brotherhood. *The ones that jus' saved yawr sweet, virgin ass!*" One of the big men shook laughing. "Those vatos were gonna make you toss some salad." The big man kept shaking, gleeful.

"So what do I owe you?"

The short man stopped walking this time. He looked at the other two men and then Shaver in disbelief. "How 'bout a fuggin thank yous for stawters?" A thick and apparent Bostonian accent melted out of the man's mouth.

"Thank you," Shaver returned tersely.

"Well, well. There ya go. I'm Pick," the man said while extending his hand.

"Pick?"

"Edward J. Pickhat. Pick for short. Listen, if you gonna fug around you can go back to your lonesome. Good luck surviving in here, fuggin' cop. We was doin' ya a favor." Shaver didn't say anything. "Pretty lucky you are that we get on wit those spics. So, the way I see it, yous owe us a favor. *Quid pro quo*," Pick said, his eyes shining. They continued walking to the other side of the yard, toward some bleachers filled with white men. As they neared, it was apparent to Shaver that all of the men were positioned in a semi-circle around one man. That one man was huge, probably six foot five. Bulky but still lean looking. He had dark brown hair and deep-water blue eyes.

"Pick, whud I tell ya about mutts?"

"This ain' no mutt, Mills. He's good, ain't ya?" Pick asked.

Shaver stood on the edge of dream and reality. These gang members were what he fought for so many years. Although he didn't target the white ones that often, it was still a tremendous adjustment. The path before him was clear at this point. He could either play along, associate with the Brotherhood, or he could go back to being on his own. In the latter scenario, he probably wouldn't last long. So, he nodded his head.

"This is the cop, huh? Whud-th'-fuck you doin' bringin' a cop over here, Pick?"

"He's good, Mills. He ain't no regular cop. You know what he's in here for?"

"I know, killin' a spic. Still a cop." Pick didn't say anything else. Everyone looked at Shaver. He remained silent as well. Talking wouldn't be redemptive, only action. Shaver knew that was coming next. Mills measured Shaver up. Some of the other gang members went back to what they were doing, playing cards, talking to each other. "You wanna prove you'self copper?" There it was, the undertow that would suck Shaver in. This yard had instantly become a case of survival. Shaver didn't say yes or no, but kept looking at Mills.

"Not the talkative type, huh boss?" Mills cackled. "I dun mind that. Anyway, Pick talks enough for the rest of us." Pick shrugged his shoulders and went to sit down beside Mills. "I got this shipment comin' in, some yay. I need someone to see it gets to its intended recipients. You game?"

Survival, Shaver thought to himself. "Yeah, I can handle it. Any unwelcome buyers?"

"Hey," Mills said, turning serious in a hurry, "We dun do no sellin'. It's trade an' barter, got it?"

"Sure, I get it. So, who'm I trading with? And who doesn't get any."

Mills' posture relaxed. "We dun sell to those gorillas. The rest is game. I'll give ya twenty-four hours to unload what you get."

"What am I gonna get in return?"

Mills spit on the ground, "Ballsy. You just got what ya gonna get. A get-oud-uh-jail-free card." Mills spoke with a strange falling off, sometimes letters and whole syllables just dropped off of the end of his words. His shirtsleeves were rolled up, revealing massive biceps. Oddly enough, his arms were clean of tattoos, as were his neck and face. "Should have the yay by 'morrow; meet me here in the yard." Mills checked out the nails on his left hand, ending the conversation.

Shaver looked at the rest of the members, but none paid attention. He took the cue and walked back to the prison compound. A full blast of sun poured down on the yard. Some prisoners gathered under the scant shade produced by the compound itself. Others sat on bleachers, soaking in the rays. Shaver could see the outside world through the chain-link fences enclosing the yard. It had quickly become a remote vestige of memory. Someone else's life, faint, barely pulsing with existence. A short burst of grief radiated out from his chest.

"You shouldn't get involved with them, any of them," a voice came from behind him. Shaver turned around and saw a woman corrections officer. She was pretty, albeit plain. Brown hair and eyes, strong but not plump—healthy.

"Get the fuck away from me."

"I know who you are. You don't have to get involved with the gangs. We'll do a fine job of protecting you."

"You don't know who the fuck I am lady. Now get away from me." The worst thing for him would be to have guard protection. It would make him *everyone's* target.

She took a step back. "I know why you're saying that, but just consider it. You get wrapped up with them and you'll never get out of here. You *can* survive on your own." She left him standing alone. He looked back over his shoulder at the Brotherhood. Pick was watching him.

* * * *

"What do you mean you've been to his home?" Mason asked.

"Just that. I've been there. It's a long story, but..." Cruz drifted off as he looked out the window behind Mason. Snow was falling, straight then swirling counterclockwise. Slowly changing direction and then spinning clockwise. He thought about the people on the street, huddled in the bluster. "...the condensed version is that the doctor held Sandra captive in his house. Martinez and I, along with two other guys, went to rescue her. That's when I was in the house."

"Timeout. This is all news to me. Someone held Sandra captive?"

"Yeah. Sandra and I went to find Martinez, so that we could track down the video." Cruz was upset about having to relive this story. "See how this devolves, constantly pulling back layers until we've been here all day talking about it?"

"Doesn't matter—this is important. Plus, it's interesting, so go on."

Cruz sighed and slipped deeper into his chair. "We tracked Martinez down at a hospital. Problem was that some henchman, who we now know was the Chief's henchman..."

"Uhh, wait a second," Mason said as he fumbled through some papers on his desk. "Tyler?"

"Tyler, right. Tyler surprised all of us. He was armed and took Sandra hostage. It's weird to talk like this, in war terms. We're pretty regular people, civilians." Cruz rubbed the chair's arms as he spoke. "Anyway, Tyler took her hostage. Then the Chief called us with an ultimatum. The video for Sandra."

"But you didn't give him the video."

"Nope. We never intended to give him a thing. We were going to go in there and blast them away to save Sandra. When I say blast it may suggest that I'm adept at those types of things, like guns and shooting them. I'm not." Mason used his lips to intimate that it didn't matter. "We went in there, Martinez did the blasting, and the Chief and Tyler escaped. We got Sandra out."

"Where was the doctor?"

"I didn't see him. I wasn't really looking either, to tell you the truth. Sandra was a terrifying sight. They had her strapped to a medical table with an overhead light pulled down to an inch from her face. All I wanted to do was save her. But that has to be it...his house, that is. Would just be too coincidental otherwise."

"How does Shaver fit into all of this?"

Cruz shook his head and reached for a glass of water. "Beats me. Not sure if Shaver and the Chief were working together at that point. They certainly had a joint interest in recovering that video. But Shaver wasn't at that doctor's house that day...at least not that I saw." Mason twirled a pen in his fingers, letting it roll off of his index, then middle, then ring finger and back to his thumb. The movement mesmerized Cruz.

"This carries significant implications. The chief of police, with an assassin henchman and an unlicensed doctor on the books? Movies are made from that kind of crap."

"Dramatic."

"We've got to track down this Tyler guy. I can charge him with assault, kidnapping, conspiracy. The charges against him aren't really what we'll be after though."

"Leverage."

"Exactly. Maybe he can help us tie Shaver to some other crimes. Hell, if Shaver had a hand in kidnapping Sandra, we'll tack those charges on. You never know what'll come from a rat. I'll give you a call when Todd and I have tracked down Tyler. Can you and Martinez go find him? A police presence would be helpful."

"I don't think this guy will go lightly. It would probably make sense to get more than me and Martinez."

"You guys work it out."

Cruz got out of his chair and shook Mason's hand. "I'll be hearing from you." Mason nodded and started typing something on his computer. Cruz left the office and headed through a labyrinth of cubicles until he found the elevator. He stepped in and headed down to the lobby. The piercing snow-ridden wind pricked his face when he opened the glass doors to the street. Hardly any people were out. Most had probably left by this time of day. The city was on a spring blizzard warning. Cruz stood there, snow steadily gathering on his shoulders, as he looked into the white wall and questioned how such horrific things could emerge from such beauty.

# THIRTY-SEVEN

The computer screen seemed to hum electronically in front of Tyler. Matter formulated pixels which coalesced into pictures, text, numbers, which Tyler converted into information. The woman was easy to find. She was on the news all the time. He would just watch her daily habits going to and leaving work. There was no problem finding the lawyer either. A quick search on the state bar's website revealed that he was the only attorney named Cruz. Got his business address from the website. Tyler didn't bother looking for the cop. The other two would lead him there. The phone rang.

"Hello?"

"It's me."

"Daddy?"

A pause. "Listen, *you fuck*," the voice hissed, "I've got one call this week so don't screw around with me."

"Not like you have anyone else to call."

"When you land in here too, I'm gonna feed you to the spics."

"You sure they'll still be hungry after tasting your sweet ass?"

Another pause as Tyler could hear Shaver breathing hard. Finally he said, "What did you decide?"

"I was on my way to start taking care of business when you called." The line went dead. "Prick." Tyler set the phone down and went back to gathering his equipment. Binoculars, a bionic ear with recorder. Conversations a hundred yards away were crystal clear with that ear. Tyler recalled reading somewhere that bears had a twenty-one thousand times greater sense of smell than humans. They could smell a carcass from twenty miles away. One hundred yards seemed peevish in comparison. Pen and paper. He put these all into a small pack and went out to his car.

The apartment complex he lived in provided protection of the masses. There was so much filth and criminal activity going on that he seemed saintly. It was like hiding a diamond ring in a bag of shit. He cranked up his car and set out for the news station. The day was young and Tyler was an early riser. From four in the morning to six he could be alone in the world as it awoke. It allowed him to avoid the herd in their daily rush to stick their heads through a yoke. It happened to coincide well with when reporters get going. He checked both ways before turning onto a four-lane road that would lead him all the way downtown.

Strip malls, fast-food joints, porn stores, thrift shops lined both sides of his path. The number of strip malls per block seemed a reasonable way to judge the makeup of a community. They housed the Indian groceries, the Somalian dry cleaners, each with some name in foreign lettering above a carefully crafted name in English, "All Season Tailor." Something innocuous and meaningless like that. Who knew if the two names even matched?

The buildings changed as Tyler drove toward the city. Building facades became renovated and shiny. Signs of gentrification emerged. Brown and black changed to white. The push to remove the poor from sight, to the outskirts of civilization, where they could collect like trash in garbage dumps. All of this facilitated by land value, capitalism. Tyler turned right into an alley that ran behind the news station. He stopped and pulled out the bionic ear. It was fun to switch it on and see what he could pick up. People were *completely* different when they didn't know someone was listening. Friends were enemies. Enemies turned out to be even worse enemies. Gossip, that's often what Tyler picked up. Men were pigs, but women were too. That's something the bionic ear taught Tyler. It also solidified his hate of other people. The sentiment that they were conniving animals, a brownish sticky substance pressed into the tread of his shoes.

He didn't pick up any chatter so he stepped out of the car and walked down the alley. He ran his hand along the grout lines in the brick facade of the news building, enjoying the roughness. The sun was just breaking the horizon, reflecting off a low-lying level of clouds. The clouds themselves radiated neon pink. Tyler came around the corner of the building and kept walking to a small park on the opposite side of the street. He took a seat on a bench in the park, partially obscured from the front of the news building.

The occasional person walked by as Tyler waited. Cars started to flow more heavily as time passed. He watched the clouds above him change from pink to a burnt orange, Monetesque in the sky. Finally, they settled on their daily color. The flow of people increased too. Tyler felt sorry for them, the walking dead. Addicted to productivity, to supposed advancement from one level of the caste to another. They woke, consumed, worked, consumed, worked, took a break, worked out, went home, consumed, slept and then repeated it all the next day. Maybe they changed the pattern two days a week, but not all of them. How did that differ from being an animal? How was that not *worse* than being an animal?

Tyler perceived his killing as a method of elevation. Out of the race to uniformity and oblivion these people so willingly participated in. He had no schedule, no office, no secretary, no Outlook and PowerPoints, no productivity meetings, no donuts on the first floor, thank-you-very-much. His life wasn't marked by the tedious passage of time. The monotonous chug of existence. Life was constantly thrilling. Tyler recognized that his way of life appealed to an animal sense as well. The predatory aspect instead of the working aspect. He identified targets, stalked them and finally hurled himself at them, his mouth clenched around their necks, both bodies breathing furiously from the chase.

She came out of the building and he recalled her allure. Not that Tyler cared on any level other than an appreciation for the creation of beauty. He was not a hetero or homosexual. Sexually, he was ambivalent, removed. All of his sexual fulfillments came in those moments when he was crouched over his victims, watching life drain out of their eyes. Despite that, Tyler could still recognize physical beauty. She had it. Glossy black hair, of medium height and perfectly figured. Her heels clacked authoritatively as she walked. Her skirt rubbed against her skin as she moved. Form-fitting, *ass*-fitting.

He stood up and walked briskly to his car while watching what car she got into. Her car crossed in front of the alley as he pulled out and fell in a couple of vehicles behind. 54XTS7. License plate number. He followed as she wound through the city. Technically, all he needed was the license plate number. That would tell him where she lived. This was the stalk though, the study of a person's small movements in their daily lives. This is what Tyler would shatter.

She slowed and put her right blinker on to parallel park. Tyler continued past her and parked around the corner. He saw her walk into a restaurant and then reappear on the patio, escorted by a hostess.

She picked up a menu, looked at it, looked at her watch, then cell phone, took a sip of water. This is what he would interrupt. The hostess reappeared with a man. Tyler took his binoculars out and focused them on their table. It was the lawyer, Cruz. He sat in a chair next to her and picked up his own menu. They laughed, he drank some water. Tyler could have used his bionic ear but it was unimportant. Plus, he didn't have to listen to see they were in love. They exchanged playful touches, laughed together, talked about people together. Tyler put the binoculars down, feeling something empty inside himself. That is what he would shatter.

\* \* \* \*

The darkness was all-encompassing. His limbs were foreign, nonexistent. All that remained was a kernel of thought, fleeting glimpses. The faintest shimmer in someone else's dream. It might be suggested that some thought would be welcome, but it was terrifying. Locked in absolute isolation, those brief moments of thought only promoted awareness of what was happening. Sound usually triggered the thoughts. From time to time voices were noticeable. They flew at him from a distance like a shout in a desert, wind-borne and solitary. He ached to reach out, to show some acknowledgment of the voices, but he had no control over any part of himself. The self-awareness was murderous. It would have just been peaceful darkness without that.

Then a collision of epic proportions, big-bang-esque, and Raul sucked in a roomful of air with one, prolonged gasp. Darkness collided with light. Senses with numbness. Silence with sound. A set of recurring sounds, beep— monitors, Raul recognized. His mind was slow. Thoughts fell into a vast chamber like individual grains of sand. They hit, echoed, and remained until the next fell. He cracked one eye open, which he shut immediately. Light burned. He requested that his right index finger move. It did. Got control of you again. Middle finger, thumb, ring finger, pinkie. Other hand. Both feet.

His arms ached and when he tried to lift himself up nothing happened. He cracked his eye open again and was able to tolerate a couple of seconds. Progress. The granules of thought were falling faster, piling up. What happened? Where am I? Am I alone? He tried to muster speech, a call out, but his vocal cords felt rusted over. He cracked both eyes, several more seconds. The beeping rose in volume and frequency. He heard rustling coming from somewhere. Then muffled footsteps. A presence. Someone was next to him.

"*Alguien llame al médico. El Señor ha regresado.*" He turned his head, more like a flop, and opened his eyes again. A woman in blue clothing stood next to him, one hand on his shoulder, the other pushing buttons on a machine. "*Con calma, Raul.*" Darkness returned.

* * * *

Cruz sat with his glass of water half-held up to his mouth. He scanned the street in front of the café. Sandra reached over and touched him on the forearm, "You all right?"

"Yeah. I've just got this overwhelming feeling that we're being watched." Sandra understood the feeling. Ever since she had been kidnapped she fought bouts of anxiety and paranoia. It was difficult for her to trust anyone, especially men. She checked out the street too. Cruz went to set his glass down on the table without looking and missed. It fell to the concrete patio and shattered, silencing the café chatter.

"Shit!" Cruz said as he grabbed his napkin and started to clean up the mess. A staff person ran out and swept the glass away, leaving just a puddle of water under Cruz. "Dammit, I'm sorry Sandra."

"No worries...we're all on edge."

"I don't get it. Even with Shaver in jail it seems like there's a constant threat."

"Shaver in jail doesn't mean this is over. He's got to have connections out here. It makes sense for us to stay vigilant." Cruz looked at her and admired her calm and strength. She was absolutely gorgeous, all facets of her, and Cruz wondered how he had missed it for so long.

"I'll be right back," Sandra said as she stood up and walked into the café. Cruz watched her and then stood up. Something overpowered him. Something rich and otherworldly. His heart pounded as he strode several feet behind Sandra. She took a quick glance over her shoulder and smiled when she saw him.

"Bathroom too?" she asked. Cruz shook his head no. She appeared slightly puzzled but continued to the women's bathroom which was around a corner from the café's main seating area. Cruz closed the distance between them and pushed the door to the women's bathroom open from behind her. Their bodies brushed together and sent electricity running up and down both of them. The bathroom was small, no one but them in it.

Sandra was startled but then melted when Cruz put his arm around her back and kissed her passionately. "Hey, I can't be seen..." Cruz ignored the comment and used his hand to raise her skirt. Her leg answered and curved around his thigh. They embraced each other in a half-starved craze. Sandra hooked her arms under Cruz's and pulled him in tight. The temperature in the room skyrocketed. Cruz felt himself become aroused as Sandra rubbed her leg and then her hand on his penis. He finished pulling up her skirt and grabbed her under her thighs, lifting her up to his waist and pressing her back against a wall. She grabbed the hair behind his head and mouthed love across his neck as he slid into her. They both groaned as their bodies swung in unison. Cruz with both hands full of Sandra's ass, squeezing tightly, as Sandra flung her head back and used it as leverage against the wall to push out against Cruz. Sweat streamed down Cruz's temples and started to bead on Sandra's chest. The rhythm became faster, harder. Their panting played off one another. The symbol of enjoyment kept taking them to higher levels of ecstasy. Cruz felt Sandra grinding into him, setting her own circular pattern to his vertical thrusts. Both of their bodies started to tense. Sandra's back arched and her nails dug into the back of Cruz's head. The sweet pain sent tremors through Cruz. They were in perfect unison now, not a single mis-step. Sandra started mumbling "Oh my god" as Cruz mustered all of his strength to pull Sandra closer. He slammed her against the wall as her fingers curled with fistfuls of hair. Her mouth opened in a silent scream as the climax ripped through every nerve, every muscle in her body. Cruz exploded at the same instant. He thrust and matched Sandra's climax, holding himself there as they shuddered together, a magnetic pulse bouncing between them. Cruz locked his lips on Sandra's who had to pull away to breath, her breath coming out in short expulsions. When her breathing slowed they kissed again, slowly, deeply. Cruz let Sandra down gently. He put out his hand and leaned on the wall. Aftershocks coursed through their bodies, an eternal release.

Cruz heard heels clicking on the tile floor outside the bathroom. When the person tried to push the door open, Cruz held it shut.

"Uhm, excuse me!"

"It's taken."

"That's a women's bathroom!"

"Get away, I'm a woman." Sandra slapped him on the shoulder.

"I'm..I'm going to get the manager!" Cruz heard the heels quickly click away as he rushed to pull his pants up and tuck his shirt in. Sandra was frantically fixing her hair in front of a mirror and then she bolted out of the bathroom, leaving Cruz with a swift kiss.

"I understand," he said, knowing that a scene like this could harm her career.

The heels were clicking back towards the bathroom. Cruz cinched his belt and opened the door to the red face of the café's manager.

"What the hell were you...well, I guess I don't have to ask that. Stay right here I'm going to call the cops." Cruz pushed the man aside with his shoulder and rushed through the café. The manager followed him, yelling. He ran forward and grabbed Cruz's collar. Cruz spun around the grabbed the man's hand, twisting his arm in the process.

"Fuck off...okay?" He stared into the manager's eyes until certain he wouldn't bother him anymore. All the people in the café stared as he hurried out the front door with a smile like a hyena's on his face.

# THIRTY-EIGHT

M artinez sat looking pensively at the desk of pictures in front of him. The police department was empty. Nightfall had come and only a few other lonely souls were left, scattered around the building. It hadn't necessarily been a welcome reception when he came back. He slipped in relatively unnoticed. Still, some watched him, one sneered. At this point he was a pariah so everyone steered clear.

He set up in one of the war rooms. It was secluded, quiet, no windows. Perfect for someone wanting to stay under the radar.

Usually pictures spoke to him. He had analyzed enough evidence to be able to create stories from the still images or written documents. The bruised faces combined with typewritten notes to weave an account. These pictures weren't talking, though.

Jerome Miller. Isabella Cordoba. Black and brown. Male and female. Connected to Shaver but by a string trailing off into darkness. He heard a quiet knock on the door. He hesitated to look up, but when he did he saw Cruz standing there.

"Hey, what the hell are you doing here?!"

Cruz stepped through the threshold of the room. "Nice hello."

Martinez shook his head in apology and stretched back over his chair, arms spread wide. Cruz stood next to the table of pictures, moving them around.

"You know, I had those in order," he said, slightly annoyed.

"Looks like you were accomplishing a lot," he said while gesturing to the mess in front of Martinez. "How about I fit some of the puzzle pieces here?"

"Go ahead."

Cruz analyzed the documents on the table and pushed one towards Martinez. "Check out Jerome's coroner report."

"Okay, I'm looking, what about it?"

"Did you have any dealings with the coroner back about this time?"

"Sure, almost on a weekly basis. What's that got to do....hey."

Cruz nodded his head.

"Who's that? Who's that there?" Martinez said pointing to the signature line on the report.

"You tell me."

"That certainly wasn't the coroner back then. Coroner was Dr. Chuck Swift," Martinez said with a furrowed brow.

"Remember where Tyler and the Chief were holed up with Sandra? The basement that seemed like a medical office?"

"Ohhh, shit. You think...this is a fake coroner then?"

"Not necessarily fake—the guy was a doctor. Just not the city's coroner." Cruz took off the hat he was wearing and set it down authoritatively on the table.

"This may implicate the Chief, but we don't care about him anymore. I mean, maybe Sandra would want to run a story on his corruption, but we're focused on the case against Shaver." Someone slid past the room and they both stopped, looking at each other but with their ears tuned to the hallway. They continued talking after sensing that the person was out of earshot.

"The only piece of the puzzle that can still talk is Tyler."

"That creep."

"I know," Cruz said. "I don't understand how he isn't locked away too. That should change soon though."

"How?"

"The DA..."

"Mason..."

"Yeah, Mason. He told me to get you and to bring Tyler in."

Martinez thought about that for a second then said, "Hell Cruz, I don't even know my status on the force right now. It's all a freakin' mess. I'm still all sorts of wound up. Carmen is begging me to take some time off. Losing Williams and Alicia weighs on me daily."

Cruz sat quietly, reading Martinez as these emotions rose to the surface and then hung in the air around them. Martinez sat shaking his head. "You know, Martinez, you were a tremendous source of strength for me throughout all of this. Doing what's right is most important—still is."

Martinez brushed a hand through his hair and then rested his forehead on his palms. "Let's go get a cup of Joe and think it out. We aren't gonna go nab him right now anyway."

Cruz appreciated the accommodation. Martinez bear hugged the documents on the desk into a pile and shoved them into his backpack. Cruz followed as Martinez led them through the old, winding corridors of the department. They reached the glass front doors of the building and pushed them open. That familiar bitterly cool air stung Cruz. He used the collar of his sweater to protect his mouth and nose. They walked out to Martinez's car which was sitting alone like an old man in a timeless train station.

"Aww, dammit," Martinez said.

"What's that?"

"I think I left my keys on my desk." They stood there in the cold about fifteen feet from the car. The next thing Cruz knew he was laying on what he thought was his back. Must have been, there were stars.

There was a totally deaf bliss. Embers spun like headless ballerinas into the night sky. Cruz had a warm feeling. He never wanted to look anywhere else. The warmth made him tired and he started to close his eyes.

Then he saw Martinez over him. Gesturing wildly. Shaking him. His right ear popped and the wailing pitch of a siren became faintly audible. Another pop and the swoosh of billowing flames came into being. He wondered what existed without sound.

"Cruz! Can you fucking hear me? Cruz, Cruz!" Three Martinez's swayed like vipers over him. Their heads vibrated and slowly consolidated into one. And then Martinez was gone. Cruz rolled over on his stomach. The black pavement was chilled and rough on his face. He pushed up with his arms and put one foot out in front of himself.

Martinez ran off around the corner of the police station about seventy feet in front of him. Cruz stood up and his left leg almost crumpled. A wobble to the left, then a sway to the right and then the earth's axis seemed to realign. He stumbled forward, picking up pace into a zombie-like jog. Tires screeched from around the corner and he saw Martinez sprinting back around the station toward him. Strange, Cruz thought, until he saw a vehicle shoot out of the alleyway and pummel through the chain-link fence surrounding the station.

Martinez grabbed Cruz as he ran by. He threw Cruz into the back of one of the squad cars and jumped into the driver's seat. Keys were hanging in the ignition. "Cruz, hold on back there." Cruz couldn't tell if it was a joke because there wasn't a damn thing to hold onto. Martinez gunned the engine and peeled out of the parking lot before Cruz could complain.

"Can you believe it? That fucker Tyler tried to fucking run me over!" Cruz nodded. "After he tried to blow us both up!!" Cruz sat limply in the back seat, jostled as Martinez sped through turns and cut over sidewalks. "You all there, Cruz? Can you hear me?"

"Yeah...I can hear you..." Cruz mustered. "I couldn't hear anything after the blast...for at least a few seconds."

"Me neither. That shit was close!"

"I still feel it," Cruz said while running a hand over his body. He looked around the headrest and saw a pair of taillights dashing away in front of them. "Why am I sitting back here?"

"Don't know. Seemed like the easiest place to swing you to." Cruz grabbed onto the two front seats, "We going straight for a few seconds?"

"Looks like it." Cruz tucked his head and pulled himself forward. His knees bumped his chest as he stepped over the center console. They swerved around another car as he plopped down into the front passenger's seat. They drifted around a corner and Tyler's car was in plain sight ahead. Martinez floored the accelerator and the Crown Vic responded with gusto.

There they were, speeding through a nearly empty city at just before three in the morning. Every now and again another car would appear and then immediately pull over. The flashing lights on their car created an eerie illumination on the surrounding buildings. Not fully lighting the buildings, but just enough light to be able to imagine things.

Tyler's car was getting larger with each cut and dash. Martinez was clearly a better driver. Probably sensing the closing gap, the chase began to move out of the city. The buildings progressively became shorter and more spread out. Both cars soon approached top speed on a two-lane road leading out to the suburbs. Martinez and Cruz inched closer.

"Car 247 what's your 20?" The shrill, electronic voice over the C.B. radio startled them both.

"About seven miles out of town," Martinez answered into a hand-held walkie-talkie.

The radio crackled and then the same voice asked, "Can you be more specific?"

"Suspect is fleeing, will get location once I've apprehended him." He set the hand-held down and turned the radio off. They were just a few feet behind Tyler's car.

They wove around cars like a pair of connected dragonflies. The road opened up two more lanes and Martinez briefly looked at Cruz, "This is our chance."

"To do what?"

"Ram this shit off the road."

"Uhm, okay." Cruz instinctively checked his seat belt and grabbed onto the door handle.

"Technically, it's a bump and not a ram. It should be pretty easy."

"You're going to flip his car? Don't we need him alive?"

Martinez's shoulders slumped. "Dammit, I hadn't thought about that. I was so pissed that all I wanted to do was flip the fucker."

Cruz was having a hard time staying put on the vinyl bench seat. The muscles on his thick forearms bulged as he threaded through the moderate traffic. What the hell are all of these people doing out anyway, Cruz thought to himself.

They neared the rear bumper of Tyler's car. Tyler must have sensed how close they were because he weaved to the left. As Martinez was about to follow him a roaring screech sounded and smoke gathered where Tyler's car had been. Now he was directly behind *them*.

"What the fuck, top gun!" Martinez yelled at Tyler's car. They both felt a bump and the rear end of their car loosened then regained traction. "You know what? I'll stop right in front of him. I'm not the one running. Hold on 'cause it's gonna get bumpy." Cruz looked around but there was nothing more substantial to grab onto than the door handle. Martinez braced and watched his rear view mirror for Tyler to approach them. When Tyler got close, Martinez centered their car on his and hit the brakes.

The impact of Tyler's car whipped both of their heads back into the headrests. Cruz could smell the burning rubber as they got pushed down the highway. The brute force of Tyler's car versus the brakes on the squad car. The brakes were slowly winning.

Martinez was doing his best to keep the wheels straight. The slightest move off-center and they would be sent into a tailspin. As their speed continued to decrease, Tyler must have realized that he was losing the battle. He stopped his car to disengage and then started to go around them.

"The *hell* you will!" Martinez bellowed. As Martinez wrenched the wheel to his right to cut Tyler off, they both caught sight of a SUV speeding down the highway. The next thing they knew, Tyler's car was sliding sideways and then flipping over. A wave of fluid flew out of the hood of Tyler's car as bits of headlights and windshield hung like illuminated fireflies in the night.

The SUV seemed little effected. It had a brush bar on its front bumper. "Get the last three!" Martinez said as he strained to see the license plate.

"Jesus. The last three of what, Martinez?"

"The license plate!" Cruz looked up but the car was too far in the distance to catch the license plate numbers.

"I couldn't get them. What just happened?" Cruz asked, in shock.

Martinez leaned back in his seat and pounded his fist on the steering wheel. "A hit."

* * * *

Sphinx lounged with his head rested on his hand watching the television. He took up all and more of the television room's couch. Legs spilling over the armrest, wide shoulders hanging over the edge of the couch.

The television was muted. He couldn't stand to listen to the commentary. Two cars sped down streets that Sphinx worked to identify. They were leaving the city, drifting turn by turn. Evenly matched and so not gaining on each other. When they reached the highway the helicopter was able to provide a steadier shot. A small circle of light illuminated the two cars as they wound through traffic.

Then the car being chased moved over to another lane and slammed on its brakes. Sphinx laughed and sat up. The tables were turned now. But the car now in front wasn't running. Sphinx leaned forward to see what was going on. The white car—the car in back—finally gave up the push and started to pull out from behind the other car.

"Holy shit!" Sphinx exclaimed as a black SUV pile-drove the white car. "Dammmmmmn. What the hell was that?!" He ran over to flip a light on, more out of reverence to the fact that this needed to be studied than to his inability to see the television. He also unmuted the action.

"We've just witnessed a catastrophic crash..." the reporter said as the white car flipped and then toppled on its roof. "This...this can't lead to anything but fatalities. The two officers appear to be unscathed as they emerge from their squad car. The SUV has disappeared into the night."

A row of squad cars arrived at the scene and officers in black uniforms melted out on the highway. Sphinx could imagine the long wail of an approaching ambulance interposed with bursts of siren chatter as it made its way through traffic. Then it arrived, the white and red hood of an ambulance spilled color into the otherwise dark scene. The helicopter hovered over the crash. A few squad cars went squealing into the night beyond the helicopter's light, presumably to find the SUV. Sphinx went to the kitchen to grab a glass of orange juice.

"3:05—dammit." He usually didn't sleep more than a few of hours, but tonight he only slept one or two. It was hard to remember. It was as if the crisp lines of his life were starting to break down around him. He slurred the facts of cases together. Sometimes he messed up his kids' names. He couldn't remember the last time he and any of his ex-wives had sex. That used to be a consistent stream.

This loss of grip on facts and reality affected his psyche. He imagined a tumor growing in his head, pushing on the part of the brain that controls memory. Whatever that part was. He imagined heart palpitations, a lack of blood flow due to high blood pressure. When his teeth ached he saw them falling out of his mouth with one powerful bite. There was no way around it— growing old sucked.

He grunted where most people would sigh and shut the door to the refrigerator. "...most likely will be pronounced dead at the scene..." Sphinx couldn't separate whether he despised the actual commentary or the way it was delivered. Those reporters were soulless. They teemed around tragedy, whiffing the air like starved street dogs.

His home phone rang. Sphinx paused mid-gulp, looking at the phone curiously. After a few rings he picked it up.

"You like that?" a voice asked him.

\* \* \* \*

Sandra stood behind the cordoned accident scene. Cruz had called her as soon as he got his bearings. People bustled around, each with their singular task. A splendor of delegation and acceptance. Martinez and Cruz sat on the back bumper of an ambulance. EMTs checked their eyes, poking, prodding, asking them to move this shoulder this way and flex that knee backwards. Red and blue lights reflected in the spilled fluids under Tyler's car.

Cruz lifted his head and smiled when he saw Sandra. He gestured for her to come over. She lifted the yellow tape and walked toward the ambulance.

"You aren't reporting this?"

"No, Charlie is," she said pointed to a row of reporters lit up by portable lights.

"Did you see the whole thing?"

"Most of it. I was just waking up when you guys were getting out of the city. What happened? Are you okay?"

"Hey Sandra," Martinez said.

"Hi Martinez. You guys okay?"

"Oh yeah," Cruz answered. "Freakin' dandy. Tyler took the brunt of it, though."

"So a random SUV plowed through him and then left?"

"I doubt it was that random," Martinez said.

"You think someone set this up?"

"Yep," Martinez said as he straightened up and stretched out. "If you all don't mind, I'm gonna head home. Maybe I can slip into bed before Carmen wakes up."

"Where do we go with this case now?" Cruz asked Martinez.

Martinez shrugged his shoulders, "I'm really not sure." He sighed. "Everyone's toast."

"Tyler's dead?" Sandra asked.

"Yeah," Cruz answered.

"They already bagged him up," Martinez added. "All right kiddos, I'm out." Martinez went to the line of cops and cajoled a ride.

"Cruz, do you agree with Martinez, that this was set up?"

"I can't see any other explanation. I mean, three in the morning and some black SUV barrels through Tyler's stopped car? That's more than coincidence. On top of that, it speeds off? A regular person isn't going to act that way. Just too much coincidence for it to be anything else." Cruz paused. "Someone doesn't want this trial to happen. Someone wants all potential voices silenced, and I think it's pretty apparent Shaver's the one." Cruz took a wet cloth and wiped his face. The only things that hurt were his lower back and neck. He felt pretty lucky. "Can we head out?"

"Sure," she said, leading him to her car. They got in and drove from the buzzing accident scene. "What's all that black soot on your clothes."

Cruz looked at her, "You didn't see that part?"

"What part?"

"When Martinez and I walked out of the police station to get into his squad car, the car blew up."

"What?!" Sandra exclaimed.

"Wow, I figured that would have been on television too. The fucking car blew up. If Martinez hadn't forgotten his keys, we would have been dead. I've still got a bit of ringing in my right ear," Cruz said while he stuck a finger in his ear and moved it from side to side.

"Then what happened?"

"Martinez and I jumped into a car and chased Tyler. It was Tyler who tried to kill us there."

"I can't believe it. I had no idea that happened...where are we going by the way?"

"My office."

"Now? It's just past four and after all you just went through? How about a cup of coffee instead?"

"I appreciate it but I've got to talk to Mason about this."

"The district attorney?"

"Yeah. He was the one that sent me to pick up Tyler."

Sandra looked at him, surprised. "He sent you? Why on earth would he send you?"

"He said Martinez and I knew the case best. It would make the most sense for us to go."

"The district attorney sent you to arrest Tyler and you end up almost blown up and then in a car chase where Tyler gets run over? Talk about coincidence."

Cruz shook his head no. "I don't see anything there, Sandra. Mason's a good man."

"Good man or not, he sends you of all people, not a cop or anything, to arrest an assassin and you are almost killed two times." Cruz didn't respond, but the suggestion bothered him a bit. So many weird things had happened in the past weeks that it was hard to know who to trust. They rode silently until they reached his office.

"Cruz, it's early still. Mason isn't even going to be up."

"I guarantee you he's up if I know his type. You have to understand— this case will be his legacy."

* * * *

Mason had a restless night. His gut was working overtime. The case lacked any definition. Pitting the testimony of quasi-vigilantes against a cop was anything but certain. When two o'clock rolled around and the hope of getting to sleep vanished, he quietly slipped out of bed. The stairs creaked as he went to grab a glass of water to break down the accumulated dryness in his mouth. He picked up a stack of research that Todd had pulled for him and slunked down into his favorite chair.

"Daddy?" Abby appeared like clockwork. She was the most concerned child Mason ever encountered. Her brother, on the other hand, was as careless and free-willed as she was attentive and attached. She rubbed both of her eyes with balled-up hands. Her dirty blond hair was bed-shaped and wild.

"Yes, hon?" he said as he went to pick her up.

"What are you doing awake, Daddy?"

He picked her up and gave her a kiss on her forehead. She folded down onto his shoulder. "Just doing some work, hon. You know daddy's work." She nodded her head but didn't say a word. She was already back to sleep. As Mason was stepping out of the room something caught his eye on the television screen. It was a car chase moving through downtown. He hurried Abby to her bedroom and went back out to the living room. After fumbling to find the remote, he turned the sound on and stood close to the television.

"...a chase that seems to have begun near the police station has taken to the streets of downtown. At this time we do not know who the police are chasing..." He watched the pursuit as it coiled and then spread out down

224

congested city streets. His gut started speaking to him again. The steady shot of the helicopter's camera belied the chaos of the car chase.

"Cruz, I hope that's not you down there."

"...for ten minutes Sally." Mason grabbed his cell phone and dialed Cruz. No answer. "Goddammit!" He watched intently as the cars burst onto the highway. "...appears that the two cars are headed out of the city, which should lessen the danger of this chase..." The cars were in some sort of standoff. The car in front was actually now in back and trying to push the squad car. When that didn't work the car pulled out into an adjacent lane.

"Oh, shit!" Mason yelled as the white car was run over by a black SUV. "Oh my God, what the hell was that?!" He paced back and forth in the room, debating whether to try to call Cruz again. He called Todd instead.

A weary voice answered the phone, "Are you fucking nuts?"

"Turn the television on."

"No, Mason, I'm freakin' sleeping. You should give it a shot."

"Listen, Todd, I'm not messing around. Turn the television on." Silence. "Todd?"

A half awake Todd answered, "Yeah?"

"What the...did you go back to sleep? Turn on the damn television!" This time a moan came through the crackle of the telephone and he heard Todd cuss as he got up.

"I swear Mason, this better be good. What channel?"

"It doesn't matter. It's on all of the stations." Mason heard Todd's television pop and then crackle the static away.

"A car accident? A car accident, Mason?! I know you didn't wake me up for this."

Mason said, "I think I know who's in the cars."

"Who?" The helicopter's camera focus shifted from the white car to the squad car. Two men emerged. "Wait. Wait, wait. Let me get my glasses because I think I recognize that person," Todd said. Mason stood with his arms crossed in the living room, posture slightly bent back from his correctness.

"Who is it, Todd?" Mason mimicked.

"Jesus, wasn't that guy in your office? Cruz, right?"

"That's right."

"Oh no. Who's in the white car?"

"I think we both know the answer to that, Todd. I'm going to clean up and then head into the office."

"It's three in the morning, Mason."

"I don't care. It's my office. I'll see you there soon."

"Not that soon," Todd said.

Mason put his glass of orange juice down on the kitchen counter and went back to his bedroom. His wife was still asleep. She had the fantastic ability to sleep through anything. Nuclear war. Two children under the age of three. Mason envied her ability most times. Other times he felt sorry for her. She was missing so much. The media-prescribed requirement of eight hours of sleep per day wrenched one third of their lives away. He got by on four a day, max. It wasn't worth trying to wake her up. He had learned that a while ago. Instead, he would leave her a note like always.

Mason cleaned up quickly, grabbed his briefcase and headed out to the garage. The world outside the garage was calm, sweet and untouched. The still untarnished morning air rushed in and wafted over him. He slid into the car seat, backed out into their cul-de-sac, then dialed Cruz again after getting out on the road.

After a few seconds Cruz answered, "Mason."

"Christ, Cruz, are you all right?"

"Yeah, just shell-shocked. What about you?"

"Me? Sure, I'm doing fine. Except that a key witness was pasted to the dashboard of his car like snot."

"It's a problem."

"No kidding. I'm headed into work. Was that Martinez with you?"

"Yep."

"How's he doing?"

"Martinez is fine. I don't think seeing someone killed has much effect on him. Especially when it's someone like Tyler."

"So, it was Tyler," Mason said, reconfirming the negative. Cruz didn't need to respond. "I can't bring the extra charges for those other murders without Tyler. My case against Shaver for killing that old man rests on a video that we may not be able to introduce and the testimony of people that may easily be discredited. This is turning south."

Cruz waited to answer. His thoughts were forming at a snail's pace. "Every case has peaks and valleys, Mason. You just hope it has another peak, preferably near its end."

\* \* \* \*

Shaver sat in his cell watching the television. It was one of the perks the guards gave him. Extra time on the yard. Extra food at meals.

He knew it may piss the other inmates off, so he kept them to a minimum.

He did take the time to enjoy this moment though. Tyler's car was smashed and laying upside down. He could imagine Tyler's shock. Completely disoriented, gasping for air. Cold chills running up and down his body. A sense of weakness and no ability to fight back. Shaver rubbed the remnant of his left eye. It was a squishy mess since the accident.

Dealing a remote knockout to Tyler made Shaver feel like a god. He had decided to take Tyler out because the cops were getting too close, and Tyler wasn't reporting any results from their earlier conversation. He picked up the cell phone he had finagled from the guards and dialed Sphinx. That one-call-a week crap wasn't going to work.

"You like that?"

"Shaver?" a bewildered Sphinx answered.

"Damn straight. You like that little accident?"

"Man, what the hell are you doing? Are you saying you had a part in that?"

"Just like you did, Sphinx."

A long pause. "It's three in the morning, what the fuck are you talking about?"

"How could I have coordinated something like that without the help of my top-notch lawyer?"

"You fuck, are you trying to blackmail me? You crazy shit, I'll just withdraw as your counsel."

"Nah, I've been reading up. Ain't that easy to get out," Shaver said as he moved from his chair to the bed. A small package with a string attached to it was sitting outside of his cell.

"Shaver...Shaver," someone called from down the cell row.

"Listen. You can't withdraw this close to trial. The prejudice you'd do me would be huge. No, you're gonna represent me. And if you don't win, I've got all sorts of shit up my sleeves for you. I gotta go." Shaver hung up the phone and tentatively moved toward his cell door. The package moved away from his cell in jerks. He stood there and watched as the package slid down the cell row again, stopping right in front of his cell.

"Shaver...take the package," a voice told him with some urgency.

"Who the fuck...?" Shaver said as he stuck his head in the thick steel bars of his cell door. He didn't know there were any other inmates housed here with him.

"It's Pick. Take th' goddamn package before th' guards come 'round 'gin."

"Forget that, Pick. I've sold four batches for you guys. That's a debt repaid in my mind. I need a two-way street."

"Every day you alive in here id our side of the street muddafucka. Take the package."

Shaver grabbed the package angrily. Just as he did the shadow of a figure passed on the far side of the cell block.

He heard a female voice say, "Hi Pick."

Pick responded, "Fuck you, bitch." The person's steps coincided with rapping on cell doors, then scraping on the walls between the cells. She was clearly coming toward him.

"Whatcha got Shaver?" It was the female cop from the yard. She had lost some of her plainness. Maybe it was makeup, a little spritz from life, whatever. Shaver couldn't tell exactly but she looked somewhat more attractive than the last time he had seen her.

"What do you want?" he said as he turned his back to her and went to sit down in front of the television.

"Already asked you that, tough guy. What'd Pick pass you?"

"Not a fucking thing. Now fuck off!" Shaver yelled.

"Oh, Shaver. I think you're confusing me for some weak bitch. Stay still right there." Shaver turned around and saw her pointing a tazer at him. It was too late to do anything. His body became stiff as a board, jaws clenched and head pushed back until his chair tipped over backwards.

"Yowch!" she exclaimed.

"Yous a crazy bitch, Melinda!" Shaver heard Pick yell. Sound was still a hundred percent there. Smell, check. He couldn't move anything though. Then his body slackened and he started convulsing on the ground. He heard the cell door open.

"Stop moving Shaver! Stop moving!" she mocked him. She had the tazer in her right hand, a baton in her left. She stood over him and put her foot on Shaver's shoulder to flatten him out against the concrete floor. Then she lowered herself onto him. Her hips were right over his neck. Her legs pinned down his arms. "One wrong move and I'll crack the side of your face open. Not that you'll be moving much in the next few minutes, but just a warnie-warning, Shaver." She set the tazer down and grabbed the ends of the baton. Then she put the baton up against his neck.

"What did he pass you, Shaver? I see everything," she said with a smile. Then she started searching his body. "Ah ha! Knew you had a package." She put the baton under her left arm and opened it. "That's a bunch of coke Shaver! My, my." Shaver could feel his finger regain mobility. "Why'd you lie to me, Shaver? I've been trying to help you out around here," she said as she swiped the package across his face. He coughed and almost choked on vomit that came up. "Thought I told ya to steer clear of the Brothers, Shaver."

She went to put the package down and Shaver made his move. He ripped one of the tazer's prongs from his neck and jabbed it into her arm. He simultaneously grabbed the tazer and activated the electric current. This time both of their bodies stiffened. Her crotch pushed down on his jaw and her knees slammed into the sides of his head. Her face was locked in a grimace. A row of white teeth about to burst from her jaw's own pressure. She collapsed to his side, both of them bouncing on the ground. Some horrific, above-ground synchronized swimming. Shaver felt an acidic foam form in his mouth and then spill out onto the floor. He was completely paralyzed.

"Hey, yous, whud th' fuck id goin' on down ther'?" Pick started to shake the bars of his cell. "Hey, hey...guards!! Guuuuuarrrds!" Red lights began to flash in the cell block. A group of five guards in helmets with plastic visors, Kevlar body vests and various weapons moved in unison towards Shaver's cell. Shaver was close to losing consciousness. He heard one of the guards mutter, "What the fuck?"

They pulled Melinda out of the cell and one of the guards screamed for medical personnel. Shaver still had the occasional convulsion as his muscles tensed and then released. His jaw felt like it had been repeatedly punched. Mobility stated to return. One of the guards grabbed the tazer and pulled the prong out of Shaver's neck. Two of the other guards secured his hands and legs with plastic ties.

Shaver managed to mutter, "She did it."

"Sure, sure, guy. I'm sure she did all of this to you for no reason. You're never gonna leave here after this."

"That bitch is crazy!" Pick screamed. "She shot his ass from outsid' the cell!"

"You'll be able to tell your story to the Warden, Pick."

"Oh, hell no!" Pick pushed away from the cell door and kicked his bed. The Warden was a damn nightmare. "Look, can'cha jus' take my statement down here?"

"Nope. Warden visit for you, Pick. I appreciate you opening that flap and letting us know you are a witness though."

"Wouldn'a fuckin' mattered. I was gonna see him anyways." Pick sat

## Derek Blass

down on his bed, dejected. He watched as they wheeled Shaver by him on a gurney. "Damn Warden. Damn yous, Shaver."

# THIRTY-NINE

"Carmen?" Raul opened his eyes and looked at the room around him. It was a hospital room, pock-marked bricks painted glossy white. The room had a single window with a view out to the *campo*. Raul turned back to Carmen, who radiated a warm smile. She rubbed his forehead and adjusted the covers.

"Where am I?"

"In the hospital, brother."

"You came from the United States to see me?"

"Of course. When the doctors contacted me and let me know you were recovering, of course I came."

"Recovering from what, Carmen?" He looked down at his arms which were covered with bandages. His left arm ached and he saw a PICC line. His chest was sore and he found it difficult to breath deeply.

"You don't remember anything?"

He shook his head, dismayed. "I feel like I've lost so much weight. Look at my *brazos hermana*."

"Raul, what do you remember?"

"Honestly, the last thing I remember clearly is being at Shaver's house. Things go dark there. I thought I was dead. Stuck somewhere."

She shook her head and wondered what he could take at this point. Then, she recalled how strong he always was, never fearful, always confident. "You've been in a coma for five weeks, Raul. About a week ago you started showing signs of coming out. I've been here since then."

He tried to move his legs but they wouldn't respond. "I can't feel my legs, Carmen. Am I on some sort of medication that does that to me?" She walked to a little cart by the side of his bed and poured him a glass of water. He took the glass with an appreciative smile. Tears began to run down her face and she quickly turned away. Raul started to lift his blanket but Carmen spun back around and held his hand.

"Don't look now, Raul."

"What are you talking about, Carmen? *De que hablas?!*"

"They couldn't do anything else, Raul. The doctors...they had no choice. They called me and told me that one leg was irrecoverable from the damage it took..."

"Irrecoverable?"

"...and the other got too infected to keep. They couldn't do anything."

Raul pushed her hand away and lifted the cover. There was nothing below his waist.

He scrutinized the emptiness for a moment. Then he put the cover down and squinted at Carmen. "It is the strangest thing, because I swore they were there a minute ago. I figured I just couldn't move them. But...they're gone. My legs are gone." He started to break down. He wept on Carmen's arm while she rubbed his back. "*Que voy a hacer?*"

"The doctors have been talking about prosthetics. They didn't want to do anything until they knew how this was going to turn out."

"I go to sleep a man and wake up a cripple. What am I going to do Carmen? They won't let a cripple on television."

"You don't know that, Raul. Let's worry about other things first, like getting you healthy again."

"Healthy?! You mean getting my torso healthy?" He tried to roll over but couldn't. "I can't even move, Carmen! *Chingado!*"

A doctor and nurse came into the room. "*Hola, cómo están?*"

Carmen flashed a fake smile and greeted the doctor. "Mister Solis, it's fantastic to see you are awake. Do you feel alert?"

"Yes doctor, I feel *very* alert. I feel like I've awoken from siesta to a damn nightmare."

"Your legs. There was nothing we could do, *Señor.*"

Raul moaned and threw his head back onto the stiff, hospital pillow.

The doctor went around Raul's body checking measurements, levels, temperatures. Analyzing beats, sounds, and pressing cold medical instruments onto Raul's brown skin. Methodical. The doctor put his clipboard down onto Raul's bed and clasped his hands together. "Rehabilitation, Mr. Solis. That will be our goal here. You can start..."

"*Mira*, fucking doctor. I don't care about rehabilitation," Raul growled, mocking the doctor's stiffness. "I only want one thing," he said while directing his gaze at Carmen. "Find me Shaver."

\* \* \* \*

Shaver sat in the cafeteria pushing orange and green bits of vegetables around a corner of his tray. The food depressed him. He looked up and saw Mills staring at him. Then Mills beckoned. He pushed his tray aside and walked over to the group. It was always a group.

"You can't shun us, Shaver," Mills said. "Everyone's always watchin'".

"I know that, but I've met my end of the bargain." Shaver looked around and caught glances from the nearby rival gangs. "If I need help again, then we'll talk."

Mills smiled a yellow-toothed grin and pulled back his stringy brown hair with one hand. "It dun work thad way Shaver. Yous our bitch. We ain't yours." Mills stood up and gestured to Pick. Pick slid down the cafeteria table and handed a package to Shaver.

"Consider id protection."

Two guards approached the table and Shaver quickly shoved the package into his pants. "Shaver, you're coming with us."

"What for? I'm just eating." One of the guards looked at him suspiciously.

"The Warden wants to see you." Pick quietly moved away from the table, joining Mills and the rest as they walked out of the cafeteria. Shaver put his hands out and the guards handcuffed him.

"All of this even though I'm a cop?"

"Shhh. That's liable to get you fucked around here Shaver."

"They all know already. Only reason they haven't touched me is because they know I'll probably kill them first."

"Anyway," the other guard started, "the Warden don't know you yet. He ain't about to take chances." The guards stood on either side of Shaver and grabbed onto his arms. They led him through the cafeteria and into the main corridor. He shuffled his feet even though he didn't have to. The guards yanked at him from time to time.

The corridor seemed to stretch on forever. It was a dilapidated prison. The paint on the walls was faded and the plaster underneath was starting to fall apart in places. The bottom half of the walls were barely green. The upper portions of the walls were grimy, full of hand prints and stains.

"Don't you guys ever clean this place?"

"For what? Y'alls comfort? Nah. This ain't a resort Shaver. Too many resort prisons around the country. Where television is expected, three-course meals like y'all got." They continued to drag Shaver through the corridors. "The Warden don't believe in all that shit. He always says that his primary concern is the taxpayers. They's the ones payin' for all this."

"What's his name?"

"The Warden?" The guard chuckled. "Just Warden to you—and the rest of us. Ain't like we're pals with the man, know what I mean." They arrived at a lonely set of double doors. One of the guards knocked.

"Yes?" a voice responded from inside.

## Derek Blass

"We got Shaver here, Warden."

"Bring him on in then." One guard pushed the double doors open while the other led Shaver into the room. Light streamed in from three windows around the Warden's office. The window directly behind him was the largest, and the setting sun shone right into it. The Warden was an older man, perhaps early sixties. Sun and wind-glazed face. A pair of penetrating brown eyes set into his rectangular head. His gray hair was partially covered by a tilted back cowboy hat, on the verge of falling off but always under the Warden's control. He had a toothpick in his mouth which he rolled from side to side with his tongue. His hands were busy cutting a cigar. He spit the toothpick out to light the cigar.

"That's all, gentlemen," the Warden said out of the side of his mouth.

"You sure, Warden?"

He looked up from his cigar. "A cuffed man. A fellow officer of the law. Not much to worry about here." The guards hesitated, but they left when the Warden gave them one more cross look.

"You like Sinatra?" the Warden asked Shaver.

"Not a fan."

The Warden went over to an old record player and picked out a record from a shelf loaded with them. He placed the record on the player and laid the stylus down onto the record with exquisite care. Familiar notes of *New York, New York* played in that wavy and old-time-comforting sound only record players could create. "When I go to your house, you can pick the music."

The Warden's office was outdated. Wood panels, an old shag carpet. He had signs everywhere. Some from his own campaigns. Others were apparently signs meant for the benefit of inmates that had to meet him. The Warden adjusted his big glasses and walked to the window overlooking the yard.

"You know, before I became the Warden, this was the third worst prison in the United States in terms of violence and drugs. In the sixteen years since I've been here, we've turned around to become the second best."

"Who's the best?" Shaver asked.

"Eh, some prison out in Tallahassee. But the point is that with the right person and the right agenda, even the biggest problem can be turned around." The Warden returned to his chair and leaned back. The cigar was pressed deep and into the side of his mouth. "The problem I'm talking about is all the goddamn immigrants coming 'cross our border. Now, I used to call them all Mexicans but apparently that ain't fucking accurate. I guess some come from

Guatemala, Honduras, El Salvador and on and on. I couldn't give two shits less. To me, they're all brown and they ain't here the right way."

Shaver shrugged his shoulders. "I think we've both seen this problem in action."

"You bet I have! This jail is sixty-five percent...brown." The Warden twisted the cigar in his mouth and continued, "I've had to change my staff to employ people that speak their damn language. In my country, no less, I have to accommodate *them*! I sit here and read the paper. I see these parasites taking jobs, causing violence, bringing drugs into the country, using our health care and finally, ending up in my fucking jail. So not only are they infesting our country—I mean look at the southwest—but *we're paying for them to do it*! It blows my mind."

"Like I said, Warden, I'm on your side. But, what's your point here?"

"Well, first, I had to drag you in here because of what you did to one of my guards." The Warden pulled something out from his desk drawer and before Shaver could react, he had the prongs of a tazer in him again.

"Goddammit, not again."

"You pull some shit like that in my prison again and I'll tazer you for an hour straight. If you don't die you'll be so fried that no one will ever get through to you again. See, the beauty of these tazers is that you can do whatever you like with 'em. If people ain't around, I could tazer you for two minutes and they wouldn't be able to tell if it was two minutes or two seconds."

"I've done it. Plenty of times."

"See what I mean? So you know. Fuck around, and I'll kill ya. But, I don't want that. What I want is for you to serve your time here until your trial is over, and then get your ass out." The Warden tapped his cigar on an ash tray and then leaned over the desk. "We need more warriors like you out there. You're never going to single-handedly eradicate that problem we're talking about. But, if you strike fear into the hearts of these immigrants, if you let them know that they ain't-fuckin'-welcome, well then, that should take care of some of the problem."

"I'm doing my part," the Warden went on. "Since this wave of shit started to come over the border I've been as anti-immigration as an elected official can be. I've reallocated nearly fifty percent of my budget to tackle issues related to the immigrants. I work with the feds to make sure every possible illegal bastard, and bitch, and kid and grandparent and whatever the else they throw at us is reported and deported." The Warden stopped for a moment. "You know, I really like that," he said while taking out a pad and pen of paper. "Report 'em and Deport 'em."

"I'm for the cause, Warden," Shaver said. "There's not much I can do while I'm stuck in here though."

"I understand that. And as much pull as I've got, all the pull in the world ain't gonna get you out scot-free. You're gonna to have to submit yourself to the mercy of twelve members of our community. Just hope none of 'em are those pansy liberals that support the immigrants! Or immigrant rights, or human rights, or any of that other shit they throw in our faces."

"Like I said, I get all this. Why'd you bring me here though?"

"Lots of reasons. To put a face to the name. To give you a warning about what you did to my guard." The Warden put his hand on his crotch and adjusted his pants. "There's one more thing."

"Oh yeah? What's that, because this has been a waste of my time so far."

The Warden leaned over his desk and grabbed Shaver by the shirt, "You be careful, Shaver! One fucking slip in here and I'll feed ya to the brown or black scum. I know you've got those brain-dead, drug-dealing Nazis on your side now, but that don't mean shit if it's up to me." He shoved Shaver back into the chair and adjusted his own collar. "You want to hear what I've got, or not?"

"Sure," Shaver said as he raised his handcuffed hands to his head and scratched.

"The grapevine tells me that your case has one big snag."

"The video."

"Yeah, the video. If they show that video during your trial, you're as good as in here with me for-fuckin'-ever."

"Ain't that hell," Shaver said while baring his teeth.

"I can keep it out."

Shaver grunted. "How the hell you going to keep a piece of evidence like that out of the trial? Give it a rest."

"The judge, he and I went to law school together. He's a connoisseur of certain...objects. I used my connections in enforcement to get him off a long time ago. Been under my thumb since then."

"Why would you use up a favor like that on me?"

The Warden pushed back toward his credenza and spun around in his chair. He opened one of the drawers and pulled out a bottle of liquor. "Whiskey?"

Shaver shrugged his shoulders. "Sure." The Warden poured some into two tumblers and handed one to Shaver. The setting sun burned the clouds outside of the office. Shaver held the glass up to his mouth and took a sip of the liquor. It set his stomach on fire. A rich, comforting tear.

"I hate the gangs in this place Shaver. They keep sendin' them to me though. I'll never be able to get rid of them. They call shots from in here to the outside, just as harmful as if they were out. I want you to get rid of them."

"Get rid of the prison gangs? I've got five weeks until my trial date. You want me to get rid of the prison gangs in five weeks?"

"Probably before that, if you want that evidence excluded."

"Man, you've *got* to be joking. How do you expect me to do something like that?"

"Shaver, you've been in a gang unit before. You know how these animals work."

"And you've been watching over these animals for years. What makes me any better?"

"You've got access to the inner belly, Shaver. That's somewhere I'll never be able to go. You plant a bomb there, take them all out."

"It's suicide."

"So is staying in this place. Your luck will run out, Shaver. Most of the inmates don't even know your history yet. Soon as they do, you and the pedophiles will be like a fresh slab of meat to a pack of wolves." The Warden took down his whole glass of whiskey in a gulp. "You got a choice. You can try to make it out of here, or you can guarantee your fate."

Shaver shot the rest of his whiskey and slammed the glass down on the Warden's desk. There were two paths in front of him, both fraught with danger. The first, staying in the prison, had a one percent chance of survival. The other, trying to start an all-out gang war in less than five weeks, maybe three percent. There wasn't really anything to ponder. A person would take any risk to get out of hell on earth. "Pretty easy fuckin' choice," he said with a whiskey-warm smile.

# FORTY

Martinez rolled around in bed. Carmen had been gone for a week visiting Raul. The bloated faces of the dead racked his brain. Jerome, Isabella, Max, Alicia and Williams. The list went on and on. The first three bothered him the most because they were unsolved. No one doubted Shaver killed Max. He was the only one with a motive to do it. However, the scene of the crime turned up nothing. The Jerome and Isabella murders carried the stench of Shaver with them, but the connections were too tenuous. With Tyler gone now, who knows if they'd ever be able to make sense of it all.

He grabbed an old T-shirt and jumped into some athletic shorts. He went to his front door and stepped outside. The cold concrete patio felt good on the pads of his feet. The street was quiet except for a pair of people taking their morning walk. He reached down to grab the day's paper and the morning breeze ran over his face. His cell phone rang before he could open the newspaper.

"This is Martinez," he answered.

"Martinez, it's Cruz. Mason is going to meet me downtown in about an hour at the Crazy Sid's coffee shop. Can you make it?"

"It's Sunday."

"He wants the story of what happened to Tyler directly from us. We've also got to talk about the trial. There's a motions hearing in about a week that you need to testify at."

"About what? The video?"

"Primarily the video. Sphinx moved to exclude it. Nothing surprising, but we've got to fight it with all we've got."

"All right then, I can be there in an hour." He hung up the phone and tucked the paper under his arm. He went inside the house and changed out of his shorts for some running pants. Kept the old T-shirt and gave his teeth a superficial brush. He pulled his lips back in the mirror to check his teeth, then stood there a moment. It had been a while since he had taken account of his physical condition. Black hair was ceding to gray in places. Bags like black half moons were starting to form under his eyes. He was still built, but his muscle tone was slowly disappearing. His brown eyes looked dull and tired. Martinez grabbed tweezers out of a cup on the sink and plucked a gray hair out of his nose.

"Damn," he said as his eyes watered.

The ride downtown went by fast. Hardly anyone was out on the roads. Plus, Carmen called him to tell him about Raul.

"He's struggling with the loss of his legs."

"I bet. That's fully understandable," Martinez said. "When do you think you'll be back?"

"I wasn't exactly going to rush back. Raul needs me, and I doubt it's safe back home yet."

"Honestly, it's probably safer now than it ever was before. The Chief is dead. Tyler's dead. Shaver's in the can. He's obviously still pulling strings from the inside, but I don't see him getting to us. If Raul needs you though, then stay down there."

"How are you holding up alone?" she asked.

"All right. I miss you, but I'm pretty self-sufficient."

"Barely. I bet there are clothes piled up around the house waiting for me when I get back."

"There are some piles," Martinez said, chagrined. She was one of the few that could break through his generally rough exterior.

"Well, leave them there for me. I'll take care of them for you." He didn't say it but he missed her immensely. That machismo thing prevented him from fully opening up, even at this stage in their marriage. Without her around, he had nobody. They exchanged goodbyes and hung up.

Martinez parallel parked into a spot in front of the coffee shop. Mason and Cruz were already waiting at an outside table.

"I came as soon as you called."

"Looks like it," Cruz said jokingly.

"Shit, you two are the *last* people I'd dress up for." He sat down at the table. Mason had a pad of yellow paper and a pen. Cruz was sipping on something. "Is that a tea?" Martinez asked incredulously.

"Chai."

"Chai *tea*," Mason chided, joining in with Martinez.

Mason extended his hand to Martinez, "Nice to finally meet you in person." They shook hands and Martinez plunked down into his chair.

"Open your horizons, fellas. Teas are a great source of relaxation. Look at the Asian cultures. They are much healthier than us and most..." Cruz saw the blank expressions on both men's faces and stopped. "That hole was getting deep."

A waitress came by and Martinez asked for a black coffee. Mason doubled up the order. "That's how it's done," Martinez said.

"Don't get all uppity and macho with me, Martinez. You forget that you're sitting at a coffee shop on a Sunday morning with two other guys. That machismo only gets you so far."

"Kidding aside," Mason said, "what the hell happened out there with Tyler?"

"You saw it, didn't you?" Cruz asked. "That's all there was to it. A car chase that ended with Tyler dead."

"Was there anything at the scene that could be helpful? Something from his car?"

"Nah," Martinez answered. "Some surveillance gear. A few guns. Nothing else helpful."

"Did someone get the guns to forensics to see if they match up to any unsolved ones?"

"I assume. I wasn't handling the scene," Martinez said.

"I don't know what to do with those cold cases anymore," Mason said.

"Jerome and Isabella?" Cruz asked.

"Yeah. They went ice cold when Tyler got run over."

"Dead ends again," Cruz muttered, visibly frustrated.

Changing subjects, Mason said, "We have a big hearing coming up next week. Judge Melburn is going to decide whether to let the video into evidence. It's time to revert our focus to this case."

"Before we move on, one thing's been buggin' me," Martinez said in a low voice. "I want one more trip to Shaver's house. He's a sociopathic killer—there's no doubt about that. Sociopaths usually keep some trophies from their kills. It's something they can go back to for their feelings of control. I've seen it in other cases. I think we've missed something big there."

"I'll help you get a warrant so you can search the house. Maybe Cruz can go with you." Cruz nodded although he was a little sick of being volunteered for things. Mason volunteered him to track down and capture Tyler and that went like hell. Now he was volunteered to go right back into the lion's den. Whether the lion is there or not didn't seem to make much difference. Who knows what secrets that house contained.

"Back to the business at hand. We've got a hearing on some preliminary matters, but also the issue of the video. Cruz, I'm going to need you to prepare Martinez to testify that he took the drive directly from the cameraman." When neither man answered, Mason added, "I hope this isn't too much for either of you. Something wrong?"

"This is very personal for both of us," Cruz said. "Martinez lost his partner trying to preserve this video. I came face to face with..." Cruz paused and the other men looked at him. They could tell he was holding something back, but a mix of early morning density and the general stupor accompanying guys and sensitive things kept them silent. Cruz went on, "The fact we are here, to this point of using the video, and that some asshole judge is going to decide if we can use it bothers me."

"Me too," Martinez added.

"Obviously, I know how this works, but I've never been on this side of things. Shoot, I'm usually the one arguing to *exclude* evidence like this," Cruz realized. "If the judge keeps the video out after all this effort, I may lose my faith in this whole process."

Mason understood their sentiment. He was frequently on the side of having excellent evidence excluded on some technicality. "I get you guys. The rules are the rules though. The chain of custody on this video is shot. I'm not expecting anything, but hopefully Judge Melburn will have some sympathy and allow us to prove that chain otherwise."

"A sympathetic judge—now that's wishing!" Cruz said.

"Sometimes that's all you've got," Mason said rather melancholy. "Next Thursday at eight-thirty in the morning. Get Martinez ready."

# FORTY-ONE

Shaver crouched next to some shaded bleachers. Signs of spring were all around the yard. The hard concrete couldn't keep back nature as her delicate fingers pushed up through cracks and blew pollen all over.

He wondered if it could be as easy as he planned. Mills, Pick and the rest of the Aryan Brotherhood sprawled out on the bleachers, wasting the day away. On the streets, these gangs killed each other for territory, women, drugs, weapons, and pride. The jail had plenty of territory, drug and pride issues. All he had to do—he figured—was stir up one of those to start the killing. It was that easy on the streets, so why would anything be different in here?

He remained doubtful despite the reasoning. His knees ached so he stood up. Mills lazily opened one of his eyes and watched Shaver.

"Whatchu so restless abou'?"

Shaver looked at Mills, not knowing he was being watched. "Nothing," he said. He got close to the ground, smelling it and doing some push-ups. Then he grunted and walked in a direct line toward the *Emes*.

Mills nudged Pick as he watched Shaver get closer to the *Eme* territory. The *Eme's* had one of the bleachers in the sun, so half of their gang was missing, scattered around places in the yard with shade. "Whud the fuck..." Mills groaned as he sat up.

As Shaver approached the bleachers he saw the gang member that had harassed him several weeks ago. He also saw that members of the Guerillas were watching him intently. Witnesses to his next act. The *Eme* members were all laying on the lower portions of each bleacher seat, the foot-resting portion. Shaver counted four of them. His pace quickened as he neared the bleachers. There was a whistle, and then he thought he heard Mills scream out, "Shaver!!"

Shaver reached the bleachers and grabbed the lieutenant. With both hands full of shirt, Shaver yanked the man from the bleachers and threw him onto the concrete. "This one's from the Aryan Brothers, you fuck." And then Shaver began to pound on his face like a jackhammer. He rained fists down on the man who had been unable to even muster a word before Shaver knocked him out. His head bounced on the concrete as Shaver developed a devastating rhythm of punches. Shaver felt blows to his own head but ignored them. Someone was trying to pull him off of the gang member but he squeezed his legs around the man's waist and hung tight.

He heard Mills and Pick screaming at him. They sounded confused.

Then the hitting and pulling on him stopped. Mills, Pick and the rest of the Aryan brothers in the yard were fighting with the *Eme*. Shaver looked down at the man in front of him, who was nearly unrecognizable. His forehead and lips were swollen in a caveman bloat. The man had spit out teeth. Some were on the ground next to him, a couple rested on his chin, stuck there by saliva and blood. Shaver rolled off of him and onto his back on the ground. He struggled to catch his breath, gasping from the effort.

The fighting was going on all around him. Mills had an *Eme* member in a headlock and was squeezing the life out of him. Pick was locked in a ground wrestling match. The familiar sirens of the prison wailed their long tones. Shaver watched as an *Eme* gang member rushed an Aryan Brother from behind with something in his hand. Turned out it was a shiv, which the gang member used to jab the Aryan Brother in the neck. Blood spurted out from in between the brother's fingers as he fell to the ground.

Then Shaver's head slammed sideways. His world grew fuzzy. Another impact and all was dark.

* * * *

The judge looked impatiently at Mason and Sphinx. "Mr. Sphinx, is your client going to attend the hearing today?"

"No, your Honor. I told your clerk that Sergeant Shaver was violently and brutally attacked while in prison. He's still recovering in the prison hospital.

"Do we need him here today for these motions?"

"No, Your Honor."

"Let's proceed then. What motion shall we start with?"

"The motion *in limine* to exclude the videotape as evidence," Mason said.

"Okay," Judge Melburn said, "I've read the fully briefed issue and stand ready to rule unless the State has anything to add."

Mason was taken aback. "Your Honor, I understood this was supposed to be a hearing on the issues presented in the motion, and that you would reserve ruling until after hearing the testimony of the State's witness. How could you stand ready to rule before hearing that witness?"

"Excuse me, counsel," Judge Melburn said angrily, "but I think I know how much evidence I need to consider to rule. I *have* been doing this for thirty-two years!"

"Your Honor, the State's entire argument against excluding the video rests with this witness behind me," Mason said, pointing to Martinez.

"I understand that counsel, and that's exactly why I stand ready to rule.

243

Do you really intend to prove chain of custody through a witness that conducted an improper and unauthorized arrest of the defendant in this case? Is *that* the testimony you hope this Court will use to deny the motion? Because if it is, I stand ready to rule."

Mason stood speechless at counsel table. In all his years of practice, he had never seen anything like this. Judge Melburn was pre-judging his evidence. "Your Honor, the State has a right to present its evidence without the Court *pre-determining* the weight of testimony. This certainly constitutes reversible error and..."

Judge Melburn shot up from his chair and pointed a bony finger at Mason. "One more word and I will hold you in contempt counsel. You do not threaten this Court with an appeal!" Mason stood with his hands on the table in front of him. He hung his head in disbelief. Judge Melburn sat back down and let out a bit of air through pursed lips. "Your gall, counsel, will not get you far in my Court."

Mason turned around to Cruz who looked equally befuddled, without a clue as to what to do. Mason next looked at Sphinx who seemed to share a feeling of disbelief. Mason didn't understand what was happening. It was outrightly incorrect, discrimination almost. "The State would still like to present its witness for the record."

"Great, waste the Court's time," Judge Melburn muttered.

Mason peeked up at the judge who was shuffling something around at his bench. The collar around Mason's neck felt like it was squeezing the breath out of him. Beads of sweat formed on his forehead. "The State calls Roman Martinez."

Martinez stood up and walked hesitantly to the witness box. Mason mustered a nod of his head and pointed to him that he was going the right way. This was a farce, Mason thought to himself. Something was going on — he had never seen a judge act like this. He looked over at Sphinx who appeared to be similarly mystified. It couldn't have been him. This had all the smack of higher powers, people beyond both of them pulling strings.

Martinez was sworn in and Mason went through his direct examination. How did you know Max Silverman? Where did he work? When did you meet him? Did he ever give you anything? When, where? Martinez did well through the line of questioning. He described that Max was able to save the original video from the camera and that he protected it up until giving it to the district attorney's office.

Judge Melburn interrupted the direct examination, "So you are a material witness in the murder of several people involved in this case, as well as the arrest of the defendant. *And* you are testifying as to the veracity of that videotape?" Mason slammed his pencil down and stared at the judge. He tried to continue his direct examination but the judge interrupted him. "I would like an answer to those questions."

"I'm not testifying as to the veracity of anything, Judge," Martinez answered. "I'm just testifying that he gave me what he said was the video of Shaver killing Livan Rodriguez." Judge Melburn grunted and motioned to Mason to continue. Mason finished his direct examination and Sphinx didn't even bother with a cross. Why rock the boat?

"The State calls Cruz..."

"Another witness, counsel? I've told you what the outcome of this is going to be."

"We have a right to put on our evidence, *Your Honor!!*" The blood had boiled right up to Mason's head. Even Judge Melburn seemed taken aback— for a moment.

"Counsel, one more outburst like that..."

Then Mason completely lost it. "One more outburst like this?!" he yelled as he flung papers over his shoulder into the gallery behind him. "Or *how about this!*" he screamed while kicking the podium onto its side. Two bailiffs rushed into the courtroom.

"Take that man into custody. I am holding you in contempt of this Court..."

"Screw your contempt! You've fixed this..."

"...and if you stop now I will only give you one day of jail time..."

"...you've fixed this hearing and the trial. You're a *coward*! An innocent man is dead and you're playing fucking games!"

"That'll be two days." The bailiffs had almost pulled Mason out of the courtroom, his mouth frothing. He grabbed onto a door frame and made one last, fruitless demonstration of resistance before he vanished. "Well, that was quite a display," Judge Melburn said with a cough. "My ruling..."

Cruz stood up, turned his back to the judge and started to walk out of the courtroom. Martinez and Sandra saw him and also got up to leave. "My ruling is that the videotape be excluded. No further demonstrations such as the State's will be tolerated in this matter."

Cruz got to the courtroom doors and pushed through them for some much-needed space. Sandra caught up to him. Her eyes were wide, outlined in black. "What happened in there, Cruz?" Martinez stood next to them silently.

"I don't know. I've never seen a judge act like that. It was obvious that the judge was biased. He ruled before even hearing evidence. I just don't know."

"Man, it's no surprise," Martinez said. "Shaver's a cop. Who knows how high his connections go. Or, who is implicated by things that man has done. It's no surprise," Martinez said with a shrug of his shoulders. "The blue line— it's more like a blue mountain."

"What do we do now?" Sandra asked.

Neither Cruz nor Martinez responded right away. They didn't have the answer. Cruz finally said something, "We put Martinez on against Shaver. That's what it's come down to."

* * * *

Shaver moaned and tried to roll over onto his side. A pair of unknown hands restrained him. He started to fight back but the person whispered, "Easy...easy. Take it easy, Mr. Shaver." Shaver cracked his eye open to a flood of world. A black woman was leaning down in his line of sight.

"Where am I?" he managed to ask.

"Shoot, the prison. The hospital in the prison. Had a nice dream that you were out, did ya?" She coaxed him to relax on his back again. Then she got on her knees and put her elbows onto his bed. "The Warden says you did good."

"Oh yeah? Those spics get beat up?"

"Oh no! Worse than that, Mr. Shaver. At least three of them have been killed since the first skirmish you started. Warden says a rival gang saw the attack as an opportunity to take over some territory. Now there are Mexican gangs fighting it out. The brothers won't let an opportunity like this pass either," she said, almost with a sense of pride.

Shaver moaned again and turned his head to look at her. She was a mid-forties woman. Cleanly pressed nurse uniform. She had some gray hairs showing on the side of her head. A worn but cunning expression on her face. "Warden says your case went well."

"What's he know about that?"

"Mr. Sphinx told him."

This caught Shaver's attention. "He talked to my attorney?" The woman looked away as if she had slipped. "Well, what did he say?"

"Said the judge did his job. The video is out."

Shaver smiled. "Freakin' amazing. This trip to the hospital was definitely worth it then."

"Mr. Sphinx also said not to get better too fast. Said it would be better if you looked banged up."

"Wait, did the Warden or *you* talk to him? You seem to know an awful lot."

The nurse flashed a coy smile at him and began to tuck the cover around his bed. "I was listening while Mr. Sphinx talked." She finished tucking and then arranged his bed stand. "Your room number is #542, same as your phone number, if people want to call you. My name's Elysa. You can ring this button up here if you need anything." She floated out of the room like an apparition. Shaver was left with only silence. Faint hums and beeps were audible if he concentrated.

"My man!"

Shaver shifted away from the phone. "What the hell?"

"Shaver, it's the Warden. Get me off intercom."

Shaver picked up the phone. "That's really loud, Warden. Should watch where you burst into."

"Awww, get your panties out their bunch. You hear yet?"

"Yeah, Elysa told me."

"So...anything to say?"

"Sure, thanks. You got anything to say to me?"

"Thanks to you, Sergeant. You really kicked this beehive good. Fuckin' spics are getting killed by their own and others. It's a lovely thing." The Warden's voice brimmed with happiness. What a lonely place this must be for the Warden, Shaver thought. Sitting in the middle of five thousand angry, criminal men. Every one of them would choke the life out of him. Him sitting there all day trying to figure out ways to further subject them to his control. His cell was solitary in comparison to the rest of them. Then again, that could be said for most people. Shaver crumpled an empty cup of water in his hand while these thoughts flowed through his mind. Some people just had more lavish cages than others.

When Shaver returned from his daydream, he realized the Warden had been talking the whole time. He was one of those people that couldn't care less whether you responded or even whether you were listening. The sound of his own voice was enough to carry a twenty-minute conversation.

Shaver heard a bit of commotion outside of his room. "Warden, gotta let you go," he said as he hung up the phone. No sooner had he set the phone down then Sphinx came storming in. Elysa followed close behind him. She tried to slow the hulking man down to no avail.

"I tried to stop him!" Elysa exclaimed out of breath.

Shaver put his hand up to stop her. "It's all right Elysa." She looked thankful and slowed to a stop before turning back out of the room.

"What the fuck do you have going on here Shaver?"

Shaver spread his hands out on his bedsheet and rubbed his legs. "This is certainly no way to greet your best client Sphinx."

"You're my *worst* fucking client, Shaver. I've been involved with some scum but the things you've got going on are beyond all of them."

"Come over here, Sphinx, closer to the bed."

"Screw that, you maniac."

Shaver smiled and shook his head while he looked down at the bed. "What'd you expect Sphinx? You expected me to sit here and play by the rules? Would you trust your fate to another man or someone else's system?"

"Guess what, that's how..."

"I wasn't actually looking for an answer, Sphinx. If you don't see that, problem number one," Shaver said as he wagged a finger at Sphinx. "Problem number two: the system and the man are fucked. Never mind that I don't trust either of them even when they work right. When they operate as they do every day, no way. I ain't the one."

Sphinx paced to the window and stood there with his hands on his hips. "You've got me in a crap position Shaver. What did you do to that judge?"

"I didn't do anything—and that's the truth."

"Who did then? That was the craziest shit I've seen in a courtroom before. He ruled before I even rebutted the State's evidence."

"Look Sphinx, just do your best job. The place you're in, it's called by the balls. Your best bet is to ride it out. You can't withdraw. Just let the bigger forces work themselves out."

"I'll tell you what, Shaver," Sphinx said as he left the window and moved towards Shaver's bed. "If I lose my license over all of this bullshit you're pulling, I'll have your heart for dinner." He stopped by the side of the bed. Shaver feigned fatigue until Sphinx got within lunging distance. Then Shaver pushed himself onto his side and reached for Sphinx's collar. He grabbed it and pulled Sphinx down towards him. Sphinx returned the favor by wrapping his two enormous hands around Shaver's neck. The men froze there, grimacing as their strength collided.

"Just try the fucking case," Shaver spat. Sphinx pushed away and broke free from Shaver. He stormed out of the room just as he had stormed in. That's how Sphinx moved.

# FORTY-TWO

Cruz waited as the guard scanned him with a hand-held metal detector. "Lift up your pant legs." Cruz complied and the guard nonchalantly waved him forward. He moved through a series of familiar corridors until he got to the "talking room," as it was called. All of the seats were empty. He took one by an end of the row and waited. Almost as soon as he sat down, he heard a faint click and a door on the other side of the glass opened. It was Mason.

Mason picked up the phone, "Hi, Cruz. What'd you need?"

Cruz shifted on the circular stool as he tried to find a comfortable position. "How long did Judge Melburn give you?"

"Two days."

"Ever been in jail before?"

"No. You?"

"Can't say that I have," Cruz said with a smirk that wasn't returned. "I need a favor."

Mason frowned. "You know, I don't exactly have spare time in here. I'm obsessed with protecting my asshole like the Holy Grail." Cruz couldn't help but laugh. "When it's you in here I'll remember that. What do you want?"

"The video."

"Oh come on Cruz. We lost, let's get over it and move on to the trial."

"I don't want it for the trial, Mason." Cruz caught Mason's full attention.

Mason looked into his eyes and saw a bit of wildness. "You're a little crazed over this Cruz."

"Shouldn't you be, too? Isn't your job to strive for justice?"

"That should be all our jobs, as lawyers."

"Well then fucking strive, Mason. We got blindsided in that hearing. I've never seen anything like that—the judge ruling without considering any evidence. Without giving us a chance to put on our side. It's a goddamn wake-up call, Mason. The system is broken. Either we play within the bounds of a broken system or we work around it. I say we work around it."

"That video is still evidence in the investigation and..."

"Give it a rest, Mason. That videotape is never going to see the light of day in this trial."

"Could be an issue on appeal. What if we need the tape on remand?"

"You mean, what if we need the tape in three years? You also mean that one of our appellate courts is going to find that the trial court abused its discretion? You know how high that standard is. Not gonna happen."

Mason squinted his right eye and ran his tongue over his teeth. Apparently this was his thinking face. "Say I give it to you, what's the point?"

"The point?" Cruz asked incredulously. He moved closer to the plexiglass separating them. "The point is to let the whole world be the judge in this case rather than some decrepit, old, white man. The point is to put this video on the tendrils of the Internet and have it burst out from where we are to the rest of the world. It will be disseminated at blazing speeds. And then they will know."

Mason shook his head as if to say no.

"You have to understand, Mason, someday everything will be on video. Everything will be recorded. The rise of the smart phone mandates it. Then there will be no police beatings in back alleys because every alley will be covered by a person on the ground or one in a building. One hundred times zoom will allow people to shoot coverage across football fields. They capture the video, post it to the Internet and in minutes, it spreads like a demon wildfire around the world. And that's just the beginning."

"I'm too old for this, Cruz. I won't live to see any of it."

"Bullshit! You're seeing it right now, Mason. The 'Internet reporters'. Photos in the morning news from viewers. The media is already riding people on the street for its news. They don't even need their own crews in the field. Someday it will just be an army of viewers giving other viewers content.

"Now you're just getting downright outlandish, Cruz. *All this* is why you want to release the video?"

Cruz leaned back from the plexiglass. "*One* of the reasons. What I'm telling you is it's inevitable, Mason. We're slaves to consumption. Media has simply turned into another form of consumption. News is sent out, bashed, mashed, stirred, and spit out. We've turned into a collective vampire, sucking the life force out of news events. A little girl is raped and killed. It shocks us the first, second time we see it. The third time we begin to get desensitized. The fourth, fifth, sixth, twentieth, hundredth times we see it? There's no reservoir of emotion for it anymore. Compare that to the times when the news you knew was your town's news. There was still the possibility to shock and awe."

"So if that possibility doesn't exist anymore, why leak this video?"

"That possibility *does* still exist, but the window is closing. This is also a much different situation. People still want to believe in police. Even with their faith in police shaken, they want to believe. They want to believe that the people lawfully allowed to carry guns, to tazer and mace people, to handcuff people and restrict their rights, are good people. That hope has been slowly eroded. The prevalence of police shootings, beatings, abuse of force, verbal abuse—all of them caught on tape—will be the end of that hope. Police will become enemies of the *citizen*. If you don't believe that, just look at how all of the minority communities view the police. *Los cerdos*, the 5-0. Every community except the white community views the police as the enemy."

After a few seconds of silence, Mason said, "Pretty good argument."

Cruz nodded. "It makes sense. Plus, there's no sense in fighting off the inevitable. Our country is browning. The world is browning. Sentiment will change. We stand at the edge of that change and have a catalyst."

"Todd has access to the video. I assume you're going to work with Sandra on this?"

"And Martinez. He feels as strongly about this as I do. Perhaps more. Remember, he lost his partner in this battle. That anger will never go away. It's smoldering inside of him and leaking this video is about the biggest 'fuck you' he can shove back at the establishment."

\* \* \* \*

Raul sat in the middle of a boarded-up apartment. Gang tags were all over the walls. A radio in the corner belted out hardcore rap. Two men sat in the apartment with him. They wore black and-white bandannas covering their faces from nose down. Each had a flat-brimmed hat pulled down low on their forehead, making little of their faces visible. A handgun rested unabashedly on each of their laps. They were close enough to intimidate but far enough away to avoid conversation.

The wheelchair was still unfamiliar to Raul. Apartments in the ghetto weren't exactly handicap accessible, so the two men in the apartment mean-mugging him had actually helped him up a flight of about five stairs.

He understood now what people meant by ghost limbs. Sometimes he would reach down to rub his leg. Twice he had tried to get up out of the wheelchair as if he could walk. Twice he had fallen.

Another man entered the room, went over to the radio and turned it down. Raul knew him only as "El Sureño." They became acquainted about ten years ago when Raul was doing a story on cross-border drug running. El Sureño had done an anonymous interview in the piece. Raul showed him respect even though the man was a stone-cold monster. He was one of the country's premier drug runners. He used thousands of *burros*, oftentimes women, who would ingest a number of condom-wrapped drug pellets before trying to get over the border. It was an inexact science, as El Sureño explained. Sometimes, the condoms ruptured, sending the *burros* to a drug induced death. Other times the *burros* couldn't handle the load in their stomachs and lost control of their bowels. Some of the *burros* tried to get away with the payload. The price of the drugs were so minimal in comparison to their ultimate selling price that the inexactitude didn't matter.

El Sureño was a ridiculous hulk of a man. Easily six-foot-five, shaved head, handlebar mustache, tatted from scalp to soles, and wide, very wide. He wore black canvas pants and a white wife-beater. The two other men in the room sat motionless, catatonic.

"What the fuck happened to you, Raul?"

"A long story, but the short of it is that I got into a gun fight. My legs got shot up. This is what's left, or not."

"A gun fight, *hombre*? Ain'tchu a reporter?" El Sureño said with a smile directed at the two men in the room. They didn't respond. Two Spartan-like figures, there to do nothing but kill should the need arise.

"I am a reporter, but I got wrapped up in something heavy."

"We all been there. What's this got to do with *La Eme*?" He grabbed a chair, flipped it around with a slight twist of his wrist and sat down.

"The man that did this to me, his name is Sergeant Shaver."

El Sureño raised his eyebrows. "Sergeant Shaver?"

"Yeah."

"Dammmn. Who's that?"

Raul chided El Sureño with a sound from his mouth. "*Hombre*, you know who that is."

"How do you know what I know?"

"I've got people everywhere. I know what's going on down at the prison. *La Eme* is in an all-out war. Survival time right now. *Nuestra Familia* is fighting you guys. You were wrapped up with the Aryan Brotherhood and the Guerillas. You're fighting a multi-front war because of that cop."

El Sureño stared hard at Raul. "You do know some *vatos*, huh?" he bellowed. "Yeah, that pig has caused us some shit. Don't matter though. *La Eme* don't get down on things like that. I just had three soldiers rob a liquor store to get into the joint. Reinforcements. You can't fuck with that kind of loyalty."

"You're going to let Shaver get away with starting these wars?"

"I didn't say that, but I also didn't say what the fuck we gonna do."

"I know what you can do."

"You gonna give *me* advice?" The emphasis on me was enough to wake the Spartans. Raul watched their fingers maneuver to better grip the guns.

"Look, not advice. Just a suggestion. A lead."

"Okay, what's your *leaddddd*? Semantic motherfucker." Raul couldn't help but be taken aback by El Sureño's use of a word that he didn't even know.

"Shaver's trial starts in four days. What better statement than to kill that *pendejo* during the trial?"

El Sureño laughed, a deep, condescending belly laugh. At that moment Raul wondered what the hell he had been thinking. This was extreme and seemed to be on the verge of backfiring. "You want us to do a hit for you?"

"Well..." Raul fumbled for the right answer, "...not just for me. For *La Eme* too."

"Listen," El Sureño said as he walked behind Raul's wheelchair and disengaged the brakes, "You worry about Raul and his little world." He started to push Raul towards the two men at the other side of the room. They both grabbed their guns and stood up. "I worry about *La Eme*. Besides, we ain't gonna do a fuckin' thing right now. *La Eme* and the Brotherhood have had a pact for years. Too much money there to fuck it up." El Sureño wheeled Raul right up to the two men. They looked into El Sureño's eyes, waiting like two Doberman pinschers for their master's order.

Raul felt his gut flip over and his heart jumped into his throat. "Damn, Raul, why you sweating?" He pushed Raul past the two men and out the front door. "Our answer is no. If you ever come back here asking me for a favor, Raul, you may leave missing another part. Don't forget that, *hombre*."

* * * *

Cruz stood behind a producer who was watching a small screen. The producer was about average height, had disheveled hair, black-rimmed glasses and a goatee. He wore a black shirt and pants so that he nearly disappeared in the dark viewing room. A seemingly infinite number of lights blinked around them. Red, yellow and green. Signifying things foreign to Cruz. Like stepping into the cockpit of an airplane and marveling at all of the switches, levers, knobs and dials.

"This video is fantastic," the producer whispered as he turned two dials one way and pushed a sliding button vertically. It was a different mentality, to be able to look at loss of life and call it fantastic. A certain hardening to life which Cruz fought off, but at the same time saw its inevitability. People in the media would call the video fantastic. People viewing it would consume it as entertainment. Another roadside crash they pass by mid-gape. "I think we can use this whole thing, Sandra."

She smiled, but not with the same depravity as the producer. "We'll be breaking this news, Eric."

Mason had put it all on the line. He'd never actually checked the video into evidence—perhaps with some inkling that it wouldn't get to the trial. Cruz's plea and the injustice of Judge Melburn's ruling were enough to force Mason's hand, and he gave the original video to Cruz.

"I know, how fantastic! We haven't had a story like this in years. Let alone be the ones to break it. This is going to do wonders for your career." A silver lining, buried deep beneath folds of bloodshed. Sandra looked at him and he gave her a supportive wink. What was actually fantastic? How Sandra looked, Cruz thought. In the time since their adventure in the restaurant bathroom, they hadn't come together that way again. There was no weirdness in the break. Both understood the attention the circumstances around them demanded, and both could subsume their desires for the time being. Although Cruz was finding that difficult as he stood there and watched Sandra in her element.

"I want to run this on tonight's six o'clock news," the producer said, frenetically. "And I obviously want you to report it. Do you have any witnesses that you can roll into the piece? Any of the people in the video?"

"Cruz here." Cruz looked at Sandra with surprise.

"Me?"

"Yeah, I think it's important to discuss the case as it currently stands. Plus, you have personal experience with how we got to where we are." Cruz had never been on television before. He looked into the recording studio next to them. It was silent and dark except for the stage.

"Sure, I can do that."

"Perfect!" the producer exclaimed. "Come back in two hours and we'll start the setup." Cruz waited for the producer and Sandra to walk out of the room. He stood there, wondering how this chess move would be received. Worried it would fall on deaf ears, people already calibrated to violence.

He dropped his head and turned to walk out of the room. Sandra was standing just inside the doorway. She grabbed his hands and kissed him on the lips. "It's going to work. Don't try to let yourself down before the video's been given a chance." He appreciated her insight. "Come on, let's go get a bite to eat."

It sounded like a good idea.

\* \* \* \*

Shaver sat in the chair next to his hospital bed, watching a small television resting on a beat-up cart. He was completely zoned out, listening to weather reports and stories about local news that didn't matter to him. A "Breaking News" banner scrolled onto the screen.

The male anchor said, "For quite some time now one of our reporters, Sandra Gutierrez, has been following a story that we quite honestly thought had died. Turns out the story was alive and well, and the facts behind it only got more gruesome. What do you have for us, Sandra?"

Sandra appeared on a split screen and Shaver jumped up as stiff as a rod. "That's right, Rob, I've been following this story for several months now. If you recall, an old Latino man was allegedly shot in cold blood by a member of the city's police force gang unit. While the story did not get much press after that, the story has indeed been going on. In fact, the officer who shot the man was only recently arrested, and he is set to stand trial starting three days from now."

"I understand that you have some breaking news on this case for us?" the male anchor inquired.

"I do Rob. We obtained a copy of a video shot at the scene of the murder. It was shot by a cameraman named Max Silverman who filmed for the popular show *Police*. He paid the ultimate price to see that this video was safe."

"You mean he died?" the anchor asked, veritable surprise on his face.

"He was killed. In fact, I was trapped in a closet at his apartment when he was killed. I had gone to his apartment to get a copy of the video. Max was visibly nervous, too paranoid I thought to myself. It was justified though. Just a few minutes after I got to his apartment, someone else arrived. Max told me to run to the closet and hide with the video, which I did. Over the next few minutes I heard the assailant interrogate Max. Then he shot him."

The anchor remained silent, stunned by these facts. "What happened next?" he managed to get out.

"There was a chase that lasted several weeks for the video I had. All of the officers that you will see in the video were killed with the exception of Sergeant Shaver and Officer Martinez. Most of them were killed in the initial days after the video was taken. After that, we were involved in our own chase to track down the original version of the video, which Officer Martinez had secured. The version I had was a copy of that original.

Sergeant Shaver was apparently taking orders from the Chief of Police to find the video at any cost, including killing us in the process. I'm sure Sergeant Shaver would have followed through if he had the chance."

"You're fucking right I would have!" Shaver screamed at the television. "I still will, you bitch!" He hurled a paper cup across the hospital room.

"I see here that you were held captive yourself?" the anchor inquired while double-checking his notes.

"I was. The chief of police and a man who worked for the Chief kidnapped me and held me hostage in an attempt to get the video."

"A man working for the Chief? So another officer?"

"This man certainly was not a police officer. I hate to use inflammatory language, Rob, but this man was an assassin. A heartless person, no semblance of emotion and wracked with sickness. Truly the most disturbing person I have ever confronted."

"And this, this...monster...he held you captive?"

"He kidnapped me, and took me to a doctor's house."

"I don't understand," the anchor said. "Why did he take you there?"

"The doctor was also working with the Chief. We have not had the chance to determine exactly what his involvement with the Chief was. All I know is that this doctor had a subterranean, mini-hospital setup in his house. That's where this monster of a man took me and strapped me to an operating table. He pulled a light down to within inches from my face, and..." Sandra started to break up.

"You pussy!" Shaver spat. "Fuck this, this is prejudice!"

Elysa came running into the room. "What on earth is going on with you?"

"Watch this!" Shaver yelled while pointing at the television.

"Just take your time Sandra," the anchor said. There were several seconds of silence while Sandra dabbed her eyes and regained her composure.

"I'm sorry, Rob. The man pulled a light down close to my face and left me there while the skin on my face started to burn. I thought there was no hope, I had lost all hope. I thought I was going to die in that place."

"But, you're here today," the anchor said, shaking off the impotence of his statement.

"I am, thanks to the efforts of Officer Martinez as well as this man." The camera panned out and Cruz came into the frame.

"And your name, sir?"

"Cruz Marquez."

"Cruz is a local attorney," Sandra said. "He and Officer Martinez rescued me from the doctor's operating room."

"Sandra, I think this is a good place take a break," the anchor said. "Viewers, do your best to absorb all of this, and we'll finish the story as well as show you the video that caused all of this when we return."

The station cut to a commercial. Shaver sat in impotent anger. "They are poisoning the jury pool with this shit! I'll never stand for a trial here!" Elysa shook her head and slowly backed out of the room. Shaver was left alone, answer-less. After a few, seething moments, the anchor was back on the television.

"Back with your six o'clock breaking news," Rob said. "Sandra, before the commercial break you were telling us about your kidnapping, and how the gentleman sitting with you, Mr. Cruz Marquez, was an integral part in saving your life."

"That's correct, Rob. As I mentioned, Cruz is a local lawyer who got wrapped up in the chase for the video."

"Mr. Marquez..."

"Cruz is fine, Rob."

"Cruz, how did you, a lawyer, end up chasing after fugitives to rescue Sandra? That seems far outside your regular job description."

"Completely. I've never done anything like this. I had shot a gun once or twice before, but at a shooting range. Certainly never pointing one at an actual person. It's been a crash course."

"From what I understand, Sergeant Shaver was apprehended and is in prison now?" the anchor asked.

"That's right. Sergeant Shaver remains in prison while his case is pending. His trial begins in three days, and just like any other person charged with a crime, he is innocent until proven guilty."

"Sure, but the video we are about to see is a relatively strong indicator that Sergeant Shaver is guilty."

Cruz had to decide how to hedge his response. "It seems that way, Rob, but I'll let your viewers draw their own conclusions."

"Fair enough," Rob said with a bit of dissatisfaction. "Let's roll that video. But first, if you have small children present or if you don't like seeing violent images, it may be a good time for you to visit the kitchen, viewers." Cruz looked at a monitor on the desk in front of them. After a couple seconds of black screen, the video started. He stared through the screen until the gunshots.

It was brutal. The old man died instantly. His face turned towards the camera. A slow stream of blood rolled out of his lower lip and over his chin. His eyes were wide open. The daughter became more visible as she lunged toward the old man's bed. Officers started to leave the room, arguing about what had happened. The cameraman did not move the camera yet. Instead, the camera caught the daughter weeping. Her tears fell on the feet of the old man as he lay cold in his bed.

The video went black.

"Fucking hocus pocus!" Shaver yelled, looking for something else to throw. "He wouldn't show me his goddamn hands!" Shaver punched at the air.

"I've never seen anything quite like that," the anchor said. Cruz felt a tear well up in his eye. He willed away the rest of them.

"Now, hopefully, our viewers can see why it was so important to find and protect this video," Sandra said. "This is the first time the video has ever been broadcast."

"Why now, Sandra?"

"I think Cruz can explain that better," Sandra answered, turning to Cruz.

"The criminal case against Sergeant Shaver has been ongoing for a couple of months. While your audience generally just catches the tail end of a case, or the trial, a lot goes into the case before that. Last week, as we neared the trial, the judge heard motions to exclude certain evidence. The video we just watched was one of the pieces of evidence that Sergeant Shaver asked to exclude."

"For obvious reasons," the anchor added.

"Yes, for very obvious reasons. At that hearing, the judge granted Sergeant Shaver's request to exclude the video. He did so on the grounds that the video did not have the proper chain of custody. Basically, it was mishandled as a piece of evidence before the case began. The real problem that we had with the judge was that he showed no inclination to take our side of the argument into account. He had *pre-determined* the ruling. While I won't speculate as to why he did that, the important thing here is that this video not be cached away in some evidence room. People need to see this video, and people need to react to this video."

"In one sense then, the judge's ruling may have been a blessing, because it allowed you to show this video now?" the anchor asked.

"It would have been better used at trial, and then disclosed afterward. I guess you can call this a distant second."

Shaver grabbed his hospital room's phone and dialed Sphinx.

"Answer, answer...answer!!"

"This is Sphinx."

"Holy shit, Sphinx! Did you see that?"

"Of course. I think the whole city saw that. I've already gotten over ten calls from attorneys asking me what the hell I'm going to do. See, here comes another."

"Well, what are you going to do?"

"I can move to change the venue, but I'm not sure how that helps you, Shaver. It's not something we'll be able to suppress. The effects will reach into the next city, the next county, the future. I'd suggest you just proceed here in town."

"That's it? That's all you can offer me with what I'm paying you? There aren't any rules to enforce here?!"

"Rules? Shaver, breaking the rules got you here. If Judge Melburn had given the State a fair hearing, that video may be in evidence now. If that video came into evidence, who knows if it ever would have been released like this. If it was released, it would have been after the trial concluded, and possibly after you had been acquitted. The effects would have been minimized. Instead, the video is released like this and I assume the public will want your blood. Hold on, I've got to let you go. There's another call coming in."

"Hold on!? What's next, Sphinx?!"

"Trial."

# FORTY-THREE

Cruz and Martinez looked at each other as the swell of people and noise grew outside the courtroom. Cruz wondered if the courtroom walls could contain both the people inside and outside. Outside, there had to be ten thousand people. Some people held picket signs reading, "Hang the Killer!!" Another read, "A Fair Trial for All!!" There were blacks, Latinos, Asians, whites, politicians, businesspeople, activists, construction workers, assistants, athletes, reporters. The crowd had split between those supporting Shaver and those not. People were shouting obscenities through a line of riot police organized for this occasion. More and more people gathered at the steps to the courthouse as time passed.

The inside of the courtroom was a microcosm of the outside, although slightly calmer. There were no picket signs and no riot police. Hushed but intense arguments took place. Then someone shattered the relative calm and screamed, "Convict this son-uf-a-bitch!!" A part of the crowd in the courtroom erupted with cheers. A bailiff promptly escorted him from the courtroom.

Cruz twisted around on his bench seat to look at the crowd. A few women were fanning their faces. The courthouse was old and stuffy without people, let alone filled to the brim. Plus, it was a pretty warm day for early spring. He saw some people taking notes on small pads of paper. The reporters took up the first two rows of seating. People were lined up along the walls of the courtroom. Some talked to one another. Others stood and shifted listlessly. Cruz heard one person ask when this was all going to start.

"This the most packed you've ever seen this courthouse?" Martinez asked Cruz.

"It's the most packed I've ever seen a courtroom, period." Cruz saw Sandra come in and look for them. He held his hand up.

She hurried over and sat down. "You won't believe this. Look at all of these." She handed them newspapers. They were from other states. Shaver was on the front cover of all of them.

"Wow, we've gone national?" Cruz said.

"That's just the start. Our station had to hire a part-time person to help with the influx of calls. We're getting overwhelmed on the networking websites. I personally got *over six hundred* emails yesterday. I've never seen anything like this. It's the main story on almost every news website I've visited." Cruz and Martinez flipped through the newspapers. Shaver's image was splashed across each of them. They all smiled at each other. "What's going on in here?" she asked, slightly out of breath from her excitement.

"It's been a madhouse. Took thirty minutes just to get through security."

"Have you guys seen the crowd outside lately?"

"We've avoided getting up," Martinez answered. "It's almost impossible to move around." Mason and Sphinx came into the courtroom. It was a quarter past eight in the morning. Jury selection was supposed to start at eight-thirty.

"How come you aren't with Mason?" Sandra asked Cruz.

"With the videotape gone, and only having a few witnesses, they don't need my help. It's better to keep it separate anyway. One attorney working on it, knowing all aspects of the case as if it were his child. That's better. Besides, that leaves me free to testify if necessary."

Mason threw his briefcase down on the counsel's table and pulled out a pad of yellow legal paper.

"Did you guys reach a plea deal?" Cruz asked facetiously. "Not that you'd want to disappoint the masses."

"No, that shithead wants a dismissal of the charges or nothing. Amazing. He's only able to take that position because of what happened with the video. So, I told the press about it. Fuck'im." Mason sat down and let out a long exhale. "Ten minutes."

"They must have devoured that."

"Yeah, they ate it up. It'll only stir the pot some more," Mason said. "Listen, all three of you," Mason said, turning to them fully. He leaned forward with his elbows on his knees, his face looked tired, worn down. "I need your help with jury selection. This judge is a joke. No jury questionnaires. Twenty minutes per side for *voir dire*. It's unconscionable."

"How can we help?" Sandra asked.

"I'll be talking to the prospective jurors, so I could use your collective eyes and ears. Watch these people when they answer my questions. Analyze their posture, their gestures, their tone. I'll be able to gather information too, but your perspectives would be very helpful. Let me know if your gut gives you a bad feeling about any of them." He pulled something out of his briefcase. "I had one of these made for you guys too."

It was a chart, blown up to about three times the size of a regular sheet of paper. "Number the chart in correlation to the prospective jurors and keep your notes on there. When it's time to use the peremptory challenges, we'll compare my notes to yours."

There was a click at the back of the courtroom. The crowd grew silent and Mason stopped talking. Cruz saw Todd slip into the courtroom and then slide into place next to Mason.

"Phew," he said.

A bailiff stood up and bellowed, "All rise for the honorable Judge Fredrick Melburn." A collective rustle took place as everyone stood up in a church-like creak of benches and crack of people's joints as they moved in unison. Cruz watched as the crotchety judge made his way to the bench, a toad in an oversized gown, he thought. The judge took the bench and told the courtroom to be seated without an upward glance.

"Appearances."

Mason stood up, "Mason West for the State."

"Sphinx for the Defendant, Sergeant Colin Shaver."

"Counsel, I see this is set for a three-day trial. If you need to ask for more time, now is the time to do it."

Mason stood up again, "Counsel for the defendant and I have discussed the issue, Your Honor, and we think three days will be sufficient."

Judge Melburn looked at Sphinx. "That's correct, Your Honor. Nothing further to add."

"Fine then. Bailiff, bring in the prospective jurors."

Sandra leaned over to Cruz and asked, "What exactly are we looking for?"

Cruz looked at the judge to make sure they weren't going to get into trouble for talking. The judge looked disengaged, toying with something in front of him. "Just give us your perceptions. Gut feelings are like gold in this process."

"I don't know this process, Cruz."

He peeked at the judge again before going on, "The process is called *voir dire*, a fancy French way of saying jury selection. Mason will get twenty minutes to talk to the jurors. In talking to them he hopes to accomplish several goals."

"Such as?" asked Martinez, now intrigued by the conversation.

"Well, the superficial goal is to select the jury. Mason will do that by asking them questions and then trying to read them for biases. It goes much deeper than that though. This is his first chance to connect with the jury. Studies have shown that jurors make judgments at the very beginning of the case. That means if a juror prejudges your client as guilty, you have to work that much harder to disprove that judgment. On the other hand, if that juror prejudges your client to be not guilty, then you just have to reinforce that prejudgment throughout the trial. Mason will weave his theme into the process, to begin to inculcate the jury."

First though, each juror had to stand up and read through a list of questions posted on a wall behind the judge. Their names, age, occupation and other seemingly tedious details. Many judges had moved away from this practice. It made the jurors uncomfortable and could set a negative tone at the beginning of the case. Judge Melburn couldn't care less. The worker gave his name, address, occupation and "something interesting" about himself. As if that would lend any humanity to the process.

The jury pool was a mix, as always. There was a male engineer, two teachers, a grocery store clerk, a doctor, two unemployed people, several businesspeople, a construction worker, a car mechanic, a jockey and one lady that described herself as an entertainer. There were others too, a total of twenty-three prospective jurors in the box. Five peremptory challenges per side left twelve jurors and an alternate. The alternate didn't know he or she was an alternate. Cruz always thought that was a raw deal. To go through an entire trial and then to be told you were the alternate and you wouldn't be deciding anything at all.

The recitation flowed through the prospective jurors until one of the teachers stood up. She was a fourth-grade teacher, plump, large glasses. Wiry, unkempt hair hung randomly around her face. Her voice barely carried over the ongoing buzz of the courtroom. Tawny Redknight.

"It's important to have followers in the jury," Cruz said.

"She's a teacher though. She can control people." Sandra whispered.

"A follower with adults, a controller with children," he responded. Cruz put a check in the box corresponding to Tawny.

The engineer stood up next. He wore an argyle, short-sleeve collared shirt. It was brown, pale blue and yellow. At least the brown matched his pants.

"What do you guys think about him?" Cruz asked. The engineer fumbled through his script.

"Can't hurt that he's black," Martinez suggested. "Maybe some sympathy points there."

"I also liked his honesty," Sandra added. Cruz added a check next to the engineer's name—Lucius Keller.

When all of the jurors finished their burdensome task, it was time for Mason to begin his *voir dire*. "Twenty minutes for the State," Judge Melburn said as he slammed his fist down on a timer next to him. It looked like one of the timers used at chess matches.

Cruz watched as Mason began his dialogue with the prospective jurors.

He was good in front of them. Serious but with a soft tone. Confident but not arrogant. Most importantly, trustworthy. He was setting himself out to be the teacher, the one who would guide the jurors to their conclusion. Sphinx was way more flash. Drama, awe. Mason would be a chalkboard to Sphinx's PowerPoint presentation. Cruz was interested to see how that dynamic played out. Jurors could be turned on or off by Sphinx's style.

Cruz took notes while watching Mason talk to the prospective jurors. Sandra whispered, "Juror number eighteen seems too into this. It looks like she's itching to be on this jury."

"Can you get a feel for why? Does she want to be on the jury to prosecute Shaver or not?" Cruz asked.

Martinez added, "She's given me a couple of weird looks. Like, 'we're in this together.' I'm not sure she knows who the hell I am." Cruz put a big "X" in the space for juror number eighteen.

They proceeded this way, tagging along with Mason through the *voir dire* until his twenty minutes ran out. Sphinx stood up next. His approach was to glamor the jury. Flash diamond studs. Wave pinstripes. Hang his left hand a little bit lower from the weight of his watch. He played the card well though. People were enraptured by a six-foot-five tall, handsomely brown, meticulously dressed man.

Cruz saw juror number seven smile nervously as Sphinx looked at her. "Sandra, watch that juror. What's your female nature tell you?"

Sandra watched her for a few seconds. "Oh boy, she's a sucker for him."

Cruz crossed number seven out. They watched as Sphinx did a number with the jury. It was masterful in some instances. He broached certain bounds in others. Cruz watched earnestly, noting when Sphinx's grandeur perturbed the jurors.

Mason turned around and showed his sheet to them. A person sitting on a bench behind them leaned into the conversation. Martinez gave him a hard stare. "I've got a large 'NO' next to eighteen," Mason said.

Cruz smiled. It was nice to have their instincts verified by another person. "Same with us."

"We thought twenty-one, the engineer, he could be a good one," Cruz said.

"I was on the fence about him. He's so damn nervous. I can't tell if its just because he's a geek engineer or if there's something more," Mason responded.

"I think he's being honest," Sandra said, lifting one shoulder to shrug off her own insecurity in being a part of this process.

"You know, I can see that, Sandra," Mason said. He put a check mark next to Lucius. "We have to hurry, Sphinx is wrapping up."

"What about the jockey?" Cruz asked. "What the hell's that about anyway? I didn't know they existed outside of the track." The rest of them stifled laughter. "What? It's weird." Cruz scratched the back of his head.

"He's bound to have a Napoleon complex. He could be the ring leader. Is that what you want?" Sandra asked.

"You guys told me to rely on my gut. I don't like him," Martinez said.

"Sometimes you need the ring leader, and I don't see much strength in the rest of them. I'm going to have to veto you guys on this one," Mason said. "What about this teacher. Tawny...Tawny Red-something."

"I like her," Cruz jumped in. "She'll follow."

"Who do we strike then?"

Cruz pointed at two. The doctor and one of the businesspeople.

"The small-business owner? Really? I liked him," Mason said.

"I don't know, Mason. But, you've done this a bunch more. I'd go with your instincts."

"We keep the business guy, we'll ditch the doctor. I think we dump the *entertainer* too."

"No way," Sandra said so emphatically that they all looked at her. "She's been there. She's been on the side of abuse. I bet she's got some intense emotions. You guys have picked mostly cold, logical people. There has to be some emotion in that group."

Mason's pen hesitated on his chart. "Counsel, your peremptory strikes," Judge Melburn demanded. Mason and Sphinx took turns calling out the number of a juror until each had used their strikes.

"Mason left the entertainer," Cruz said.

"Her name is Dawn."

"More like Diamond," Martinez said sarcastically.

"Wait till she's our winner," Sandra said. Cruz noticed she was taking some ownership and he liked it. Mason sat down with a huff.

"We got to keep all the ones we wanted," Cruz said.

* * * *

Tawny sat in the middle of a small, crowded room of prospective jurors. The temperature plus nerves plus tight quarters made it all nearly unbearable. She took the note card with her juror information and fanned herself. She used her other hand to play with the tag hanging off of her purse handle. A Mexican man sat to her right. He was in overalls and had a hat pulled down low over his eyes. He stared into nothing. A white man sat on her other side. He had his iPhone turned sideways and was typing furiously. The clerk had told them no phones. She considered saying something to the man, but then thought better of it. Despite this hesitation, she started to reach her hand out to him to say something but stopped. Sensing it, he looked at her. She turned away, red-faced.

They had been waiting for over an hour in that sweltering room. Amazing it was so hot this early, she thought to herself. Was supposed to get to eighty by mid-day, uncharacteristically warm for this time of year. The note card told her to get there by seven. Once they arrived, the clerk told them that court would start at nine a.m. So they waited around for no apparent reason.

The door to the room cracked open. Everyone lifted their heads, but the door just shut again. Tawny went back to toying with the tag. She thought about her students who she hated leaving with substitute teachers. They were her kids, her wards. The substitute was nice enough but it was always hard when the normal rules were suspended for a day. The kids felt they had carte blanche when she came back.

The door popped open again. A woman came in that Tawny didn't recognize—she wasn't the clerk. "Numbers twenty-eight forty-three, twenty-eight forty-nine and twenty-eight fifty, you're excused". Tawny scanned her card. Twenty-eight fifty-one. Typical. "Those people with numbers I didn't call, you're staying here." The woman started to walk back out of the room.

A woman in a white blouse and black skirt called out, "Wait! What about the rest of us?" The other woman ignored her and continued out of the room. "Oh my god! She just ignored me!" the woman whined. She was probably in her forties, the whiny woman. Pretty but tight-skinned and seemingly tight in other areas. Tawney laughed at her own description. A few people looked at her. Damn, it was out loud! Her face turned red again.

The woman came back into the room. "Twenty-eight sixty-two through eighty-four, you're excused. The rest of you are in the pool." One man threw his card on the ground. Others sprung up and hurried out of the room.

"Looks like we're the ones," an awkward-looking black man said to her. She half-smiled and clutched her purse a bit closer.

"At approximately quarter to nine we will call you into the courtroom. The judge will give you instructions as to the proceedings and how you will be selected to be a juror." The woman delivered this information like she was reading off a menu. "Any questions?" The whiny woman made a move as if she was about to talk but was shut down just as quickly by an evil eye.

It was eight-thirty.

"I just can't believe this," a man said. This was the first time Tawny had looked at him. He was absolutely tiny. "I've got races on all these days. They better let me out of this!"

"What kind of races?" the man to Tawny's right asked. He had grime under his nails and his overalls were spattered with paint. She found it hard to believe that someone would come to a courthouse looking like that.

"Horse."

"You got bets?"

The small man looked bemused. "No, I ride them. Like a jockey, you know? On the horse's back?"

"Ahhhhh, *un caballero!*"

"Sure, that too."

"I've never seen one of you in real life, like outside of the horse."

"Believe it or not, we exist in the same realm as you non-horse riders," the jockey said sarcastically.

The woman in the white blouse said, "I ride horses." The jockey glared at her, but then must have decided to drop the whole conversation.

They sat there in silence until another door opened. A skinny man in a brown uniform came into the room. His last name was printed on a badge. Craven. "Go time, jurors. Come on through this door and another bailiff will escort you to the jury box." He held the door open with one arm. Tawny couldn't see into the courtroom but heard its bustle. The jurors stood up and looked at each other before the jockey let out an exasperated sigh and barreled into the courtroom. Tawny brought up the rear of the column.

Her first glimpse of the courtroom was surprising. In many respects it was beautiful. Very high ceiling with thick, white crown molding. Gold accents all around. Tall, rectangular windows covered by velvet sashes. The bench seats were hand carved out of thick wood. She got to the jury box and noticed that all the seats were taken. Dismayed, she started to look for somewhere to sit and saw that jurors had spilled over into seats in front of the jury box.

"Hey—lady," the awkward black man said. "Here, you take mine." She started to wave her hand in the air as if to say "no," but he insisted. She sat down in the chair while the black man sat in one of the folding chairs in front of the jury box. The chair was actually plush. There was a brass foot rail in front of her. Maybe this wasn't going to be that bad.

She peered to her left and saw a cantankerous-looking old man sitting high above them. He wore a black robe and already had his gavel perched in the air. He motioned to the black man to hurry and sit down.

"Ladies and gentlemen, you have been charged with what many agree to be the onerous task of serving on a jury. Welcome," the judge started. "This case is set for a three-day trial. We will start with the jury selection process. In that process, the attorneys for the State and the defendant will get twenty minutes each to talk to you and ask questions." The judge waved his hand in the general vicinity of the courtroom as if to direct the jurors' gaze toward the attorneys.

Tawny looked to her right where two big desks rested with a podium in between them. At the desk on her left was a dark man, although not black. He was very big, and aggressive looking. On her right was the other attorney. He looked older, more broken-in, and had sandy blond hair which was still thick and brushed to the side. Tawny liked his look, it was simple and comfortable.

"Juror number one..." The bailiff standing next to the jury box pointed to a man seated at the opposite end of the jury box from Tawny. "...please stand up and give your answers to the questions behind me." This was the first time Tawny had seen those questions. They were going to have to stand up and read these out loud? She immediately became hot and felt her chest moisten.

Juror after juror stood up and gave their information. All of them recited the information as fast as possible, like shy students in her classroom. The train of embarrassment rolled her way until it was finally her turn. She stood up with her purse clenched to her chest. Her glasses slipped down along the sweat on her nose.

"Tawny Rednight, school teacher, thirty-four years old. I like my students and the Harry Potter series." She sat down just as quickly as she had spoken and pushed her glasses back up the brim of her nose. The blond attorney got up next. His name was Mason West and Tawny was right, he was pretty comfortable. He possessed a calm demeanor and even spoke directly to her once. He asked whether she had any students of color, to which she answered she did. In fact, their school district was made up of over sixty-two percent Latinos. She saw him scribble something down.

The man sitting next to her called himself a long-distance truck driver. He looked wholly disinterested. When the aggressive attorney began his own inquiry, he asked the truck driver what he thought about immigration. The man looked into the gallery as if to make sure no illegals were present and then said, "They don't belong here, do they?" The attorney, he had a catchy name, Sphinx, asked another question. "Are all the Mexicans here in this country illegals?" To which the truck driver responded, "I doubt it, but I can't tell. Can you tell a Chinaman from a Jap?"

Once the two attorneys finished, the judge explained that there was a peremptory strike process. Apparently, each attorney would get five strikes. That would leave thirteen jurors. One alternate out of the thirteen. Both attorneys were huddled at their desks. This was the first time Tawny saw the accused man. He was seated next to the attorney Sphinx. He looked up at the jurors and caught her gazing at him. It sent a shiver down her spine and her eyes darted away.

The image of his face was burned in her mind even after shifting her vision. A long scar ran down his forehead and to his left eye, which was covered by a patch. His hands resembled concrete blocks on the end of a tree limb. There was a general aura of coldness around him. She glanced back and felt relieved that he wasn't still looking at her. She felt the net of focus loosen and watched as both sides worked furiously on their selections.

The prosecutor called out a number and the truck driver next to her stood up. He slid out of the jury box and as he did said to her, "Thank Jesus for that." Then the other attorney called out a number. The young man who had identified himself as another teacher stood up and left as well. He had said he liked, "Democracy and a fair police force." When the defense attorney asked him if he knew about this case, the man answered affirmatively. Tawny must have been out of it because she hadn't heard anything about this case. She didn't pay much attention to the news anyway.

The attorneys went back and forth with their selections. When they were left with only two strikes each, Tawny started to wonder if she was really going to be left on the jury. It kind of made her feel good, as if in not being stricken, she was selected. She looked around at the other people remaining and saw the jockey and the woman with the white blouse. The nice black man who had given her a seat also remained.

She heard the prosecutor say, "Eighteen." No one got up immediately. The judge said, "Juror eighteen, you may leave." A woman finally rose from her seat. She was lanky and a bit crazed-looking to Tawny. While she stood up, she didn't move from her seat just yet. Instead, she peered at the judge, who seemed mildly amused by this occurrence. Then the woman started yelling.

"These police officers do what they can! You don't know what they deal with on a daily basis!" She was generally directing this tirade to the people in the gallery, most of whom were deflecting the words by directing their attention elsewhere. Two of the bailiffs jumped to action and grabbed the woman.

"I will put you in county jail if you don't stop this right now!" the judge yelled. The woman paid him no attention, "The dead man was just a leech! Living on our system, a drain!"

"That is quite enough!!" the judge yelled as he stood up and slammed his gavel down on the bench. The woman stopped talking but struggled with the bailiffs. They got a hold of both of her arms and dragged her out of the courtroom. The judge managed to slap a day in jail on her before she was fully out. He turned to the remaining jurors and said, "You will disregard what just happened. The case you may hear is controversial, but it is your imperative, your duty, to have no prejudgment when this case starts." He sat down and adjusted his robe. "Go on, counsel." The attorneys struck three more people without incident. Tawny looked around, a bit shocked. She was on her first jury.

# FORTY-FOUR

The judge let them take a break after the attorneys finished jury selection. It was actually an exhausting procedure for everyone involved. Even Shaver found himself fatigued. The breaks didn't mean anything to him. He didn't smoke, he had no one to talk to. They were actually more isolating than when everyone was sitting around him, constantly keeping him at the periphery of their attention.

The hoard of people filtered back into the courtroom as the judge directed the prosecutor to begin his opening statement. Shaver watched as the prosecutor swayed in front of the jurors, like a multi-headed snake. He began with an introduction to the case, combing and plucking the jurors in preparation for the evidence he was to present. The man was convincing, Shaver thought to himself. A ball of nerves shuddered momentarily in his stomach before he suppressed the emotion.

Then the prosecutor told a story of that old man, undoubtedly woven together from equal parts bullshit and fairy tale. A transparent attempt to rile feelings that left Shaver feeling ill. As if these people cared about that man.

"Don't be confused, ladies and gentlemen, this is a case about murder. Don't be fooled either. There was no defense, no justifiable use of force here. Instead, an old man was murdered in his bed." The prosecutor turned and pointed at him. "This is a cold-blooded killer, capable of aiming directly at a helpless man's chest," the prosecutor raised his arms as if holding a gun and came right up to Shaver, "and pulling the trigger three times. No hesitation. No remorse."

Shaver bore a hole through the prosecutor with his eyes. The two men stood staring at each other. Far too long. Mason broke the contest first—out of necessity. He redirected his attention to the jurors and continued. "This is a monster that needs to be put away for the rest of his life. The State is asking for murder in the second degree. The State is asking you to protect your fellow citizens from sharing Mr. Rodriguez's fate."

As the prosecutor wrapped up his opening, Shaver heard an extra amount of commotion behind him. He looked and saw that people were standing up and rushing to the windows. This seemed to awaken the judge from his reverie. He pounded his gavel a couple of times, but almost the entire gallery was crowded around the windows at the back of the courtroom. "Bailiffs, go settle these people down!" A woman shrieked and

271

fainted. Two of the bailiffs pushed through the crowd and created some space around her.

"Don't even think about it," Sphinx said to Shaver.

"What're you talking about?" Shaver asked as he looked at all of the bailiffs dealing with the crowd around the windows.

"What's going on back there?!" the judge bellowed.

"People are fighting!" someone screamed.

"Who?!"

"Everyone!" someone cried back to him. "People are fighting each other...the cops are fighting the people! It's a sea of bodies! It must have tripled in size since this morning!"

Shaver started to go to see for himself until the judge screamed out to the bailiffs, "Bailiffs! Secure the prisoner!" Three of the bailiffs came to their senses and redirected their attention to Shaver. Just then the a chorus of footsteps sounded from down the marble hall outside of the courtroom. They stomped in relentless unison until they burst through the courtroom doors. Six policemen stormed in.

"Your Honor, we need to stop this trial right now!"

"For what?"

"Have you seen what's going on outside?" another officer asked incredulously. "Let's get you out of here." Half of the officers stood by the courtroom doors and the others moved toward the judge.

"There is no way," Judge Melburn said. "This trial will continue!" Where the gavel failed this statement did not. The officers halted in their tracks. The people who had been watching what was going on outside stopped and looked at him.

"Your Honor, you can't be serious," one of the officers said in a high-pitched voice.

"Well I can and I am."

"There is a mob outside fighting to get in here. People are getting attacked, smothered and trampled in the process. It's all we can do to stop them from getting into the courthouse—so we need to get you out now!"

"You do your job and stop them. We'll do our job in here and continue this trial. There will be no intimidation of my courtroom," Judge Melburn said with a bit of reckless pomp. The attorneys, the jurors and the gallery looked at him in astonishment. Shaver was the only one that appeared unaffected. In fact, he looked pleased.

"No, this isn't right," a man said as he came toward the bench. "You need to get us all out of here! I just came to watch a trial, not be a part of a siege!" A bailiff put his hand into the man's chest. "Listen, you can't stop me! I want out!" Some of the other people voiced their agreement with the man.

The judge slammed his gavel down, but it may as well have been a plastic toy. "Everyone will sit, and everyone will be quiet!" Shaver smiled but kept his calm. The jurors were always watching. That's what Sphinx told him.

Sphinx stood up and said, "May I proceed, Your Honor?" The judge nodded. A deep, low-toned boom went off outside and sent a light vibration through the courtroom. The hanging chandeliers slowly rocked back and forth. People in the gallery huddled together.

Sphinx moved to the podium, set down some notes, and then dove into his opening statement. "One man's word versus another's. That's all you're going to get in this case. One of those men, Sergeant Colin Shaver, sitting right here, is a fourteen-year veteran of the police force." Sphinx moved around as he spoke, as fluid as water through a creek. He used hand flourishes, dramatic expressions. It was a good show. "He has been *serving* and *protecting* this city against its worst elements. Its cancer." He moved toward the prosecutor.

"Now, this man wants you to believe that Sergeant Shaver, after fourteen years of service without reprimand, snapped and shot an innocent, helpless man in the chest three times. How's he going to prove that to you?" Sphinx pointed at Martinez, who Shaver had not looked at since the trial started. He did now. That little shit enraged him.

"He is going to use the testimony of this man, and this man only. He may parade some experts through here. Some serious, plain-looking expert from the State to talk about ballistics. You can't forget though, it's all about this man's word," he said pointing at Martinez, "versus Sergeant Shaver's word."

"Who is this man? This centerpiece of the State's case? Unlike Sergeant Shaver's fourteen years of service, Officer Martinez has six years. Unlike Sergeant Shaver's years of service without reprimand, Officer Martinez has twice been reprimanded for insubordination. Let's talk about breaking the rules while we're at it. The man that the State is going to use as the core of its case, the core of its argument that you should convict Sergeant Shaver of second degree murder, *can't even follow rules.* On at least two occasions, when his superiors told him what to do, he refused. More importantly, in this case *he broke all of the rules.*"

"There is a simple rule of law called chain of custody. You may have heard of it or seen it on television in your favorite legal dramas. The rule deals with evidence and how that evidence must be protected. Why do we have this rule? To protect people who have been accused of crimes from having tampered or inaccurate evidence presented against them. To make sure that what you see is fully accurate. Why? Because at the end of all of this," Sphinx said with a sweep of his arm across the courtroom, "you're deciding this man's *life*," he said while moving to stand behind Shaver.

"Officer Martinez broke that cardinal rule of chain of custody. He tampered with evidence related to this case. He demonstrated his comfort with breaking rules in other ways as well. Officer Martinez led a group of vigilantes, including his criminal brother-in-law from Mexico and the man you see sitting next to him, Cruz Marquez, to Sergeant Shaver's house. As if hunting prey, he cornered Sergeant Shaver in his house and then nearly killed him while trying to take him into custody!" Sphinx had strewn together those sentences in excitement and ended almost out of breath. "There is a process we use when apprehending alleged criminals, ladies and gentlemen. A process guaranteed to us by the laws of this country! It's called a warrant! Officer Martinez was willing to violate *that* rule of law as well!"

Sphinx stopped to take a drink from his water glass. It was also a moment for absorption, to let the weight of his words fall over the jurors. He pulled at one of the cuffs on his suit jacket and then set the glass down. Another tremor from outside the courtroom made the water in his glass ripple.

"It's fitting, isn't it, that there's so much chaos outside. Chaos is what marked the indefensible hunt for Sergeant Shaver. Much like the crazed crowds that howled around the burning corpse of an accused witch, the State is on a witch hunt for Sergeant Shaver. There is no proof that Sergeant Shaver committed any crime. There is no certainty as to *what* gun, of the five officers that were at the scene, shot Livan Rodriguez. The State has to prove its case beyond a reasonable doubt, and this case is chock-full of doubt. On your verdict form, 'no' to second degree murder." Sphinx returned to his seat and leaned back.

"I don't think they have a chance," he said to Shaver.

\* \* \* \*

Sandra stood on the courthouse steps and looked at the swell of flesh below her. She pulled a long, black wisp of hair away from her face and adjusted the collar on her suit jacket. The crowd stretched two blocks back, and covered every square inch of the park in that area. She had never seen anything like this. Four rows of police in riot gear positioned themselves at the bottom of the courthouse steps. The sun was halfway to the horizon and splashed shadows along the buildings encircling the park.

The crowd of people went crazy when she came out of the courthouse. She almost turned back to go inside, but Cruz was right behind her. Sandra noticed that his tie was loosened and the sleeves of his shirt were pulled up his arms. He pointed to an area for disabled people at the front of the mass of people. It was too loud for them to communicate clearly. They got to the designated area which was actually full of reporters. Each of the reporters was desperately trying to report above the screams of the crowd.

Two separate chants were going, sometimes audible individually but usually a muddled slur of indecipherable vowels. "Gas the pig" and "Free Shaver." A reporter tried to grab Sandra by her arm but Cruz deflected the man's hand. He put his body to her side and shielded her through the crowd. They finally got through and took a minute to survey the mass. People were still arriving. Their sheer number was daunting. It seemed that at any moment the thin thread of civility that existed could break and send the crowd into a state of bedlam.

The police set up a makeshift headquarters comprised of an enormous white tent. Officers surrounded the tent, as if under attack. They carried automatic weapons and many of them had gas masks hanging from their belts. Body armor protected their arms, legs and chests.

"This is ridiculous," Sandra said to Cruz, still having to raise her voice to be heard.

His face looked excited. "This is *amazing*! Look at all these people." He stood in the middle of a road that had been blocked off, with his arms crossed, analyzing.

"I never would have imagined..." Sandra started.

"Me either. I just can't believe all these people are here. There must be fifteen thousand people—I don't know. I've never seen a gathering like this." Someone came up to them and asked where the "anti-Shaver" groups were. Cruz pointed them in the right direction.

"Let's walk to the news station. I've got to get back there to deliver my report."

"Have you ever seen coverage like this? By the way, where's Martinez?"

"I thought he was behind you?"

"Hmm, maybe he stayed inside," Cruz said. "So, have you ever seen this many people? This many news stations?"

"I've never seen this many. I bet there are around a hundred different stations there." They churned against a steady flow of people.

"It's especially telling that people are still walking there," Cruz said as he turned around and took a couple of steps backwards. "It's five-thirty! These people look like they're going to stay overnight." Indeed, some people were carrying sleeping bags, pots, and tents stuffed into tight little sacks. "Hold on —look at this." Sandra stopped and turned around too. She saw a head bobbing through the crowd, coming at them. It was Martinez. He reached them out of breath.

"Christ," is all he managed to say between breathes. His hair was crazed and puffy, and the suit jacket hanging in his hand scraped the ground as he bent over.

"Yeah, you've got quite a stage, Martinez."

"You guys missed it. The judge is crazy." Martinez stood up straight and put his hands over his head. "That damn crowd was hard to fight through."

"Wait, what did the judge do?"

"He shortened the trial."

"What?!"

"Yep. He must have seen what was going outside. A few minutes after he left the bench and you guys split, he came back out. He said that due to the circumstances, he was shortening the trial to two days. He talked to Mason and the other attorney about what witnesses they each have. Mason said just me and one expert. The other attorney said just Shaver. I think that kind of surprised Mason."

"So then he shortened the trial to two days? You mean, two days after today?"

"No! Two days as in, today was the first. He said that we would get through the three witnesses tomorrow and then do closings. The attorneys are still there with the judge working on jury instructions. Mason said he would call you in a few hours, but that he didn't anticipate getting out of the courthouse until about nine o'clock."

"Can the judge do that?" Sandra asked. She was walking in front of the men to make sure they didn't run into anyone. They were completely engrossed in the conversation.

"Absolutely," Cruz answered. "If it isn't going to prejudice either of the parties, then the judge can do it. So Sphinx said he's going to call Shaver?" Martinez nodded. "That's rare." They reached the front of the news station and stopped in a circle, looking at each other. "Are you ready?" Cruz asked Martinez.

"Ready? All I'm gonna do is tell the truth. Mason and I went through my examination a lot. I know what Sphinx is going to beat me up on. Shit, we heard all about it in his opening. None of that changes what Shaver did."

"Guys, I've really got to get inside. This is probably going to be the biggest report of my life." They had walked several blocks away from the courthouse.

"Can we come in and watch?" Cruz asked.

"I'd love that," Sandra said with a look of relief on her face.

"Actually, I've got to get some food and then rest," Martinez said. He gave Sandra a hug and wished her good luck. Then he walked away, moving sideways in the thinning crowd of people.

* * * *

Tawny sat in the jury deliberation room with everyone else. It was a meager step above the waiting room they had been in that morning. People were starting to get restless. Her stomach grumbled. Six o'clock and they hadn't heard anything from the judge. He told them they had to stay because of "developments."

"You know, the only fucking development I want is dinner and my bed," a man said from the water jug at the back of the room. He filled his glass and then stood there staring. Everyone else was silent. Tawny forgot the man's name but remembered he said he was in insurance. He had a black tie on with a cream shirt and matching black pants. His clothes were clean and neatly pressed. Everything about him was neatly pressed but plain. "Am I the only one who's pissed here?" he asked quizzically.

The black man who previously offered Tawny his seat shook his head. "Nope. I'm pissed too. But what the hell are we gonna do about it?" The insurance man didn't respond and slouched back into his chair.

"I haven't even been able to get in touch with my family," the whiny woman said. Tawny remembered her name—Rebecca. "They won't let us make phone calls in here. How are we supposed to let our families know what's going on?" No one responded to that either.

Tawny watched as the jockey walked back and forth across the room. He stopped and looked up at her. "You got a problem?"

"Uh, no. No, not at all. I was just thinking."

"About what?"

"Well, whether anyone else caught the news on channel nine last night."

The jockey looked around and when no one answered, he said, "I didn't see it. Doesn't look like anyone else did either. Why?"

277

"I only caught the tail end of it, but did you recognize that woman sitting behind the prosecutor today? The Mexican woman with the short black hair..."

"Yeah, kind of a hard one to miss," the insurance man chortled.

"She's a reporter for channel nine. I caught the very end of her story and basically just heard the anchor say something about a video."

"Her story was about this case?"

Tawny shrugged her shoulders and pulled away a piece of hair that had gotten stuck on her lip. She got embarrassed with this amount of attention, but at the same time didn't much mind. It was the dichotomy of the adult geek. "I don't know because I didn't hear enough. But, I'm assuming that if she's sitting right there in the courtroom..."

"And they said something about a video?"

"I heard '...video excluded from evidence.' That's it. I paid no more attention to it. I hate the news. It just gets me so down so I try not to watch it except for..."

"Has anyone else heard about this?" the jockey asked, interrupting Tawny. No one indicated they had. "I guess we'll see what happens during the trial then."

Tawny shook her head, taking a bit more of an assertive tone. She didn't like being cut off. "The lawyers didn't mention anything about a video today. If there was a video of what happened, and we were going to see it..."

"...it would have come up," the jockey finished, jumping in again. Short man syndrome, she thought to herself.

The door opened and the judge came in followed by a bailiff. Tawny kind of likened him to her father. They both had creased faces with shiny, taut skin. Yellowing teeth with thinning, but not balding, hair. The judge wasted no time in getting to his point, "I have good and bad news for you. First is the good news. I have spoken with the lawyers in this case and we will be doing this trial in two days. In other words, tomorrow will be the last day the lawyers present evidence to you. After that, you deliberate."

The insurance man muttered, "Thank God."

"The bad news is that I am going to sequester this jury."

The jurors gave each other a collective "huh?" The judge explained, "It means you will be kept at a hotel, not far from the courthouse. You are to have no contact with anyone, except one two-minute phone call to your families to tell them what's going on. You are *not* to watch television. You are *not* to read a newspaper. Do *not* talk to anyone other than jurors. And, when you talk to one another, do *not* deliberate until you have heard all of the evidence. There

278

will be bailiffs with each of you at all times except when you are in your rooms. In fact, none of your rooms will have televisions. *Do you all understand?"*

"How can you do this?" the whiny woman asked. "I have a family!"

The judge's upper lip twitched a bit and he answered without looking at her. "I understand this will be an inconvenience to some of you, but we have to get this right. There is simply too much media coverage, too much garbage being shoved down people's throats."

"Why is this such an important case?" the black man asked. Tawny had talked to him before they came into the deliberation room. His name was Lucius.

"That's something I cannot answer, sir. Nothing about the case other than procedural issues. Is there anything else?" the judge asked his bailiff. The bailiff whispered something into his ear and the judge said, "Oh, yes! You will all be compensated for your lodging and will be provided two meals. The hotel will send a shuttle over for all of you soon. Thank you," he ended in a sing-song voice and walked out of the room. At least they got a couple of meals, Tawny thought to herself.

The insurance man stood up. "Aren't *any* of you going to get mad? This is infuriating!" He went over to the door where the judge had exited and cautiously opened it. Seeing nothing he turned back to the rest of the jurors and spit out an exasperated, "...fuck!"

"Listen son, calm down and watch your tone around the ladies." The voice came from an old man that Tawny had barely noticed until now. He wore a green and white flannel shirt with a pair of faded jeans and suspenders. He had a bushy, curled mustache that almost hid his upper and lower lips.

"Just because you don't have anything going on old man, doesn't mean the rest of us can afford this time off."

"Hey," Lucius said, "the man's right. You just need to calm down." And with the sentiment turned against him, the insurance man took his seat. Tawny looked around the room. Small wall sconces cast a dim light on the other jurors. They were seated around the perimeter of the room, everyone facing each other. Her eyes rested on a younger man, his head bobbing to some imaginary tune.

"Well, I for one think he did it," came a voice from Tawny's left. It was Dawn, the fake entertainer, and real stripper. This was the first comment anyone had uttered regarding fault. Tawny immediately saw the insurance man and Rebecca pull back, as if to draw a line.

"Based on what? You haven't even heard them tell their sides of the story yet. Plus, we're supposed to wait to talk about the case," the insurance man said.

"Oh hell, who needs to hear their sides? The lawyers told us what we were gonna hear. There ain't gonna be no surprises. Screw the judge and his rules too," she said while scratching her neck. She wore a pair of black, stretch pants and a T-shirt that was purposefully torn down her chest. Three earrings hung from both ears and made clinking noises anytime she moved. She popped her gum constantly. Tawny hated that noise almost more than anything else. "Plus, the damn cops in this city are bastards. They'll do things like this. I had one girlfriend that was attacked and raped by a cop. He threat'nd her if she ever told anyone, she'd be dead."

"This is like an episode of tales from the hooker," the insurance man said under his breath.

"What'd you say, you scrawny little man?" Maybe she couldn't hear it because of the incessant chewing, Tawny thought. The man just hung his head and stared at the ground. "That's what I thought, you two little pricks running around here like y'all are the bosses," she said while looking at the insurance man and then the jockey. "Truth is, ain't no one gonna control me." The broken English made Tawny sad inside, but she did feel a small laugh surge through her lungs. "You feelin' me, girl?" Dawn said to her. Tawny just smiled.

"You've got to listen to what the men say tomorrow though, darling," the old man said.

"I know, you sweet thing. What's your name again? Why don't we start there? We don't even know each other's names."

"I'm Earl, darling. Earl." Just as the insurance man was looking around to see if he should participate, the bailiff came back into the room.

"Time to go, folks." Dawn stood up first and got close to the bailiff as she crossed through the door. She stopped and tugged on his shirt. "Big ol' man like you has got to know who did it?" The bailiff took her hand and gently moved it away.

"No, ma'am. I don't know a thing except that your shuttle is here." Dawn pouted a bit and then continued on out of the room. Tawny was amazed. This was the jury of your peers. This was the group of twelve people set to decide that man's fate.

# FORTY-FIVE

Cruz, Martinez and Mason sat around a patio table at Mason's house. He sent his family away during the trial in an effort to protect them from the abounding idiots. The change from three to two days was a strain and a relief at the same time. A strain because he wasn't prepared to cram everything into that short of a time frame. A relief because the trial was eating away at his strength even a day in.

That was a new enemy, the elephant in the room for Mason. He couldn't last at this much longer. The trials felt more and more drawn out. He started to lose grasp of all the facts, all the nuances of matters. Working twice the amount of time was the only way to keep it all straight, and that took a toll on his marriage. He stood in front of the tall mirror in his room each day, naked, analyzing the deterioration of his body. His gut protruded. His cheeks were starting to sag. His pectoral muscles looked more like breasts than muscles.

The mirror in the bathroom was no greater help. He stood in front of it and examined his teeth, which despite his best efforts were turning slightly yellow. Lines zagged across his face like fish under water. His eyes looked haggard most days. There was still a glowing ember deep within him, to prosecute, to bring the criminals in society to justice. However, the ember was fading and would have to be passed on to someone else soon.

A glass of whiskey on the rocks sat in front of each of them. Mason picked his up and watched the light brown liquid play among the cubes of ice.

"Mason, why so solemn?" Cruz's voice stirred him from his thoughts. He looked up and pulled back the corner of his mouth but said nothing.

Trying to redirect the mood surrounding the table, Martinez said, "So, what's the order of things tomorrow?"

When Mason didn't pick up the conversation, Cruz said, "We go first. I assume Mason is going to briefly put on the expert regarding ballistics and then use your testimony. Right, Mason?"

"Yep, that's what I was thinking," Mason responded, finally looking at them.

"You know you've got this in you, right, Mason?" Cruz said. Both he and Martinez peered at Mason to get some semblance of how he was feeling.

"Oh, I know. It's just one more day of trial. No big deal." He took a sip of his whiskey. "It's really the bigger picture. I'll be honest with you guys— this shit makes me feel old." He let a grin out with the admission, enough to set the other men a little bit more at ease. "My battery's on low, fellas. I'm not sure I've got another one of these in me, but I don't want to go out a loser either."

"Wait," Martinez started, "you're conceding defeat?"

"No...come on. It's not like that. But I've been around long enough to have seen this play out. Without the video, this is a very, very difficult case to prove. People aren't prone to putting a cop away for thirty years when the only evidence against him is another person's testimony. Sorry, but that's just reality."

"Mason, you're gonna crush Shaver on cross," Cruz said. "What we lost with the video we make up, even if not to the same degree, on his cross examination. You *do* have a chance to go out on top, and that cross examination is your chance!"

Mason hadn't really looked at it that way.

"There is so much you can do to whittle away his credibility on cross. You can bring out his violence, his hate of minorities." Cruz's own comment made him flash back to his youth. The incident with his friend lying next to him, hanging on to life. He recalled Shaver's face then. "There's something I haven't told you guys" They both looked at him. "When I was a teenager, my friend and I had a run-in with some of the city cops. My buddy split, took off when the cops drove in front of our house. I had no idea why he did, or why I followed him. They ended up catching us and they just about beat my friend to death."

Mason and Martinez kept listening. Cruz was visibly shaken up. "The cop that beat my buddy, that took joy in seeing us cry in fear, was Shaver."

"What?!" Martinez exclaimed.

"Cruz, why didn't you tell us about this?" Mason asked.

"Hold on," Martinez said, "This fucking Shaver? The one in this case?"

"Yes."

Martinez threw his hands in the air. His brown skin turned red. His eyes narrowed and turned the same color. "How can you be sure?"

Cruz looked at him sideways. "It's not something you forget. His face was etched in my mind all this time. When I saw him at his house, I almost puked."

"I can't believe you haven't told us this before," Mason said again. "How have you been sitting there silently?"

"It's *my* damn issue, isn't it?" he said, his own face burning crimson. "Plus, it had nothing to do with this case."

"Well, you can't be sure of that," Mason said.

"Are you gonna try him for a crime that I say he committed fifteen years ago? Come on. It's irrelevant to this case."

Mason had to agree with that, but it was still inconceivable to him that Cruz remained silent about it for so long. It was a remarkable display of repression. Mason had never gone through anything that traumatic. He went to ask another question but Cruz held his hand up, cutting off the conversation.

Cruz said, "Back to the case, because we don't have time to sit around flabbergasted. I'm simply trying to let you know what Shaver is truly like. This was not a one-time incident. This was most likely something he did with frequency. So, I think you can elicit that in his cross examination..." Martinez slammed his glass on the table and went inside. "Fuck, what's the big deal? It's not the end of the world."

Mason looked at the young attorney. He was clearly talented but also had so much room to grow. There was leadership potential in Cruz, if he stepped out of himself a bit more. There was no doubt the young man was a bright star.

"I think you're right, Cruz. I'll try to elicit those emotions from him. No guarantee though."

"Of course not, but I have confidence in you." That was nice to hear, because Mason wasn't feeling so stellar. "What demonstratives are you going to use?"

"Todd created a chronology of events that will be a primary piece for me. I have pictures of forensic evidence, the spent shells, Shaver's gun. I'll use most of them during the expert's testimony." Martinez pushed the sliding glass door back open and tripped onto the patio.

"Goddammit!"

"Hey, you aren't getting drunk, are you?" Mason asked.

"No," Martinez answered indignantly. "Just missed that damn step." Mason and Cruz kept looking at him. "Get outta here! I've barely had half my drink."

Mason slipped a bundle of documents over towards Cruz. They were shrunken copies of the demonstratives.

"How bad's it gonna be tomorrow?" Martinez asked.

Mason slowly took his glasses off of his face. "The truth?"

"Of course the freakin' truth. I need to be prepared for this."

"Pretty damn bad. Sphinx is a good lawyer," Mason said. Cruz watched Martinez's face for changes in expression. "Quite honestly, there's a whole bunch of shit to toss at you. The association with your wife's brother, Raul. The chase for Shaver. The arrest. You're in for an ass-whooping." Martinez shrugged his shoulders and leaned on the wall.

"He can get those things, but that doesn't change what happened at Livan Rodriguez's house."

"That's exactly right," Cruz applauded. "Doesn't change the fact that Shaver walked into that man's house and killed him in cold blood. All Sphinx will be trying to get at is your credibility. And I don't see how Sphinx has a chance to bring your credibility as low as Shaver's will be. That whole 'man in blue' thing isn't going to last long at all."

"All right then, one more question. You think we're gonna win?" Mason and Cruz looked at each other. It was impossible to predict how a jury would come out. A jury was like a black box. You could do your best to get the right elements in there, but once deliberations began the chemistry project took over. Some personalities did well with others. Some personalities clashed. Other personalities took over while some remained weak. Juries were comprised of victims and aggressors much like the greater society. The victims blamed outside forces, usually beyond their control. The aggressors were unwilling to bend to fate. How the jury comes out often depended on the mix of these subtypes of people.

"Well?"

"Fifty-fifty," Cruz finally answered. Mason just looked away.

# FORTY-SIX

Not that bad, Tawny thought to herself. They got a meal at the hotel and then a decent room. She was sure some of the jurors lost their minds without a television, and it was undoubtedly something she would hear about. She had just read a book and fallen asleep to the heavy sound of the inhale and exhale of her breath.

The ride over to the courthouse was groggy and silent. The only person who looked more put together than yesterday was Rebecca. She was sitting in the front seat of the van, as uptight as ever. Tawny sighed and dug through her purse for some gum. The insurance man was sitting next to her. She extended her hand with a piece of gum in it. He shook his head no without saying anything else. Jerk.

The courthouse sat on a full block of the downtown area. There were two entrances and the bailiff said they would be using the back one to avoid the congestion. Tawny figured he meant the morning commute congestion. That was until they got about half a mile away from the courthouse.

The streets were packed with people. Cars were stuck, emitting wisps of exhaust up in the morning air. Emergency vehicles pulled up onto sidewalks with their lights flashing aimlessly. Tawny stopped chewing her gum and looked down at her watch. A few minutes past eight in the morning. This couldn't be right, she thought to herself. She'd never seen anything like this.

The van came to a stop behind a long row of cars that were honking like geese in flight. People rubbed up against the van as they scraped past. There were all sorts of homemade signs. Just about every right or interest was represented. It didn't seem like an upbeat atmosphere. In fact, the tension was tangible even inside the van.

The van driver picked up a walkie-talkie and spoke to someone named Chad. He asked for an escort at their location. Tawny was looking out of the window when all of a sudden a camera popped into her face. It surprised her enough to send her reeling back onto the insurance man.

"Watch yourself!" he said as he pushed her away. Then more cameras popped up like like moles peeking their heads out of the ground. One became three which became ten. They surrounded the van and Tawny heard someone scream, "It's the jurors!" The van started to shake a little bit as more and more people accumulated around them. It was rocking back and forth slowly, like a ship on a lazy sea. Tawny moved away from the window as men and women plastered their hands and faces against the van. A small child sat perched on her father's shoulders, looking strangely calm.

285

## Derek Blass

The van driver called Chad again. Much more urgent this time.

Then the screaming started. Rebecca yelled when a man slammed his hand against her window. People outside were screaming to put Shaver away, to stop the reverse discrimination and let him go, to not fuck up the decision. Underlying the screams were thuds. The van sounded like the inside of a taut drum as people slammed their fists on its steel outer skin. Everyone inside the van was awake and fully alert at this point.

"Get us out of here, driver," the jockey said. Tawny noticed that Dawn had taken a hold of the insurance man's arm and smirked at the irony. Like grabbing onto a twig while falling through a tree. The driver tried to pull out from behind the row of cars and get onto the sidewalk, but the mass of people pushed back. Tawny saw a set of emergency lights coming their way.

"Here comes the escort," she said lightly. As the three motorcycle cops got closer, the van started to shake more violently. It was almost as if the people sensed their chance to yell at the jurors was ending soon. The child on the father's shoulders had disappeared. Tawny looked around the various windows of the van, concerned about the child but seeing nothing. The van was shaking enough now from side to side that they all slipped on the bench seats.

The motorcycle cops lost momentum. Their lights weren't making forward progress toward the van. Tawny could see the three cops waving people back to no avail. A van followed about fifty feet behind the motorcycle cops. It shot out chunky waves of siren wails. Then it stopped and started to shake a bit. People were pushing it back and forth too.

Some of the people around Tawny's van were caught in the mayhem. They had scared faces, bulging from the pressure of the people around them. She watched as one woman started swinging her elbows to get room. Others seemed to be taking advantage of the mayhem. They bore wicked smiles while pushing against the people around them. This created a mixture of willing and unwilling participants in a veritable mosh pit.

Tawny heard a faint *thu-thump*. This occurred several more times over the next few seconds. She saw smoke start to rise from various places around the van. She imagined that the friction of all these people had started a fire. As the smoke spread so did the people. People close to the van started to cough and pull their shirts over their faces. Tawny saw a column of spartan-like riot police creating a rift in the crowd. They marched in formation, slowly eating their way through the mass of people who were now trying to find cover from whatever was in the smoke.

The insurance man was leaning across Tawny now. His mouth agape. The column came closer and closer to the van until the front of it, three police officers, reached the driver's side window. They stopped to verify that the column was still intact and then proceeded to pass the van. The officers moved like a centipede through dirt.

When the end of the column passed, the driver started the van again. They crept behind the officers, watching the mass of people around them disperse. Every couple of minutes or so the column would stop to shoot off some more canisters into the crowds.

When the van finally made it within eyesight of the courthouse, Tawny could not believe what she saw. What was visible of the ground was littered with empty bottles, paper, clothes, and scraps of food. The ground usually disappeared in the swell of people though. Heads bobbed and jostled as far as Tawny could see. Police in full, black riot gear mixed with soldiers in tan uniforms. There was a wall of fifteen-deep national guardsmen posted in front of the courthouse.

When the mass caught wind of the slowly moving group of officers and its trailing payload, a cheer started from afar and then overwhelmed the van like a shock wave.

"Oh my God," the insurance man said. All of the jurors shared his sentiment and clustered together in the van. They could do nothing but watch thousands of sets of eyes turn to look at them. The sound of the column's feet hitting the ground in unison was all but washed out now. Cheers and chants emanated from the crowd. Lights and cameras pointed at them as both sides looked at each other in surprise.

The van finally turned the corner to the back of the courthouse. This area was shut off except to police and military personnel. The column broke off from the van, still in formation, never relinquishing its image of force.

Once the van went into the underground parking lot, Tawny felt like she could breathe again. Bailiffs slammed the doors to the lot shut and swung an enormous metal bar in front of the doors to keep them closed. One of the bailiffs hurriedly approached them from the other side of the lot.

"Let's get going. The judge is waiting."

"No rest for the weary, huh?" Tawny said. A few of the other jurors grunted to agree with her assessment. They followed the bailiff to the open elevator. It's dim light spilled out just into the dark garage. They all squeezed in and stood shoulder to neck, elbow to breast, as the elevator seemed to struggle under their weight. A ding sounded and they got off on the first floor.

The bailiff beckoned them to hurry, but no one really did. The stress of getting to the courthouse left them all exhausted.

Another bailiff opened the courtroom doors and Tawny could see that the judge, lawyers and gallery were all in place.

"So nice of you to join us," Judge Melburn said.

"Great way of getting us over here," the jockey shot back.

"Who does the State call as its first witness?" The judge had not even waited for all the jurors to be seated. A loud cheer and wailing horns sounded just after the judge stopped talking. "Hold on a moment. Bailiffs, I want you to confiscate every person's cell phone in here. Someone must be communicating with people on the outside." He paused as the bailiffs looked at him to see if this order was for real. They already had plenty on their plates. "Who is it? Which one of you is communicating—texting is probably what you are doing—with the outside?" No one responded. "Bailiffs..." Judge Melburn said with a wave of his finger towards the crowd.

This interlude gave Tawny a moment to pull a tissue out of her purse and dab her forehead. The bailiffs went around collecting people's cell phones. Once the tedious process was completed, the judge sat back in his chair and repeated his earlier question, "Who does the State call as its first witness?"

"Dr. Rajeed Ganesh." Tawny watched as a younger Indian man stood up from the gallery and walked to the witness box. He had a brisk, slightly nervous pace. He gripped a binder under his left arm and adjusted his glasses with his other hand. Once seated in the witness box, the clerk of the court made him swear to tell the truth and nothing but the truth. This was just as she imagined it in her dreams last night.

\* \* \* \*

Cruz pushed his way through the seemingly endless crowd to get to the courthouse. Sandra followed behind him, holding onto his hand. Martinez was off to their side somewhere, cutting his own path through the thicket.

They stayed a half of a mile away from the courthouse with the anticipation that yesterday's crowds would lessen by the morning. That was entirely incorrect. Most of the night they heard people, bustling like locusts, milling around their hotel. Their hotel was actually the center of the chaos. Most of the media covering the event were staying there. Anytime they stepped out of their room they were bombarded with questions and cameras. Even Sandra, used to the spotlight, was growing tired of the coverage.

The media presence at the first day of the trial was nothing in comparison to today. Vans encompassed the hotel, which was large in regular times, but dwarfed now. Satellite dishes perched on the top of most of the vans, sometimes extending towards the sky, other times rotating to pick up their signal, but always in motion like antennae on bugs. Cruz had seen all sorts of badges hanging from people's necks. Local and national, big and small news stations alike. Reporters from New York, California and Florida The hotel lobby was awash with different cultures and languages and smells.

He and Sandra pushed out of the hotel at about eight in the morning. Most members of the media were already awake, or never slept to begin with. They sat in the hotel restaurant, sipping coffee while ignored cigarettes burned in ashtrays next to them.

The streets were packed. Not with awake people. Most of the people were still asleep. The rustling from the night before must have been the setup of this makeshift village. Some people had no tent, just a sleeping bag. They lined the sidewalks of every visible street. It wasn't until Cruz and Sandra got a few blocks away from the courthouse that people were awake, packing up their gear and starting to meander with the rest of the herd.

Two blocks away from the courthouse, the crowd was at a dead, packed standstill. Martinez had run to catch up with them and they all looked at each other silently. Cruz could see over some of the crowd, but the bottom quarter of the courthouse was cut off by heads. Martinez shrugged his shoulders and started to push through. When people got pissed he just flashed his badge. Cruz and Sandra followed behind Martinez for as long as they could until they eventually got split up by people filling the space left by Martinez.

Cruz looked at his watch and saw they had fifteen minutes until the trial was supposed to restart. He figured Mason was losing his mind with Martinez not being there. He looked up and saw they still had at least half of a block to go. The people standing around had grown so cramped and pressed together that they couldn't move even if they wanted to. Cruz yelled out to Martinez who screamed back. He was stuck too.

When they stopped, the pressure from behind began to build. More and more people were arriving and pressing against those in front.

"Cruz, this is getting tight," Sandra said. He nodded, acknowledging her while looking around for a solution. A woman screamed out to stop pushing. Cruz saw a man next to him who looked pale and weak. He watched as the man's knees buckled and he lost consciousness. The man didn't completely fall to the ground. Instead he was supported by the people packed in around him. Someone yelled for a doctor.

"Martinez," Cruz screamed, "Need you to do something!!" The people around him looked back and then two roaring shots rang out. The crowd's natural instinct was to move backwards, toward the empty space behind it. Cruz grabbed onto Sandra tightly and they cut across people to where he thought Martinez was. They saw Martinez running ahead of them, brushing off people moving the other way, and holstering the gun he just fired.

They started sprinting toward Martinez. Sandra kicked off her shoes and was able to keep pace with Cruz. The courthouse was within distance now, but the crowd started to slow in its retreat. Once the imminent danger was gone, the empty spaces started to fill back up. The crowd had spread as if a bomb went off in the middle of it, but was now congealing around the empty center. The pathway to the courthouse was quickly closing, and Cruz saw Martinez bent over on the first courthouse step catching his breath.

"We've got to hurry!" Cruz yelled to Sandra. He tucked his head and grabbed her forearm, essentially dragging her along. He reached the edge of the crowd just as it closed, his arm still clasped onto Sandra's. Sandra was behind two men who he shoved aside.

"What the fuck..." Martinez said.

"I don't know," Cruz answered. He looked at Sandra whose face was smeared with a mixture of sweat and tears. She looked much more delicate without shoes on. "Let's get in there." He shot a glance to his right and saw a commotion on the street next to the courthouse. Smoke was rising in various areas along the pavement.

Martinez flashed his badge and they moved through a thick wall of national guardsmen. The halls of the courthouse were empty and silent. Their steps rang off of the marble floors and echoed down the hall. Sandra's little feet slapped along on the cold surface. Mason was standing outside of the courtroom, with a stern look on his face.

"Why aren't you in there?" Cruz asked.

"Where the hell have you guys been?" he responded. Sandra stepped out from behind Cruz and put a hand on his shoulder to balance while she put her shoes back on. It clicked with Mason when he saw Sandra. "Man, what happened?"

"When did you get here? You didn't have to deal with the crowds?" Sandra asked.

"No, not really. Most people were asleep, camped out, when I got here. Probably about six in the morning."

"Well, that explains it," Sandra said, drifting off.

"It was...difficult...to get over here," Martinez said.

"You guys are lucky. The jury hasn't arrived yet. Apparently they were held up too."

"You know, I saw some commotion and smoke rising on the street over there," Cruz said, pointing behind him.

"That smoke is probably some sort of tear gas," Martinez said.

"They'd use that on civilians?"

"Sure, whatever works."

Mason opened the door to the courtroom. Cruz adjusted his suit and tie, then turned around to see if Sandra was all right. She pulled down her skirt a bit and ran her hands down the front of her suit jacket then smiled at him. They walked into the courtroom and took a seat behind Mason's setup. The judge was sitting at his bench.

When they settled in, Mason came and knelt by their side. Cruz saw that his hair was bushy and wild, untamed from last night's sleep. His blue eyes looked sharp, focused. "I want to introduce you to someone," he said. "Right behind you is Dr. Rajeed Ganesh." They all turned around to look at a small Indian man sitting there with a notebook clutched to his chest. He looked very nervous.

"Pleasure to meet you, doctor," Cruz said, extending his hand. The doctor shook his hand with a limp, damp hand. Cruz looked at Mason and they exchanged a thought without any words. A bailiff came out from the judge's chambers and whispered something to Judge Melburn. Cruz could see the judge nod his head and then return to the distractions in front of him. Mason took his seat at counsel's table and leaned back. The old chair creaked under the new weight.

The courtroom door cracked and then opened fully. The jurors stood in a line behind a bailiff. Cruz saw that the short man, the one who had identified himself as a jockey, was standing at the front of the line. He wondered if they had already selected him as the foreman. Cruz studied each juror as they came into the courtroom. The only one that made eye contact with him was a pudgy woman, fidgety. Redknight was her last name. That much stuck with him.

"Who does the State call as its first witness?" Judge Melburn asked before the jurors were situated. Cruz looked over at Sandra who was texting something furiously. The crowd outside screamed and Judge Melburn's face contorted. He screamed something to the bailiffs about confiscating phones, about how the gallery was communicating to the outside. Sandra looked mortified until she saw Cruz grinning. He made a motion to her for her to hide the cell phone in her blouse.

Judge Melburn repeated his question to Mason who then called Dr. Ganesh. The man virtually stumbled over his feet to get to the witness box.

His voice cracked when he answered "yes" to the swearing in.

"Dr. Ganesh, please introduce yourself to the jurors."

"Dr. Rajeed Ganesh. That is R-a-j-e-e-d G-a-n-e-s-h," the doctor said, spelling his name out for the court reporter.

"Dr. Ganesh, begin by telling us a little bit about your education." Cruz searched through his jacket pockets for a pen while the doctor listed his education and qualifications. Washington University undergrad, M.D. at Duke. He was now the city's forensic pathologist.

"Just what is a forensic pathologist, Dr. Ganesh?"

"Forensic pathology is a specialization," he started. "I do things such as autopsies to figure out the cause and manner of death. When, for instance, you see that someone committed suicide on television," he said, turning to the jury, "I will usually be investigating a case such as that."

"Do you investigate homicides?"

"Oh yes, that is one of the most common investigations that I perform. Although, the most common of my investigations are simply related to natural deaths."

"How many homicides do you investigate, say, on a yearly basis?" Mason asked.

"In this city?" Dr. Ganesh asked while he thought about the answer. "Probably about fifty a year, give or take." The doctor reached for his glass of water. Cruz listened as Mason went through the steps to qualify Dr. Ganesh as an expert. Sphinx chose not to *voir dire* Dr. Ganesh, which surprised Cruz some.

"When did you get involved in this case?"

"Sometimes I will go to the scene of an incident, which I did in this case. I was called out soon after it occurred actually. I studied the scene and rode back to the morgue with the body."

"Did you notice anything unusual during your initial investigation?"

"No. The older man had apparently suffered gunshot wounds, although I did not know for sure how many at that point because he was still clothed. The man had nothing in his hands or around him that would constitute a weapon. He was just lying in his bed and..."

Sphinx jumped up and bellowed, "Objection! Your Honor, what the man had around him or did not is irrelevant!"

"Your Honor," Mason said, "the State has a right to put some flesh onto the bones of this story. The Defendant cannot expect to try this case in a vacuum."

"Overruled."

"You can finish your sentence doctor," Mason said. Cruz watched as Sphinx stewed over his pad of paper. Shaver looked remarkably calm, staring into oblivion. His hands were placed neatly on the table in front of him.

"He was just lying in his bed and appeared not to have moved before being shot."

"How do you know that?"

"Oftentimes, people will be frozen in contorted positions when the victims of a violent crime..."

Sphinx shot up and objected again. The judge overruled him again.

"...but this gentleman, Mr. Rodriguez, was just laying on his back, looking quite peaceful actually. We recovered the spent shells to conduct a ballistics analysis and transported Mr. Rodriguez to the city morgue."

"What do you do once you have a corpse back at the morgue?"

"We do an intake—name, age, address, et cetera—and then we find a storage unit for the body until I am able to perform an autopsy."

"How long until you start the autopsy?"

"Generally pretty soon after the intake. It is important to perform the autopsy relatively quickly. The process usually takes a couple of hours, especially in a case such as this where there were three gunshot wounds."

"Dr. Ganesh, can you please describe to the jury what you found when you performed the autopsy on Mr. Rodriguez?"

"It was relatively simple. He suffered three, close-range shots to his chest. The bullets caused a tremendous amount of damage. Any one of the bullets on its own most likely would have been able to kill Mr. Rodriguez. He died immediately."

"Were you able to tell where the bullets came from?"

"You mean, directionally?"

"Your Honor, I am going to object to this line of questioning. Dr. Ganesh was admitted to testify as an expert in forensic pathology, not ballistics or crime scene investigation," Sphinx said. He moved to the podium and blocked Mason from the microphone.

Mason laughed and said, "Your Honor, despite defense counsel's suggestion, I went through Dr. Ganesh's qualifications both as a forensic pathologist and a ballistics expert. He has been qualified as an expert in both areas in courts of this state on many occasions."

"I didn't hear that testimony, Your Honor..."

"Mr. Sphinx," Judge Melburn said in an agitated voice, "Overruled! You will allow this witness to continue to testify without these baseless objections. I heard the testimony as well and accepted his expertise in both specialties." Turning to Mason, he said, "You may proceed." Cruz liked the exchange. The more Sphinx irritated the judge the better. A judge could not directly decide the case, but if Sphinx pissed Judge Melburn off, that would only help rulings turn more in Mason's favor.

Mason flipped through his notes. "Can the court reporter please read back the last question?" Mason asked. The court reporter stopped typing and read Mason's last question back to him. "Okay, so I meant directionally to begin, Dr. Ganesh."

"The three shots all came from above Mr. Rodriguez, and from close range."

"Now, could you tell what weapon they came from?"

"Yes. The police department issues two types of weapons primarily. The first is a standard issue, Glock 23 handgun. The second is a weapon only issued to members of the department's Special Weapons and Tactics team. It is a submachine gun called the Heckler and Koch MP5. The evidence indicated that the three wounds were made by rounds from a MP5."

"Taking a step back, doctor, was the Defendant a member of the S.W.A.T. team?"

"Sergeant Shaver was a member of the S.W.A.T. team and the leader of his sub-team. I pulled records from the personnel division to confirm both of these facts."

"We know these wounds were caused by the MP5," Mason said, "but do you know which officers had those guns on the day that Mr. Rodriguez was shot?"

"I was able to figure that out as well. The city's police department tracks which officers in the S.W.A.T. team take which weapons when responding to a call. The city implemented this tracking procedure approximately ten years ago to track weapons usage. On the day in question, hold on one moment..." The doctor dug through his records. "On the day in question there were five officers that responded as a part of Sergeant Shaver's team—Officers Williams, Martinez, Tomko and Lindsey and Shaver himself."

"And, by the way, where are those officers today?"

"Objection! Irrelevant!"

"What is the relevancy of where the other officers are, Mr. West?" Judge Melburn asked.

"The jury has a right to know why Officers Williams, Tomko and Lindsey are not here to testify, Your Honor."

"Overruled, but I will be paying close attention to this testimony, Mr. West."

"Can I answer?" Dr. Ganesh asked.

"You can," Mason said.

"Officers Williams, Tomko and Lindsey were killed shortly after the incident involving Mr. Rodriguez."

"Do you know how that happened?"

"Objection!"

"Sustained. I do not see that having any bearing on this matter, Mr. West. Move on."

"Getting back to the day at Mr. Rodriguez's house, Dr. Ganesh, which officers were carrying an MP5?"

"Sergeant Shaver and Officer Martinez." Cruz heard a low, collective gasp from the gallery. Jurors looked at each other with raised eyebrows.

"Were you able to conduct any tests to determine which of the guns, either the one the Defendant was using or the one Officer Martinez was using, was shot?"

"Unfortunately, no. By the time we obtained the guns, they had both been disassembled and cleaned before being checked back into inventory."

"Is that standard operating procedure?" Cruz saw Sphinx start to rise to object but then decide against it.

"If the officers went out and did not have to discharge their weapons, yes. However, when an officer discharges his weapon the department has a strict protocol to follow. This includes submission of the weapon to ballistics immediately."

"Did that occur in this case?"

"No. Neither of the officers turned in their weapons."

"That means one of the men is lying and did not follow protocol on the day in question?"

"It seems that way, yes."

"I have no further questions, Your Honor."

Sphinx stood up and threw his pad of paper onto the podium. "Let me understand a few things here, Dr. Ganesh. Most importantly, you have no idea whether Sergeant Shaver's or Officer Martinez's gun was the one that discharged into Mr. Rodriguez, correct?"

"I cannot tell from the evidence I had which gun it was."

"So that's a yes."

Dr. Ganesh looked uncomfortable. "I guess you could say that."

"You have no expert opinion then as to whether Mr. Rodriguez was shot by Sergeant Shaver or Officer Martinez."

"Objection," Mason said, "asked and answered."

"As I said before, the evidence would not allow me to make that conclusion. I only know that it was either Sergeant Shaver or Officer Martinez."

Sphinx flipped through the pages in his notepad. The silence was broken by thumping coming from outside of the courtroom. Cruz ignored the sound and focused intently on Sphinx's cross-examination.

"You know what, Your Honor? I have no further questions myself if that is Dr. Ganesh's only conclusion."

"Would the State like to redirect?" Judge Melburn asked Mason.

"No, Your Honor."

"Next witness then."

"The State calls Officer Roman Martinez." A cheer broke out from the crowd outside the courthouse again, following another secret text from Sandra. Judge Melburn scoured the courtroom with his eyes. Cruz smirked at this man's vain attempt to exercise control. It was amusing and simultaneously depressing to see a man of his age not having learned to let go of certain things.

Martinez rose from behind Mason and gave Cruz a quick look of reassurance. He made his way to the witness stand and was sworn in. Martinez looked calm, his jet-black hair slicked back, matching his black suit. Cruz thought he appeared credible, controlled. The true test would arise on cross-examination.

Mason stood beside the podium for this direct. He leaned casually, hands clasped together and resting on the edge of the podium. The court reporter stared at him, waiting for his first word. Cruz looked at the jurors, who were all captive.

"Officer Martinez, can you please introduce yourself to the jury?"

"Sure. Officer Roman Martinez. I'm a six-year veteran of the city's police force. My last two years have been as a member of the S.W.A.T. team."

"What did you do before becoming a police officer?"

"I served in the Army for seven years as a communications soldier attached to a special forces squad."

"Service is in your blood then."

"Yes, it sure is."

"Were you recognized in any way while in the Army?"

"I was. I received the Army Commendation Medal and the Purple Heart."

"The Purple Heart? So you were wounded?"

"I was wounded while serving in Iraq during the first Gulf War."

"How were you wounded?"

"The short story is that I was shot in the ankle by an enemy. I ended up needing a bone graft and several surgeries to correct the injury, which still is not a hundred percent."

"I assume you were honorably discharged?"

"Yes."

"When did you join the police department?"

"I went to the academy a couple of years after I was discharged from the Army. I needed to heal before putting myself through that type of physical work. The academy was about six months long and included tough physical and mental testing."

"Mental?"

"Rules of law mainly."

"When you completed that training, what happened next?"

"I passed the required tests and began my field training. Patrols mainly. The worst shifts in the worst parts of town."

"Is that what they do with most new recruits?"

"The ones they think can handle it. In some ways, it was harder being on those streets than in war. Your own people were attacking you. They hated you even though you were trying to help."

"When did you start working with Sergeant Shaver?"

"Pretty much when I was assigned to S.W.A.T."

"Was there a process for becoming a member of that elite team?"

"Oh, yeah. You had to prove yourself in combat situations, had to pass extra physical and cognitive tests. There were several tests dealing with all types of firearms. Then you had to be political."

"What do you mean, political?"

"Lots of guys want to be S.W.A.T. To put it bluntly, you had to know which ass to kiss." A couple of the jurors laughed. Judge Melburn looked like he was going to rouse himself but instead slunked back into his chair.

"Did the Defendant lead your team the entire time you were on it?"

"Actually, he was reassigned for six months during my time on the team."

"For what?"

"He got into..."

"Objection, objection Your Honor!" Sphinx said as he stormed past the podium and halfway to the bench. The bailiffs looked at him quizzically. He slid to a stop on the polished marble floor after becoming aware of where he was and just where he was storming.

Judge Melburn looked at him quizzically. "Your objection?"

Sphinx cleared his throat and readjusted his jacket with both hands. "Yes, Your Honor. Irrelevant." Cruz looked at the jurors who seemed more perturbed than amused. He knew jurors could sense if someone was trying to hide facts from them. Too many objections could make it feel that way.

"Does the State have any compelling reason to introduce this evidence?"

"I'll withdraw the question," Mason said. It was a nice move. Willingness to decline a fight went over well with jurors. "Let's move on to the day in question Officer Martinez. When did your team get the call to respond to Mr. Rodriguez's house?"

"Seems like it was about two-thirty in the afternoon. It had been a slow couple of days before that. We were called out on one other d.v.—er, domestic violence—but that was it. The call came in and we geared up. This was during the time of the *Police* shows, so we had to wait a couple of extra minutes for the cameraman to get ready."

"What *Police* shows?"

"The shows you see on T.V. You know, where the camera follows cops on their beats. Ours was just a special S.W.A.T. edition."

"All right, and what was the cameraman's name?"

"Max."

"So you loaded up and headed to the house?"

"That's right. It was about a ten-minute trip in the armored rescue vehicle from our station. We got there and Sergeant Shaver gave us our orders. Essentially, who was supposed to go where. He told me to take the rear of the house."

"Who else was there with you?"

"At the rear? I know Max was there. Then I think it was Lindsey and Williams. Tomko and Sergeant Shaver usually stuck together."

"They were close?" Mason asked.

"Always. Tomko was his right-hand man. So, we waited for our count, the time we were supposed to breach, and then breached."

"What did you find when you entered?"

Martinez laughed and pushed back from the witness stand. "Nothing, nothing at all. The house was empty where we entered. Silent. We moved down the hall, in formation, until we got to the main living room. That's where they were."

"Who was there?"

"The old man, Mr. Rodriguez, and his daughter."

"What was her name?"

"We never got her name. At least I didn't. Everything kind of fell apart after things went down."

"Before you go there, where were Tomko and the Defendant?"

"Standing there, in the living room. Mr. Rodriguez was lying on his bed. He was quiet and looked to be asleep, although I don't know how he would have been with all the commotion of the breach. That's probably what pissed Sergeant Shaver off."

"That Mr. Rodriguez was asleep?"

"No, that Mr. Rodriguez seemed to be faking it. No way he was asleep."

"What happened after you all ended up in the living room?"

"The daughter was on the floor, on her side and grasping at the foot of the bed. She was just recovering from the flashbangs that we tossed into the house. She was crying, clearly hysterical from the sight of us once her eyes adjusted. It was understandable, you know? Five men in black armor, masks pulled over our faces, guns drawn, and a cameraman to boot."

"Hold on. Can you explain what a flashbang is for the jurors?"

"Sure, flashbangs are shaped like cylinders and kind of look like grenades. They are true to their name. Once deployed, they emit a burst of high intensity light and a deafening bang. The combination will stun just about anyone—there's really no defense to it. When the people inside the building are stunned, it's safer for us to go in."

"Okay. Once you all entered the room and saw just Mr. Rodriguez and his daughter there, did anyone declare the room secure?"

Martinez paused for a second, thinking about his response. "I don't think so. I don't remember hearing that. It was more confusing. We had expected some sort of altercation, but it was pretty calm except for the daughter freaking out. We all stood there for a minute or so, trying to figure out what was happening. That's when Sergeant Shaver started honing in on Mr. Rodriguez."

"What do you mean by that?"

"I think the old man was pissing Shaver—Sergeant Shaver—off. He was just lying there. He hadn't moved at all since we entered. Sergeant Shaver started jabbing at him with the barrel of his gun, the MP5 that Dr. Ganesh was talking about earlier."

"Did Mr. Rodriguez respond at that point?"

"Nope."

"Was he alive?"

"Oh yeah, he didn't look dead or anything. He had opened his eyes, but appeared to be in some sort of catatonic state. Excuse me," Martinez said as he drank some water. "Sergeant Shaver jabbed at him a few more times and told him to get his hands out from under the blanket that was covering him. This made the daughter go off. She started wailing, hitting at our feet. She told us that her father didn't speak English. Shaver yelled at her and told her to shut up. His attention diverted to her at that point and he started to mess with her. He grabbed her hair, got really close to her. She was screaming and he was loving every second of it." Cruz saw one of the woman jurors pull her sweater tighter around her chest. She had a look of disgust and fear spread on her face.

"Did the Defendant stop harassing the people at any point?"

"It didn't seem he would. He was escalating the violence by doing sick things like licking the daughter. When I saw that I had to stop him. I didn't think he would stop on his own."

"What did you do to stop him?"

"I lunged toward him, leading with my shoulder, to try to knock him away from the daughter. When I did, the old man stirred from his position. That's when Sergeant Shaver wheeled around and shot—several shots with a few hitting the old man in the chest."

"And then it was over."

"And then *that part* was over," Martinez corrected.

"Did the Defendant ever say anything to you about why he shot Mr. Rodriguez?"

"I doubt he cared that he shot Mr. Rodriguez. He called the old man an illegal and pestilence. All that would have been important to him was that he had rid the world of another illegal. Sergeant Shaver did say something about the old man causing the incident, but I don't see how. Mr. Rodriguez was old, unarmed and stunned from the flashbangs."

There was a break in the testimony as Mason looked at his notes. "Your Honor, I think this would be a good time to take a break. We've been going for a while here."

Judge Melburn squinted at a clock on the wall and then nodded his head. "Ten minutes." The people in the gallery stood up and went to the windows at the back of the courtroom. Cruz tapped Mason on the shoulder and motioned he was going to go outside. Sandra followed him.

"How do you think it's going?" she asked.

"Not bad. I think Martinez is credible. He paints Shaver out to be a monster, which he is. By the way, who is helping you with the texts outside?"

She pulled her cell phone out from her purse and waved it proudly. "Let's go meet my correspondent."

"But the testimony starts back up in ten minutes."

"He should be on the steps. It'll only be a minute." Cruz followed her through the long hallway to the front doors of the courthouse. He pulled back a thick, wood door and the mid-morning light swept into the hallway. There was actually a hush outside. The people had settled down overnight, and the excitement of the event had transformed into the grind of the wait.

The crowd picked up the movement and twenty thousand people, looked silently, expectantly at Cruz. He let Sandra squeeze out behind him, hardly able push the door against the stare of the crowd.

"Just creepy," Sandra said as she scooted down the fifty or so stairs to the street. Sandra hugged the wall of the courthouse as she went, trying to be less visible to the crowd. She met a man who was dressed in a cream suit. His black hair was slicked back like a gel helmet. Big, white teeth gleamed when he smiled. Sandra waved Cruz down to join them, which he did reluctantly. He watched the crowd and felt its energy pulse up through the wall of national guardsmen.

Cruz got to Sandra and the plastic-coated man. He extended his hand to Cruz. "Andre Cisneros. Muuuucho gusto," he said in a baritone voice. Cruz didn't like this guy already with his Mexican monster-truck-rally introduction.

"Cruz Marquez." The man went back to talking to Sandra, groping her with his eyes. They were talking about how her break of the news story had spurred a national barrage. The horrific account of what Sandra went through plus the chase to get the video is what sent a local story over the top. Sandra told him what was going on inside the courtroom. Most reporters couldn't get into the court because Judge Melburn had limited the people in the gallery to those present on the first day of trial. This had sparked outrage in the media community. Stories like these made money, lots of it.

Andre took notes furiously. He was cheesy even when doing that. Extra energy, bouncing his pen on his pad of paper when asking questions, flashing that shit-eating grin. Cruz wondered if the man was actually this onerous, or if it pissed him off to see anyone else enjoying their time with Sandra. A little jealousy was healthy, he thought.

Clouds were rolling over the high roof of the courthouse. Cruz stood there impatiently. He wanted to get back inside to see how Martinez was doing. The clouds looked ominous. Sure enough, the sound of thunder groaned from somewhere in the distance. People in the crowd looked up, questioning their allegiance to the resolution of this issue. Banners that hung taut the day before had corners falling off of their supports. Tents slanted sideways under the weight of the crowd. The fickle attention of people was waning as time passed.

The conversation between the two finally seemed to be wrapping up. Cruz took the chance to jump in and suggest that they get back to the trial. The crowd exhaled as hope of some news dissipated. Cruz walked briskly in front of Sandra back to the courtroom. When he cracked the door to the court, he saw that Sphinx was already in his cross-examination of Martinez.

"The State's attorney made a big deal about your service on the police force. You're aware that Sergeant Shaver has served fourteen years in the department, correct?"

"I didn't know the exact time, but that sounds accurate."

"That's over twice as long as you, right?"

"Yes."

"And you..."

"That doesn't diminish my service though. I wasn't finished."

"I apologize for interrupting then. I was going to ask about the description of your time in the academy. One of the things you brought up was testing on rules of law. Did those rules of law include how to perform a legal search and seizure?"

"They did."

"And what you needed before arresting someone?"

"That too."

"Okay, we'll get back to that later."

Cruz could already feel the force of Sphinx's cross. It was like a jackhammer chipping away at a carefully built castle wall.

"I want to talk about the day that Mr. Rodriguez was shot. You said that you and Sergeant Shaver were the only ones that checked out the MP5s from inventory when you left on the call, right?"

"No, I think Dr. Ganesh said that."

"You remember his testimony to that effect though," Sphinx said without missing a beat. Cruz noted a golden rule of cross-examination—always get the witness to agree with your statements.

"I recall Dr. Ganesh saying something to that effect."

"I want you to take a look at this document, Officer Martinez," Sphinx said as he gave a document to Mason and then walked another copy up to Martinez and the judge. "Do you know what that document is?"

"It looks like a log for the inventory at the department."

"Have you seen these logs before?"

"We see them every time we check equipment out," Martinez answered as he looked up.

"Your Honor, I move to introduce this document as defendant's exhibit number one."

"Any objection from the State?"

"Yes, Your Honor. Foundation to begin with. Officer Martinez does not keep these records, so how could he know if this is the actual record from that day? Hearsay also."

Judge Melburn turned his attention to Sphinx who said, "Officer Martinez has just testified that he saw this type of log every time he checked equipment out. He recognized and authenticated it as one of their inventory logs. That is sufficient for its introduction. As to hearsay, this is a business record and so it is excluded from application of the hearsay rule."

"I'm going to allow the document into evidence," Judge Melburn said.

"The defense moves to publish to the jury."

"Go ahead," the judge said.

"Does the date on that log appear to be for the day you all went to Mr. Rodriguez's house?"

"Yes, I believe so." Sphinx had projected an image of the log onto a big screen next to the jury box, which they were all reading.

"What gun does it show Sergeant Shaver checking in that day?"

"It reads one MP5."

"What gun does it show you checking in that day?"

Martinez took a moment to look at the log, then he briefly looked at Mason before answering, "I don't see a log for me checking in my weapon."

"So, you didn't check your weapon in that day?"

"Objection, Your Honor, asked and answered," Mason stood up and said.

"Sustained."

Sphinx went back to his counsel table and pulled another document out from a folder. Cruz could see delight in Shaver's eyes. Sphinx went to Martinez and handed him a copy of the document. "Officer Martinez, can you tell me what this document appears to be?"

Martinez read the piece of paper and then put it down. "It looks like the log from the next day."

"Your Honor, the defense moves to admit this document as the defendant's exhibit number two."

"Any objections?"

"Same objections as to the previous document," Mason responded in a slightly defeated tone. He knew he would lose the objection, but he had to preserve the record for any possible appeal.

"Overruled," Judge Melburn said matter of factly.

"Officer Martinez, I am going to hand you this document which has been marked as the defendant's exhibit number two while my paralegal publishes it to the jury." The document was again projected on the big screen. "Please read the log for that day pertinent to the S.W.A.T. team you were on."

"There is one entry, for me, for the MP5," Martinez said disgustedly. The people in the gallery shuffled, creaking the old wood benches. Cruz looked at Martinez intently and then at Mason. This log issue was a fact that had escaped all of them—except for Sphinx.

"That means you didn't check your MP5 back in until the day after the incident, correct?"

"It seems that way although these inventories aren't always accurate."

"What evidence do you have that the inventories are not always accurate?"

"Mainly accounts from the inventory officer, Officer Tulite."

"Do you have any reason to believe that the inventory you see here in the defendant's exhibit number two is inaccurate?"

"No, other than what I just told you. The problem with that day, after Sergeant Shaver shot Mr. Rodriguez, is that it was hazy. I had never seen a civilian murdered like that." Sphinx had made a critical error in asking an open-ended question like that. He knew it and tried to move on quickly.

"Let's turn to the day in question and the incident itself, since you provided a nice segue." Sphinx took a position in front of Martinez with his arms crossed. "Both you and Sergeant Shaver had MP5s on the day in question, right?"

"Pretty sure that's been established."

"Is that a yes?"

"Sure."

"You allege that Sergeant Shaver shot Mr. Rodriguez, but it could have just as easily been your MP5 that shot him, right?"

"No, that's ridiculous. Shaver shot him, no question."

"You don't have any evidence that Shaver shot Mr. Rodriguez, do you?" Martinez stared hard at Mason. He wanted so badly to disclose the fact that the video existed. It was bullshit that Sphinx could use a rule of evidence to get around the video. Mason stared back at him and Martinez could barely discern Mason shaking his head no.

"Besides what I saw, no."

"In fact, the only evidence you *or* the State have against Sergeant Shaver is your word, correct."

"I don't know what evidence the State is going to present. I just know that I saw Sergeant Shaver kill Mr. Rodriguez in cold blood."

"But, it just as easily could have been you, right?" Martinez just shook his head. "Officer Martinez, answer the question."

"No, it could not have been me." Sphinx smiled and moved on.

"We already established that you did not check your MP5 into inventory as required. After the incident involving Mr. Rodriguez, you went after Shaver for some time, didn't you?" Sphinx was walking a fine line. If he stepped too far over it, the door to explaining the existence of the video would swing open.

"Sergeant Shaver was actually chasing after me for a while."

"When the tables turned, you started chasing Sergeant Shaver to apprehend him."

"There came a time where we had to arrest Sergeant Shaver for his crime."

"Who was the we? Other members of the police force?"

Martinez pursed his lips, knowing that this issue backed him up against a wall. "It was me, an attorney, and some other people."

"That means you were going to effect the arrest with civilians?"

"That's how it worked out."

"And you didn't have a warrant to arrest Sergeant Shaver, did you?"

"We had a warrant on its way, but there was an emergency situation that required us to effect the arrest immediately."

Sphinx picked up a piece of paper and asked his next question, "This emergency was a Mr. Tyler Smith?"

"What do you mean?"

"The emergency you are referring to, it was saving Mr. Smith?"

"We had reliable information that Sergeant Shaver was holding a person as a hostage."

"Mr. Smith."

"Yes."

"And isn't it true that Mr. Smith had tried to kill you before you went to save him?"

"That is true."

"What you are trying to tell me and the jurors is that you forced your way into Sergeant Shaver's house to save a man that had tried to kill you?"

"Whether he tried to kill me or not is irrelevant. It was a hostage situation."

"It wasn't just a convenient way to arrest Mr. Shaver?"

## Derek Blass

Mason stood up and said, "Objection, Your Honor, argumentative."

"Sustained. The jury will disregard counsel's last question."

"In your opinion then, Officer Martinez, you didn't violate any rules when arresting Sergeant Shaver without a warrant?"

"That is..."

"When you stormed Sergeant Shaver's house with flashbangs and automatic rifles."

"If you let me finish, no, I didn't violate any rules."

"How many people were there when you effected this illegal arrest?"

"None, because there wasn't an illegal arrest."

"How many people were there, Officer Martinez?"

Martinez let out a sigh and looked up towards the ceiling as he counted. "I think, about eight people."

"Were any of them officers?"

"No, as I said before."

"In fact, weren't some of them criminals?"

"I don't know any of their backgrounds." Cruz did not like how the cross examination was going. He tensed in his seat.

"Was there a Luis Gutierrez in your group?"

"I don't recall anyone with that name."

"Were you aware that he had been convicted in Mexico of a double homicide, but was released early due to his political connections?"

"Like I said, I don't remember all of the people that were there."

"How about Simon Morales?"

"Nope."

"Did you know he was one of the F.B.I.'s most wanted drug runners operating at the Tijuana border?"

"No."

"If you didn't know these people, who was your connection to the criminal underbelly of Mexico?"

"I didn't know everyone there."

"But you knew a man named Raul Solis, correct?"

"Yes, he is my brother-in-law."

"Was he the one that brought those criminals along to illegally arrest Sergeant Shaver?"

"Objection, Your Honor!" Mason yelled. "This cross examination has gone on like this long enough. Counsel's questions are argumentative and ignore the answers that Officer Martinez is giving."

"I am simply ascertaining who Officer Martinez took with him to perform this illegal arrest, Your Honor. If he had used other police officers, as required, this wouldn't be an issue."

"I'm going to overrule the objection, but let's get on with this, Mr. Sphinx," Judge Melburn said in a raspy voice. It was a napping voice.

"My last question, Officer Martinez. What rule didn't you violate in the time between when Mr. Rodriguez was killed and you arrested Sergeant Shaver?" Cruz sat up in his seat. This was a tremendous gamble on Sphinx's part, to ask such an open-ended question. Martinez contemplated the question.

"I maintained my integrity and made sure that the man who murdered Mr. Rodriguez is sitting here on trial today." Sphinx calmly picked up his stack of papers and sat down.

"The State's next witness?" Judge Melburn asked.

Mason rose from his chair and leaned on the counsel table. "The State rests, Your Honor." It was a difficult thing to say, especially where there just weren't many witnesses to call.

"The defense?"

Sphinx leaned over to Shaver and whispered something. Shaver shook his head and the conversation continued between the two. "Your Honor, can the defense request a brief recess, please? Five minutes is all we need."

"Five minutes. Everyone remain where you are, no milling about." Judge Melburn went back into his chambers. Sphinx approached one of the court's bailiffs and asked to be allowed to speak with Shaver outside of the courtroom, in confidence. The bailiff looked at some of the other bailiffs who shrugged their shoulders. Sphinx grabbed Shaver by the bicep and led him out into the hallway.

"Shaver," Sphinx started, "You don't need to say a thing. There is enough reasonable doubt in this case for you to be acquitted ten times over!" Sphinx looked back at the courtroom to make sure no one was around to hear the conversation. "I *promise*, you can *only screw things up from here*. Trust me and give this to the jury now!"

"I want my story to come out, Sphinx. I want the chance to say something!"

"You'll get that fucking chance when you are acquitted and you go onto every fucking morning, afternoon and evening show in the fucking world!" Sphinx yelled. He was raining spit as he spoke. "This is *not* the time to speak up!"

"But what about my story?"

Sphinx pulled Shaver farther away from the doors to the courtroom. "Your *story*?! You mean the story that you shot that old man in cold blood? The story that you may have killed the cameraman that caught you shooting the old man? The story that you may have killed other police officers, and that you may have called for hits from your prison cell? *Those fucking stories, Shaver*?!"

Shaver smiled and said, "You don't believe all that, do you?"

Sphinx pulled his head back from Shaver. "I've worked with a lot of sick fucks, but you're at the top of that list."

"I'll take that as a compliment."

"Don't. I'm not here to be your friend. I'm here to get you acquitted, that's my job. At most, our interests are temporarily aligned. But don't confuse that for friendship or camaraderie. I'm not like you."

Shaver's face turned red, he thrust his hand out and grabbed Sphinx by the collar. He pushed Sphinx back against the cold hallway wall and said, "Kidnapping people isn't a crime? I know the things you've done, Mr. Sphinx. You're far from clean. Spare me your *fucking* lectures."

Shaver let Sphinx go and walked back into the courtroom. Sphinx adjusted his clothes. "Fucking asshole," he muttered as he turned to head back in himself. They entered the courtroom just as Judge Melburn was taking his seat at the bench.

"Has the five-minute recess brought any enlightenment to the defense?" he asked.

Sphinx looked at Shaver. Cruz had been watching the interplay and guessed that Shaver wanted to testify. He was an attention monger like that.

"The defense calls Sergeant Shaver, Your Honor." Mason had been hunched over his counsel table until Sphinx's words reached his ears. Some higher power had just provided a chance for redemption.

Sphinx stood up and moved slowly to the podium. His face had lost most of its color, and he fidgeted with documents while Shaver was sworn in. Sphinx raised his head and realized that everyone was looking at him, the courtroom silent and ominous. He cleared his throat and said, "Sergeant, tell the jury a little about yourself."

The two did a forced dance through Shaver's direct examination. Performing a direct examination of your own client when you are a criminal defense attorney, is almost unheard of, and certainly not practiced much. Shaver explained his time on the force and how he rose from a beat to a gang unit to S.W.A.T.

Sphinx exhaled some of his pent-up air because Shaver was actually doing a decent job. He was credible, and had seemingly softened some of his rough edges for this moment.

"Why was your S.W.A.T. team called out to the Rodriguez's house that day?"

"Obviously, we don't get called out for every domestic violence call," Shaver started. "But, when there's a potential hostage situation, including arms, that's when they get us out there."

"And you guys can be first responders?"

"Not often—we usually support the first responders. But, on the day we went to the Rodriguez's house, the regular cops were spread thin with other things in the city. We got there fast, and we were the first."

"Describe the protocol when responding to an armed hostage situation."

"We treat it like a mini-war. Diversion, confusion, and hopefully submission without needing to discharge our weapons. So, we create sub-teams, get into position, breach with diversionary tactics like flashbangs, and raid the building."

"Is that what you did in this situation?"

"It's exactly what we did."

"What did you find when you got into the house?"

"The threat was supposed to be from the daughter's husband—but he wasn't there. It was just the daughter and her father. We still had to secure the area though, so I asked the father to get up from a bed he was lying on. I did that several times but he didn't respond."

"What was his daughter saying?"

"I had no idea. I don't speak that language."

Sphinx winced. "By that language, you mean Spanish, right?"

"Yeah, sorry, Spanish."

"What was she doing while talking to you?"

"She wasn't talking, she was screaming. Real animated. I didn't understand a thing she said, and her father still wouldn't move. He had his hands under a blanket and I started to get concerned that he may have something under there."

"What do you mean?"

"He could have had a knife, a gun, anything. You can never be sure," Shaver directed this last statement at the jurors.

"When Mr. Rodriguez would not respond to you, what did you do?"

"I tried to poke him, to get him to move. I just wanted him to respond.

The daughter became more emotional when I started doing this, and it felt like things were getting a little bit out of control. So I was going to cuff her and then deal with the father. When I reached down to handle her, Officer Martinez lunged at me. At the same time, I saw the old man finally move, and Martinez discharged his gun in our struggle."

"How many times?"

"I don't remember the actual number of bullets fired, but I do know that three of those shots hit the target."

"Mr. Rodriguez, you mean."

"Yes, three shots hit—Mr. Rodriguez. Unfortunately."

"You said unfortunately. Do you regret what happened?"

"I do. I regret that we couldn't communicate with the family better, and I regret that he was shot."

"After this all occurred, what did you do?"

"Followed the required procedure. Turned my gun in to inventory, wrote a report on the incident. Everything should have been normal, except that Officers Martinez and Williams split off from the team at that point."

"Now, we haven't heard much about Officer Williams. Who was he?"

"A black cop in our team."

Sphinx saw one of the jurors, the engineer, frown at Shaver's response. His luck had run long enough, it was time to wrap up the examination before Shaver said something devastating.

"Was Officer Williams a part of the group that ended up hunting you down at your house to arrest you?"

Shaver furrowed his eyebrows. "Well, no, but before that Williams and Martinez..."

"He wasn't a part of that group then," Sphinx said, trying to cut Shaver off and get him to follow the lead.

"Like I was saying, Williams and Martinez split off, and then Williams was involved in the murder of one of my other officers."

"That part really had nothing to do with the Rodriguez case though, right? And, it's probably part of an ongoing investigation so you can't talk about it?"

"Who's to say what I can and can't do anymore? I've been locked up in jail since that unlawful arrest at my house. An investigation? No idea whether that's happened or happening."

"I think that wraps up my examination, Your Honor."

"Hold on, because I'm not done," Shaver said. "Those two...officers..."

Shaver managed to push out, "...attacked and killed Officer Lindsey. Then Officer Martinez hired a gang of criminals to chase me down to my house. I was shot multiple times," Shaver said as he actually stood up and pointed to where he was shot.

"Are you finished?" Sphinx said.

"I just wanted to say that I've been a good cop for a long time—over a decade. Never been involved in anything like this."

"Thank you, Sergeant," Judge Melburn said. "The prosecution, I assume you have some questions of Sergeant Shaver?"

"I do, Your Honor," Mason said while trying to control his excitement. To cross-examine a criminal defendant was a rare occurrence, and in this case spawned from Shaver's stubbornness.

"Good late morning, Sergeant Shaver."

"Hello."

"Let's start with what you did at the Rodriguez's house. You were positioned at the front of the house with Officer Tomko, right?"

"Correct."

"Any specific reason it was Officer Tomko?"

"He was like my lieutenant...my right-hand man."

"So you and your right-hand man stormed the front, while Officers Martinez, Williams and Lindsey breached the back, correct?"

"Yes."

"Was there anyone else present?"

Shaver paused and glanced at Sphinx. "What do you mean?"

"I mean, on the team you brought to the house, was there anyone else there besides the officers we mentioned?"

"Objection, Your Honor. Request to approach the bench," Sphinx said.

"Come on up, counsel."

Mason and Sphinx walked up to the judge and huddled over a small microphone which was there for the court reporter's benefit.

"Your Honor, Mr. West is going down a path that ends in the excluded video," Sphinx whispered so the jurors couldn't hear. "What relevance is there to the cameraman being at the scene?"

Judge Melburn turned his attention to Mason. "What relevance counsel?"

"Video or not, Your Honor, I *do* get to inquire as to where that cameraman is today. Almost everyone in this case has disappeared, to put it mildly. I can inquire and attempt to impeach Sergeant Shaver's credibility using that information."

Judge Melburn squinted at Mason. The rest of the courtroom sat in silence, desperately trying to hear what the judge and attorneys were talking about. "I'm going to let you ask your questions, but you stay the hell away from that video, counsel."

"Understood," Mason said, although the anger of that ruling still burned in the pit of his gut.

"Sergeant Shaver, you can answer my last question."

"There was also a man there, named Max."

"And who was he?"

Shaver hesitated again, which was fine with Mason. It only lent more suspense to his answer. "A cameraman for a show called *Police*."

"He's no longer with us, is he?"

"I don't know what you mean," Shaver said, getting irritated. Mason noted the inflection change in Shaver's voice. It was clear he didn't like having to answer Mason's questions.

"No longer with us...as in deceased, passed, *dead*."

"I think you're right. He died."

"That's glossing over his death, Sergeant. He died shortly after the incident with Mr. Rodriguez, correct?"

"I believe so, yes."

"What was the cause of his death?"

"I have no idea, that wasn't my case."

"You didn't know that he was shot to death in his apartment?"

"I didn't," Shaver said through clenched teeth. His face had changed, from the forced placidness to angular annoyance. He tapped the witness box with one of his fingers, and fixed an unflinching glare on Mason.

"Turning briefly to Officers Williams and Martinez, you stated that they killed Officer Lindsey. Remember that?"

"I do, they shot him in cold blood."

"We'll get to that. First though, where was Officer Lindsey shot?"

"On his body? It was a head shot."

"No, no. Sorry, I wasn't clear enough. Where, as in location. Where was he when he was shot?"

"Don't remember that either. Some house."

"Okay, let me try to help you refresh your recollection, Sergeant, because you may have forgotten that you gave a brief statement to the media on the day Officer Lindsey *and* Officer Williams were shot. The statement was given at..."

"I do remember now."

"Ah, see, sometimes we just forget these details. Where was it then, Sergeant Shaver?"

"At Williams' house."

"In your direct examination, you testified that following the incident Williams and Martinez essentially split off from the team, right?"

"That's right, they distanced themselves from the rest of us right away."

"What were Officers Lindsey and Tomko doing at Officer Williams' house then?"

"Well...I hadn't talked to them, but I assume they were trying to get back in touch with Williams...I wouldn't know though because..."

"Did they try to call Officer Williams?"

"They did, actually, but he wouldn't answer."

"He didn't answer and tell you all to, as politely as I can put it, go to hell?"

"I don't recall that."

"At the house, who shot who first?"

"Williams shot Lindsey first."

"And then who shot Officer Williams?"

"Officer Tomko."

"Did Officer Tomko tell you why Officer Williams shot Officer Lindsey?"

"Objection, hearsay!" Sphinx blurted out, as much because he had a viable objection as to interrupt Mason's momentum.

"Overruled."

"Can I answer?" Shaver asked the judge, who nodded yes. "He didn't."

"Hold on, you never asked him what happened?"

"I asked him, and he said that Williams shot Lindsey, unprovoked."

"So, Officer Tomko told you that Officer Williams just came into his house shooting, no questions asked, no explanation?"

"That's what he said."

"Officer Williams' wife was at the house during this shootout, right?"

"That's what I remember."

"Who got to the house first—Officers Tomko and Lindsey?" When Shaver looked like he was going to hesitate again, Mason held up a slim stack of papers and said, "And if you need help with any of this, Sergeant Shaver, let's just refer to your report from that day."

Mason could see the "fuck" form on Shaver's lips. "They got there first."

"They got there first, and only Officer Williams' wife was there, right?"

"Yes."

"Just to be clear, they were inside the house before Officers Williams and Martinez arrived, correct? Is that your understanding?"

"I don't know that."

"But, the shooting took place inside the house, right?"

"Correct." The courtroom could see the noose tightening around Shaver's neck.

"And you just said that Officer Williams came into the house shooting, right?"

"Look, that's what Tomko told me. I wasn't there."

Mason smiled. "What Officer Tomko said is good enough for me, Sergeant Shaver. If what Officer Tomko said is true, that Officer Williams came in shooting, it seems logical that Officers Tomko and Lindsey were already in the house, right?"

"I guess."

"And if Officer Williams came in shooting, presumably there was a reason, right?"

"With someone like him, who knows."

"What do you mean, someone like him? Do you mean because he was African-American?" Mason guessed that *wasn't* what Shaver meant, but he had the opportunity to push a button.

"Why would I mean that? I mean he was a hot-head. Anyone can have a bad temper." Shaver grabbed the pitcher of water in front of him and poured a glass.

"Just to wrap this up, and get the story straight, you're saying that Officers Tomko and Lindsey went to pay Officer Williams a friendly visit, and that he ended up shooting Officer Lindsey in the head, unprovoked?"

"That's what I'm saying."

"What happened to your eye?"

The sudden change in topic caught Shaver off-balance. He reached up and touched his eye patch while looking at Martinez.

"I was in a car accident."

"Again, Sergeant, that unfairly glosses over facts, doesn't it?"

"What do you mean?"

"How did the accident occur?"

"We were in a high-speed pursuit, and our car flipped over several times."

"You were in a high-speed pursuit of Officer Martinez, *weren't you?*" Mason said with some force.

"Yeah, we were chasing Martinez."

"Tomko was with you, correct?"

"He was."

"So you weren't always this lamb being chased by the big, bad wolves were you?"

"Counsel!" Judge Melburn screamed before Sphinx could even get his objection out.

"That...Martinez broke off.  He and Williams killed Lindsey and shot Tomko.  We *had to* chase him down!"

"Oh, you were chasing him to arrest him for the murder of Officer Lindsey?"

Shaver sat back in his chair. "Yeah, that's right."

"Did you have a warrant to arrest him?"

Shaver's face contorted.

"Sergeant, easy question.  Did you have a warrant to arrest Officer Martinez?"

"No, we didn't have a warrant."

"That's something you're complaining about in this case, right?  That you were supposedly hunted down to be arrested without a warrant, right?"

"Sure is."

"But you're comfortable with the fact you did the same thing to Officer Martinez first?"

"Martinez was a part of killing Lindsey, so yeah."

"And Officer Martinez told us that you killed Mr. Rodriguez, so it seems like fair's fair, right?"  When Shaver didn't respond, Mason added, "Add to that, when Martinez was running away, he didn't have a hostage, did he?"

"No, he didn't."

"Because he was on a motorcycle, right?"

"He was."

"What about when you were arrested, who was with you?"

"A guy named Tyler."

"Friend of yours?"

"I wouldn't say a friend—he was there trying to help me defend against Martinez and his crew though."

"A person, not your friend, was in your house about to risk dying for you? That's what you're saying?"

"Correct," Shaver responded. His face was completely red at this point. Mason stood coolly at the lectern, enjoying the cross-examination like a cat pawing at a wounded bird.

"How did you know Tyler?"

"We both worked for the Chief of Police," Shaver said. Before he could retract the word "work," Mason jumped to his next question.

"Worked? I know how you worked for the Chief, indirectly. He was your boss. How did Tyler—and I believe his last name is Smith—how did Mr. Smith work for the Chief?

Sphinx rose from his seat. "Your Honor, I'm going to object to this entire line of questioning. It is irrelevant to the issues in this case."

"Overruled, counsel. This goes directly to the defendant's credibility, plus he opened the door."

"I'm not sure exactly what he did."

"Even though he was there to help you save your life, and you worked for the same person, you don't know what he did?"

"That's what I said."

"I'll tell you something, Sergeant Shaver, I have looked at the City's payroll and I don't see Mr. Smith's name anywhere."

"I couldn't tell you anything about that."

"The other thing I can't reconcile, and by reconcile I mean make sense of..."

"I know what the hell it means." Mason looked up from his notes and smiled at Shaver again. The courtroom held its breath as the confrontation between these men continued to escalate.

"That thing I can't make sense of...before he was released, Mr. Smith explained to the investigating officer that you held him hostage, bound is the word he used. When it became clear that you were going to be attacked, you took off his bindings and made him help you, isn't that correct?"

Shaver wasn't aware that Mason knew this much. "We were both in it, so we..."

"*Hold on*, what do you mean *both* in it? At this point, you've testified that Officer Martinez was coming for *you*."

"Tyler was wrapped up in something else, and we were both being hunted."

"Do I assume correctly that whatever he was wrapped up in, that you're now using as an excuse for holding Mr. Smith hostage, you don't know what it was?"

"That's right, I don't know what he was doing."

"By the way, where is Mr. Smith today?"

"He's dead."

"You know how he died, right? Essentially run over by a SUV while in the middle of a police chase?"

"I knew that."

"And you had nothing to do with that, right?"

"Objection!" Sphinx yelled. "That is an improper inference, Your Honor!"

"Sustained. You do not have to answer Sergeant Shaver," Judge Melburn said.

Mason flipped a page in his binder and shook his head while doing so. "Let's turn to the day in question, the day with Mr. Rodriguez, okay?"

"Be happy to."

"Did you pick Officers Martinez and Williams to be on your team?"

Shaver shot out a puff of air and answered, "No."

"Someone from the department forced them on you?"

"Yeah, the Chief."

"But they were just as competent as the rest of your team, right?"

"Competent at what?"

"Physical requirements..."

"Sure, Williams was a freakin' ape, a physical specimen. Didn't make him smart though."

"So, Officer Williams, the African-American member of your team, you refer to as..."

"Look, why don't you save your breath and just say black? I'm white, he was black, Martinez is brown. All that other junk, not necessary."

Sphinx stood up again and said, "Your Honor, we have been going for a few hours straight here, and lunch is impending. Can we take that break?"

"Your Honor! I'm in the middle of my cross-examination, at a critical juncture in the testimony. This is *not* an appropriate time to take a break," Mason responded.

"I agree counsel, you may continue."

"I will stick with my terminology, Sergeant Shaver, if you don't mind." Shaver sneered at Mason and waited for the next question. "Let's cut to the chase here. You and Tomko breached the front of the house, right?"

"Yeah."

"And the rest of the officers, along with the cameraman, breached the rear, correct?"

Shaver leaned closer to his microphone and slowly said, "Correct."

Mason figured this was the time to spring the trap. Shaver was tired, testy and getting loose with his answers. "Is it your position that Officer Martinez killed Mr. Rodriguez?" Mason asked incredulously.

The grin on Shaver's face disappeared. He sat there, looking conflicted for a few seconds until he said, "That's right. Martinez shot him."

"You claim that Officer Martinez shot Mr. Rodriguez, and yet he has never been the subject of an investigation into the matter, has he?!"

"He hasn't but..."

"And in all of your testimony today, you *never once mentioned* you were trying to apprehend Officer Martinez for supposedly killing Mr. Rodriguez, did you?!"

"I said that we were trying to get him when we flipped our car!"

"For his supposed involvement in the shooting of Officer Lindsey, Sergeant Shaver! Do you recall that? You never mentioned you were trying to arrest Officer Martinez for the death of Mr. Rodriguez!"

"Well, I guess I forgot..."

"Just like you forgot to tell us that you were holding Mr. Smith hostage, right?"

"I didn't forget to tell you *shit*. You're trying to spin this so you can get that smelly..."

"Your Honor!" Sphinx called out, trying to stop Shaver.

"...Martinez off the hook. I stood there, while that ass shot the old man, plain and simple." Shaver pushed the microphone away from his mouth.

Mason glanced at the jurors, who were all glaring at Shaver. His work was done. "Those are all the questions I have."

"The defense has no further questions either, Your Honor," Sphinx added. Technically, Sphinx had the right to perform a re-direct of Shaver, but that could be suicide. Why give Shaver the opportunity to shoot himself in the other foot.

# FORTY-SEVEN

Tawny sat in the jury deliberation room with an empty paper cup in her hand. They had just finished eating the meager, court-provided lunch. No one said much since the attorneys finished their closing arguments and the judge read them their jury instructions. Tawny looked at the juror notebook in front of her, uncertain what she thought about the case.

"You know, that Sergeant was a real racist," the insurance man said, breaking the silence.

Tawny agreed with his sentiment, but was surprised to hear it coming from him. Overall, she felt like she trusted that Officer Martinez, but Sergeant Shaver's attorney had definitely cast doubt on whether he did the right things.

"Like that attorney, Mr. Sphinx, said in his closing, if Officer Martinez was willing to break all these rules to get Sergeant Shaver, who knows if he's telling the truth?" asked Lucius, the engineer. "At the same time, my gut tells me that Sergeant Shaver did it. I don't see murder in that Officer Martinez's eyes. The other cop looked menacing and cold."

"Let's look at these notebooks," the jockey said, attempting to take control of the decision-making process. "They have our standards in there. Unfortunately, I don't think 'gut' qualifies, although I'd say my gut agrees with yours." They all shuffled to find and open their notebooks, except for Tawny. Hers was already open and she was reviewing a page entitled "Burden of Proof."

"It says in here that the State has the burden of proving beyond a reasonable doubt that Sergeant Shaver intended to kill Mr. Rodriguez, but did not plan to kill him," Tawny said.

"Well, if what Officer Martinez said is true, that seems pretty clear-cut," the jockey said.

"And reasonable doubt is what?"

"Turn to the next page," Tawny answered. "Reasonable doubt is a fair, honest doubt based on the evidence produced at trial. Reasonable doubt must be based on reason and common sense, not on conjecture, speculation, possibilities or imaginary scenarios. We must be satisfied that no reasonable person would doubt that this person is guilty."

"What happens if we got a reasonable doubt?" Dawn asked.

The jockey looked at her sideways, wondering if the question was for real. When he realized it was, he answered slowly, "Then we can't convict the policeman."

"Oh." Tawny looked around the room to get a hold of who these people were. So far she had met Dawn the entertainer, Lucius, the old man, the insurance man, the jockey and Rebecca. There were five other people though, and she thought they should all know each other.

"Before we move on, we don't all know each other. I know some of you, but not others," she said, looking at a man in nice pants and a suit jacket. Another man sat next to him in athletic pants and a windbreaker. It seemed strange to Tawny, given that it was pretty hot outside.

"I'm Carlos," the man in the suit jacket said. When Tawny kept looking at him expectantly, he said, "I own a small business."

She looked at the man next to him. She had perfected this polite yet demanding stare with her students.

"Jeff. I'm a trainer."

There were three women sitting on the other side of the jury room from Carlos and Chuck. Tawny noticed that they had already formed their own little clique. One of them said, "How about we just decide this? I don't think we need to be friends to do that." The other two women giggled nervously when she said it.

"Fine, have it your way," Tawny said.

"What do we look at first?" Carlos asked, perhaps trying to ease the tension.

"There isn't too much evidence," Lucius said. "We've got testimony from three witnesses is all."

"And it really comes down to two," the jockey added. "I mean, the expert witness told us that it was either Sergeant Shaver or Officer Martinez, right?" Tawny and the others agreed. "He couldn't tell us which of their guns it was. So it boils down to the officers' testimony."

"I liked Officer Martinez," Dawn said.

"See, that's the type of emotion that shouldn't come into play," the jockey said.

"Hold on a second," Tawny started, "a big issue with Officer Martinez is going to be credibility. If he is credible, then we can believe his story. While Dawn didn't use that word, I think that's what she was saying, right Dawn?"

"Yeah, thanks," she answered with a smile.

"I've got a big problem with the credibility of a police officer that is willing to break the rules," the insurance man said. "Now, don't get me wrong, I thing the Sergeant is a snake. But, if Martinez was willing to arrest him without a warrant, who's to say that he wasn't arresting him just to cover his own ass?"

"Do you really believe that?" Lucius asked. "I can't believe that he would have gone to all that trouble to frame the Sergeant."

"Oh come on!" the insurance man exclaimed. "If you kill someone, you don't think you'll go to the end of the world to cover it up?"

"Guess I've never thought about it like that. I believe in the inherent good quality of people, and Officer Martinez seemed to have that to me. He may have been caught up in a few technicalities, but that prosecutor showed us the Sergeant is a *damn liar!*"

"I believe that people are motivated by greed and self-interest, and I have a doubt whether Martinez wasn't just covering his ass!"

"Sometimes we project," Lucius said coyly.

"Whatever, man. All I'm saying is that we have a standard here...reasonable doubt. I've got some damn doubts, okay? And they are based on the evidence given us. What about the whole gun thing too?"

"That was actually what seemed fishy to me," the jockey said.

"I don't think it matters," Rebecca piped up and said. "I'm sure Officer Martinez was in a haze, like he said. Just because Sergeant Shaver got his gun checked in that same day doesn't mean Officer Martinez was the shooter."

Her words ended and then silence returned to the room. They all sat there, considering the options before them.

"One other thing. What motive would Officer Martinez have to shoot that man?" Lucius asked. "There was none that I could tell. So he would just have to be a cold-blooded killer? Killing for sport? I don't see that at all. On the other hand, it was pretty damn clear that Shaver didn't think much of us black or you brown folk," Lucius said, looking at Carlos.

"But do you have a reasonable doubt based on the evidence we saw, that maybe, just maybe Martinez *did* shoot that man?" the jockey asked. "Even if it was just an accident." Tawny squirmed in her seat. She was having trouble deciding this one as well. Lucius didn't answer the question.

\* \* \* \*

Cruz stood next to Mason and Todd, chatting with them about the case when the jurors started to come back into the courtroom.

"That was fast," Todd said. "What the hell does that mean?" Cruz's shoulders dropped a little bit.

"Could be that it was so clear-cut they had to convict him," Mason answered rather emptily. Judge Melburn returned to the courtroom with a big smile on his face.

"I am happy to see you have returned in a timely fashion," the judge said. "Please, everyone in the gallery take your seats. Counsel, return to your tables." He waited for people to stop their conversations. He displayed some modicum of patience as he felt ahead of the curve with the jury returning so quickly.

Cruz went back to his seat and Sandra grabbed his hand. She shot an anxious look at him. He squeezed her hand and said a quick Hail Mary in his head. He didn't know where it came from, and he forgot a couple of the words, but the uncontrollable nature of the whole event prompted the prayer. The jurors had taken their seats.

"Have you chosen a foreperson?" Judge Melburn asked.

"We have, judge," the jockey said as he stood up. So it *was* the jockey, Cruz thought to himself. He had speculated the jockey was the one taking control all along. Cruz looked around for Martinez. He found him, standing by the courtroom doors.

"Has the jury reached a verdict?"

"We have judge," the jockey said. One of the bailiffs approached the jockey and took the verdict form. He walked it over to the judge who opened the form and took a few moments to read it. Cruz put his hand on Mason's back. He tried to convey nothing but positive thoughts. He looked over at Shaver who still looked calm and disassociated. Sphinx was grinding a pen in his mouth.

"How do you find as to the charge of second degree murder?" the judge said. Chatter, movement, breathing in the crowded courtroom came to a screeching halt. People sat on the edge of their seats, digging their fingernails into the old wood and straining their ears to hear the verdict.

"Not guilty." The two words fell like anvils. Cruz dropped his head and tears formed in his eyes. Sandra threw her arms around him and started to cry as well. Mason pounded his fists down on the table. The gallery erupted. Some people cheered, others screamed bloody murder. Lost in the mix of noise was Judge Melburn banging his gavel. Cruz looked over at Shaver through a veil of tears and the man was the same, emotionless. A remote, heartless human being, stranded on his own island of hate.

The crowd outside could sense that something had happened. Sandra openly took her cell phone out and texted Andre the news. Moments later the crowd erupted. Cruz went to the back window as the crowd outside revolted in waves extending away from the courthouse. Sirens immediately began to sound. Men screamed into bullhorns. The lines of national guardsmen on the steps of the courthouse braced for the worst. Cruz turned around to see that the judge was gone. Shaver and Sphinx were gone too. He pushed through he people that had gathered behind him and ran out of the courtroom. Sandra saw him moving and tried to keep up.

Cruz caught a glimpse of Shaver's back just as he turned for the front doors of the courthouse. He sprinted to catch up, not sure what he would do if he caught up, but sprinting nonetheless. He slid around the corner and then jetted to the front doors. Shaver and Sphinx were already outside. He barreled through the doors and was momentarily stunned by the sun. That's when he heard a crack. His shoulder suddenly burned hot. He grabbed at his shoulder and came away with a hand of blood.

"What the..." But before he could get the sentence out, two more cracks sounded. Cruz fell to the ground. His shoulder was howling in pain. He felt weak and heard thumping sounds as police shot canisters of tear gas into the crowd, which had gone mad like a disturbed anthill. Sandra fell on top of him and whispered to him, "Cruz, are you okay?" He felt everything start to go black around him. His head fell to the side, the sharp edge of a stair pressing into his temple. That's when he saw Shaver sprawled out on the steps. A line of scarlet blood was streaming down from where Shaver rested. Sphinx was off to the side, crouched behind one of the columns supporting the courthouse. Cruz fought off the darkness and strained to see beyond Shaver. There was a commotion down toward where he remembered the handicap area being. A man was fighting off several policemen as they picked him up out of his wheelchair. Sandra looked over to see what was going on, and when she saw who they had, she screamed, "Raul!!!!"

# EPILOGUE

# REVELATION

Sphinx rested with his head propped up on the palm of his left hand. He aimlessly stirred his coffee and watched steam rise from the cup into the air. "Appropriate metaphor for life..." he muttered.

"What's that?"

Sphinx looked up at Cruz, mildly abashed after letting that thought escape his mind. "Oh, nothing. Where were we?"

Cruz shifted in his seat and leaned over toward Sphinx. "Look, I appreciate you invited me this time instead of kidnapping me, but stop wasting my damn time. I've been watching you ruminate over a cup of coffee, which is black as tar and yet you're stirring it as if it's loaded with cream and sugar. Cut the melodrama and get to the point."

"You're right...but I need to give you some background first."

Cruz sighed and crossed his arms. This was pure Sphinx—Spotlight Sphinx—Cruz thought to himself with a half-hearted chuckle. When Sphinx didn't start talking, Cruz gestured to him to go on.

"I was disconcerted by the trial and how it unfolded."

"Your client's death too...?" Cruz said pointedly.

"Not so much." Cruz quickly raised his eyebrows. "The trial, the trial, the trial. There was something wrong with it."

"You mean the plain obviousness of it being fixed?"

"Fixed? That's more for horse races or boxing matches. It was...altered."

"Semantics. I don't care what you call it, the judge's preclusion of that evidence was downright...hold on. Let me pry into the vortex that is Sphinx's mind. You're upset, aren't you? Personally upset, not about anything related to anyone else, such as your client."

Sphinx raised the glass of hot coffee to his lips in a smooth swing of his arm. The dark liquid slightly burnt the roof of his mouth as it rolled into his throat. "I can neither confirm nor deny that emotion."

"For fuck's sake, Sphinx. You're acting like a prima donna. This is all about you and how upset you are that you didn't win on the merits of your skill? I should have known."

"Don't go that far."

"Stop being such a kid. You had this nagging feeling that you won because of higher forces, assuming there could be a higher force than *the Sphinx*. So, did you invite me here to shed some tears and get this out? You know I'm not your friend, right?"

"In any event, you can cut out the criticism." Sphinx looked around at the busy café. The people's swarm was enough to generate a low-level white noise, sufficient to mask their conversation. "I started digging a bit and the ground fell out from beneath me like sand."

"Digging at what?"

"The case, Judge Melburn, our facts, everything. I spent nearly a week straight pouring over the case documents. I should have moved on, but something wouldn't let me."

"Sphinx, that's called conscience."

"It's a bitch. Day and night I looked for something to justify my own work and the reason we won. But I couldn't find it. We won because that video was excluded, plain and simple, and I had no idea why it was excluded until I got to Shaver's trial notes."

"He was taking notes during trial?"

"Yes, almost a full yellow pad. Ramblings, sketching, thoughts on jurors, the judge, *me*."

"How were his notes relevant to the video though?" Sphinx looked into Cruz's eyes with an intensity and simultaneous softness, almost an "I'm sorry," that caught Cruz off guard. "You aren't going to cry, are you?"

Sphinx snickered and pulled a piece of yellow paper from a pocket inside his suit jacket. He put the paper on the table in front of himself, paused a moment, and then slid it over to Cruz with all the ominousness of an undercover delivery of a package of top secret information. Cruz put his hand on the piece of paper and just as he was about to pick it up, Sphinx stopped Cruz with his own hand. They looked at each other—one man bewildered, the other impassioned.

"You need some context first. I was alone, confused and trying to figure out what had happened. I played no part in any of it."

Cruz removed his hand from the paper and sat back, his sunken eyes peering at Sphinx. The week since the trial had offered no catharsis or rest for him either. Raul was facing charges of first degree murder. The case against him seemed to be tight. His only defense was heat of the passion, based upon the loss of his legs. It was an attenuated argument since so much time had passed between when he lost his legs and when he killed Shaver. Cruz tried to explain this to Carmen once, but she just shook her head and wept. For what it was worth, Raul seemed at peace with his decision.

Sandra had been elevated to a position of deity within the news station for uncovering such a hog of a story. She was promoted to the female anchor on the evening news, and in the midst of a drunken wake after the trial, Cruz proposed to her. He reconfirmed the intention with her the next day when they both weren't so trashed, although both of them had kept the engagement secret so far.

Martinez retired from the police force, overwhelmed with a mixture of shame, pride, satisfaction and disappointment. Shame from being associated with a monster like Shaver, and the shame which he unfairly squared on his shoulders related to the trial loss. Cruz rubbed his forehead as these thoughts coursed through his mind. He and Martinez had met to take an aimless stroll through the drenched city a few days after the trial and the morning after a nightlong thunderstorm. Cruz recalled the thick, refreshing air refilling him with some semblance of life and hope. Martinez explained that his ultimate disappointment did not derive from the trial. Instead, he felt as if he did not fulfill a promise to Williams—the promise that release of the video would reach international magnitude.

With all of these competing thoughts, exultations and sorrows racing through his mind, Cruz lowered his voice and sternly said to Sphinx, "You've missed something throughout this entire process, Sphinx. The importance of the video can't be overshadowed by your own ego. It was a symbol of injustice—the murder of a hapless member of our society by another member of our society wielding all of its power. Sure, this happens on a daily basis amongst civilians, but to have what should be a most trusted member of our society commit a crime like this...what does it say about us? Is everyone touched by darkness? Isn't there a group of men or women outside the influence of hatred and discrimination? A very fine thread of hope existed in our society that the answer is 'yes' and that perhaps police officers are those people." Cruz paused before concluding, "The video demonstrates that the thread of hope has been cut, and that we can trust no one in this world."

"Hobbes finally wins out..."

Cruz fell silent, as did Sphinx. "What happened?" Cruz asked quietly.

Sphinx locked his arms in a circle around his cup of coffee. A woman bumped into Sphinx as she walked past and startled both of them. Returning his attention to Cruz, Sphinx said, "I had to search, Cruz. I was desperate to know how things happened. When I saw that note you're holding, I had to search." Sphinx flicked his hand at the piece of paper as if to prompt Cruz to finally open it. So Cruz did.

The piece of paper was folded neatly lengthwise and then again crosswise. Cruz slowly pulled the corners of the paper apart, in a show of reverence to Sphinx. Once he finally got it open, he had to let his eyes and mind adjust to the scrawl. There were scribbled drawings of towers and large, unending mazes. Words were scattered around the page like the remains of the ocean's contents on a beach. Near the bottom-middle of the page was a sentence, the words clearly written, almost with computer-like precision. "Warden did his job with the judge." A shiver bolted down Cruz's back and his heart fell into his stomach.

Sphinx, seeing the pallor cast over Cruz's face, went on, "I felt the same way. Something was wrong, Cruz, do you understand that?"

Finding his voice Cruz responded, "I do now..."

"Not the whole thing, Cruz—not the whole thing. That little piece of damn paper drove me to dig further into the quicksand. I went to Shaver's house."

Cruz's cell phone rang. It was Martinez.

"You can take that, I need a refill of this coffee."

"No," Cruz said as he silenced the phone, "go on."

Sphinx rattled the cup of coffee around in his big hands and said, "Shaver mentioned a list once during trial. It was almost like something uttered while he was asleep. It sounded like '...list'll get me out'. When he said it I saw him freeze, but I was too immersed in the trial to think more of it. In fact, it had completely disappeared from my consciousness until I saw that piece of paper. I went to his house looking for that list."

"Did you find it?" Cruz asked with bated breath.

"I did, and I don't want it anymore." He hurriedly took a square, leather-bound notebook from his jacket pocket and shoved it towards Cruz.

"Hold on! Why don't you want it? Shouldn't you be trying to protect your client?!"

Sphinx scoffed and jammed his hands into his pockets. "He's dead and I've got a shrunk heart, goddammit. I need to do something so just take the damn notebook." When Cruz hesitated, Sphinx added, "Take the damn thing before I change my mind!" Sphinx sat there, a man obviously embroiled with competing emotions of good and bad. It was powerful to watch someone choose good.

Sphinx stood up, took his hands out of his pockets and leaned on the table. "That list, Cruz, that list could have been very valuable to me. It's everything. Your release of the video, it made a local sensation of a story and even garnered national attention. But, the information in that notebook implicates so much more. The horror in the delicate words of those pages will shock *the world.*" Sphinx seemed to be possessed, confused by the words streaming out of his mouth.

"We—Martinez and I—knew some sort of list existed. The Chief told us, but we had no idea what it was about."

Cruz's words seemed to knock Sphinx out of his trance. He straightened up and adjusted his tie to tighten more closely around his neck. He looked dismayed by the fact that it had been loose in the first place. "I don't know if that's the same list, but you should be thanking me for bringing this notebook to you first in any event." A scowl manifested on Sphinx's face like a cloud covering the sun. "You're lucky I was so generous with you, Mr. Marquez."

Cruz looked at Sphinx with some surprise and amusement at the change in his tone. With a smile, Cruz said, "Sphinx is back."

"I've no idea what you're talking about," Sphinx said with his own attempt at a smile, which the two shared for a fleeting moment before Sphinx spun around on a dime and walked out of the café.

Cruz remained at the table, alone, the sounds of the café replaced in his mind by racing thoughts. He opened the first page of the notebook and read.

*Accounting of Work Performed*

*Dr. Xavier Kastenoff*

*Sheryl Petrow*

*Mark Lunstrom*

*Harvey Theobald*

The list under Dr. Xavier Kastenoff went on for many pages, and then a heading for Sergeant Shaver started, went on for several pages, and the notebook ended with a list apparently related to Tyler Smith. The list contained people's names, their places of employment and home addresses. Cruz flipped all the way to the end of the notebook, bewildered by its contents, until he saw an inscription on the inside back cover.

*To YOU. If you found this notebook, then I am dead. But, the remains of my work and the work of the other men listed in this* notebook will take years to find..

The souls in this book were consumed,
burned, buried, stuffed into bags part by
part, and disposed of in an array of other
manners. All on behalf of Chief Edwin
Colgate, whose reasons for disposing of the
souls knew no bounds.

We were all monsters, and if you're
reading this, at least one of us has tasted
justice.

--Dr. Xavier Kastenoff

# THE END

# AFTERWORD

Thank you for reading *Enemy in Blue*! Much has happened since I released this, my debut novel, in May of 2011. Almost a year later, over 5,000 copies of the book have sold, and it has reached #2 in all legal thrillers on Amazon on multiple occasions.

The support from my readers has been phenomenal. THANK YOU ALL. I also appreciate the fact that so many people have chosen to challenge themselves with the subject matter of this book. Some acknowledge the issues raised, some do not, but in either case I am happy to have so many people at least contemplating what's going on around us.

My next book, which revs up four years after *Enemy in Blue* ends, will be out by May 1, 2012. Cruz, Martinez, and even a surprise character return. I promise plenty more thrills and suspense in *Allegiance*! As a reward for finishing, here are the first pages of *Allegiance:*

\* \* \* \*

Blown sand stung his face like tiny darts shot from an invisible enemy. He lay prone in the desert, his tan and chocolate fatigues doing little to combat the heat that emanated through the earth. A row of ants marched just beyond his shadow, providing him a distraction as he waited for his targets to crest the hill in front of him.

He turned his head when he heard the howl of wind from his left—the incessant source of the sand. Grainy pellets struck the back of his cap and then subsided. He looked back at the hill and thought he saw the hazy outline of a person's head, surely a mirage. With a quick snap, he pulled binoculars from a side pocket and propped up on his elbows.

It was the top of a person's head, the molecules around the figure shimmering in the distant heat wave. The rest of the body appeared slowly as the head bobbed from side to side. Bushy, caterpillar eyebrows poked up. A glossy, heat soaked face took form.

He put the binoculars down and whispered to the woman next to him, "¿Hay más?"

She put her own binoculars down and pulled the bandanna from her mouth. "Many more." He looked back at the hill and four other people surrounded the man struggling up the incline. They all panted and struck various poses while catching their breath—hands on knees, hands behind head, crouched down with head between legs.

# Derek Blass

"Go time?" she asked.

"Let them get closer," he answered. The group of people was about four hundred yards away. He watched them as they battled the intense heat and worked to recoup their energy. The sun's unrelenting rays beat down on them. Their lips were chalky white and their normally brown skin was pale and sickly—initial signs of heat exhaustion.

They managed to press forward though, a testament to the oft-forgotten or unused human will. When they neared a little over two hundred yards away, he turned to her, gave a quick gesture with his head in the direction of the group of people, and picked up two jugs of water. She grabbed her bag of food and jogged toward them. He followed behind her, the water sloshing in the jugs and making balance challenging over the uneven desert terrain.

The people froze when they saw these two figures coming their direction. A man, the same one who first crested the hill, put his hands out to his sides to get the rest of the group to stop. He stood alone, the tip of a triangle.

When they were just about to reach yelling distance from the group, they all heard a crack, like a distant tree branch falling. Both he and the woman froze. Another crack and one of the jugs of water spun out of his hand. Water gushed out onto the sand, creating a silhouette on a golden background. Then it seemed as if a shooting gallery erupted. He fell face down, the desert floor grinding against his cheek.

The lead man in the group of people waved his arms in the direction of the firing until one of the bullets connected. He screamed as his hand was ripped off. A second shot and he was silent, lifted into the air, angelic for a moment before crashing to the ground.

With the jug of water by his side, the man in fatigues grabbed the woman's foot. She glanced at him, a look of terror in her bloodshot eyes. The bandanna had fallen off of her face, revealing her trembling lips.

The sound of firing ended as abruptly as it had started and was replaced by the crescendo of engines. The grumble grew louder until he worried they were going to get run over. Without moving his body he shifted his head to look in the direction of the engines.

Three tan jeeps bellowed across the ripples in the desert sand. He could smell trace exhaust fumes. The jeeps closed on him and the woman until the last moment. The unrefined roar of the engines deafened every other sound, including his own breathing. The lead jeep braked, spun sideways, and sent up a plume of dust and sand which enveloped them.

The crunch of several footsteps were all he could make out in the dust around them. Then, nothing but a face emerged from the brown cloud, peering at him from several inches away. A copperish-brown stream of spit shot from the person's mouth.

"Well, look like we got two-of-'em angels."

The man couldn't see the butt of a rifle swing up and then come down toward his face until the last moment, which coincided with the world turning black.

* * * *

Another of the wonderful benefits of writing this book has been meeting a host of wonderful authors. One of them stands out in particular: Carolyn McCray. If you enjoy thrillers, then check out a gritty police procedural from her (under her pen name Cristyn West) entitled *Plain Jane: Brunettes Beware*. Here's a teaser:

#1 Bestselling Police Procedural and Hard-Boiled Mystery…

Plain Jane: Brunettes Beware. A Patterson-style thriller with a dash of Hannibal.

In the words of New York Times best-selling author James Rollins (Devil Colony)…**"Wickedly macabre and blisteringly paced, PLAIN JANE marks the debut of a thriller for the new millennium. Brash, funny, terrifying, and shocking, here is a story best enjoyed with all the lights on. Don't say I didn't warn you!"**

A quick overview of Plain Jane…

A city paralyzed by a serial killer stalking the night, taking a most gruesome trophy. The only thing standing in the murderer's way is an F.B.I. profiler…recently released from a mental institution.

Plain Jane combines the swift pace of Patterson with the macabre of Harris.

## Derek Blass

More Praise for Plain Jane...

"A perfect mix of suspense, romance and phenomenally developed characters. I heeded the warning of the reviewers preceding me, and chose a day that I wanted and was able to get lost in a story.

Cristyn West, you have spoiled me for other crime novels that I may read in the future, setting the bar quite high."

Kara Haas (@karahaas)

THANK YOU AGAIN!